LESLIE PARRISH

AUTHOR OF *COLD SIGHT*

When does a chilling gift
become a deadly curse?

EXTRASENSORY AGENTS

COLD TOUCH

"Leslie Parrish keeps
me riveted, keeps me
guessing, and keeps me
coming back for more!"
—*NEW YORK TIMES*
BESTSELLING AUTHOR
LARA ADRIAN

SIGNET
ECLIPSE

SIGNET ECLIPSE

$7.99 U.S.
$8.99 CAN.

ISBN 978-0-451-23300-4

5 0 7 9 9

S ▷ EAN

"A romantic suspense genius."
—Reader to Reader Reviews

PRAISE FOR THE NOVELS OF LESLIE PARRISH

Cold Touch

"Fresh, exciting, truly thrilling romantic suspense . . . the Extrasensory Agents series delivers outstanding paranormal intrigue from a sharp, creative new voice in the genre."
—Lara Adrian, *New York Times* bestselling author of the Midnight Breed series

Cold Sight

"Well-written, guaranteed to keep readers on the edge of their seat. Filled with many plot twists, readers are going to have a tough time putting this one down!" —Fresh Fiction

"This story is action-packed and the romance is just right. Ms. Parrish has written a story that will hold your attention from the first page and keep it until the last word is read. Her characters seem so real that they will draw you into the story." —Night Owl Romance

"This is an entertaining paranormal whodunit starring an intrepid reporter and a man with telemetric extrasensory psychometric abilities." —Genre Go Round Reviews

"Dark, emotionally compelling romantic suspense with a light paranormal element. I opened this book and didn't close it again until the last page had been read." —Book Binge

"Parrish blends her suspense and paranormal elements well, and I found this dark thriller immensely addictive . . . romantic suspense with an edge to it." —All About Romance

"The only cold thing about this witty, steamy, and totally engrossing novel is the high-powered air conditioner you'll need to sit under while reading it . . . a nonstop ride."
—Romance Novel News

continued . . .

COLD TOUCH

EXTRASENSORY AGENTS

LESLIE PARRISH

A SIGNET ECLIPSE BOOK

SIGNET ECLIPSE
Published by New American Library, a division of
Penguin Group (USA) Inc., 375 Hudson Street,
New York, New York 10014, USA
Penguin Group (Canada), 90 Eglinton Avenue East, Suite 700, Toronto,
Ontario M4P 2Y3, Canada (a division of Pearson Penguin Canada Inc.)
Penguin Books Ltd., 80 Strand, London WC2R 0RL, England
Penguin Ireland, 25 St. Stephen's Green, Dublin 2,
Ireland (a division of Penguin Books Ltd.)
Penguin Group (Australia), 250 Camberwell Road, Camberwell, Victoria 3124,
Australia (a division of Pearson Australia Group Pty. Ltd.)
Penguin Books India Pvt. Ltd., 11 Community Centre, Panchsheel Park,
New Delhi - 110 017, India
Penguin Group (NZ), 67 Apollo Drive, Rosedale, Auckland 0632,
New Zealand (a division of Pearson New Zealand Ltd.)
Penguin Books (South Africa) (Pty.) Ltd., 24 Sturdee Avenue,
Rosebank, Johannesburg 2196, South Africa

Penguin Books Ltd., Registered Offices:
80 Strand, London WC2R 0RL, England

First published by Signet Eclipse, an imprint of New American Library,
a division of Penguin Group (USA) Inc.

First Printing, July 2011
10   9   8   7   6   5   4   3   2   1

To Caitlin—thanks for your invaluable help in keeping me on track with these books. Oh, and thanks for being such a wonderful daughter, too!

And to my editor, Laura Cifelli—thank you so much for challenging me to expand my writing into the world of the paranormal. I've loved working on this series and would never have attempted it without your encouragement and support.

ACKNOWLEDGMENTS

Sincere thanks to Julie, Janelle and Karen, who, as always, were there to help me untangle my big ball of plot at a moment's notice. And to Bruce, who was always standing by as my sounding board.

Thanks also to Googlemaps for giving me the amazing ability to walk the streets my characters walked.

Though this story is set in the real—and lovely—city of Savannah, I have taken some liberties with its history, politics, topography and geography for the purposes of this story. Thanks for understanding.

Prologue

Twelve years ago

"He's gonna kill you."

The boy's voice shook with both sadness and fear. And with those four whispered words, Olivia Wainwright's faint hope of survival disappeared.

The boy, Jack, was he a victim, too? She wasn't sure. She only knew that during the three terrifying days she'd been tied up in this hot, miserable barn, his sharp, angular face was the only one she'd seen. She'd caught brief glimpses of him in the shadows when he shuffled in to bring her water or sometimes a handful of stale nuts that she suspected he wasn't supposed to share. Once, he'd even come close enough to loosen the ropes on her wrists and ankles a little, so at least she had some circulation again.

But he hadn't let her go. No matter how much she'd begged.

He was a couple of years younger than her, twelve or thirteen, maybe. Skinny, pale, with sunken cheeks and deep-set eyes. While he was free to go in and out, she suspected he was a victim, too—of abuse, at the very least. The kid looked beaten down, his spirit crushed, all memories of happiness long gone.

Olivia began to shake, long shudders making her bound legs quiver and her stomach heave. She'd eaten almost nothing for days, yet thought she'd be sick.

This wasn't supposed to happen. She'd tried so hard to be strong, to think positively. Her parents loved her, and they had a lot of money. Of course they'd pay the ransom. She'd told herself it would all be okay. But it wouldn't be okay. Not ever again.

"When?" she finally asked, dread making the word hard to push from her mouth.

"Once he makes sure they paid the ransom money."

"If they're paying the money, why is he going to kill me?" she asked, the words sounding so strange in her ears. God, she was fifteen years old; the very idea that she would be asking questions about her own murder had never once crossed her mind.

Four days ago she'd been a slightly spoiled, happy teenager looking forward to getting her driver's license and wondering how much begging it would take to get her overindulgent parents to buy her a Jeep.

Now she was wondering how many minutes she had left on this earth. She could hear a clock ticking away in her mind, each tick marking one less second of her life.

"He don't want any witnesses." Jack leaned back against the old plank-board wall and slid down it, like he couldn't hold himself up anymore. He sat hunched on the backs of his bent legs, watching her. A shaft of moonlight bursting through a broken slat high up in the barn wall shone a spotlight on his bony face. Tear tracks had cleared a path through the grime on his bruised cheeks, and his lips—swollen, bloodied—quivered. "He's afraid you can identify him."

"I can't! I never even saw his face."

That was true. She'd never gotten a glimpse of the man who'd grabbed her from her own bedroom. Liv had awakened from a sound sleep to find a pillow slapped over her face, a hateful male voice hissing at her not to scream or he'd shoot her and her sister, whose room was right next door. Their parents' room was on the other side of the huge house, and Liv didn't doubt that the man would be able to make good on his threat before anyone could get to them.

A minute later, any chance of screaming had been taken from her. He'd hit her hard enough to knock her out. By the time she'd awakened, she was already inside this old abandoned barn. Jack was the only living soul she'd seen or heard since.

"I'm sorry."

"Let me go," she urged.

He shook his head, repeating, "I'm sorry."

"Please, Jack. You can't let this happen."

"There's nothin' I can do."

"Just untie me and give me a chance to run away."

"He'll find you," he said. "Then he'll kill us both." His voice was low, his tone sounding almost robotic. Like he'd heard the threat so many times it had become ingrained in his head.

"When did he take you?" she asked, suddenly certain this boy was a captive as well.

"Take me?" Jack stared at her, his brown eyes flat and lifeless. "Whaddya mean?"

"He kidnapped you, too, didn't he?"

"Dunno." Jack slowly shook his head. "I've been with him forever."

"Is he your father?" she persisted.

Jack didn't respond, though whether it was because he didn't know or didn't want to say, she couldn't be sure.

"Do you have a mother?"

"Don't remember."

"Look, whoever he is, you have to get away from him. *We* have to get away." She tried to scoot closer, though her legs—numb from being bound—didn't want to cooperate. She managed no more than a few inches before falling onto her side, remnants of dry, dirty old hay scratching her cheek. "Come with me. Untie me and we'll both run."

If she *could* run on her barely functional legs.

She thrust that worry away. If it meant saving her life, hell, she'd crawl.

"I can't," he replied, looking down at her from a few feet away. His hand rose, like he wanted to reach out and touch her, to help her sit up. Then he dropped it back onto his lap, as if he was used to having his hand slapped if he ever dared to raise it.

"Yes, you can! My parents will help you. They'll be so grateful."

"I can't."

Again that robotic voice. Like the kid was brainwashed. If he'd been a prisoner for so long he didn't remember any other life, she supposed he probably was.

He reached into the pocket of his tattered jeans, pulling out two small pills. "Here," he said. "I swiped 'em from the floor in his room. He musta dropped 'em. I think they'll make you sleep, so maybe it won't hurt."

A sob rose from deep inside her, catching in the middle of her throat, choking and desperate. "How will he do it?"

The boy sniffled. "I dunno."

"Not a knife," she cried, panic rising fast. "Oh, please God, don't let him cut me."

She hated knives. In every horror movie she'd ever seen, it was the gleam of light shining on the sharp, silvery edge of a blade that made her throw her hands over her eyes or just turn off the TV.

"He don't use a knife, not usually," Jack said.

His consoling reply didn't distract her from the implication: She wouldn't be the first person to die at her kidnapper's hands. He'd killed before. And this boy had witnessed those killings.

"Don't let this happen, Jack, please." Tears poured out

of her eyes as she twisted and struggled against the ropes. "Don't let him hurt me."

"Take the pills," he said, his tears streaming as hard as hers. "Just take 'em."

"You should have brought the whole bottle," she said, hearing her own bitterness and desperation.

"If I could get to a whole bottle, I woulda swallowed 'em myself a long time ago."

That haunted voice suddenly sounded so adult, so broken. The voice of someone who'd considered suicide every day of his young life. What horrors must he have endured to embrace the thought of death so easily?

It was his sheer hopelessness that made her realize she *hadn't* given up hope. She was terrified out of her mind and didn't want to die, didn't want to feel the pain of death—*oh, God, not a knife*—but she wasn't ready to give up, either. No matter what she'd said, if he had a bottle of pills in his hand, she didn't think she would swallow them, not even now with death bearing down on her like a car heading for a cliff.

She wanted to live.

"Where you at, boy?" a voice bellowed from outside.

Jack leapt to his feet, his sadness disappearing as utter terror swept over him. That terror jumped from his body into hers, and Olivia struggled harder against the ropes. Like an animal caught in a trap, she could almost smell her own extermination barreling toward her.

She tried to keep her head. Tried to think.

If her captor didn't know the boy had warned her, maybe he'd let his guard down. Maybe she could get him to untie her, maybe she could run. . . .

Or maybe she really was about to die.

"Please," she whispered, knowing Jack wanted to help her. But his fear won out; he didn't even seem to hear her plea. He had already begun to climb over the side wall of the stall, falling into the next one with a muffled grunt.

No sooner had he gone than the barn door flew open with a crash. Heavy footsteps approached, ominous and violent like the powerful thudding of her heart.

Through the worn slats, she could see Jack lying in the next stall, motionless, watching her. She pleaded with her eyes, but he didn't respond in any way. It seemed as though the real boy had retreated somewhere deep inside a safe place in his mind, and only the shell of a human being remained.

Her kidnapper reached the entrance to the stall. Still lying on her side, Olivia first saw his ugly, thick-soled boots. She slowly looked up, noted faded jeans pulled tight over thick, squat legs, but before she could tilt her head back to see the rest, something heavy and scratchy—a horse blanket, she suspected—landed on her face, obscuring her vision.

Confusion made her whimper and her heart, already racing, tripped in her chest. She trembled with fear, yes. But there was something more.

Hope.

He didn't want her to see him. Which meant he might have changed his mind. Maybe he knew she couldn't identify him, and he was going to let her go.

"Up you go, girl," he said, grabbing her by her hair and yanking her to her feet, holding the small blanket in place. He pressed in behind her, and she almost gagged. The cloth over her head wasn't thick enough to block the sweaty reek of his body or his sour breath—the same smells she'd forever associate with being startled awake in the night.

Forever? *Please, God, let there be more than just tonight.*

"Looks like your Mama and Daddy ain't sick'a you yet. They're paying over a lot of money to get you back."

"You're going to let me go?" she managed to whisper, hope blossoming.

"Sure I am, sugar," he said with a hoarse, ugly laugh.

Olivia forced herself to ignore that mean laugh and allowed relief and happiness to flood through her. She breathed deeply, then mumbled, "Thank God. Oh, thank you, God."

Ignoring her, he kicked at her bare feet so she'd start moving. She stumbled on numb legs, and he had to support her as they trudged out of the stall—her shuffling because of the rope. His grip on her hair and a thick arm around her waist kept her upright as they walked outside into the hot Georgia night.

At least, she thought she was still in Georgia. It smelled like home, anyway. Not even the musky odor of the fabric and her attacker's stench could block the scent of the night air, damp and thick and ripe like the woods outside of Savannah after the rain.

Maybe she was still in Savannah. Close to her own house, close to her family. Minutes away from her father's strong arms and her mother's loving kiss.

Despite everything—her fears, the boy's claims—she was going to see them again.

Suddenly, he stopped. "Where you been at?"

A furtive movement came from nearby. Jack had apparently scurried out of his hiding place. "Watchin' the road."

Suddenly, Olivia was overwhelmed with anger at the boy, fury that he'd scared her, even more that he hadn't helped her escape. Over the past few days, there had been any number of times when he could have released her, but he hadn't done it.

Then, remembering the blank, dazed expression, the robotic voice, she forced the anger away. He was a little kid who'd been in this monster's grip for a whole lot longer than three days. She couldn't imagine what he had endured. Once she got home, she was going to do what she could for him. Help him get free, find out who his people were. She had to; otherwise that blank, haunted stare and bruised face would torment her for the rest of her life.

"Good. I'm gonna need your help in a li'l while. Once I take care of this, I want you to get some plastic and roll her up good and tight to bury her. You know what to do."

And just like that, her fantasy popped. He wasn't hauling her outside to let her go. Jack had been right all along. Olivia shuddered, her weak legs giving out beneath her as the world began to spin and the faces of her parents and little sister flashed in her mind.

"Get me my hunting knife."

Her every muscle went rigid with terror. A scream rose in her throat and burst from her mouth. He clapped a hand over it, shoving the fabric between her split lips. "Shut up, girl, or it'll go worse for ya." Then, to the boy, he snapped, "Well? Get goin'!"

"Knife's broke," Jack mumbled. "I was usin' it to tighten up the hinges on the barn door, and the blade snapped."

Her kidnapper moved suddenly, the hand releasing her mouth. A sudden thwack said he'd backhanded the boy. Jack didn't cry out, didn't stagger away, as far as she could hear.

"What am I supposed to do now?" the man snapped.

Jack cleared his throat. For a second, she thought he had worked up the courage to beg for her freedom, that he would try, however futilely, to stand up for her.

Instead, in that same brainwashed voice, he made another suggestion. And her last hope died.

"Why don't you drown her?"

Chapter 1

Present day

Pulling into the gravel parking lot of a burned-out honky-tonk on Ogeechee Road, Detective Gabe Cooper eyed his watch, then the temperature gauge on the dash of his unmarked sedan. Six twenty-five a.m., eighty-two degrees. Humidity about eighty percent.

It was gonna be a hell of a day. Or a day in hell. With any summer in Savannah, there wasn't much difference, and this August heat wave had already been one for the record books. Not just for the high temps but also for the crime rate. Because with heat came anger; with anger, violence. And, more than anybody on the Savannah-Chatham Metro PD would like to admit, that violence ended in death. Which was why he was here, outside what had once been Fast Eddie's Bar and was now one giant hunk of burnt.

Killing the engine, Gabe pushed his dark sunglasses firmly over his eyes, then glanced out the window at a car that had just pulled in beside him. His partner, Ty Wallace, had gotten the call on his way in to the central precinct, too, and had detoured to meet him on the scene.

Theirs weren't the only vehicles present. The fire department had reportedly gotten the call at around three a.m., and it had taken crews from two stations to beat the flames into submission. Now, the smoldering ruins of a once troublesome hangout were ringed by a handful of trucks, a squad car, a fire chief vehicle, and a crime scene van that said forensics was already on the job. From up the block, an early-bird crew from one of the local news stations ogled everything, hungry for a story to lead off the seven a.m. broadcast.

Fortunately, the few sad, ramshackle houses nearby remained quiet, either abandoned, or their occupants were sound asleep, tired out after the middle-of-the-night fire excitement. The only close neighbors likely to be attracted to the action now would be watching from the afterlife: The North Laurel Grove Cemetery cast its shadow of eerie-genteel Southern death over the entire area from directly across the street.

From what he'd heard on dispatch, the initial call had sounded like just another random fire, possibly an arson case. The kind where some roughneck got mad about being cut off, then flicked a match on a tank of propane and roared away into the night. Then they'd found the body.

Too early to say who it was, how they'd died, or who'd lit the match. But things had definitely gotten a lot stickier.

Stepping out of the car, he braced himself against an assault of pure heat against his air-conditioned skin. A sheen of sweat immediately broke out on his brow. The scorched air was sharp in his nose, the smoky embers leaving a haze that rose to meet the one falling from the humid sky. But even that didn't quite cover up the smell of old paper and damp cellar that seemed to permeate the state in August.

The keening screech of a million cicadas deafened him for a moment. Oblivious to man's drama, the insects drowned out the chatter of the on-site responders and the rumble of a city waking up to another steamy morning.

Summertime in Georgia. You had to love it 'cause

you'd just go crazy hating it. Never having lived any-where else—he'd been raised on a farm less than a hundred miles from here and had gone to community college, and then the state university, SSU, right here in Savannah—he didn't know how he'd react if a summer day didn't include sweat and haze and hot air in his lungs. And bugs . . . Lord knows, you couldn't forget the bugs.

"Beats some Northern city with ten feet of snow in the winter," he reminded himself. Besides, while Savannah might have cockroaches as big as his hand, he wouldn't trade them for dog-sized rats in someplace like New York.

Eyeing the smoke still rising from the charred, blackened remains, he found himself hoping this was an open-and-shut kind of case—arson as revenge, owner caught in the wrong place at the wrong time. He didn't know if his boiling brain was ready for much more than that this early, especially with no coffee.

"Hey there, partner," said Ty, who'd hopped out of his car with his typical jaunty air. His freshly shaved head gleamed, and his light-colored suit was crisp and fresh. As usual, the guy looked like he'd stepped off the cover of *GQ*.

Gabe, on the other hand, could maybe pose for *Field & Stream* on his very best day. A suit-and-tie kinda guy he wasn't, though, of course, he'd made the tie concession since earning his shield three years ago.

"Lucky us—getting to work in the great outdoors this fine morning," his partner added. "One of the best parts of the job, isn't it?"

"Cheery SOB," Gabe muttered, knowing the man was trying to get a laugh out of him.

"Broughtcha somethin'," Ty said, lifting his hand to reveal a large, plastic cup containing some beige Slurpee-like confection topped with whipped cream and chocolate syrup that wouldn't be consumed by any self-respecting coffee drinker.

He grimaced. "No, thank you."

"That's mine." Ty placed the drink on the car roof and bent back inside. When he stood, he held a foam cup, the steam rising out of the tiny sippy hole at the top.

Ahh. Perfect. His partner might have peacock genes, but he did know Gabe well. Didn't matter if the heat index was two below molten lava, he needed his coffee hot and dark to start the day. "Thanks. You're forgiven for sticking me with the report on the liquor store holdup so you could go out with that tranny you met at the racetrack."

Always good-humored, Ty grinned. "She was all woman, partner. Just big and fierce."

Gabe knew that; he'd just been giving his partner shit. Ty was purely straight. The younger man loved women, probably a little too much, considering how many different ones seemed to drift in and out of his life. Gabe had been warning him that one day he was either gonna get the Bobbitt treatment, or else he'd fall crazy in love, for real, with a woman who wouldn't let him touch a hair on her head.

Watching him take a sip, Ty gave him a sly look and asked, "So, whaddya say? Is it strong enough to float an anvil?"

Gabe chuckled. One thing he had to say for his young partner, he sure was tenacious. Ty had picked up some book of Southern expressions and was forever trying them out. He had moved here from Florida, which any Georgian would tell you was about as much a part of the true Deep South as New York City. Tired of losing the argument that south of the Mason-Dixon Line meant *Southern*—which it didn't—the man was blasted determined to fit in like a born-and-bred Georgian, one colloquialism at a time.

"Y'all just about got that 'un right," Gabe said with a grin, letting his own Deep South accent, which he usually kept under control, slip out. "But remember, it's pronounced 'tuh' not 'to.'"

The younger man saluted. "Got it."

Leaving their cars, the two of them approached the scene and were greeted by a sweating firefighter wearing about forty pounds of gear. The red-faced man eyed Ty's froufrou drink, and without a second's hesitation his partner wordlessly handed it over. "For you."

Pain-in-the-ass clothes-and-women hound or not, Ty was one hell of a nice guy. In the year that they'd been partnered up, Gabe had come not only to respect him but also to like him more than just about anybody else he knew. Of course, that didn't stop him from giving the rookie detective shit just as often as he felt like it.

"Thanks," the firefighter said, sounding truly grateful. His soot-smeared hand shook a little with visible exhaustion as he lifted the icy drink to his mouth and gulped.

"So whadda we got?" Gabe asked after the exhausted firefighter had sipped deeply.

"Remains were found hidden inside a wall. Looks like they'd been there a long time."

Taken by surprise, since he'd expected an arson victim who'd gotten trapped by the flames or smoke mere hours ago, Gabe frowned. "How long?"

"Skeleton long," the main replied with a shrug.

Meaning years. Talk about a cold case turned very hot.

"The body musta been wrapped up in plastic or something, which pretty much melted under the flames. But there wasn't much corpse left to melt from what I could see. Just bones."

"You found the remains yourself?" Ty asked, jotting a few notes in a small notebook.

"Uh-huh," the firefighter said. Offering his name and badge number, he added, "We were walking down the site, just to check for any hot spots. Didn't think there were any victims—the owner lives nearby and came in right away. Said the bar had been closed for an hour and nobody shoulda been here."

Gabe glanced around the parking lot and spied a dejected-looking older man with long, graying hair. His loose shorts, T-shirt and flip-flops said he'd dressed and gotten here in a hurry. "He the owner?"

"Yeah, that's him, Fast Eddie himself. He's been wailing 'bout some cracker who was hassling a waitress the other night."

Gabe couldn't prevent a tiny, reflexive stiffening of his spine at the casual, derogatory slang. Pure product of his upbringing, he knew. He was long past being bothered about the fact that he'd been labeled a cracker, a redneck, or just a white-trash bastard as a kid, having grown up on a dirt-poor farm with his racist asshole of a grandfather.

Huh. He couldn't even imagine what the old man would say if he knew Gabe's new partner was a black man. If Gabe had actually spoken to his only living relative once in the past seven years, he might be tempted now to call him up, just to tell him that.

"Fast Eddie suspects the guy came back tonight and set the blaze for revenge," the firefighter added.

Maybe. But judging by what they'd heard so far, this "cracker" probably hadn't been the one who'd left a plastic-wrapped skeleton on-site, unless he had a twisted sense of humor and a liking for dramatic calling cards. "Okay, we'll talk to him, get a description of the guy."

The firefighter finished the drink Ty had given him and mumbled, "Thanks, man. I owe you one."

"No problem."

"Next one's on me, I swear," he said with a grin. But

it quickly faded. "Hell of a thing, finding something like that. Never seen anything like it. Who'd expect to stumble over a bunch of old bones stuffed inside a wall?"

The big man looked shaken. Working homicide, dealing with bodies had become an unpleasant habit for Gabe, but this guy might never have seen human remains before. Firefighters went into their field to save lives, while cops like Gabe eventually got used to the fact that they spent more time helping victims after crimes were committed than before.

The old adage said an ounce of prevention was worth a pound of cure. But in this day and age, with budgets stretched so thin that states were sending IOUs instead of tax refunds, cops were badly outmanned and often outequipped. Playing solve instead of prevent seemed to be the name of the game everywhere, including Savannah.

"Where exactly did you find 'em?" Gabe asked.

"The masonry was still intact in the corner of what was once a storage room, but, fortunately, not the liquor storage room, or we might not'a found anything at all. We got this wicked bitch under control right before she made contact with about fifty cases of beer and dozens of bottles of Jack, Johnnie and Wild Turkey."

That would have been bad. Real bad. The dead over at Laurel Grove Cemetery might have been rattled out of their graves if that room had gone up.

"Looks like the body had been wedged up against the wall between two studs, then closed in with drywall. Once the wall came down, the bones did, too."

"You'd think they'd have noticed the smell," Ty muttered.

Maybe. But in a bar filled with the smell of beer and sweaty bodies, maybe a nasty odor coming from a packed storage room wouldn't have stood out too much.

Thanking the firefighter, Gabe nodded to a man

who'd just exited the ruin—Wright, one of the crime scene investigators. Good. In fact, he was probably the best. Wright wasn't a grandstander or a typical science geek. He was friendly, though methodical and thorough, never missing a thing. Every cop in homicide hoped he'd be the one they drew on a case.

"Mornin', detectives," he said, heading straight to his van and talking over his shoulder. "I don't have anything yet."

"You're losing your touch then; figured you'd have the vic's name and driver's license number by now," Ty said with a grin.

Wright, usually good-natured, didn't laugh in response. Instead, he shook his head in disgust. "This poor kid was too young to have one."

A kid.

"Damn," Ty mumbled, rubbing a hand against his jaw.

Wright reached into the van and hauled out a sizable equipment case—he'd apparently gotten here just ahead of them and hadn't done much more than walk into the building and take a look. "He's been there a long time—years probably. Judging by the size of the skeleton, I'd say he was around ten, maybe twelve when he died. Somewhere in that range."

Gabe steeled himself against the instinctive mental rebellion that went with the idea of a little kid being murdered and stuffed into a wall and focused on doing his job: finding out who'd done it. "Male?"

"Pretty sure, not one hundred percent yet because of the soot and the melted plastic, but it looks that way. Coroner'll be able to confirm it."

"Any sign of trauma?"

Wright shrugged. "Like I said, I can't see much yet. The skull is intact; so's the rib cage. If there was any remaining flesh or organ matter, the fire burned it away, along with whatever clothes he'd been wearing." He shrugged. "Just have to wait and see what the coroner can find regarding cause of death. I sure hope he can find something."

"You'n me both," said Gabe, preparing mentally to walk into the ruins to see the crime scene for himself. In any old murder case, finding evidence after a number of years was tough. But after a fire? Talk about finding your needle in a stack'a needles.

Whether the bar had actually been the place of the murder was still very much in question, though he tended to doubt it. What would a young kid be doing inside a rowdy hangout? More likely the boy had run afoul of somebody connected with the place, somebody who'd done a little creative construction work to hide evidence of his crime.

He glanced across the parking lot toward the owner, noting Ty was doing the same thing.

"Think we're gonna need to talk to him," Gabe murmured.

"Uh-huh." Ty frowned, any evidence of earlier humor having evaporated with the knowledge that they were dealing with the murder of a child, the worst-case scenario for any cop, as far as Gabe was concerned. Though he'd worn the uniform for a few years in Florida, Ty's detective badge was pretty new, so this could very well be his first case involving a kid. Sucked to be him today. And even though he'd been on the job long enough to have seen a few cases he'd rather never have known about, frankly, it sucked to be Gabe today, too.

Since her own murder, at the age of fifteen, Olivia Wainwright had experienced more deaths than she could ever remember. Not that she tried to remember. Why would anyone choose to? Bad enough that she did what she did, that her own brush with death seemed to have opened some portal into a darkness she had never fully understood, even if she had finally accepted it.

But some experiences never left. Some sensations seemed to have been forever imprinted onto her cerebral cortex. Sense memories clawed at her brain even in her sleep, often causing her to wake up in terror, sure she was being shot or choked or beaten—murdered.

Because she had been. Not once, but many times.

She'd felt the agony of a bullet tearing into flesh, the pressure of hands wrapped around her throat, the thud of fists battering her body. Then there were the accidental deaths—sometimes those had to be investigated, too. So she knew the crushing sensation of a human form being twisted around the steering column of a small car, and sometimes still tasted the vile black smoke inhaled by a man trapped in a burning building.

Not once, but many times.

Although the horrific deaths she experienced now weren't her own, it never got any easier. In fact, each time was just a little worse than the last, each connection just a hint more terrifying to make. Because she'd been brought back. Saved. Those other victims hadn't.

It always took a while to move past one of her shared-death experiences and required a great deal of determination and mental will. Until she did move past it, she never got much peace or rest.

Lying alone in her bed just after dawn on Monday, Olivia tried to even her breathing and still her racing heart. She had jerked out of sleep, the overwhelming sensation of falling making her reach out and grab for something—anything—to prevent her from splattering on the hard ground. Dreams of falling weren't uncommon for anyone. But they probably didn't hold the clarity that Olivia's night terror just had. It had been so real, so incredibly real.

"Because of Bernie Ratzinger," she whispered, hearing the quaver in her own voice.

Beside her, Poindexter, her cat, lifted his head and

opened one sleepy green eye. She reached for him, sinking her fingers into his fur, stroking him back to sleep, though she knew slumber would elude her until she rid herself of the sad final minutes of Bernie Ratzinger's life.

Bernie had been a banker with a serious gambling habit who'd been playing a risky game with his employer's money. When that game had ended with a Go-Directly-to-Jail card, he'd taken another way out—off the top of a fifteen-story high-rise on Bryan Street.

His wife hadn't believed it was suicide. She'd been sure Bernie had been murdered by someone who'd been even more deeply involved in the embezzling scandal. She'd come to eXtreme Investigations—the paranormal detective agency Olivia worked for—and asked them to prove it.

Olivia's boss, Julia, knew the widow personally and had wanted to help her out. The husband's life insurance policy wouldn't pay off in the case of suicide. If Olivia had been able to find any evidence that Ratzinger had been pushed off that building, evidence that could be corroborated by the rest of the team, the widow and her children would be much better off. So Olivia had agreed to do it.

She'd known the moment she touched his corpse that it had, indeed, been suicide.

Olivia had connected with him, almost *become* him, during the final two minutes and ten seconds of his life. And, like always, once that connection had been made, she couldn't break it until the very end. So she'd been with Bernie for every one of those awful final seconds.

She'd looked down at feet pacing that roof as if they were her own. Had heard his words as he talked to himself, working up his nerve to jump. No one else had been there. Not another person's voice, not a footstep, not a hand in the dark—neither a helpful nor a murderous one. Just Bernie and his rantings about his fear of prison and his anger at being so stupid and his sadness at what he'd done to his family.

She hadn't been inside his head. That never happened, so she couldn't read anybody's last thoughts. She could only experience what they experienced through their own sensory input: what they saw, heard, tasted, smelled. And felt—physically, not emotionally.

Honestly, she wouldn't have needed to share his thoughts to understand what Bernie was feeling and thinking during those final minutes. Nor did she really have to hear his words. The man's condition had been made clear by the sick clenching in his stomach, the tightness of every muscle, the sobs, the sting of tears in his eyes. The way his arms shook and his hands trembled as he prepared to hoist himself out onto the ledge.

Shivering lightly, she let the rest of the memories in, little by little. Though the temperature in her bedroom was comfortable, she easily recalled the sensation of hot night air stabbing at her face as she hurtled off the roof. The trip down had been an incredibly fast one, the ground looming ever larger with each foot she and Bernie fell out of the sky. His long scream of remorse as the human survival instinct kicked in suggested that in the last seconds of his life, he had wished he could turn back the clock so he could take it back, not make that fearful leap.

He had died almost instantly, so there had been very little pain. Just that fear, that awful, bone-deep terror during the short but still interminably long descent.

Not his terror. Hers. He'd been her first jumper. That was the problem. It wasn't as easy to get past this one because she was dealing with something new.

"Time to let it go, Liv," she reminded herself.

Breathing deeply, she utilized a few relaxation techniques she'd acquired over the years. Aidan McConnell, a psychic she worked with at eXtreme Investigations, had once told her he tried to visualize building an enormous cement block wall to serve as a barrier between him and any invasion into his psyche. Olivia didn't require a barrier, however. She didn't have to keep anything from coming in. She just needed a way to get it out.

Relaxed, she visualized gently falling rain, a slow, soft shower. Only when she could almost feel it against her skin did she allow herself to fully acknowledge the fear, remember the pain. She let it take her for a second. When she'd fully embraced it, come to terms with the horror, Olivia let the rain pour in, let it flow over her, seep into her pores to carry away all that was dark, grimy and awful. She focused on being washed clean, on the reality that she was fine and safe and not at all frightened. Slowly, each of those dark feelings began to float away with the water, long rivulets escaping her subconscious to evaporate in the daylight of reality.

Eventually, she began to feel back in control, normal—or her version of it, anyway.

"Oh, great," she said with a weary sigh, glancing at the gleaming green numbers on her bedside clock. She wondered if there was any point in even trying to go back to sleep for the fifteen minutes she had left before the alarm went off.

Outside, a motor suddenly whirred and whined. The landscaping guy who cut almost every lawn in the neighborhood was starting super early these days to beat the heat, noise ordinances be damned. And oh, what a noise it was. Now she *knew* there was no point trying to go back to sleep.

Slipping out of bed, she beelined for the shower. A real one was now just as necessary as her mental one had been. Her memories had been washed clean; it was time to finish the job with real water on the rest of her body.

Water. Funny that it was her coping mechanism now, considering it was also her number one terror. Not warm showers, of course, but cold, black, fathomless pools. Once upon a time, when she had been young and normal, it had been the swipe of a sharp blade across her skin that had instilled the most terror in her. Now, it was water.

"Not gonna think about that," she mumbled as she turned on the shower, then got right in, not even waiting for it to get hot. It was going to be another scorcher outside, and being pelted with cool liquid seemed the wisest way to start the day.

Afterward, while she got ready for work, Olivia turned on the radio, wanting to catch the weather forecast. It was masochistic, she knew, but hey, a high of 97 beat one of 102 any day. And, despite the fact that a lot of people probably considered her a ghoul, she was an optimist—or at least a realist with optimistic leanings.

"And now for the local news, here's an update on our top story: an overnight fire at a bar near the Laurel Grove Cemetery."

Olivia stiffened, dropping the towel she'd been using on her hair. Her mouth went dry; her pulse sped up. The visceral reactions were familiar, occurring whenever she heard anything to do with Laurel Grove. The very name conjured up a litany of dark images, unearthing memories she would much prefer to keep buried.

Black night, creaking, rusty gates, tiny bugs and creatures skittering across her bare, ragged feet. Struggling to breathe—trying to remind her body how it was done—with air so humid it was like inhaling through a blanket made of wool and soaked in syrup. The uneven ground, the twisted trees and tangled Spanish moss sending strange shadows in every direction.

The graves. Oh, God, the graves. Every one seemed to bear her name; each crypt had invited her to enter and lie down there with the cold dead, since that was where she rightfully belonged. And so she'd. . . .

She shook her head hard, struggling to focus on the

bright and sunny now, not the dark and bleak then. Escaping the mental effects of that horrific night had taken a lot of time and effort, not to mention therapy. While her friends in high school had been staying after school for cheerleading practice, she'd been heading to a shrink's couch. It had taken sacrifice and grit, but she'd survived. So she refused to give those memories any power over her now.

Yet the dark thoughts persisted.

"As reported earlier, fire crews responded at about three a.m. to this two-alarm fire which destroyed a popular hangout on North Ogeechee Road. We're now hearing that human remains have been found on the site."

Fire—smoke inhalation. What an awful way to die. Olivia knew that better than most.

"But an inside source tells us that the remains apparently were hidden at the site several years ago. A small skeleton was found walled up inside the burned-out structure."

Shock made her slowly lower herself to the bed, and she barely heard the voice on the radio as it continued. She was too focused on what the deejay had already said: *A skeleton. Walled up for years.* Twelve years, perhaps? Was it even possible?

"There's no way," she told herself. "How many people die in Savannah every year?"

A lot. God knows, in her line of work, she knew a lot about death and murder. So the idea that this particular victim could possibly be connected to *him* was incredibly slight.

A small skeleton. There for years.

Olivia shook her head, angry at herself for thinking those thoughts. It had been over for twelve years; she needed to leave the past in the past. She turned off the radio, no longer worrying about the weather. Hot was hot, and she would dress appropriately.

Forty-five minutes later, she left her Victorian District house to head to work. But somehow, instead of skirting Forsyth Park to Abercorn so she could head north to downtown, she found herself going south. She didn't even think about it, didn't recall making a conscious decision to do it, right up until she hit West Thirty-first and turned right.

"What are you doing?" she mumbled, not sure what had compelled her to come this way.

Then she saw the sign for Ogeechee and realized where her subconscious was taking her.

Go there, Olivia. You have to see for yourself.

Why she had to see, she didn't know. Nor was she entirely sure whose voice that whisper in her brain had sounded like. Not really hers, it was as if she were being directed by someone else altogether. Someone who wanted her to find out what was happening at the scene of that fire and whose skeletal remains had been found there. *His?*

As she drew closer, she saw the news vans parked at the corner. Onlookers who had gathered on the sidewalk across the street from what had once been Fast Eddie's were staring avidly at the police and fire investigation officials who filled the scene.

"Make a U-turn and go back," she told herself, knowing she wouldn't want to turn right and drive past Laurel Grove, which she always took great pains to avoid.

But she didn't turn around, and she didn't turn right. Instead, she pulled over and parked behind a WJCL van, with its antennas up and a cameraman and reporter standing nearby.

She sat in the car for a minute, her hands clenching the steering wheel. Something had drawn her here, something compelling and insistent. Rationally, she knew that made no sense, but how long had it been since anything about her life made a whole lot of sense?

Whatever instinct had brought her here, she wasn't content to watch from the car. She cut the engine, then stepped out into the hot, bright morning and walked up the sidewalk. She saw the onlookers blocking the path. Saw the vehicles and the twirling lights and the reporters. But her mind didn't really register any of that other than as obstacles to move around. So she moved around them, silently, almost as if in a trance. Then farther, stepping down off the curb, drawn irrevocably closer to that burned-out shell across the street.

You have to see, have to make sure. You must find out what happened to him.

"Hey, lady, what the hell are you doing?!" a voice yelled. "Watch out!" The shout was quickly followed up by the blast of a horn and the loud squeal of tires on pavement.

As if she'd been slapped out of a daze, Olivia blinked and swung her head around just in time to see a car barreling down on her, so close she could see the driver's huge eyes and his screaming mouth. Shocked into near immobility, all she could do was throw her hands up in a self-protective gesture, even as her brain screamed at her to move.

Waiting for the crunch of steel on her body, knowing this time the pain would be hers, she gasped when someone tackled her around the waist, hauling her out of the way. Her rescuer stumbled several feet, carrying her along with him. He held her close, his back to the street, shielding her, as if determined to provide one final barrier between her and the vehicle—the vehicle that skidded to a stop right where she'd been standing.

It had all happened in less than ten seconds.

"Jesus, that was close," a man's voice said, low and thick, close to her ear. She felt his breath on her cheek and his big, hard form pressed against every inch of her.

"No kidding," she whispered, feeling as though she'd

suddenly awakened from a dream, like this morning's, when she'd been falling through the air. Only this had been no dream—she could have been killed.

Swallowing hard, she peered around him, seeing a car angled across the opposite lane, its driver shaking a fist at her. The crowd on the corner was abuzz, and the cameraman had swung his equipment around, all bearing witness to what could have been her death.

Good Lord. She'd walked right into the middle of the road, into oncoming traffic.

"Are you okay?" her rescuer asked.

The powerful arms that had hauled her out from in front of the oncoming car released her, and she dropped onto her toes. Olivia hauled in a deep breath, then nodded once, still too shaken to even look at him fully. "Yes." She lifted a hand and pushed her hair back off her face, feeling the cold sweat on her forehead. "Thanks to you."

"You stupid bitch, what the hell were you thinking?" someone screamed.

Her savior, who was still so close she could feel the brush of his pants against her bare legs, swung around and pointed at the man. "Get back in your car, sir."

"She walked right out in front of me!"

The man reached for his belt, pulled off a leather wallet and flipped it open to display a badge. "I said, get in your car and move along. You're blocking traffic."

The driver ignored the order. "Are you gonna charge her with something?"

The stranger took one step toward the vehicle, his powerful body rigid, his shoulders bunching against his brown suit jacket. "If you say one more word, I'll ticket you. You were driving like a maniac through a crime scene, and if you'd been paying attention to the road rather than what was going on across the street, you would have seen this pedestrian in plenty of time."

The man's eyes widened, and his face flamed, confirming what the officer had said. Still, Olivia knew she'd been responsible for the near miss. She'd walked right into the path of the car, focused solely on whatever force seemed to be tugging her toward the burned-out ruin.

She stepped toward the officer. "It was entirely my fault."

That seemed to mollify the driver, as did the subsequent apology she offered him. He gave her a single, harsh nod, then got back into his car and drove away. Slowly.

Once he was gone, the cop turned back toward her. For the first time, she was able to look at him, face-to-face, and for a second, her breath caught in her throat. Her legs, which had been firmly planted on the ground once he'd set her down, wobbled just a bit, and both her X chromosomes went on alert, reacting to his mighty Y one.

The man wasn't so much handsome as incredibly good-looking, rugged and utterly masculine. His face was strong and determined, his nose a little crooked like he'd taken a few hits in his day. That was a nice change from the more plastic, perfect male faces she'd seen. She'd grown up around rich lawyers and politicians; a nose job was generally a prerequisite before the launch of any political career.

The stranger's jaw was strong, jutting; the mouth wide and probably incredibly attractive when he smiled. Which he was not. His light brown hair fell a bit shaggily over his brow, and his dark green eyes seemed to see more than the average person's. He wasn't excessively tall, just of average height, but his body was big, compact, incredibly muscular and intimidating.

No wonder he'd been able to pick her up so easily and haul her out of harm's way. He was built like a gladiator.

Olivia usually dated lean, softer-looking men. But for

the life of her, she suddenly couldn't remember why. Because this one had her stomach—not to mention her female parts—fluttering with just one long look.

"Are you sure you're okay? I didn't hurt you?"

Hurt her? He might have just saved her life. "I'm fine, thank you. I can't believe I was so oblivious."

He took her arm and steered her toward the curb, making sure she stepped up onto it. Then, glancing around, he stepped back, bent and scooped up a pair of dark sunglasses off the street. They must have fallen off his face when he'd rescued her. They were now missing a lens. And the other was badly scratched.

"I'm *so* sorry," she told him. "Please let me replace those. Were they prescription?"

"Nah." He shrugged, tucking them into his suit pocket. "No biggie. I'm so hard on 'em I stock up at the dollar store."

He had a nice voice, she realized, when he wasn't barking at people. His soft drawl said he was a Georgia native—maybe not Savannah, more country—but still attractive, sexy.

"You, uh, wanna tell me what had you so fascinated that you almost walked right up to the pearly gates and introduced yourself to St. Peter?" he asked, his voice low, lightly amused. But his stare remained keen, assessing.

She licked her lips, glancing past him at the fire scene, where emergency responders continued to work, making sure the area was secure. "I, uh . . . ." What could she say, that she'd heard about the fire on the news and had driven down here because she had this strange mental compulsion? Savannah police already thought those associated with eXtreme Investigations were bonkers; why on earth would she add to that conclusion? "I just saw the activity and came over to see what was happening. I didn't even realize I'd actually stepped out into traffic." A weak excuse, and she doubted he entirely bought it.

He didn't. "That's all? You wouldn't have any information about the fire, would you?"

She evaded the question. "I heard you found human remains inside."

His eyes widened, and his jaw dropped briefly. "How the hell . . ."

"It was on the radio."

"Damn it," he snapped. "Are you kiddin' me?"

"No, I'm afraid not," she said, realizing his anger at having a leak on the scene might work to her advantage. He looked ready to go rip somebody a new one, which meant he might not be too interested in questioning her further.

That was a good thing. She suddenly wanted to get out of here, to forget she'd ever come down here. Whatever strange force had made her come here had nearly gotten her killed, and she wasn't interested in heeding it anymore.

The officer was glaring toward the news truck, then glancing over his shoulder at the site across the street, already distracted, his mind back on his job.

"I'm so sorry I took you away from your work," she told him. "I promise I'll stick to the sidewalk from now on."

He nodded absently. "Yeah, you do that, please. Have a good day, ma'am."

"You, too," she said. "And thanks again."

"Take care now," he said; then he turned, looked both ways, and jogged across the street. He immediately engaged in a serious conversation with a uniformed police officer, forgetting about her and her near miss.

But Olivia had the feeling she wasn't going to soon forget him. Not only because he'd saved her life but also because he'd done it without even thinking about it, without giving a thought for his own safety. He'd been decisive and powerful, forceful and strong. She wasn't used to being around such men, men who could easily swoop in at a dangerous moment, pick a woman up in his arms and carry her away as if she weighed next to nothing. Like a hero, a real one.

"You're watching too many romantic movies," she mumbled. "He's just a man."

No, he wasn't. He was the man who'd saved her from a lot of pain or worse and whose name she didn't even know.

It doesn't matter; you'll never see him again, she told herself as she got in her car, determined to drive straight to work without any more detours.

Somehow, though, she didn't find her own words comforting. In fact, she found them pretty damn depressing.

Chapter 2

Though the week had started out badly, it was finishing off pretty well. First of all, Olivia had had no more bad dreams since Monday morning. Second, she and the rest of the eXtreme Investigations team had helped solve a case involving a missing woman. And third, it was almost the weekend, and she hadn't had one additional near-death experience—hers or anyone else's.

No, not a bad week at all.

"Especially considering you started it by almost becoming roadkill," she mumbled as she finished showering Friday morning.

She'd thought about the near miss several times, though she hadn't mentioned it to anyone. Not only because she still felt foolish about walking out in front of a speeding car but also because of that strange, urgent compulsion that had drawn her to the scene of the fire.

Then, of course, there had been that good-looking cop who'd saved her.

She would have liked to have met him under different circumstances and wished she'd gotten his name. At the very least, she'd like to replace his sunglasses, dollar store or not. She'd been keeping an eye on TV news stories about the case but hadn't seen him in any of the coverage. A couple of cops had been quoted in the paper, but there were no clues that would help her identify the man who'd saved her life.

Nor had the articles contained much additional information about the crime itself. So far, the police had been pretty closemouthed about the case, beyond finally acknowledging that there had, indeed, been human remains found on the site.

Frankly, she'd feel better when those remains were identified, so she could stop this crazy wondering that had plagued her since Monday.

"Best to just let it go," she told herself. Looking back on it, that weird urge she'd had to go down there the other day seemed more than a little ridiculous, not to mention embarrassing.

Wrapping her hair in a towel and donning a robe, she headed downstairs to the kitchen, needing a cup of coffee to get her going. It was a bright, sunny morning, sunlight spilling through the bank of windows running across the width of the kitchen. Poindexter had already staked out his favorite spot on the windowsill. When she'd gotten out of bed, he'd been sleeping on her pillow. Now he was sleeping in a shaft of sunlight, the key word being *sleeping*.

"Feels good, doesn't it, Dex?" she said. "But only because you don't have to go out in it."

He offered her his standard, baleful kitty stare, reminding her who was top dog around here, then dropped his head back onto his paws.

It suddenly hit her. She'd become a cat lady: a single, living-alone, muttering-to-herself, hadn't-been-on-a-date-in-months, hadn't-had-sex-in-far-longer-than-that cat lady.

She chuckled in spite of herself, knowing how that would have horrified her late grandmother, the one who'd left her this house. Olivia Wainwright, daughter of a multimillionaire, granddaughter of a former senator, cousin of a current one, descended from a long line of Southern debs and socialites . . . a spinster. Frankly, she suspected her grandmother would be more horrified by that than she would by the fact that her granddaughter had an unhealthy connection with the dead and worked with a bunch of eccentric paranormal types.

After setting the coffeemaker, Olivia stuck a piece of bread in the toaster, if only to keep herself from reaching for a donut when she got to the office. Julia brought them in almost every day—a habit that had lingered from the other woman's previous days as a Charleston cop. Of course, a donut obsession wasn't the only thing that had stuck around after Julia left Charleston. Her last partner had, too. Not that he could be seen by anybody but Julia.

Ghosts. Huh. Once upon a time, the very idea would have made Olivia laugh in outright disbelief. That was before she, herself, had become a semiregular in the land of the dead. Now, it wasn't that tough to believe anything. eXtreme Investigations was staffed with the best of the paranormal best.

There was Julia, of course, her boss, who was seldom without her ghostly best friend. Aidan McConnell's psychic visions had proved remarkably helpful in solving crimes. Mick Tanner's ability to touch something and know its entire history had led them all in some interesting directions. And Derek Monahan's ability to see a murder victim reenacting his own death again and again added to the power of Olivia's own shared-death experiences.

"Crazy stuff," she muttered. But all part of her life now.

Not really thinking about it, she picked up the remote and flipped on the small TV that stood on a corner counter just in time to hear a news anchor say, "Coming up after the break, the latest on remains found after Monday's fire at a bar on Ogeechee Road."

Her stomach tightened instinctively, her mind immediately tripping back to those surreal moments Monday morning when she'd felt like somebody else was propelling her body to that crime scene. Olivia was used to feeling like she'd stepped into other people's bodies; the feeling that someone else had taken over hers was something she didn't like. Not one bit. Especially since it had nearly gotten her killed.

You should turn it off. You don't need to be thinking about this.

But of course she didn't.

The news program segued into a long commercial break, but the cheerful jingle of a national fast-food joint didn't distract her. Instead, despite all her efforts, her tension rose.

After pouring her coffee, she buttered her toast and took a few bites. She stopped chewing as soon as the familiar news program logo reappeared.

"And now, more on a story we broke Monday morning, about a fire at a bar called Fast Eddie's, which revealed a disturbing discovery: human remains concealed inside a wall. This morning, sources inside the Savannah-Chatham Metropolitan Police Department are telling us that the remains most likely belonged to a child."

Olivia swallowed hard, her hand shaking a little, or a lot, judging by the coffee that sloshed out of the mug and hit her skin. Lowering the cup to the counter, she absently reached for the sink, turned on a stream of cold water and let it run over the side of her stinging thumb.

The news anchor introduced a reporter who was delivering a live update from outside one of the local police precincts. The perky-looking woman gave her intro and then introduced a police officer, whose image soon filled the screen.

"You," Olivia said, the word riding out of her mouth on a pleased sigh.

Because there, easily recognizable, was the man who'd

saved her from a run-in with a car. The bottom-of-the-screen graphic identified him as Detective Gabe Cooper.

"Gabe." A nice name. She liked how it felt on her lips.

Cooper squinted at the camera, his rugged face bathed in harsh morning sunlight. *Probably because some clumsy idiot made him break his sunglasses.*

Dark smudges under his eyes and a weary slump to his broad shoulders said he hadn't been sleeping well. She wondered if anybody surrounded by crime and murder ever could.

"Detective Cooper, can you give us any more information on the victim?" the reporter asked. "We're getting reports that you have identified a child?"

"No, that is incorrect," the detective said, almost cutting the reporter off. She sensed Gabe Cooper didn't like reporters. "We haven't *identified* him at all. The coroner's office has confirmed the skeletal remains found at the scene of the fire belonged to a male child, likely Caucasian, approximately ten to twelve years of age."

Olivia slowly lifted her hand and turned off the faucet, then reached for the remote and jacked up the volume. Her heart had begun to thud a little harder, her pulse picking up its pace.

A boy. Ten to twelve years of age. *God.*

"Has a cause of death been determined?"

"I'm not at liberty to discuss specifics of the murder investigation. But we do need the public's help with the actual identification," the detective said.

"What about dental records or DNA?" asked the reporter, as if reading off a *CSI* script.

"We're working on those," Cooper said, "but this child doesn't appear to have had any dental care in his short life."

The reporter nodded, looking pious and sympathetic. She obviously wanted to appear saddened rather than merely thrilled at scooping the other local stations this early on a Friday morning by landing an interview with the lead detective on a tragic murder case.

"They're not all media cockroaches," Olivia reminded herself, remembering she and the other agents at eXtreme Investigations no longer loathed all members of the media the way they once had, mainly because of Aidan McConnell's new girlfriend, Lexie, a reporter.

"His remains also appear to show signs of regular and extended abuse."

Olivia's mouth had gone dry, but she didn't lift the coffee cup because she had the feeling her suddenly churning stomach would reject anything she tried to swallow.

Abused. Neglected.

"Judging by some property records we've discovered, we suspect this boy might have been hidden in the wall twelve years ago, during a renovation after a previous fire."

Twelve years.

Was this really possible?

"Whoever this boy was, his life was very difficult," Cooper said, his voice thickening, as if he were taking this case personally. "We want to catch whoever did this to him. Badly."

"How can the public help?" the TV reporter asked.

"A forensic artist has created a sketch of what the victim might have looked like at the time of his death." Then the detective stared into the camera, intensity revealed in a pair of attractive green eyes. "If you recognize this boy, or if you recall a child you might have suspected was being abused who has since disappeared, please contact our office."

The screen split. Olivia held her breath, waiting for what she knew would appear beside the live scene outside the police station—the drawing. It wouldn't be perfect, of course, based merely on the shape of the skull, the measurements between the eyes, the prominence of any bones. She knew that and was prepared to find nothing familiar in the impersonal sketch.

After a brief technical pause, an image appeared. She stared at it.

A sound filled her kitchen, making Poindexter leap up and run out of the room. It took a second before she realized it had been her own voice, emitting a long, helpless moan.

"Again, if you have any information or think you might recognize this child, please contact the authorities," the reporter said, the voice merely a dull background noise now because Olivia's entire focus remained on the drawing.

As expected, it was basic. Simple. Like any of the dozens of police sketches she'd seen before but, of course, *not* like any of the dozens she'd seen before.

The shade of the hair was wrong, as was the eye color. But the face . . . Oh, God, the face . . . Those prominent cheekbones, the thin, sallow cheeks—like those an abused, neglected child might have. The deep-set eyes, the small mouth, the hooked nose. All of it familiar. So damned familiar.

Olivia stared at the face for as long as it remained on the screen, awash in mental images of the last time she'd seen it. Her memory inserted sunken, too-old-for-their-years brown eyes, a smattering of freckles over pale, bruised cheeks and a mouth twisted with pain, sadness and mistrust.

She knew this face, knew this boy. It was the same one she'd dreamed about, the one she'd searched for again and again over the past twelve years.

Her killer. Her tormentor. Her savior.

Jack.

Why don't you drown her?

He'd sentenced her to death in the most awful way

imaginable. And then he'd brought her back from the other side. She owed him everything and had long told herself that someday she would find him, would repay him.

Once she'd been rescued, the authorities had listened to her story and had tried to locate him. But eventually, when the leads went nowhere and the case had been deemed otherwise closed, they'd lost interest. Then her father had hired private investigators. And once she'd grown up and moved out on her own, Olivia had done the same thing.

All for nothing. They'd been searching for a child who'd probably died not long after he'd helped Olivia escape from their captor. While she'd been filled with hope that she'd be able to repay the greatest debt of her life, he'd been rotting away inside the wall of a bar just a few miles from where she lived.

Olivia couldn't think for a moment, oblivious as the picture faded and the anchor moved on to the next bit of dishy city news. She just stood there, frozen, letting it sink in, letting herself accept that he was gone, murdered all those years ago.

And when it did sink it, when she swallowed that reality like a bitter, rancid hunk of meat, the only thing she could do was lean over the sink and vomit up her breakfast.

By Friday afternoon, Gabe was beginning to regret releasing the sketch of their young Jimmy Doe to the public, but not because it hadn't generated any tips. In fact, it had brought hundreds, all of which had been duly recorded and then delivered to him to sort through.

The problem was, there were too many, and none of them looked very promising. It seemed like every family with a missing son had called in from all over the state. Hell, all over the East Coast. Many were desperate parents, hopeful and pleading, thinking they might finally get a response to a long-unanswered question. Those he could understand.

It didn't end there, however. There had also been the lonely souls who called in on *every* tip line just to have someone to talk to. The vengeful exes looking to put somebody they'd once loved into a brief jam with the authorities. The suspicious neighbors who were just sure the guy next door would do something like that to a kid. There were the sick pranksters, the inevitable false confession from some poor crazy son of a bitch who'd gone off his meds, and on it went.

Ninety percent of these were a waste of his time, and the other ten long shots. Still, no matter how implausible, every call had to be evaluated, which would take up a lot of man-hours. *His* man-hours. There was no task force working this old, cold murder, just him and Ty, plus whoever else was willing to help them out while also dealing with their own workloads, which were all just as heavy as steamy Savannah boiled over into tense, angry Savannah.

It only takes one. He kept reminding himself of that every time he lifted the phone to return a call to somebody who might know something important.

"Hey, Cooper! Somebody's here to see ya," a voice called.

Lowering the phone back into its cradle, he looked up at Kinney, a longtime patrolman whose shitty attitude had kept him from ever climbing the SCMPD ladder. The barrel-chested man was old school—racist, sexist, always smiling but as quick to stab you in the back as to offer you a hand in friendship.

"Who is it?"

Kinney wagged his bushy eyebrows. "A woman. She says she won't talk to nobody but you. Hot, juicy little piece."

"Classy as ever, Kinney," he muttered in disgust.

Hard to insult, the man simply shrugged. "She says it's about some fire you're workin'. I put her in interview two," Kinney added.

Gabe nodded once, figuring the woman might be another reporter. If so, he couldn't help wondering why she'd just shown up rather than calling first. He didn't have a lot of time to deal with impromptu interviews, but he couldn't deny being curious about the woman who'd insisted she talk to him and only him. Sounded like a little more than a media request.

Ty had gone out to grab a late lunch, so Gabe headed alone down the long hallway to interview room two. He rapped once on the door, then pushed it open, his gaze immediately moving to the woman sitting at a small, bare metal conference table.

Surprise shot through him at the sight of her. His feet hesitated for the briefest moment, causing a tiny misstep between one stride and the next. Because it was *her*, the redhead who'd stepped into oncoming traffic Monday and had almost paid for it with her life. The woman he hadn't been able to stop thinking about since, the one whose face he hadn't been able to get out of his mind.

In his memory, though, her eyes hadn't looked like this. They were green and huge, yes. Beautiful, heavily lashed, expressive. But now they were reddened and luminous with recently shed tears. This woman looked like she'd been crying all morning and no amount of eyedrops could have disguised that.

"We meet again," he said.

She nodded, then reached into her purse and pulled out a small box. "These are for you."

When he saw the label, he had to laugh. "You really didn't have to replace them. I was serious; they were dollar-store throwaways."

"It was the least I could do. Thank you again for what you did."

Even as she said it, he knew that replacing his broken sunglasses wasn't the reason she'd come here. The woman's slim throat quivered as she swallowed. Then she licked her lips nervously, and Gabe's heart skipped a beat. Not only was he damned glad she'd waltzed back into his life—since he'd been kicking himself all week for not getting her name—but he also thought she might be ready to tell him what she'd really been doing outside Fast Eddie's Monday morning.

His excitement grew, as it always did when he sensed he was on the verge of some kind of break in a case. If this attractive woman had been crying like her heart was fit to break and had then come here, insisting on seeing him in person to talk about the bones found after the fire, she might have recognized the sketch from the news. Might have known that boy enough to be well and truly grieved at his passing.

Might be here to give him just the lead he'd been hoping for.

The woman managed a small smile as she gracefully rose to her feet and extended her hand. "I saw you on the news. Your name is Detective Cooper?"

"Guilty as charged, ma'am," he replied, his voice low, unthreatening. He wanted to keep her calm and relaxed while she told him whatever she'd come here to say, not only because he hoped he could use the information but also because, like most men he knew, Gabe was completely useless around a crying woman.

Not that she looked on the verge of crying again. That stiff spine and lifted chin showed grit. Like somebody who had a job to do and aimed to do it, no matter how much he or she might hate it. He didn't know this woman from Adam, but already he respected her, at least a little.

"And you are?"

"I'm Olivia Wainwright," she told him.

Their hands came together. His, he knew, big and rough. Hers, much stronger than he'd have imagined. Soft, yes, and small, but her grip was firm, as confident as any man's. The pretty mouth—full lips—didn't tremble, nor had her voice quivered. Those tear-moistened eyes seemed to be the only chink in her armor, and he'd bet she would graciously accuse him of seeing things if he dared to ask her why she'd been crying.

"Thanks for coming in," he replied when their hands slid apart.

"Thank you for seeing me."

Niceties—check. If they were anywhere else, and there weren't a child's murder to investigate, he'd happily keep right on chatting like they were just two strangers meeting for the first time. But they didn't have that luxury. "How can I help you today, assuming there are no speeding cars heading in your direction?"

She smiled slightly, a strained one, but he did note that her tense shoulders might have relaxed the tiniest bit. "I came to see you because I think I might be able to help with the case you talked about on the news this morning. About the murdered boy?"

Still speaking slowly, conveying a casual, laid-back mood he definitely didn't feel, he said, "Is that right? Well, that is good news. Hey, listen. I was just fixin' to have some coffee. You want some before we get down to business?"

"No, thank you."

"Okay, then, let's have a seat."

"Your coffee?"

He waved an unconcerned hand. "It'll keep."

"Very well," she said, drifting back to her chair. She cast him a slightly suspicious glance, and he wondered if he'd overdone it with the folksy Southern manner. It worked on most people when he wanted it to, and right now he wanted her comfortable and relaxed. But she had heard him in his blunt, no-nonsense glory on TV this morning. Plus she looked a little smarter than the average bear.

Smarter, cooler, all put together.

Again he noted the smoothness of her movements, the way the air seemed to part around her rather than her pushing through it. It suddenly occurred to him that she moved like water, flowing from position to position, and he wondered if she was some kind of dancer.

Though, to be honest, she hadn't shown much grace when strolling into the path of that car. He didn't even like to think about what she might look like now if he hadn't grabbed her out of the way. He just thanked God he'd been nearby and had seen what was about to happen.

One thing was sure, this Olivia woman was not, as the piggish Kinney had said, some "juicy little piece." There was an elusive quiet quality about her, nothing at all in-your-face. But she was definitely attractive, with beautiful red-gold hair that hung in a silky curtain down her back.

Redhead with big green eyes—a deadly combination for any man.

The rest of her was just as distracting. Her soft, heart-shaped face was a little too sweet to be called beautiful, her body more slender than curvaceous. Her tasteful jewelry, small handbag, ivory-colored dress and high-heeled shoes didn't scream that they'd come with a very high price tag, but oh, did they ever whisper it. Which meant old money. Old Savannah money, he'd be willing to bet, having heard that unmistakable lilt in her voice.

Gabe was good with accents. And though hers was buried beneath probably at least six years of higher education, he definitely caught the melody line at the bottom of the orchestration.

"Now, what is it you wanted to tell me?" he asked.

She got right down to it. "I think I knew the boy in the drawing."

His heart lurched, though he didn't show it. "Is that so?" Reaching into his pocket, he pulled out a small notepad and pen, and flipped the pad open, wanting to make sure she knew this was slow and easy, unthreatening, nothing to get upset about. Because, damn, he did not want any tear fests in interview two.

"His name was Jack. At least, that's the name he was going by when I knew him. I suspect it wasn't his real one."

"Why is that?"

"Because I think he'd been kidnapped."

That startled him, and he stopped writing.

"I believe he was being held captive by the same man who kidnapped me."

Not only wasn't he writing, now he actually dropped his pen. "Beg pardon?"

She sighed, as if realizing she was not going to be able to simply dump him in the middle of her story but would have to go back a little, or a lot. So that's what she did.

"A little over twelve years ago, when I was fifteen, I was kidnapped right out of my bedroom in the middle of the night." Staring hard at him, she added, "It happened here in Savannah and wouldn't be hard for you to verify that I'm telling you the truth. You might even remember hearing about it on the news."

"I moved here eleven years ago."

"It was a pretty big story," she said, not sounding proud of that but in fact rather bleak.

Considering twelve years ago he'd still been scrabbling to survive, counting down the days until high school graduation so he could get out from under his grandfather's thumb, he'd have to say he hadn't been a big follower of the news, national or state. Big news to him in those days was when he actually managed to go a week without the old man trying to smash a board upside his head.

"I was taken for ransom money. I was . . . my family is well known."

While she spoke, he finally remembered where he had heard the name Wainwright. Not much giving a damn about politics, it had taken him a few minutes to put it together. It could be her father who was currently serving as senator from the great state of Georgia, but for some reason he didn't think so. Maybe it was her grandfather, uncle or cousin? Someone like that.

"I get the picture."

Looking relieved she didn't have to cop to being a rich, spoiled brat, she continued, talking about enduring a horrific ordeal like she was relating the key plot points of a movie she'd just seen. Impersonal. Detached.

He supposed she had to be. Letting something like that remain a prominent, active part of your psyche would probably drive a person nuts.

"And you never got a look at your kidnapper's face?"

"No. He covered my face when he took me. The boy was the only one I saw until . . ."

"Until?"

"Until right before I escaped. But I didn't see the man, even then."

She went on. And as the story unfolded, he found himself less interested in taking notes and more interested in learning what made this woman tick. How had she come back from something like that, being kidnapped right out of her bed as a teenager, then getting away with the help of a strange boy a few days later? Hell, he dealt with people all the time who excused their crimes by saying they just couldn't get over daddy leaving mommy for his assistant. So what made her the calm, cool exception?

Then he thought about it, wondering if she'd just done what he had: decided to live as a sort of fuck-you to the past. Not letting it drag you down was the best revenge, right? And letting some awful memory distract you from living whatever life you had left was a sucker's play. He was no sucker, and he sensed Olivia Wainwright wasn't, either.

"So this Jack, you say he was, what, guarding you during your captivity?"

"Sort of," she admitted. "Although, as I said, I think he was a prisoner, too. He'd obviously been abused; he was all bruised and scarred. And I heard him being struck." She shivered, as if that sound, that crunch of fist on flesh, still echoed in her mind.

"Did you ask Jack who this man was, why he was with him?"

She nodded. "He didn't remember any other life, said he'd been with him forever. But he did not say the man was his father. He'd just been captive so long, I honestly think he was brainwashed. That's how he sounded, anyway. Flat, emotionless. Hopeless."

A lump formed in Gabe's throat, one he couldn't swallow down. What she was describing could certainly fit the abused child he'd been picturing since the autopsy report had come back. Whoever that boy was, he'd had so many broken bones—most of them not properly reset—that Gabe suspected he'd been beaten every week of his young life.

"I know Jack didn't like having to be an accomplice in this; it wasn't like he had any choice. He hated that I was tied up and terrified. He brought me food and water."

"And eventually, he even helped you escape?"

For the first time since she'd begun quickly skimming

over her ordeal, the redhead's eyes shifted. She glanced down at her own hands, which were clasped on top of the table. A surefire indication that she was hiding something or else was about to tell an untruth.

"Something like that," she murmured.

He breathed a sigh of relief that she hadn't lied. No, she hadn't told him the whole story—he imagined there was a lot more to tell—but he liked that she hadn't taken a step into deceit.

Her story was, as she'd said, easily verifiable, and, of course, he was going to have to verify it. He'd like to trust her, but even witnesses to a crime that took place yesterday got details wrong today. He saw it all the time.

This could also just be a product of survivor's guilt or of wanting the answer to a question so badly, you saw similarities where none existed. She'd showed up at the scene on Monday, long before the sketch had been made, based on . . . what, nothing but a report of an old skeleton?

This was looking more and more like a long shot. Maybe she'd seen what she wanted to see in that sketch. Memory could be a tricky thing; it could create scenes that hadn't happened or leave out details that it didn't necessarily want to remember. Frankly, he suspected there would be a lot a young woman wouldn't want to remember about a kidnapping ordeal that had gone on for days.

Fifteen years old and taken right out of her bed. Jesus. She was lucky she'd gotten away because the far more likely scenario was that she would have been killed. Or, like one of the more well-publicized kidnapping cases in recent years, she might have been kept in sexual servitude for years. He couldn't help wondering if that's why this boy, Jack, had been kept alive.

Though revolted, Gabe forced his instinctive emotional reactions away, thinking of all the possible explanations for the mysterious Jack. There was one big one. Could the boy actually have been the son of Olivia Wainwright's kidnapper? And if he were, did that make his whole sad tale better or worse? He honestly didn't know. But being a blood relative of somebody did not, by any means, guarantee a life free from abuse and pain. He knew that far better than most.

He also knew he had to keep an open mind and acknowledge that, even though her memories might have played tricks on her, her story *could be* entirely true. That boy's face may have been imprinted on her mind, and the forensic artist might have been able to draw him accurately enough to be identifiable. Stranger things had happened. He'd learned in his career to never rule anything out until he had hard evidence on which to base his decision.

God, he hoped it was true. He would really like to have just been handed his first solid lead in this murder investigation. Going back to her kidnapping case would be like finding a secret staircase in a huge house. It could take him down hallways he'd never have thought to explore. Including right to her own kidnapper, who might very well have murdered his young accomplice for helping Olivia to escape, not that he was about to mention that possibility. Why add to her guilt by pointing out something he'd lay money she had already considered?

Honestly, at this point, he wasn't placing bets one way or another. But he certainly hoped she was right. Not only would it make his job easier, it also might give her a little closure he suspected she badly needed.

"The news said he was hidden in that bar that burned down?" she said.

"That's correct. He'd been entombed right behind the drywall."

She blanched, and he kicked himself for being so blunt. But she didn't back down. "When you say entombed, do you mean the killer built a wall around him? He didn't just stash him in a crawl space or something?" she asked, a frown line appearing between her eyes.

"He worked hard to conceal him, making the wall look like part of the construction."

"That would take some time," she murmured, the frown deepening.

"I suspect this guy knew what he was doing."

In fact, he'd already been gathering information from the contractors on every person who'd worked that reconstruction job. That was a chore, considering the way the construction businesses had collapsed when the economy did. A lot of the workers had already been transient types, going up and down the southeast coast looking for work during the busy hurricane season.

"Did you happen to see any construction equipment when you were held? Anything that would indicate he worked in that field?"

"No, I didn't." She nibbled the corner of her mouth, trying to work it out, then mumbled, "But if he were a carpenter or something, that would make sense, wouldn't it? Then he could build something like that very quickly."

She sounded like she was trying to convince herself, more than him, and he found himself wondering what else she hadn't told him. It sure sounded like she had some time line in her head and was trying to make sure all the pieces fit.

"Could be. Or a handyman, somebody who knows a little about a lot of things," he said, not wanting to get her hopes up but not wanting to dash them, either.

"I'm sure you're wondering if my mind is playing tricks on me," she said, as if noticing he'd been carefully evaluating every word she said. "If I'm really remembering his face or just projecting it onto that drawing."

"Maybe. It's been a long time. Hell, I can barely remember what my last girlfriend looked like, unless I look at a picture of us together." Shrugging, he added, "Of course, that'd be impossible, since she ripped 'em all up when she dumped my sorry ass."

A tiny smile played on those pretty lips, as he'd wanted it to. She might have sounded calm and cool while relating her own horrifying ordeal, but he knew it had dredged up some stuff she'd probably rather have kept buried down in the black muck of lost memories. He wanted to bring her back into the light, and if playing self-deprecating good ol' boy accomplished that, that'd be just fine with him. Lord knows he did it enough. Seemed some people equated an accent and a little Southern color with stupid, and sometimes it paid to have a perp underestimate the cop who was questioning him. Gabe had learned that real quick.

"At least she didn't burn them."

He lifted a wry brow. "That came after the ripping."

"Where did the picture of your face as bull's-eye on a dartboard come in?"

"Hey," he said, pretending to take offense, "did *you* teach her that?"

"*Angry Ex-Girlfriend Secret Handbook*."

"Guess I missed that one."

"Guess you missed the 'Secret' part, too," she told him, actually sounding amused.

"Is there a chapter in that book about cutting up all a guy's clothes and dumpin' 'em on the lawn?"

"Depends on whether you're dating a real woman or a *Fatal Attraction* applicant."

"Just kidding. She didn't cut 'em up."

"Dumping them on the lawn?"

"I'm gonna have to take the Fifth on that one."

Her eyes gleamed, but now it wasn't strictly due to the moisture that had filled them not so long ago. There was good humor there, too. He was glad she hadn't stopped to evaluate that, figuring she'd start feeling guilty at the very thought of smiling given the roller-coaster ride of emotions she'd probably been on all morning.

"Please don't even try to tell me you guys don't have a secret coded playbook, too," she said, sounding accusing. "Somehow the word got out that a guy should drunk-dial his ex in the middle of the night to accuse her of breaking his heart."

"That I didn't do. May've gotten drunk a time or two, but I deleted her number from my address book the day after she deleted me from her Facebook friends list."

She snickered, as if finding it hard to believe he had one. That was perceptive: He didn't.

"Whew. Glad to hear you rose above the impulse."

"How about you?"

"I'm not the Facebook type. I try to stay as disconnected and hard to reach as possible."

He didn't point out that he could understand why, given her past. Any kidnapping victim would be pretty damn protective of his or her privacy, he suspected. "I meant the drunk-dialing."

"I rarely drink." The quirk of her lips said she was teasing him, pretending she didn't understand the question at first. "Okay, I've had to have my number changed once or twice."

He'd just bet she had. The woman was bright and warm, not to mention incredibly attractive. He didn't doubt she'd broken some hearts in her day. Having known more than a few crime victims, he had to wonder if she had a hard time really trusting anyone. Most did. Which could lead to some broken hearts if somebody decided to take it personally.

He'd already snuck a quick glance at her left hand and seen a big, antique-looking silver ring that looked like it had been inherited, not slipped on by a fiancé. At least, that's how he preferred to think of it, though, having known her all of twenty minutes, he couldn't say why.

"So, tell me, Miz Wainwright, is there a chapter in there about ordering gay porn and big-woman skin mags and having them delivered to your ex-boyfriend at work? Because if so, that's some seriously bad advice and can get you arrested."

Whistling, she replied, "She sounds like she was a real piece of work."

"Nah, not speaking from personal experience. It'd be pretty stupid to do that to a cop."

"Oh, so *you* ordered the gay porn and big-woman skin mags?"

"Ha-ha," he said with a wry grin, liking how quick-witted she was. Especially liking that the evidence of those tears was growing dimmer with every word she spoke.

"So when was this devastating breakup?" she asked, though whether it was to be polite, or because she was really interested in knowing, he couldn't say.

"Year or so ago. And to be honest, it wasn't that devastating."

"Not even to her?"

"I don't think so. She was all about settling down and having babies and being with somebody who didn't risk getting shot every day when he left for the office. Ended up engaged to a guy who runs a bookkeeping business up'n Brunswick."

"Somebody nice and normal," she murmured, sounding thoughtful.

He leaned back in his chair, hearing it creak, and crossed his arms over his chest. "You sayin' I'm not nice and normal, Miz Wainwright?"

A faint sheen of pink might have appeared in her cheeks, and she smoothed her dress, suddenly looking a little more prim and uptight. Embarrassed. Rich Southern ladies didn't usually go around insulting people, and she apparently thought she had. "Sorry. I didn't mean . . ."

"I'm kidding," he said, gentle and earnest. "Because you're right. I don't live a lifestyle that can be called in any way normal. No homicide detective ever could."

"I agree. Nobody surrounded by death all the time could ever be said to have an entirely ordinary, sane existence," she said, that thoughtful tone returning to her voice. "That's what I meant. Again, I'm sorry if I sounded snotty."

"You didn't."

"It's just, normal's not in my vocabulary, either."

He doubted that. Olivia looked about as normal a member of the Southern elite as anyone he'd ever known, even if she did have a kind streak and spoke in a down-to-earth way that didn't quite match the dollar signs under which he suspected she'd been born.

Then he remembered her background, the whole reason she'd come here today.

Hell. No, *normal* wasn't necessarily the word to describe this woman's life, and it hadn't been, not since she was fifteen years old. And nothing could make an ivory-towered princess come down to earth faster than realizing she was just as likely to be a victim of crime as any normal person born into a middle-class lifestyle. In her case, with those dollar signs attached to her name, probably even more so. He doubted she'd have been awakened in the middle of the night by a kidnapper if she'd been the daughter of a truck driver and a high school teacher. She'd seen darkness most people couldn't even imagine.

Even as he thought it, he saw the way her shoulders gradually slumped as she came to the same realization. Her smile faded. A low sigh emerged from her mouth. It appeared distraction time was over; her mind was heading back toward business.

"Thanks," she whispered.

"You're welcome," he replied, knowing exactly what

she meant. She appreciated the distraction. The brief segue into *normalcy*. "And for the record?"

"Yes?"

"I'm so sorry about what happened to you," he said, almost surprising himself with the tender note in his own voice. But it was only the truth. He hated even picturing those awful days, and wished he could turn back the clock and change things so she'd never have to know about such ugliness. No innocent kid ever should.

"You're really a nice man, aren't you?" she asked.

Feeling stupid for having opened his mouth, he muttered, "Don't let it get around."

"Our little secret," she said, not laughing, sounding more thoughtful and appreciative than anything else. Then she shook her head, as if shaking out any distractions, and got back to the reason she'd come here. "Now, as to whether I'm basing this just on my memory of what Jack looked like, let me just point out a couple of things." She raised her hand, ticking off points like a lawyer presenting closing arguments in a case. "The boy I remember seemed to be about twelve or thirteen years old, in line with what the coroner said about the remains you found."

"He said nine to twelve."

"So he was small for his age. Or mature beyond his years—probably with reason."

He nodded, conceding the point.

"You said you think this might have taken place twelve years ago, around the time the bar underwent renovations after a previous fire?"

"It's a theory."

A pretty solid one, actually, considering what forensics had discovered. They didn't believe the body had been disturbed since it had been put inside that wall—at least, not until the fire—and that it had been there for the full period of decomposition. Some tests they'd run on the bones as well as on a few flecks of the clothing and plastic that remained put the time period at no less than a decade, and it was doubtful somebody had moved the boy and walled him up after he'd started to decompose.

Building permit records had indicated a major renovation twelve years back . . . long before Fast Eddie had ever bought the place from the former owner, who'd since died. And the blueprints on file with the county showed the addition of the very storage room where the boy was found. It was circumstantial, but, like a lot of circumstantial evidence, it all certainly led to a picture that seemed more likely than not to be the truth.

"My kidnapping happened twelve years ago last spring."

"The timing does seem to fit." Still, he didn't want her to get her hopes up that her long-held mystery was definitely solved. "But a lot of children go missing each and every year. The chances of it being this one particular boy . . ."

"I know," she murmured.

"Listen, how about I go get the file, bring back the sketch so you can give it a closer look?" And also, he knew, so that he could take a quick look at this woman's history, just to confirm everything she'd said. Not that he doubted her—he didn't. But he had the feeling there was more to learn about Olivia Wainwright.

Rising to leave the room, he paused, his hand on the doorknob, when she spoke again.

"There's one more thing."

"Yes?"

She swallowed, a visible gulp of grit to go on with something that bothered her. Gabe geared himself up to hear it, sensing they'd come to something big. Something major, in fact. He loosened his grip on the knob.

"This bar, this Fast Eddie's, it's very close to Laurel Grove."

"The north section, yes."

Another deep swallow, and he'd swear her hands shook the tiniest bit on the table. She confirmed it by clenching them together again, each long, slim finger twining into another until she looked like she was gonna do that kid's rhyme about the church and the steeple. Like if she didn't have something to hold on to—her own other hand—she might falter or lose her nerve.

Finally, she got down to it. "I've been there, Detective Cooper."

He hesitated, not entirely sure why that mattered. Hell, in point of fact, she'd pretty well been there just Monday morning.

Then she laid it out.

"I was found the fourth morning after the kidnapping, wandering around in Laurel Grove Cemetery. Naked, filthy, badly injured, and nearly out of my mind after having spent the entire night among the dead."

Chapter 3

Tyler Wallace had never been much of a reader, other than doing what he had to for school and work. But as he quickly skimmed through Olivia Wainwright's case file, he found himself thinking he needed to check out more fiction books. Because, man, did her story ever read like one. He couldn't bear to put it down.

When he'd returned from lunch and heard his partner was interviewing a woman about the Jimmy Doe murder, he'd instinctively turned to join him. But no sooner had he reached the hallway when Gabe had come out of the interview room, appearing deep in thought. He also wore that excited look that said he might be on to something.

Hearing the *something* was the twelve-year-old memory of a kidnapping victim who thought their vic might have been a kid who'd shared her darkest nightmare didn't inspire a lot of confidence. In fact, the whole thing sounded far-fetched or, at best, a total shot in the dark.

Still, Ty had been every bit as hopeful that they'd finally gotten a break. This case was getting to him on a personal level. It had been since they'd first heard that firefighter talk about finding those little bones and had gotten worse when he'd read the autopsy report. Because they weren't merely talking about the tragic murder of a boy, they were talking about systematic abuse of a kid throughout much of his short life.

So, yeah, as Gabe had warned him it might, this case had started to mean something to Ty. And it meant a lot to his partner. Even the thinnest lead deserved every bit of respect they could give it. Which was why, together, they'd come back to the bullpen to pull up the report on the Wainwright kidnapping. After doing a little more poking around about Ms. Wainwright, Gabe had frowned, then headed back in to talk to their witness, asking Ty to finish reading over the case file without him.

It all read pretty normally . . . until it got pretty damn freaky.

"Kid *told* him to drown her," Ty mumbled, his eyes drawn back to one portion of the victim's statement.

Any way of dying was bad, death being the main problem with it. But, in Ty's opinion, some means of getting there seemed a lot worse than others. For him, drowning had always ranked as one of the worst ways to go. It was right up there with being tied down to a set of train tracks, watching a big old freight train barreling down on you. You'd know what was happening, but would have a hell of a time surviving without help.

Though, to be fair, both were slightly less awful than being eaten by a shark—also too easy to be aware of and tough to escape.

But *being* drowned as opposed to accidental drowning—that was some heavy shit. To think about somebody holding you down in water, on purpose, until you stopped struggling—what would it take to survive that? And what kind of person would you become afterward?

Honestly, part of him wanted to meet this Wainwright woman just to see if she had a whole Elvira, Mistress of the Dark thing going on. Because something like that would have to scar someone for life, put him or her on a first-name basis with the Grim Reaper.

Then there was that graveyard business. Talk about a nightmare after a bad dream. It was like escaping from

Michael Myers only to land in a nightmare with Freddy Krueger.

When he'd first moved here, he'd walked around Laurel Grove as well as some of the other old cemeteries. Like the city's famed squares, they were part of Savannah's unique charm, or so he'd heard. Though, honestly, he had to question the sanity of anybody who would call a cemetery charming.

To give credit where it was due, if there was one thing the South did well, other than sweet tea and NASCAR, it was death. They knew how to take a biological function and make it mysterious and eerie, each grave telling a story, every headstone seeped in history and ritual.

Though not as big as the city's more famous cemetery, Bonaventure, Laurel Grove was still a sprawling site, shadowed with massive, moss-draped trees, all bent and gnarled like giant arthritic limbs. Gated family plots with rust-encrusted wrought-iron fences vied for space with maudlin mausoleums dripping with marble vines, cherubs and angels. Headstones that had once been black or white were now a mottled gray color, about the shade of two-day-dead skin. And for every twenty graves with bouquets of plastic flowers or small American flags on them, there would be one with a chicken claw, a bit of eggplant or some strange brown powder. *Voodoo*.

Amid the commonplace surnames were others that stood out, repeated again and again in testimony to the rich father-to-son tradition around here. Whole sections of the cemetery bore eternal witness to some of the city's most respected families.

Of course, stones in the older part of the north cemetery wouldn't include the names of any black folks. Segregation had been alive and well in Savannah, even when it came to burying, and Laurel Grove South was where they'd have stuck a Wallace like him if he'd died a century ago or, hell, probably fifty years ago.

One walk-through had been enough for him. Ty had been raised in Florida and far preferred going to theme parks for entertainment rather than graveyards. He'd take a giant cartoon mouse over marble-carved, weeping angels any day.

The Wainwright woman hadn't had the choice. It had been made for her. Run or die.

Those places were bad enough during the day, when other mourners were around, but nighttime, all night long, a teenage girl alone? Worst of all, spending an entire windswept night there after being kidnapped, abused, and brought back from the brink of death?

He couldn't even imagine it. Frankly, he didn't even want to try.

Olivia hadn't intended to be so dramatic when telling Gabe Cooper about the final hours of her long-ago ordeal. He'd left right after she'd said it, leaving her to stew, feeling stupid. She'd probably sounded like some phony fortune-teller relaying a ghost story when she'd only wanted him to hear her own certainty, her reasons for being so sure she could help him.

Mainly, she'd wanted him to trust her before he found out the rest, before he found out who she really was and what she did for a living. Knowing he was headed back to his desk to get the sketch—and, undoubtedly, to do a little research on her—she'd felt compelled to show him just how deeply affected she was by this whole situation.

Judging by the visible clenching of Gabe Cooper's jaw and the way his eyes narrowed as he offered her one brief nod, she'd made her point. He might suspect her memory was faulty, but he could no longer doubt she passionately believed what she was telling him. After her surprising admission, he'd left the room without another word, leaving her to wonder just how bad it was going to be when he came back. *Probably pretty bad.*

"You should have brought somebody," she told herself, though she didn't know who.

Her sister had called this morning, after seeing the local news, her mind obviously going the same way Olivia's had. But Liv had downplayed the whole thing and definitely hadn't told her she recognized the boy in the sketch. Brooke was recently engaged. And though Olivia considered her sister's fiancé a complete ass, she still didn't want to do anything to intrude on the younger woman's excitement over making wedding plans.

Nor did she want to drag her parents into this. Her kidnapping had wrought enough havoc on them, including the breakup of their marriage. Well, at least, that's what she thought had caused it, though they insisted otherwise. Still, it was hard to argue with the fact that as soon as Olivia had recovered from her ordeal, her mother had packed up her and Brooke and, over her father's loud objections, moved them to Tucson for several years. The destruction of even a happy marriage had been painfully easy when husband and wife lived on two different sides of the country and one blamed the other for their child's kidnapping.

Her mother's eventual boyfriend hadn't helped matters. Nor had her father's eventual girlfriend. And yet neither one of them had taken the oh-so-final step toward filing for a divorce.

God, wasn't Thanksgiving a convoluted mess in the Wainwright house nowadays?

In any case, no, she didn't want to involve them. Her parents would go into protector mode. Her sister would just worry. Her senator cousin and his ambitious wife would shudder at the thought of all that unpleasantness being dredged up again only a year away from the next election. That was it for family.

Nor could she have brought one of her colleagues. Considering the Savannah authorities didn't have much

use for anybody who worked for Julia Harrington at eX-
treme Investigations, it had been bad enough for Olivia,
one of them, to come in unannounced.

Coming alone to this squat, cold police building on
Bull Street had taken a lot of will. If she'd stopped to
think more about it, or if she'd told anyone else what she
planned to do, she might not have gone through with it.
Yet she was glad she had, even if the uniformed officer
who'd shown her to this room had been a little slimy, his
milky eyes way too intrusive, his hand too quick to move
to the small of her back when he ushered her in.

But as for Detective Gabe Cooper, it had been a completely different story.

The man had saved her life or darn near close to it.

Even if he hadn't, though, even if she'd never met him
before today, she had the feeling she'd still have trusted
him. Maybe it was because this morning during that TV
interview he'd looked so strong and resolute despite his
physical weariness. Or it could have been because he'd
so obviously tried to lay on some Southern charm in order to relax her, as if he knew she'd been crying her face
off half the morning. Being honest, she had to acknowledge one more possibility: It could have been because
she was just so damned attracted to him. Not just because of his looks but also his personality, his ease with
people—with her.

Then there'd been that sweet, unexpected moment
when he'd told her how sorry he was about what she'd
been through. Olivia had heard a lot of people rehash
the story over the years, saying what an awful thing it
was. But she couldn't remember anyone saying quite
those words in quite so tender a way. He had a very kind
streak, this big, tough cop. He was quickly working his
way around every last one of her defenses.

Olivia wasn't usually the type to let her guard down
around good-looking men. God knew she'd been the tar-

get of a number of them. Most of them saw dollar signs where her eyeballs should be or wanted her family's political connections more than they wanted her. Or, if they did take the time to really get to know her and found out what she could do, they usually got scared and ran like she was Wednesday Addams and she'd just introduced them to Cousin It.

Gabe Cooper seemed different. Within a mere half hour she'd found herself liking this man a lot. He was easy to talk to, reasonable, friendly. And he obviously cared about the same thing she did—finding out what had happened to the boy who had saved her all those years ago.

She only hoped her instincts were right and he didn't prove to be one of the suspicious, judgmental types who could turn on a dime. Like the ones who'd nearly ridden her colleague Aidan McConnell out of town on a rail last spring after a bad turn in a child murder case.

She needed Detective Cooper to be much more than that. Even if he was the open-minded sort and didn't come back in here telling her to get out and take her woo-woo reputation with her, he was probably going to have some serious reservations about granting the request she intended to make when he came back. She didn't know anybody who wouldn't. Because it was a biggie.

The minute she heard footsteps approaching the door from the hall, she stiffened in her chair. And as soon as he stepped back inside, his face stern, his mouth looking like it had been carved out of pure granite, she let out a long mental sigh. *He knows*.

She couldn't help feeling a surprising rush of disappointment, knowing whatever sparks of interest or friendship or attraction had flashed between them a few minutes ago were now gone, lost forever. Sharp, realistic, blunt police detectives didn't get involved with slightly eccentric paranormal investigators with a thing for death.

Not that she'd really been thinking they might have gotten personally involved beyond a *wonder what it would be like* moment or two. But it might have been nice for the entire team to actually get along well with somebody in the police department. The fact that he was pretty damn sexy wouldn't have hurt, either.

"Well, you're still here," he said, eyeing her as he pushed the door closed.

"Did you think I wouldn't be?"

His shrug said the thought had crossed his mind.

"It doesn't make me an unreliable witness," she told him, cutting through any pretense or preamble to the conversation she knew they were going to have.

He didn't jump to the bait. "What doesn't?"

"What I do for a living."

Looking resolute, stiff, he approached her, eating up the floor in three long strides. He pulled out the metal chair opposite her. It scraped across the faded linoleum, emitting a long, low squeal that made her flinch. Spinning the chair around, so its back touched the table, he straddled it, resting his arms loosely on the back. Then he placed a few sheets of paper on the table between them. "If you say so."

She did. Sort of. Only she couldn't protest, considering what she really wanted from this man, because her profession was definitely going to come into it sooner or later. "I didn't say anything because . . ."

He threw a hand up, palm out, stopping her midsentence. "Look, I don't care what you do from nine to five," he said matter-of-factly. "You came in here only as a former crime victim and as a witness, and that's all I'm interested in hearing about."

Which was fine. Good. Perfect.

Except for the fact that it wasn't entirely true. She

wasn't here strictly as a crime victim and potential witness. In fact, sooner or later—probably sooner—she was going to ask him to trust her to do something most people would find utterly horrific and ghoulish.

"I don't care if you say you can look into a bunch'a tea leaves and tell me who was on the grassy knoll when JFK got shot," he added. "The only thing I'm concerned about is the case I'm workin' on right this minute."

Spoken like a stubborn, nose-to-the-grindstone skeptic. *Damn*.

He'd left here ten minutes ago someone she thought she could trust, someone she suspected might even trust her. He'd come back a suspicious, doubting cop.

She felt the loss somewhere deep inside, wondering why it always came back to this. Why she could still be surprised by people's reactions to what she could do and what she had done. Not, she suspected, that he knew all that. He had probably just seen eXtreme Investigations as the name of her employer and formed as much of an impression as he needed to.

Olivia Wainwright: Rich. Spoiled. Freak. Next?

"Fine," she said, crossing her arms and lifting her chin. He wanted to play this cool and professional; that was just fine by her, at least for a little while. Until she got around to telling him why she had really come here today.

As if realizing he might have come off a bit judgmental, Cooper sighed heavily. "Look, I know one of the people you work with, okay?"

"Is that a good thing or a bad one?" she asked. Considering he worked for the SCMPD, she suspected she already knew the answer.

"Actually, I thought Aidan McConnell got a lousy deal on the Remington case. That was some shoddy police work, and I think he was made a scapegoat to cover some asses."

"Yes, he was," she murmured, surprised a city detective would admit such a thing.

Aidan had caught the blame for steering local police in the wrong direction during the search for a missing little boy. When the child had been found dead, Aidan had been blamed by the press, the family, and the authorities. Lately, though, due to some diligent investigative work and well-placed whispers in the right ears, the case was being reexamined. The city was rife with rumors that the child hadn't merely wandered away and gotten trapped in an old freezer at all. Which everyone who worked with eXtreme Investigations had already figured out—the boy's mother had killed him. They just couldn't prove it. Yet.

"He and I have crossed paths on the job once or twice," he added, "and he's been helpful. So can we get past any idea that I think you're a whack job looking for attention?"

Her jaw dropped open.

Wincing, he clarified. "I mean, if that's what you thought I was thinking."

"It wasn't."

"Good."

"Until now," she mumbled.

Ignoring her last comment, he lifted the sheets of papers from the table and quickly flipped through them. "Here's the sketch," he said, pushing the drawing she'd seen on this morning's news over the table to her. Then he pulled out another sheet—a printout of a police interview—and placed it before her as well. "And your original statement about this boy, Jack."

"You read my case file?" she whispered, feeling her stomach turn over. Not just at having to revisit that night but also at the thought that *he* already had.

He shook his head. "No, it's pretty big. I printed it out

but just grabbed this page where you gave the description of the boy for right now."

She managed to hide a sigh of relief. It was one thing for him to know she worked for eXtreme Investigations; it was another for him to read exactly what had happened. Then she'd go from poor-little-kidnapped-rich-girl to poor-little-kidnapped-and-murdered-rich-girl. That familiar look of pity and horror would cross his face, the same one she'd seen on just about everyone else's who'd ever heard the whole story.

He frowned. "But I will have to read through the rest of it. Is there anything else you want to tell me?"

She thought about it, wondering how much to reveal. Then she decided to reveal nothing, at least not right now. Once she made her request, she would have to give him some more answers, if only to explain what she thought she could accomplish. And why. But for right now, she'd just as soon not don the freak cloak and instead work on rebuilding whatever sense of trust might have been forming between them before he'd left the room.

"Not just yet."

"Okay," he said, a tiny line furrowing between his eyes, as if he were disappointed in her answer. "Now, I'm inclined to think you might be on to something. The description you gave then sounds a *lot* like this," he said, tapping the tip of his finger on the drawing.

She glanced at the artist's rendering, which had already imprinted itself on her mind, and then scanned her own words, trying to hear them in her young, fifteen-year-old voice. It was like reading a book, a piece of fiction drawn out of the dark imagination of some anonymous writer. Separate from her, not at all a part of who she was now.

And yet she knew that when she went to work, when

she did what she did, it was this girl, this terrified, broken fifteen-year-old, who always showed up for duty.

"I gotta say, you gave a really good, solid description, especially after what you'd been through, Miz Wainwright."

"Olivia," she murmured, pushing the printout away with her fingers. "If we're going to be discussing the most personal, dark details of my life, you should call me by my first name."

He didn't respond, didn't say her name but didn't refuse to, either. "I know it took a lot for you to come here and talk to me about this," he said, his tone gentle again, some of the belligerence he'd been wearing like an invisible shield since his return disappearing. "If it matters, I think you did a brave thing."

"Thank you."

"Are you ready to see it all the way through? Get justice for this boy?"

Olivia tilted her head and eyed him. "I think he's a little beyond justice, but I can't deny I'd like to find out once and for all what happened to him."

"What do you mean?" he asked. "It's never too late for justice."

"It is for Jack. If this played out the way I think it did, it's not as though you can do anything to his killer." Seeing his confusion, she suddenly realized he hadn't read far down in her case record at all if he didn't even know how the whole thing had ended. "You obviously *didn't* read much of that file, did you, Detective Cooper? Why? Were you too distracted when you Googled me and saw the name of my employer?"

He didn't flinch at the accusation, replying evenly, "Like I said, I printed it out but only grabbed the sheet with your description of the boy to help prompt your memory. I figured I'd be hearing the whole story from you."

"Sorry," she said knowing she was being a little over-sensitive. "The point is, my case was closed long ago."

"I could tell that much by the file name."

"But do you know why?"

He stiffened. "Tell me it's because the guy was caught and is now in prison serving as some in-house gang's blow-up doll."

She shook her head. If only it were that easy. If she could have asked the monster who'd taken her what he'd done with her fellow captive, she would have done it ages ago. "He's not."

Cooper was intuitive; he immediately knew what she was getting at. "Don't tell me."

She told him. "The man who kidnapped me and probably murdered the boy who helped me was killed in a shootout with police several hours after I escaped."

He muttered a curse, looking frustrated, almost angry. He ran a hand through his thick hair. It stuck up a little, making him appear almost boyish, though the expression on his face was anything but. He looked like a man deprived of achieving his lifelong goal, and she sensed that he was sorely tempted to launch out of his chair and stalk around the room.

Obviously Gabe Cooper took his cases very seriously. And some of them, like this one, a little personally. She wondered just how far he'd be willing to go to solve one that had become so important to him. *Hmm.*

"The authorities later identified the man who'd been killed as Dwight Collier," she added. "He was an ex-con, with a long rap sheet of minor offenses. A loner, no known address, I guess because he was living out in the woods with the boy."

"Son of a bitch," he muttered, sinking, all the anger disappearing to be replaced by utter disappointment. "I'm sorry. It's not that I'm not glad they caught the bastard who did this to you. It's just, I was happy to finally have some kind of lead in the case."

"I know. But this might not be over yet," she said, her tone low. Even as she said the words, she wondered if she was making a mistake, opening a door she might someday regret opening. Because as desperately as she wanted answers, a churning in her stomach hinted that maybe they would only lead to more questions.

She plugged on, anyway. She'd never know the truth if she didn't at least try to push for it. "I might be able to confirm who this boy was and how he died."

"We know how he died," he interjected, sounding suspicious. "He was strangled. The coroner said the hyoid bone was broken."

She closed her eyes briefly, feeling sick. Olivia had experienced strangulation before. Having to look directly into the face of the person who was killing you made the experience beyond awful. But there were worse things than that. Staring into the void of unresolved memory, living an eternal mystery, waking up night after night seeing the face of someone you desperately wanted to save but having not the slightest clue how to do it—all that was worse. If going through with this experience gave her the answers she needed, if it gave her peace, it would be well worth one hundred and thirty seconds of fear and pain.

"I still think I can help you," she insisted. "Part of me feels sure the remains you found belong to this mystery boy I knew. But another part . . ."

"Is wondering about the timing?" he asked, immediately leaping upon what had been bothering her about this whole thing.

"Yes," she admitted, glad he'd seen the difficulty, too. "I've long thought Collier must have killed Jack right after he found out I'd escaped. I figured he ditched his body, then moved the trailer where they'd been staying, went to collect the ransom money and was shot by police."

"Not much time in that scenario for somebody to build a wall around the boy's body."

"Exactly." That was the only thing that didn't fit, the only fly in the ointment to this whole scenario she'd painted in her mind to answer all those old questions. "The bar is close to the cemetery I stumbled into, so it wasn't far from his campsite. That makes me think it's not impossible."

She didn't like to think *how* close that bar was to the cemetery. God, imagine if she'd come stumbling out onto the street rather than hiding all night? The first person she'd run to for help might very well have been the one she'd been trying to escape.

The thought made her sick even now, all these years later.

"But it is a long shot," the detective said. "I mean, if he knew you'd gotten away, why would he go through with the money drop?"

She shrugged helplessly. That was one of the many questions. "But he *had* to have found out I was gone before he went to get the money. As I mentioned, he moved the camper. It was there when I ran, and the next day it wasn't."

"Did they ever find it?"

"No. The police theorized that he ditched it somewhere in the Okefenokee and it just disappeared into the swamp."

They'd also theorized that Jack had been in it at the time. Now, though, she had begun to doubt that very much.

"Which makes the time line that much tighter," he said. A muscle in his jaw worked, like he was clenching his teeth. She had to wonder if he was reevaluating what he'd thought about her possibly being "on to something." Because it sure didn't seem very likely, on the surface.

Yet, deep down, something still told her she was right. She couldn't explain the timing—yet. But she knew that face. Everything else fit, right down to the strange, otherworldly compulsion she'd felt to go to that scene Monday morning, as if fate itself were telling her she was finally coming to the end of her twelve-year-long search.

There was one more thing, one other possible explanation for all these questions about the time line. That other possible explanation made it imperative that she find out the truth, one way or another. Because for years she'd assumed the kidnapping monster had worked alone, aside from his poor, brainwashed sidekick.

But what if he hadn't? What if somebody else had taken care of disposing of Jack's body and the camper? What if there was an accomplice out there, somebody else who might yet face justice for what had happened to Jack—and to her?

She had to know. *Had* to.

"Maybe he wasn't working alone," she whispered. "Maybe somebody else helped him, then covered all this up after he'd been killed. That person could still be out there."

He didn't try to talk her out of the idea or tell her it was a crazy one. Because he had to know it wasn't crazy; in fact, it made a lot of sense. Terrifying sense.

"I can help," she told him again, hoping he'd hear only the sincerity in her voice, not the hint of desperation she suspected was there as well. "I'll know if it was Jack you found in that wall. If it wasn't, I might be able to give you some new leads to figure out who he was. If I'm right, and it is Jack, well, at least I'll know for sure and won't have to spend the rest of my life wondering about him." *And can perhaps find out if someone else was there, bearing witness to his murder.*

The detective was no longer frowning and frustrated;

now he looked curious and a little skeptical. "You can do all that, huh?"

She nodded.

"How?"

Swallowing and hoping her voice didn't shake, she answered him with the truth. "I can't really tell you that. I just need you to trust me."

"Trust you to do what?" he asked, looking suspicious.

"To give me a few minutes alone with the remains."

"You're such a shithead. I can't believe I cried at your funeral."

Julia Harrington didn't look up as she mumbled the words. She was too busy trying to focus on her job, not on her silent business partner, who, annoyingly, had been anything but silent since he'd arrived. He'd been trying to talk her into leaving work and going to the beach.

As if she wanted to be breaded in sand to go along with living in the frying pan that was Savannah, Georgia, on any August day. Yeah. Right.

He was completely unfazed. "You need to get a life."

"No. What I need to do is finish this report," she retorted, focusing on the screen of her computer, not on the man leaning indolently against the closed door of her office. He'd popped in a few minutes ago, unannounced as usual, offering no explanation about where he'd been for the past six days. Not that she'd ask for one. Sure, she was curious. But, no, she didn't have time to get sidetracked by one of his adventure tales.

"Why don't you get a dog? That would give you something to do."

"I have plenty to do," she said, absently pointing at the piles of paperwork on her desk.

"I mean other than work. Imagine a cute little puppy to come home to at night."

Knowing he wouldn't leave her be until she gave him her full attention, she tore her gaze off the screen, preparing for the jolt that seeing him always gave her.

Jolt.

God, he was so gorgeous, so utterly, incredibly beautiful to look at: thick brown hair, laughing dark eyes shot with gold, a face that should have ended up on a movie screen rather than a police identification badge. Morgan Raines had been the most glorious male specimen she or just about any other woman would ever see in her lifetime.

He was still that man, that same perfect sexy man, his looks frozen in time, all forward momentum stopped by a madman's bullets: four to the chest.

If he'd been on-duty and wearing his vest, he would have survived with bruises and a few broken ribs. Being ambushed outside a restaurant late one night, however, he'd had nothing but a thin shirt for protection. Well, and Julia. But she hadn't been enough, either.

Thank God real life wasn't like the movies, nothing like that creepy kid who'd declared *I see dead people.* If she had to see Morgan now the way she'd seen him in the last seconds of his life, with those gaping wounds, the blood pumping out of him with every beat of his heart, she would have broken apart with grief long ago. Well, she had broken apart with grief, at least for a while. Then he'd returned, sort of, and put her back together again.

"So. Whaddya say?" he asked with a wide grin. "Lab or golden retriever?"

"You'd scare it to death."

"I would not," he said, stiffening, indignation lacing his voice. "I like dogs."

"I don't think dogs like your kind."

"That's very bigoted. You're a ghostist."

She rolled her eyes.

"A dog would be good company for you."

Groaning, she considered sticking earplugs in her ears, but knew then he'd just do that freaky thing where he talked inside her head. "Better than you? Yeah, I'd say so."

"I'm wounded, Julia," he said, flashing that ultrasexy grin that still had the ability to stop her heart after all these years. *Ten. I've known him for ten years. Two when he was alive, eight since he was murdered.* "You know how sensitive I am."

That note of mischief in his voice and the aggrieved tone almost brought a smile to her lips, as she knew he wanted. "You're as sensitive as a pit bull," she said.

If it were possible, Morgan Raines was more of a cocky, sexy smart-ass in the afterlife than he'd been in his real one. And that was really saying something.

Huh. Did this count as his afterlife, since it was still her real one? One of the many things she hadn't figured out about this exceedingly strange relationship.

"See? You do have dogs on your mind."

Gritting her teeth, she glanced at the clock, saw it was well after three and groaned. "I mean it; I need to get this done. Just give me twenty minutes to finish, and then I'll let you analyze my life and tell me how poorly I'm living it."

"Those who are alive usually do," he said, managing to sound pious, which didn't suit him. Throwing himself back on the love seat that stood in the corner, he added, "I'm so bored!"

"So go find a Christmas tree and perch on top of it."

"Ha-ha. I'm not an angel."

"No, you're a devil," she said, not believing she'd let him suck her into this conversation.

"There's no such thing."

"How do you know?"

He suddenly frowned, his brown eyes darkening to

near black as he became very serious, indeed. "Because nothing in creation could be as bad as an evil man."

Their stares met, his good humor melting away along with her irritation. Yes, they knew a lot about evil men. More than most ever would. Among those men, the one who had killed him and the ones who had hired him. *Someday, I'll find them. I swear it. Someday.*

Instead of making that promise again, she merely whispered, "Touché."

His frown still in place, he nodded once, then crossed his arms and stared out the window, letting her get back to work. She hated to leave things on that note, far preferring a mischievous ghost to a melancholy one. But his moods were always mercurial; he was an eternal twenty-six years old, energetic, hard to keep down.

Funny, when they'd met, he'd been the older one, the experienced one who'd taken her, the fresh-out-of-college rookie, under his wing. Now she'd moved past him, right into her thirties, growing, maturing, aging. She had a business and a mortgage and a lot of responsibilities to go with them, while he would be forever young. Free.

Dead.

Throwing off the thought, she turned back to her computer, needing to finish this report she'd been typing. It was for a client who was looking for her missing sister-in-law, who had disappeared weeks ago. Bad enough to tell the woman she was correct in her suspicions that the sister-in-law had met with foul play. Worse to tell her that the woman's husband—the client's own brother—had been the one who'd made her disappear. Then again, if the client hadn't suspected her brother, she would have gone directly to the police with some evidence she'd discovered, rather than to a group of private detectives, especially a group of private detectives as specialized as eXtreme Investigations.

"Specialized? I think you mean ostracized."

"Stop it, Morgan," Julia snapped, knowing he'd already gotten over his brief bout with the dead-guy blues. "Get out of my head." He couldn't do it often, especially because she was very careful to guard her thoughts, but obviously her stress was speaking loud and clear.

"*Shh*, pipe down," he said, laughter evident in his voice. "Do you want our new receptionist to think you're crazy and quit the first week on the job?"

"I *am* crazy," she muttered.

"Nah, if you were really crazy, you'd think you were perfectly sane."

Maybe. Or maybe she'd just gotten really good at convincing herself Morgan was here because she so wanted him to be. But, if the issue had merely been about not being able to let him go, wouldn't his "ghost" have been around since right after his death?

It hadn't been. In fact, he'd been gone for months after he'd been shot down in the street. She'd almost begun to think she really could go on living without him, if only so she could catch the men who'd killed him. Then she'd come face-to-face with a punk aiming a gun at her, and who should show up to save her life but her old partner. Her old love, Morgan Raines.

"If I weren't really here, could I do this?" he asked.

She sucked in a breath, watching as he lifted a vase filled with fresh flowers. "If you drop that, you're going to clean it up." Julia glanced at the closed door, wishing she'd locked it, since she was the only one who could see the solid-looking man holding the vase. If her new receptionist walked in now, she'd see a vase of pretty roses floating a few feet off the floor and would either faint or quit on the spot.

The woman wouldn't be the first to run out screaming at the stuff that went on around here. Hell, sometimes Julia herself was tempted to. After all, *she* didn't have any powers; she couldn't do anything like what Aidan, Mick, Derek or, God help her, Olivia, could. She just had a relationship with a dead guy. One guy. There were no other ghosts in her world. Sometimes, like now, even one was way too many, and she wondered what it might be like to have a normal life.

Then Morgan put the vase down. Winking, he flashed her that unbelievable smile, the one that had claimed her heart long ago when they'd met on the job with the Charleston PD. And Julia mentally acknowledged what she'd known since the day she'd first seen his ghost, backing her up the way he always had when he was alive: Normal was way overrated.

"Oh, hey, I forgot to tell you something."

Julia went back to her typing. "Uh-huh?"

"Your friend, Olivia? Something's up with her."

That caught her interest, mainly because Olivia had done something she'd never done in the more than two years she'd worked here. She'd called in sick. "What?"

"I'm not sure. But somebody's been looking for her, trying to get at her."

"Somebody . . . like who?" she asked, wishing he would just get to the point.

"Well," he replied, "somebody . . . like me."

Chapter 4

"Just wait until you get a load of this."

Startled, Ty looked up, realizing his partner was back again from his latest interaction with their new witness. This time, though, Gabe didn't look hopeful about having a break in their case. Instead, he looked both angry and a little disgusted. Ty couldn't remember ever seeing that expression on his face before. While his partner could be a total hard-ass who was absolutely fearless on the job, for the most part, Gabe Cooper seemed most natural when doing his you-can-trust-me-I'm-just-a-good-ol'-boy thing.

"What's up? You get anywhere with the Wainwright woman?"

"You're not going to believe what she wanted me to let her do," his partner said, throwing himself down into an empty chair. He quickly explained the woman's bizarre request, adding, "Is that whacked or what? I almost fell outta my chair."

"What'd you do instead?"

"What do you think? I ended the interview and escorted her to the exit."

Too bad. Ty was very curious about the woman. "She say why she wanted to see the remains for herself?"

"No," Gabe snapped, "but I assume it has something to do with the fact that she works with that paranormal detective agency, eXtreme Investigations."

Ty had heard of the outfit, though only in the most general how-stupid-is-this-shit terms most cops used when talking about psychics. As for Ty? Well, he wasn't gonna call himself a believer, but he wasn't a skeptic, either. Some mysteries couldn't be explained by normal means. As far as he was concerned, the idea of somebody having the brains to read another person's mind was no crazier than thinking man might soon figure out a way to travel outside the solar system. Yet one concept was laughed at, the other considered a likely possibility in the future.

"I think I'd like to get a look at this woman," he admitted.

Gabe had grabbed his laptop off his own desk and began punching on the keys. Then he turned the thing around so Ty could see the screen. It was a Web site for the paranormal detective agency and included pictures of the staff.

Ty couldn't help whistling. Olivia Wainwright was a beauty—a little skinny, maybe, but pretty in a fragile way. Part of him wondered if that's what had Gabe so riled up: worrying that such an attractive, delicate-looking female might be as nutty as a Snickers bar. But he didn't think that was it. Gabe had never been one to let any kind of personal life interfere with his work.

If, that is, he had a personal life. So far, in the year they'd worked together, Ty hadn't seen much evidence of one.

"There's more." His partner was tugging a cell phone out of his pants, staring at it, then at a small white business card he held in his other hand.

"What's that?"

Gabe tossed the card onto the desk. "I guess you'd call it a character reference."

Glancing at the name and title, Special Agent Steven Ames, Federal Bureau of Investigation, Atlanta office,

Ty could only shake his head in confusion. "Who's this guy?"

"The FBI agent who handled her kidnapping case. Apparently they still keep in touch, and she's sure he'll 'vouch' for her. Before she left, she asked me to give him a call."

Gabe muttered something else under his breath.

"Huh?"

"I said I guess he works with Mulder and Scully."

Ty snickered. "At least she came prepared, knowing you'd need convincing."

"I thought she was gonna call Daddy and ask him to lean on the chief."

"Wainwright . . . she connected to *that* Wainwright?"

"I think so." Gabe plunked some keys on his laptop and made a sound of disgust. "Yep. Her grandfather was a former senator, and the current Senator Wainwright is her cousin."

Ty whistled. "Do you really think she'd call in that big a favor, all so she can feel up some old bones? That's pretty fuckin' morbid, man."

"I don't know how far this one's willing to go. She seems like a very determined woman. And it's not just that she wants to examine them, she wants to be alone when she does it."

That sounded sick, twisted, and if it were anybody else, Ty would probably be advising his partner to ignore the crazy psychic. But he couldn't deny that he felt curious about what this woman could do. After all, he'd read the whole file; he knew what she'd been through, what she'd seen, felt, experienced. Did he really think spending a scary night in a graveyard had opened up a gateway between the woman and the afterlife? No. Not really. But, if her statement was to be believed, she *had* been dead herself that very same night. Two minutes dead, at least.

He didn't think his partner knew that, however. Ty

wondered if it would make any difference if he did. No, he didn't suppose the story would suddenly turn Gabe Cooper into a Casper believer, rushing out to load up on rock salt for his shotgun. It might make him look at the woman who seemed to be driving him a little crazy in a slightly different way, though.

She did seem to be driving him a little crazy. Why else would his usually calm, laid-back partner be so worked up about what she wanted? Yeah, it was off the wall. But this was Savannah, where law firm porters walked invisible dogs for twenty years after the canines had died, if you believed that Kevin Spacey movie. They weren't talking about her getting some kind of sick thrills off seeing a fresh body—most people wouldn't know the bones were human if the skull weren't there. Besides, all he had to do was say no. But it was as if Gabe were personally upset about the request having been made. Interesting. Very interesting.

"Hey, Cooper, you make a date with that foxy redhead?" a smarmy voice asked. *Kinney*.

Ty frowned in distaste. The patrolman tried to watch his tongue whenever the company was mixed, but Ty had no doubt the *n* word flew left, right and center when the man left here. Not to mention lots of crass names for women. He was an equal opportunity piece of shit.

"She came in with some information on a case," Gabe said, his tone hard. Ty suspected his partner didn't like the other cop any more than he did, though they'd never discussed it.

"Well, if you decide to bring her in again and need some help friskin' her, be sure to let me know, y' hear?" the man said, laughing at his own dim wit as he turned and left.

"Slimeball," Gabe muttered under his breath.

Ty nodded, then said, in complete solemnity, "About as useless as tits on a boar hog."

Surprised into laughter, Gabe gave Ty a thumbs-up. "You nailed that one, son."

Ty grinned. He was *so* getting the hang of this Southern thing. "Now, what's the plan? Sit here and pretend you never met her, or are you gonna get back to work?" he prodded.

Gabe's amusement died, and he shot Ty a quick glare as Ty had expected him to. He had begun to suspect his partner was a little more personally interested in this witness than he should be after just meeting her today. And that it was his interest making him react so strongly to what might otherwise have just come across as a strange request from an eccentric local.

"I'm getting to it," Gabe said with a sigh. Then he muttered, "She sure is ballsy."

Admiration. He heard it in the other man's voice as loud and clear as he heard the irritation. Ty wanted to laugh. All the shit he'd taken from Gabe about his own dating record, and his partner was the one who'd gotten all hot 'n' bothered by a witness.

From where Ty was sitting, he figured Gabe oughta just ask the woman out and be done with it. Doubting his partner would appreciate that advice, however, he wisely kept his mouth shut. Finally, though, Cooper pushed his chair back and rose to his feet.

"You going to call her and bring her back in?" Ty asked.

"Nope," Gabe said, glancing at the business card. "I guess I'm gonna get in touch with this FBI agent and then try to decide whether I need to call somebody from the nearest mental hospital to see if they're missing a patient."

Gabe wasn't too keen on calling up some FBI agent, asking him questions about Olivia Wainwright. Not when he'd felt pretty sure he had all the answers he needed about the woman—that is, right up until she'd blindsided him with her request to spend a few minutes alone in a room with the remains of some poor murdered kid.

What he didn't know about women would fill an encyclopedia, but he sure thought he would know a crazy one when he met her.

You're not being fair. That little voice in his head, the one he liked to call his backup detective, wasn't going to let him get away with that. With reason; he *wasn't* being fair.

Because he was skeptical? Because he believed in evidence he could see, examine and process? Because he definitely did not believe in people who sold otherworldly services to the gullible and the grief-stricken the way huckster funeral home directors sold them fifty-thousand-dollar mahogany caskets? Or because he had found Olivia Wainwright to be a damned attractive, interesting woman—right up until she'd gone all Bellatrix Lestrange death eater on him?

Shoving that thought out of his head and deciding he'd been watching too many Harry Potter movies on cable, he punched in the number on the business card. He didn't know whether to be relieved or disappointed when he got a recording.

He left a detailed message and his contact information, then disconnected, wondering what to do next. Wait for a response? Talk to his lieutenant about the whole mess? Or just wait for a call from the senator's chief of staff or the chief of police?

He groaned, each alternative sounding worse than the last. He didn't like to think she had walked out of there and started calling every number in her address book to line up an army of bigwigs demanding that he give her what she wanted, but it wasn't impossible.

Almost against his own will, he flipped the business card over and looked at the address and phone number scrawled on the back of it—Olivia's. She'd asked him to get in touch after he'd had a chance to think about her request. Now he just needed to figure out what he was going to do and how to do it tactfully.

Thank her for her assistance and never see her again?

Thank her for her assistance and refer her to a psychiatrist?

Thank her for her assistance and ask her to dinner?

Or simply say yes, she could see the skeleton and see what happened?

Decisions, decisions.

Before he had to decide anything, however, he overheard a woman's high-pitched, persistent voice. "You don't understand. I need to see that detective from the TV!"

The voice had come from the outer vestibule, which was open to the public. There was nothing threatening about the tone or the words, but he'd swear he heard a hint of desperation.

"Trouble?" Ty asked.

"Seems par for the course today," he said. He got up and followed the sound of the voices, Ty right behind him.

"It's about the boy, the one they found after the fire."

"Ma'am, like I told you," explained the desk sergeant, looking a little exasperated, "Detective Cooper is in a meeting. If you'd like to speak to . . ."

"Nobody but the one on the TV!" the woman said.

Wanting to help derail the situation, he walked over and interjected, "It's okay, Sarge." Then he turned to the woman. "I'm Detective Cooper. You were looking for me?"

The woman, who looked to be in her midforties, had a long face prematurely wrinkled and gouged with heavy frown lines on the brow. The unmistakable scent of beer wafted from her rumpled clothes, and her lank hair car-

ried the heavy reek of cigarette smoke. She wore the
description "rough life" like it was stamped on her skin.

She turned her bloodshot eyes on him, studying him
with hope but also with a hint of mistrust. "You're the
one who was on TV?"

"Yes, ma'am." Gabe pushed his preconceptions away,
knowing it probably hadn't been easy for her to walk
into a police station like this. "What is your name?"

"I'm Sue-Ann Bowles. You really are workin' on that
case, 'bout the boy found Monday?"

"Yes, Miz Bowles, I am." He gestured to Ty. "This is
my partner, Detective Wallace."

She didn't reply but instead glanced down and opened
a large purse that hung at her side. She dug in it, then
pulled out a small square picture, ragged, faded, its age
etched in every crease. "Here."

The photo itself was old, though the child depicted in
it was not. He was a cute kid, probably in first or second
grade, with a gummy gap where his front teeth should
have been, brown hair, freckles. If you were to peel off
about a decade's worth of hard living and the bone-deep
sorrow from this woman's face, he'd even say there was
a resemblance.

"That's my Joey."

He knew what she'd say next. Her Joey was among
the missing, and she feared he was the one whose remains had been found at the fire site.

"He was eight when he got took, right outta the play-
ground near our house. I didn't even notice he was missing until an hour after suppertime." Her voice drifted
away, years of guilt evident in the visible gouges of time
and self-loathing she wore on her face. "My husband
told me I shouldn't let him go down there alone, but he
begged and begged."

Lifting a hand, he put it on her bony shoulder, knowing he couldn't offer her anything else but a hint of hu-

man connection. God, he couldn't even imagine it. What, he wondered, had this woman been like before her child was kidnapped? Had she been on a collision course with the dark side even then? Or had she been a normal, hardworking mom who loved her son, her husband and her home, who'd had no idea she was about to take a hard right turn into the agonizing abyss of lost-kid land?

"That was eight years ago," she whispered. "Eight years he's been gone."

Eight years. Probably not the same boy, then. As much as he wished he could help her and could use the help on the case, he had to be honest. "Miz Bowles," he said, speaking carefully, "I think it's very unlikely that your son's remains were the ones we found this week."

The woman snatched the picture back. "I know that. I ain't stupid. Joey got found four years back in an old apartment buildin' up in Augusta."

Gabe was hit with two strong emotions: sorrow for her, of course, but also confusion.

"He was hidden under some floorboards and hadn't been dead more'n a few months."

He and Ty shared a glance, both seeing the commonality that must have driven her here. But, heaven knew, hiding bodies in buildings wasn't exactly a unique way to dispose of them, though it was a pretty stupid one. Some shrink or FBI profiler would probably have something to say about what it meant—guilty conscience or some such. But as far as he was concerned, it just meant dumb-ass killer who left more evidence to be used against him later. Which was A-OK with him.

"Afterward, I did some reading on the computer at the library and found out about another case. A boy named Brian Durkee from Marietta. His body was found in 2003."

Gabe crossed his arms, noting that Ty was leaning

closer, getting more interested, in spite of the spiderweb-thin connection this woman was making.

"He was white, too, with light brown hair. Had turned twelve a few weeks before he died, just like my Joey." Her voice grew louder as she spoke. "And he had been kept alive for a while—years even—before he was murdered!"

Interesting. He couldn't deny that much. But not earth-shattering. Sadly, kids were kidnapped all the time. Statistically, it was usually a custody issue, but there were random psychos who went out trawling for kids. It was a sick fact of life.

"You don't see it," she said.

"I do, ma'am. It's just . . ."

"Two boys," she snapped, "and with this one you found, that's three." She raised her hand, three fingers jutting straight out to illustrate her point. "All from somewhere in the Southeast. All about the same age. All lookin' alike. All kidnapped, held till they was about twelve, then murdered and their bodies stuffed inside a wall or under a floor or somethin'."

Startled, he asked, "What?"

She shook her head, hard, as if angry at herself for not mentioning it. "The Durkee boy, he was found inside a compartment in a movie theater in Myrtle Beach."

It may have been that this grief-stricken woman was seeing coincidences, but, to be honest, Gabe couldn't help seeing them, too. When she laid it out like that, it was pretty damned surprising. And, strangely, the one thing he kept coming back to was Olivia Wainwright's face when she mentioned her fear that the man who had attacked her had been working with an accomplice, who'd perhaps gotten away.

What if she's right? What if he's still out there and has been since the night she escaped?

"Even the timing adds up to something going on. The

first one found in '03, my Joey in '07, now this new one. Seems to me some crazy psycho is killing boys every four years and nobody seems to care nothing about it!"

Gabe froze, doing the math rapidly in his head. The woman had come here thinking the remains they'd found had been of a boy killed recently. She apparently hadn't listened closely to the news report and didn't realize those remains were roughly . . . twelve years old. Which put that murder somewhere around 1999. Four years before the Durkee boy. Her son's had been four years after that. The final piece of the puzzle was infinitely more worrying.

Because it had been four years *since*.

"Jesus," Ty whispered. Apparently he'd been hit with the same awful implication.

If this convoluted tale was true—a big if—the timing couldn't be worse. Because if some psycho really was kidnapping boys, aging them, then killing them every four years, he might be out there, right now, with another victim. A victim who might not have very long to live.

And he suddenly had to wonder: Despite her unusual methods, might Olivia Wainwright be the key to finding him?

Olivia hadn't known what to expect when she'd asked to examine the remains found after the bar fire. It hadn't, however, been that the lead detective on the case would practically pick her up and push her out of the interview room in his rush to get away from her, like she was contagious, her madness catching. Yet that's what he'd done.

"You could have given me the benefit of the doubt," she muttered, still bothered by his reaction, hours later. He hadn't even asked her why, hadn't demanded an explanation. He'd heard her proposal, decided she was— what had he called her?—a whack job, and said goodbye.

After leaving the police station, she'd been so bothered by the whole thing, she hadn't even thought about going in to the office for a while. That, despite the fact that Julia had called and left two worried messages on her voice mail this afternoon. She had called her boss back, assuring her she was fine and would tell her what was going on soon. Then Liv had come home and busied herself doing laundry and washing her kitchen floor—anything to avoid thinking for a while.

It hadn't helped. She'd thought. A lot. Mainly about him.

Why she'd been so upset about the good-looking detective's reaction, she couldn't say. It had felt almost personal. She'd expected suspicion, perhaps. Disbelief. Not dismay. But dismay was what she'd swear she saw in Cooper's eyes before he'd launched himself out of his chair, thanking her for her time and saying he'd be in touch.

Digging out Steven Ames's business card had been an impulsive act. She hadn't seen or spoken to the FBI agent in at least two years, though he used to call to check up on her once every six months or so. She honestly didn't know why she still had the man's card in her wallet. Or why she'd thought of him when she realized Detective Cooper might need some outside convincing to let her do what she knew she had to. Now, though, she decided the impulse had been the right one. If there was anybody who would want to know for sure whether Dwight Collier had had an accomplice, it was Special Agent Ames.

She used to think Ames had taken a fatherly interest in her. Now, though, she had to wonder. Had he ever really, fully believed it was over? Or had those phone calls, that tenuous connection, been maintained because, deep down, he feared it wasn't?

Ames had thought from the time he'd come to Georgia to work on her case that the man responsible for her kidnapping had committed that kind of crime before. Not just with Jack, but other for-ransom jobs on the southeast coast. Kidnappings of people with wealthy family members, all of which had ended in murder. Except hers.

Not for lack of trying.

Looking back, she remembered how surprised he'd been when he'd read the profile of Dwight Collier, the man Savannah police had killed that night twelve years ago, when he'd come to pick up the ransom money. The agent had acted as if he just couldn't believe the petty thug/drifter could have been working his kidnapping schemes for several years, staying ahead of the police and the FBI. Ames, more than anyone, had wanted her to study pictures of the man, to see if there was anything at all familiar about him.

She'd agreed, but it hadn't helped. There hadn't been anything familiar. Nothing to rule him in or out, actually, as the monster who'd taken her from her bed. Having heard but not seen him, she'd had no way of knowing for sure without hearing his voice. Even that might not have been enough, since she'd heard him say so little and then only when she was terrified.

Not that he'd been alive to say a word.

Of course, that had all been before she'd known about the dark ability she'd acquired during the last night of her captivity, so she had never considered examining Collier's remains, just to be sure. By the time she had discovered what she could do, a year after the kidnapping—*God, Grandmother, I'm so sorry I got hysterical at your funeral*—Collier had been cremated, his ashes spread who knew where.

For years, she'd accepted what the police and her family and almost everyone else had told her: Her attacker was dead. Now, though, she kept thinking about those small remains, entombed in a wall. She kept considering that night. The locations. The time line. And she had to wonder if Ames had been on to something all along.

Deep in thought, she hadn't even heard anyone approaching the front door of her house until the doorbell rang. Poindexter, who'd been delicately licking his paw as he watched her clean, hopped down from the top of the entertainment center and sauntered toward the door, putting on that feline *I'm-not-up-to-anything* air.

"Forget it, cat," she muttered, knowing he would love to dart outside. During his last joyful romp out of the house, he'd found himself a comfy spot right on top of the cage housing a rabbit owned by the little girl next door. Hearing his plaintive, hungry meows from all the way up on the balcony off her bedroom, she had raced into their backyard to retrieve him. She'd been caught red-handed by Lenny, the lawn guy, who'd eyed her in shocked disapproval from behind his push mower.

Wonderful. Just what she needed to enhance her reputation: the pale, secretive redhead with a bunny-stalking black cat who trespassed in other people's backyards.

She'd been very careful to make sure he didn't escape again.

Scooping him up, she held him tightly, made sure the door's chain was fastened, then pulled the door open and peeked out. She didn't know who she had expected, Julia maybe? The UPS man?

Definitely not Detective Gabe Cooper. Yet there he stood, the strong, solid form unmistakable. His shoulders and hair—i.e., the back of him—were the first things she saw. While he'd waited for her to answer, he'd turned to look around the yard, so he faced away from the door. That gave her a moment to note the way the lazy, end-of-the-day light brought out gold highlights in the thick, coarse hair.

When he didn't turn around, she took another moment, still peering through the few inches of open doorway, mentally noting a few more things—really attractive, interesting things.

Olivia's breath got trapped in her throat as she again acknowledged the breadth of those shoulders, which were covered in a lightweight dress shirt. He'd eschewed the loose-fitting, slightly rumpled suit jacket he'd had on earlier, and she couldn't say she minded. As impressive as he'd been at the police station, he was even more so, now. The powerful creature free from his cage.

All broad at the top, he was slim-waisted, positively lean at the hip, and his trousers did nice things to the taut backside. His long legs were slightly bowed, braced apart, and with his one fisted hand on his hip, he looked almost like a sea captain at the helm, master of all he surveyed.

You've got to stop reading those epic historical novels, a voice in her head whispered.

They were her secret indulgence, and swashbuckling pirate stories her favorite of all. She couldn't imagine what people who probably thought of her as the chick who got off on dying would make of her being a closet romantic.

Finally managing to breathe again, she took one more rueful look, then gave herself a little break for being wowed. Because Gabe Cooper was absolutely stunning to stare at from behind, and every feminine inch of her responded instinctively to all that strength, the male power evidenced by the rock-hard form.

But it was time to stop playing voyeur and let him know his knock had not gone unanswered. Carefully balancing Poindexter under her arm, she gently pushed the door in a few inches, slid the chain free, then reopened it all the way.

He still didn't notice, probably deafened by the early-evening cicadas that were serenading the entire planet from this little piece of Georgia. His attention remained focused on the treelined yard, the quiet street and the nearby houses. She wondered what he was thinking, if he'd made any more judgments about her based on the fact that she lived in a big house on an exclusive street in the Victorian District.

She also wondered what he'd say if she told him she'd inherited the house and everything in it from her paternal grandmother. The house had been in the family for generations and traditionally had been passed down to the oldest daughter or granddaughter. Her father had only had a brother, so it had come to her in a trust when she'd been only sixteen. She loved the old place but had to work a full-time job just to afford the taxes and upkeep on it.

Realizing she was already on the defensive, she shoved all random thoughts aside and cleared her throat. "Detective? What are *you* doing here?"

He spun around, eyeing her from behind a pair of dark sunglasses, familiar ones, the ones she'd handed him earlier today. He was probably wearing them to break the ice—a backhanded way of thanking her—because he didn't technically need to have them on. Not here on the porch and not this late in the day.

But he didn't take them off, which was just as well. The man's eyes were a little too distracting. Of course, that just left the rest of his face to look at: the strong nose, slashing cheekbones, truly sensual mouth.

Hell. She really didn't want to like his looks, not after he'd treated her like some kind of leper this afternoon.

"Would you believe I was in the neighborhood?"

"No."

"Well, how about that I needed to see you?"

"Why? Did one of my neighbors call and say my cat's been stalking their bunny?"

One corner of his mouth went up. "You know, that sounds like a euphemism. A kind of salacious one."

"*Ooh*, big words for Mr. Average Joe street cop," she said, knowing she sounded bitchy but unable to help it.

"Can you take out the angry eyes, Mrs. Potato Head, and just let me talk to you?"

She clamped her lips together, tempted to laugh, which wasn't fair when she wanted to stay mad at him. "So talk."

"I'm sorry I showed up unannounced. I did try calling."

She'd ignored the phone, not even glancing at the caller ID, sure it was her sister calling to talk about her latest wedding plans. Olivia wasn't much in the mood for cheerful, happy-happy-joy-joy sister talk. It was going to be hard enough to go to the engagement brunch tomorrow and face the family with all this going on.

"How about letting me in so we don't give your neighbors more to gossip about than your bloodthirsty cat?"

Oh, she had no doubt they would already be burning up the phone lines if he were in a marked car. Fortunately, the sedan parked out front was plain, unidentifiable as a police vehicle. She hoped.

"Please, just give me a chance," he added, his tone gentle, reminding her of the kind streak beneath that tough outer shell.

"All right, come in," she said, stepping back and letting him enter. Poindexter stiffened for just a moment, eyeing the newcomer. When Olivia firmly closed the door, the feline lost interest, leapt from her arms and sauntered away, ignoring their visitor, obviously not caring that he could be an ax murderer or something. A guard cat, he wasn't.

"I didn't think I'd ever see you again," she said.

"Yeah, well, believe me, I wasn't expecting to come here, either."

She stared at him. Hard. "So why did you?"

He finally pushed the glasses up, revealing those springtime green eyes. Such soft, gentle-looking eyes, meant for a man of good humor. Which she definitely hadn't seen much of in him, with the exception of those brief moments of near flirtation back at the station. It was those moments she'd replayed in her head more than once since she'd gotten home. She'd found herself wishing, not for the first time, that they'd met under different circumstances.

When he didn't reply right away, she prodded, "Are you here to Baker Act me right into the psych ward?" She was trying to be light but heard the edge in her own voice. He'd hurt her earlier. That he'd had the power to hurt her after she'd known him such a short time surprised her, but it was true.

"Nah," he said. "You could go around calling yourself Mrs. Santa Claus and nobody in Savannah'd raise an eyebrow."

"But they will if I say I can use my psychic abilities to help in a murder investigation?"

He sighed, obviously realizing she had her defenses up big-time. "Which is why I came. I'm here to finish our conversation."

"The one we couldn't finish because you practically threw me out of the police station?"

He nodded, not denying it. "I regret that, and I apologize. You caught me off guard."

She liked that he'd admitted it and apologized. And for the first time since she'd opened the door, she realized what a big step it had been for him to come here at all. A few hours ago, he'd looked at her like she was a lunatic; now he was in her house, all big, tough cop.

He looked completely out of place surrounded by her late grandmother's fussy antiques, the dark burgundy walls, gold drapes, and delicate china figurines on some of the tables. She might have claimed title to the house. But she hadn't yet claimed clear possession of it, hadn't put her own stamp on it. Redecorating the whole thing would be a long, slow, expensive process; she had to do it little by little.

While her father would have given her the money to do it, she preferred to make her own way. Freeing herself from his financial support had been one of the first steps she'd taken to declare her independence, physically and emotionally. She'd decided a few years back that the time had come to stop letting what had happened to her as a teenager dictate how she would live her life. Putting an end to her parents' overprotectiveness had been step one.

"Let's go in the other room," she said, gesturing toward what had once been a parlor and was now a nice-sized den. It was the one area she had been able to afford to redo since moving in, and she immediately saw his stiff form relax a little as he beheld the big, overstuffed couch and solid, blocky wood furniture. She sensed that, like most big, strong men, he didn't quite know how to act around fragile things . . . or women.

Hmm. She wondered what he'd think if he realized she wasn't nearly as fragile as she looked. He wouldn't be the first man to make that mistake. She just wondered if he'd be the first to decide that was a very good thing, not a bad one.

Men often wanted to change her, wanted her to go back to the wealthy life she'd left behind. So far, none had liked her exactly as she was or accepted what she could do. Might he be the exception to the rule? More important, why did she care?

"Have a seat." Playing hostess to someone who thought she was a few cards shy of a full deck felt a little strange, but she was, after all, Southern. "Would you like something to drink? Sweet tea? I brewed some this afternoon."

"You regularly offer sweet tea to people who toss you out of police stations?" he asked with a small lopsided grin.

"Do you regularly toss people out of police stations?"

"I'm usually more focused on keepin' 'em in."

"You pretty well sucked at that today, didn't you?"

"Yes, ma'am, I guess I did."

"Was that a yes or a no on the tea?"

"No, thanks," he said, sitting on the sofa. Then, with no further niceties or preambles, he bluntly got to the point of his visit. "Tell me why you need to handle the remains."

"I told you, I think I can . . ."

He put up a hand, stopping her. "I know what you think you can find out. I want you to tell me exactly what you plan to do and why you think it'll work."

She sat down on a chair on the other side of the low coffee table and stared at him from a few feet away. Olivia found herself looking at those flecks of gold in his green eyes, seeking warmth, compassion. Wondering if she could trust him.

A whisper repeated in her mind. *Olivia Wainwright: freak of nature.*

Sometimes it was an old lover's voice saying it. Sometimes her former best friend from college or kids she'd known in high school. They all pretty much sounded the same. Revolted.

Fortunately, there were other voices in her life now, voices saying positive things, telling her she wasn't crazy and that the things she did were for a reason, served an important purpose. Julia's was a constant reassurance, as were those of the other agents at work.

And then there was her own voice. She'd come to accept herself, what she did and why, and these days the voice she most heard telling her to keep going, that what she did was right and necessary, was hers. That knowledge renewed her confidence. She doubted Gabe Cooper would ever be one of her biggest fans. Still, she had to try.

"Did you call Agent Ames?" she asked.

"I left a message. Now, you gonna answer my question?"

She crossed her arms over her chest, rubbing her hands against her upper arms. The room suddenly felt cold, even though it got the most late-afternoon sunlight, being on the back of the east-facing house. "You won't believe me."

His eyes narrowed. "Try me." When she still hesitated, he grudgingly added, "I want your help. I think I might *need* your help. But I have to understand."

Sitting back in the chair, she replied, "If you want to know what I can do, you have to know why I can do it. Which involves what happened to me that night, the night I escaped." Doubting it, she had to ask, "Did you read the whole file after I left?"

He shook his head firmly. "I was going to, but my partner, who had read it, suggested I hear the whole thing from your mouth first."

His eyes shifted to the mouth in question. Her mouth. And she suddenly realized something: He was aware of her, too. He didn't necessarily like it or want it to be, but at least some of his obvious tension came from the fact that the attraction she'd felt for him wasn't one-sided. That flirtation back in the interview room hadn't just been about putting her at ease and getting her to relax. She'd lay money on it.

Olivia couldn't help smiling just a little, suddenly feeling better about what she had to do. All because he'd stolen that quick, totally male look at her mouth, as if wondering what it might taste like. A man who thought about kissing her even after hearing what she wanted to do with a bunch of old bones had promise.

"Okay, then," she said, unable to help moistening her lips with her tongue. "I'll tell you."

After a quick flash of heat as he again gazed at her mouth, he gave her the full force of his attention. She saw nothing in his stare but interest. Keen, unflinching interest. No derision, no immediate skepticism, though she didn't doubt he felt it. Mainly she saw patience—she suspected this man had a lot of that.

Really, she had no other choice. The detective wasn't going to give her what she wanted until she shared her deepest, darkest secret with him. Which meant she had to go back in time. Back to that night, to that one moment, that awful, hateful moment when her old life had stopped and her new one had begun. Back to the five words that had changed everything she thought she knew about the world: What was evil and what was good; what she could survive and what she couldn't; who she'd become.

Five little words.

Why don't you drown her?

Chapter 5

Twelve years ago

Olivia tried to run.

When she heard the boy's brutal suggestion that her attacker drown her, then heard the man's answering laughter, her body reacted independently of her brain. Panic sent her spinning wildly. Like a bird caught in a cage, she tried to fly, oblivious to whatever was barring her, needing just to escape. She threw all her weight forward, desperate, not even deciding to do it until it was done.

To her surprise, her sudden lunge caught her captor off guard. Thinking she was totally subdued, broken, he hadn't realized she still had real fight in her. His firm grip broke and she plunged forward, free. *Free!*

But not, of course. Her hands remained tied behind her back, her feet lashed with rope, her face still covered with the blanket. She was completely lost and terrified.

Still, she didn't give up, driving forward into the blackness, the rope at her ankles lax enough to allow her to shuffle several inches at a time. The rough ground stabbed at her bare toes, sharp sticks and rocks piercing her flesh. Her long, filthy nightgown whipped around her legs, trying to trip her up. On the third step, her feet tangled, sending her plummeting facedown to the ground. Unable to put her hands out to break her fall, she hit hard, feeling sure she'd broken her nose and a few of her teeth. Blood gushed in her mouth, dripping over her lips, the salty, metallic scent filling her nose.

Sobbing with the pain, she continued to move, desperate, still in a blind terror, needing to *go*. She started to crawl, propelling herself on her torn-up knees. *Inchworm, inchworm . . .* the childhood song screamed crazily in her head. Or she screamed. Or the night did.

"Stop it, little bitch," the man snarled, pouncing on her, driving a knee into her back, before she got more than a foot or two.

She struggled, twisting, kicking.

"Stop wiggling or I'll make it worse on ya."

How could it be worse?

He smacked her hard on the back of the head, then roughly ran his hand down her hair, yanking a handful of it. Holding her head back, he tore her tattered nightgown off her body, then thrust his other hand between her thighs, yanking them apart. Thick, rough fingers groped at her crotch, tearing her underwear off, too, leaving her naked to the cool spring night.

Olivia screamed, knowing what he meant by worse. "No!"

"I'll fuck you and then the boy'll fuck you and then I'll kill you anyways," he hissed. "Now shut the hell up and stop fighting."

She shut up. She stopped fighting.

He rose, pulling her by the hair. Her mouth throbbed, blood spilling down her chin, and she spat out something small and hard that she suspected had once been part of her front tooth.

Surreal. Everything, the whole world tilted and wobbled, up becoming down.

I'm going to die. I'm going to die. I'm going to die.

The horse blanket fell, but his fingers were twined so tightly against her scalp that she couldn't turn as much as an inch to see him behind her. Blinking, she instead looked forward, dazed and confused. Everything she saw told her it was useless to scream. Nobody was around, who would possibly hear?

Beside them was the rickety old barn, its faded wood planks rotting and dangling by broken hinges. Bleached with sun and age, thinned by bugs and heat, it looked ready to fall down in a strong breeze. At any time during the days she'd spent in there, she probably could have kicked her way out if she'd tried, though, with her guard and the bindings, she probably wouldn't have gotten far. Still, oh God, did she wish she'd tried.

Several yards away stood a banged-up pickup truck and a rusty mobile camper, the top popped up. Other than the two vehicles, nothing but wilderness. Not a building, not a vehicle, not another man-made thing as far as she could see. Just enormous ancient trees blocking much of the cloud-swathed sky. Whatever farm or plantation this barn had once belonged to had been abandoned or reclaimed by the ground from which it had been birthed. All that was left were the barn and the woods. Nasty, thick, Georgia swamp-woods, the trees heavy with moisture from a recent rain. Enormous spiderwebs filled the branches, glimmering like freakish silver necklaces in the pale, watery moonlight. She could practically see their occupants, brown, furry spiders as big as her fist, but she didn't even flinch.

She'd once been deathly afraid of spiders. That had been before she'd known what real fear was. Now, she'd grab them with her bare hands if she thought it could help her escape. Nor did she hesitate at the thought of running through the slimy muck beneath those ancient bent trees. The area was probably filled with gators and snakes, yet if she had a chance, she'd take it.

But she was out of chances, and all three of them knew it.

Her captor said something, but she couldn't hear it.

Bullfrogs croaked so loudly she couldn't have heard her own whimpers, and she couldn't stop thinking how strange the air tasted. Musty and damp, rich with muck and the decay of rotting limbs and dead animals and turned earth. And blood.

She didn't want her last breath to be of this air. Just as she didn't want her attacker's face to be the last one she ever saw on this earth.

It won't be. The boy's will.

Jack. She shifted her eyes, seeing him watching from a few feet away, wondering if he felt her hatred. Her rage.

He flinched.

Yes. He felt it. *Good.*

"Get over there. I'm gonna need you to help hold 'er," the man snapped.

Jack stared at her, hesitated. Then, when the man barked something else, leapt to do his bidding. All the while, Olivia dangled from the roots of her gripped hair, her back pressed against the massive body that reeked of sweat and filth.

He dragged her to the rain barrel, a huge, old-fashioned one that stood as tall as her waist. Bugs and mosquitoes rose from the murk, not liking to be disturbed. A thin coat of slime and algae gleamed green against the brackish water, and it stunk the way a standing pond did in high summer.

She couldn't help it, instinct made her squirm, try to kick. He hissed something in her hair, reminding her he'd rape her if she didn't quit, but she couldn't make herself stop. Couldn't submit to that dark, black pool that looked like the opening to a cave that led straight to hell.

"Hold her!" he barked, and she felt smaller hands grab her arm.

She tried to yank away, more repulsed by *his* touch

than she was by the man's. Because he had betrayed her. Utterly, completely betrayed her.

But there was no time to think of that, no time to again accuse him with her eyes, or plead or beg or scream. Because that powerful hand was pushing her head down . . . down . . . until she saw the reflection of her own eyes shining back at her from the moonlit surface.

She panicked, sucked in a breath to scream. Thinking better of it, she instead clamped her mouth shut to conserve the air.

Then she was in it.

Warm and thick, viscous, not like water, more like blood. Arching her back, she tries to lift her head, her body instinctively striving to stay alive. The grip remains merciless in her hair, and her head stays beneath the surface, no matter how much she twists and splashes.

She holds her breath. Oh, how she holds it.

Unable to help it, she opens her terrified eyes, sees nothing but the black. Bubbles escape her closed lips. She clenches her mouth tighter, wriggling, jerking. Her lungs ache, her heart races, her blood surges through her veins as if knowing it's making its last delivery of oxygen to her starving organs.

Her muscles clench, then cramp painfully. In the blackness before her eyes, she suddenly sees her father's face. Her mother's. Her sister's.

The boy's.

Such anger. Such pain. Hot fire in her chest. The urge to open her mouth and suck in her own destruction is strong, relentless.

She has heard drowning is a peaceful death.

That is a lie.

Her body rebels until her chest cavity feels on the verge of implosion. Her mouth opens, her lungs clench, working independently of her mind, groping, demanding what they need.

She tries, struggles to hold on to that last breath, which has long since been robbed of its life-sustaining oxygen. Her cells begin to die. The images in her mind fade. Her lips part, more bubbles as the dead air leaks from her lungs.

At last, helpless against millions of years of evolution, she inhales.

Oh, God, the agony! Unlike anything she's ever imagined.

Her heart continues to beat, though her mouth and lungs are filled with filthy water. She hears her pulse in her head: ker-thunk, ker-thunk, ker-thunk.

Slowing. Weak. Kerrrr-thuuuunk. Kerrrrr—

Then nothing. Silence. The heartbeat is gone.

And soon, so is she.

Present day, Friday, 7:25 p.m.

"You *died*?"

Gabe didn't think his body could get any more tense, but right now he felt ready to snap in half. Shock rolled through him, horror making his breath slow, as hers had done while she relived the nightmare.

She hadn't *just* died. She had been murdered. A lovely, innocent fifteen-year-old girl, brutally, ruthlessly, painfully murdered.

Throughout Olivia's recitation, during which she had closed her eyes and verbalized some awful picture playing in her mind, he'd found himself leaning farther forward in his seat, his elbows gouged into his knees, his hands clasped together. Shocked into silence, he had been aware of nothing but her voice. He hadn't even really been thinking, just watching and listening as Olivia uncovered her long-buried memories, giving them life, giving them power.

That power abused her. He could see it in the paleness of her face, the way her mouth trembled and her nails dug into her own flesh as she tightened her arms around her middle.

"Oh, yes," she finally replied in a voice that quivered almost as much as her lips did. She gazed at him with watery green eyes. "I was dead for a little over two minutes."

"Lord in heaven," he muttered, stunned out of the immobility the horrifying story had brought on him. He didn't think about it, didn't wonder what he was doing or if he should do it. Instead, he found himself launching out of his seat, then dropping to his knees in front of hers. Grabbing her icy-cold hands, he wrapped them in his, watching shivers rack her slim body.

As much as he felt connected to her, given the personal, intimate secrets she'd shared with him today, Gabe had no idea if she lived here alone or if some boyfriend might come storming in at any moment. But he didn't care. She needed human connection. And he was there to give it to her.

Dropping her hands, he reached for her, wrapping his arms around her and tugging her up. Then he slid into her chair, bringing her onto his lap. She didn't protest. Instead, she slid her arms around his neck, dropping her head onto his shoulder and curling into him like it was the most natural thing in the world. Hell, maybe it was. The specter of death made every human being long to grab at life, didn't it? To hold someone, touch a warm body, hear another's heartbeat, share a breath and acknowledge that, for one more moment, whatever mysteries lay beyond this world had been held at bay.

But for her, they hadn't. She'd crossed over that boundary, explored those mysteries and was, to this day, haunted by them.

"I'm sorry," he whispered against her soft hair, "so damn sorry, Olivia." He drew small patterns on her back

with the tips of his fingers, reminding her she was connected, wanting to impress on her the fact that she was
not alone, not still wandering in that darkness.

They stayed that way for several moments, during
which he felt her rapid, shallow breaths slow against his
neck. One of his hands was cupped over her shoulder, his
thumb brushing the pulse point in her neck, where he
could feel her frantic pulse slow.

She was okay, returning to normal. Whatever terrors
tormented her, they had been put back in Pandora's box,
at least for now.

Good. That's what he'd wanted. But he realized something: The return of normalcy also made him acknowledge how good she felt pressed against him, curled on
his lap. She was small, though not tiny, fitting perfectly
against him, her soft curves melting against his harder
angles.

It had been a long while since he'd been so close to a
woman, and frankly he didn't remember it being quite
this nice. He wasn't sure anyone had ever felt as good in
his arms as Olivia did.

That realization brought all kinds of images to mind.
Images of her turning around to face him, leaving him
free to tangle his hands in her hair and pull her down for
a warm, wet kiss. He liked kissing—it was one of his favorite things to do—and he suspected Olivia's mouth
would taste just about perfect.

He was suddenly terribly aware of her soft breasts
pressing against his chest and the curve of her bottom
against his thighs. The tender embrace was feeling different. Her breaths were getting choppy again, and he suspected her pulse was speeding up, too. As was his.
Whatever this feeling was, it was catching. It leapt between them for a few seconds, and he'd bet her thoughts
mirrored his own. *This is too soon. She's a witness. She's
vulnerable right now.*

All of the above, and that meant it was time to let her go, even if it was the last thing he wanted to do. He dropped his hand. She lifted her head. Their eyes met, her expression searching and appreciative. She silently thanked him, and he just as silently said it was okay. Then she rose to her feet and moved to the couch, taking the spot where he'd been sitting.

Offering him a shaky smile, she finally broke the silence. "I didn't stay dead, of course."

He managed a faint smile, too. "If you did, you're the most solid ghost I've ever seen."

One brow went up in challenge. "Have you seen many?"

"Not a one. You?"

She shook her head. "That's my boss's thing, not mine." Her smile faded, as if she'd suddenly remembered that *her thing* was what had brought him here. And they still hadn't quite gotten to it. Yeah, he understood a lot more about what had happened to her. But how it had changed her, what abilities did she think the experience had given her? No clue.

"Listen, before we finish this, how about a drink?" she asked, getting up before he'd even responded. "I could use a glass of wine. Are you off-duty, Detective? Can I get you a beer?"

"My shift's over; to be honest, I came here off the record. So, yeah, a beer would be great, thanks. And please call me Gabe." She'd been curled up in his lap five minutes ago, and if she'd stayed there another ten seconds, she probably would have felt his body reacting to that. So, yeah, they oughta be on a first-name basis.

She didn't go far, just to a wet bar in a corner. He liked this den area; not only did it have a big screen, the bar and a small refrigerator, but it also had none of that frilly, girly stuff that had marked the rest of the house he'd seen so far. It was a room you could live in, not one you had to tiptoe through to get somewhere else. He liked that the pillows were big and squishy, the pictures on the wall of sunny meadows, not plastic fruit. This room, he suspected, was the one she really lived in. Which made him wonder who lived in the rest of the museum.

Opening the fridge, she retrieved a beer and a half-full bottle of white wine. She poured herself a drink, then returned and handed him the beer. The tips of their fingers met on the slick, cold glass, and she didn't let go of the bottle immediately. Such a slight touch, but he felt it way down deep. Every touch seemed a little more important now, though he couldn't say why. Maybe it was because she'd opened up to him. Maybe it was because he'd held her. Whatever the reason, he was more aware of her than he had been before. Whether that was a good thing or a bad one, though, he just couldn't say.

"Thank you," he finally said.

She let go, turning away while he twisted the cap off the bottle and took a deep sip. Once she'd sat down, smoothed her skirt and sipped her wine, she nodded once, silently letting him know she was ready to continue whenever he was. He'd done enough pushing for one day, however, and was content to let her take the lead. He hoped they'd already gotten past the worst part but honestly wasn't entirely sure.

Though, really, what could be worse than experiencing your own death?

"Okay, where were we?" she finally murmured.

"You were about to tell me how Jack saved you."

She sucked in a breath, obviously surprised he'd figured that out.

It hadn't been hard. "You sounded desperate to know what happened to him earlier today, like you owed him your life. But when you just told me what happened that night, it sounded like you had gone to your grave hating him. So I suspect he's the one who hauled you out of it."

She nodded, cupping her fingers around her glass, staring into the pale liquid. "Yes, he did. I remember taking a breath, inhaling that water. Then blackness. Absolutely nothing."

"No bright light or long tunnel?" he asked, not teasing, not one bit.

She shook her head. "Sorry. If there was, I don't remember it. Not a thing. The first memory I have after drowning is of being rolled onto my side so I could vomit up a bunch of water, then trying to remind my body how to breathe."

"He'd performed CPR?"

"Don't ask me how an abused, terrified boy did it, but yes. He brought me back to life."

"Where was Collier?"

Another sip, another long, introspective silence. "Gone. Jack said he'd left to get the ransom money, telling Jack to bury me."

He shook his head, having a hard time imagining it. "How long were you . . . ?"

"As I said, on reflection, I'm sure I was clinically dead for two minutes, ten seconds. I don't know if my brain waves had actually stopped when Collier pulled me out of the barrel and tossed me to the ground. But my heart had, and he certainly thought I was all the way gone."

"Maybe you never . . ."

"I did," she said. "Trust me on this. I would have been pronounced dead in any hospital."

He didn't push it.

"Anyway, Jack revived me. I started to breathe, then clawed at him, screaming how much I hated him." Her voice broke, this memory seeming worse than the other horrific ones she'd already shared, the final, brutal straw. "Then I looked at his face and saw huge tears rolling down his dirty cheeks." Her eyes drifted closed but not quick enough to stop a tear of her own from slipping out.

That tiny dot of moisture gave testament to a lot of pent-up grief. "He told me he was sorry for suggesting the man drown me, but said he'd seen something on TV about CPR and thought he might be able to do it. It was all he could think to do."

Gabe shuddered, not even wanting to calculate all the things that could have gone wrong. "That's one hell of a risk."

She scraped the back of her hand over her cheek casually, pretending she wasn't catching a tear. "I know. But he thought the odds were better with that than letting Collier cut me up, as he'd intended to." She said it matter-of-factly and apparently didn't notice him flinch. "Jack knew I wouldn't have much time. As soon as he thought I was dead, Jack reminded Collier he had to leave to stake out the drop spot and said he'd take care of getting rid of me. I can't imagine how hard it was, worrying he might not actually go."

But he did. Miraculously, shockingly, the monster had left in time for some poor, brainwashed, abused kid to resuscitate his intended victim.

She took another sip of her drink, deeper this time, and curled up in her seat, tucking one leg beneath her. "I begged him to come with me. Literally grabbed his hand and tried to drag him. But he wouldn't. He was terrified."

That was, on the surface, hard to grasp. Having worked with some really screwed-up victims, though, he thought he could understand it. *The devil you know . . .*

"He said that if he came back and Jack was gone, Collier would know right away he'd helped me escape and would hunt us both down. There was no phone, no buildings anywhere we could see. Even Jack wasn't sure where we were. By staying, he could cover for me until I'd gotten to safety. Say he'd buried me or whatever."

"What did he think would happen when the media reported you'd been found?"

"I don't know," she whispered. "We were young, both terrified, panicked. We were thinking of the next ten minutes, not the next ten hours."

He nodded, understanding. Trying to think rationally at such a moment, well, it was amazing she had survived. It would have taken some kind of miracle for them both to.

Maybe there would have been one, if the kidnapper hadn't returned soon enough to realize what Jack had done. Collier had been killed by police later that night . . . if only he hadn't come back before going to pick up the money, Jack might very well have been saved.

Funny, how he was thinking of this whole scenario as such a likely one or, at the very least, remarkably plausible. A part of him had already accepted it.

"So you ran for your life."

Her mouth trembled the tiniest bit. "Yes."

And, he assumed, she'd never seen Jack again. At least, not until she saw his face in a forensic artist's sketch. Or believed she had.

"I thanked him, told him I'd come back for him, and took off. I ran for a while, then found a place to hide and stayed there, shivering, all night long. I didn't come out until dawn." Her voice faltered and her hand, the one holding the wineglass, trembled. "Looking back, I think Collier must have come back soon after I'd gotten away and realized what Jack had done. So he killed him and took the body with him when he went."

"*And* the camper and all their stuff?" he pointed out, still hung up on the timing of this whole thing.

She nibbled the tip of her finger. "I sat down with a piece of paper and figured out the time line. It would have been tight, yes, but not impossible. He could have killed Jack, ditched the camper, brought the body back into town and walled it up, then gone to the ransom drop point. He had hours—seven or eight at least."

He could see by the twist of her mouth that she was regretting those hours, every one of them, that she'd spent hiding. Poor, terrified kid.

"It wouldn't have saved him," Gabe murmured, leaning forward in his seat, wanting to make sure she really heard him—and believed. "If you'd kept running, been rescued right away, it *still* would have taken a long time for the police to figure out where you'd been."

A scared kid, running in the dark, after what she'd been through? It probably would have been morning, anyway. "It wouldn't have made any difference for Jack. You know that, right?"

She managed a short nod. But he didn't imagine his words would help. She hadn't set down that heavy load of guilt; he doubted she ever would, not until she found out for sure what had happened to the boy. He hoped to be able to help her with that, especially now that he knew her horrific story.

"So, what about his truck?" he asked, still piecing it all together in his mind.

"The police found it at the bus station a few days later and figured Collier had parked there and walked to the drop site, wanting to scope things out since he knew I'd gotten away."

He made a mental note to look into that. "Was it registered to Collier?"

She shook her head. "Stolen two years before from out of state."

Damn. So many leads that went nowhere, so many unanswered questions. If only the police had managed to take the man alive.

"What do you think, Gabe?" she asked, his name sounding really nice on her lips. "Do you believe me? Do you think I could be right, that he walled Jack up?"

Yeah, actually, he did. Somehow, he'd begun to believe in her. Maybe because she was so sure, her description so dead-on. Maybe because of the mother who'd come to the station today with her theories. Whatever the reason, he strongly suspected the Jack whom Olivia had known was the boy whose bones he'd looked at four days ago.

"I do," he admitted. "He couldn't risk burying him. He knew you'd be bringing the police; that's why he got rid of the camper." Which would have been the natural place to leave the body. But plenty of tourists and hunters visited the swamps, and he couldn't have known the camper would never be found, especially if it was ditched quickly and at night. Walling up his victim at a work site like something out of a Poe story might have sounded a little safer at the time. And hell, maybe he'd wanted to kill time, wanted to listen to the news reports or even scan police radio traffic to see if anybody was talking about picking up the missing Wainwright girl. His confidence could have built with every hour that he didn't hear that news until he'd decided to make a try for the ransom.

"The police did find the site," she said. "There wasn't much. Some footprints, tire tracks, trash that made it look like they'd been staying out there for a while. Little else."

Suddenly remembering what she'd told him that afternoon, he said, "Was it somewhere near the cemetery? That's where you were found, right?"

Her already pale face went the tiniest bit whiter, which just served to emphasize its delicate lines. The high cheeks, huge eyes, those pretty, trembling lips. "The old barn was in a big wooded area west of Laurel Grove North. I actually made it as far as the cemetery during the night. By that point, I was jumping at every noise and just wanted to hide."

Her throat worked as she swallowed, and, for the first time since his arrival, she turned her gaze away, not meeting his eyes. This wasn't fear. It was humiliation. Shame. That was clear in the small, quiet whisper. "So when I found an old run-down crypt with a broken capstone, I pulled it open, crawled inside and hid until daylight."

"Jesus, Mary and St. Joseph," he muttered, repeating his late mother's favorite saying, which she'd used when she didn't know what to say. He didn't punctuate it by making the sign of the cross, as she would have; there was no religion in the expression. Just pure, utter shock.

How much agony had this one woman—girl, at that time—been expected to survive? And where on earth had she come up with the strength, the utter grit, to survive it?

"I'm sorry," he whispered, not knowing what else to say, hoping she hadn't interpreted his outburst as a sign he was judging her for choosing to curl up with the dead in order to save her own life. He wasn't. In fact, the only feeling he had right now was admiration that she'd dug so deep and found such stamina to fight for her own survival.

"Thanks," she said with a nod, confirming she didn't think he'd been criticizing the choice she'd made at a desperate moment. "The next morning, when it was light, I crawled out. A caretaker spotted me stumbling around, called nine-one-one, and I was rescued." She lifted her hands in a helpless shrug. "There's not a lot more to tell. The rest you know. Collier was killed, and the police never found Jack. Twelve years went by. Then, this morning, I saw his face on the news."

Had that just been this morning? Had he really not even known her name one day ago? That seemed impossible. Wrong, somehow, on a deep, primal level he couldn't quite understand.

He knew her now, though, knew her better than most people did, he'd wager. While he'd come here determined to make her prove she wasn't frigging crazy, now he would dare anyone to suggest she was. And yet . . . *and yet . . .*

She'd told him everything that had happened to her but still had explained nothing about the end result. Oh, sure, he had his suspicions that her back-from-the-dead experience and her subsequent night spent in the embrace of some old skeletons had combined to make her think she had some kind of psychic ability. Whether it was real or not he wasn't willing to say. He was the biggest skeptic on the planet and would never have believed that an abused, kidnapped, twelve-year-old boy could have schemed to have a girl drowned just so he could later save her life. And that it would *work*. So what did he know?

Finally, as if knowing his mind was again churning, she sighed deeply, shaking her head to force out all those dark, unpleasant thoughts and prepared to give him one more explanation. The big one. "As for what I can do and why I want to examine the remains?" she said slowly, as if wondering if he really wanted to know.

"Tell me."

"You remember how I said I was dead a little more than two minutes?"

"I remember." *Vividly*.

"Well, Detective Cooper, since that night, I've had the ability to touch human remains and relive the final minutes of someone else's life. See what they saw, hear what they heard." She cleared her throat. "Feel what they felt. Which means if Jack's bones are the ones you found, I'll know it. Give me two minutes and ten seconds, and I promise you, I'll *know*."

He hesitated, staring, not sure he'd heard right. Once he'd absorbed the words and saw she meant every one of them, he spun them around in his mind, thinking about everything that had happened. Everything she'd been through. Everything he knew about this woman so far.

Then, when it had all fallen into place, he handed her his empty beer bottle. "I think I need another drink."

More than a drink. Maybe a lot of them. Not because he didn't believe her but because somehow, deep down in his true skeptic's heart, a part of him really did.

Or, at least, was considering it.

Though it sometimes seemed like he was remembering a scene from a movie or a TV show, the boy felt pretty sure his name had once been Tucker and that he'd once had a mama and a daddy and a big sister.

Some Tucker had, anyway. Maybe it had been him. Maybe not. He couldn't hardly remember anything anymore, beyond the rickety old trailer with the roaches living in the walls. And the dead grass outside. And the heat, the never-endin' heat.

Once, maybe, he'd lived in a place that got cool inside even when it was hot out. Not anymore, though. Now it was always hot. Day and night. *Always*.

Like now. As he stirred the pot of canned ravioli on the portable camping stove in the kitchen, he couldn't help thinking about what it might be like to go jump in a cold swimming pool. Or the ocean, maybe.

That other Tucker had gone to the ocean a couple of times, he thought. More often, he'd swam in a lake. There'd been a rope hanging from a big old tree that used to let him swing out over the water like he was a bird flyin' through the air. He'd always been afraid to let go, even though sometimes he wondered if he could maybe just keep on flying rather than falling down and makin' a big splash. He'd be afraid, terrified, but also excited and pretty sure he'd be fine. That, just like always, he'd land safe in the water, and his mama would smile and clap her hands, and his daddy would laugh and give him a big okeydoke sign with his fingers.

He'd lived with his family in a pretty house near a field full of apple trees that his daddy grew along with peaches and cherries. He didn't like the peaches, but he thought he used to climb up to snitch apples on his way home down the long gravel lane that led from the school bus to his house. He also sort of remembered the way his big sister would run home fast, her braids flying out behind her, leaving him in her dust, his shorter legs unable to keep up.

Sometimes in his dreams, he found himself running and running but never getting anywhere.

Just dreams. Like Tucker. Like his old life.

Now he was Jack.

"Damn it, boy, I told you to have my supper on the table!"

He cringed, tucking himself into the corner between the stove and the flimsy wall that separated the tiny kitchen from the just-as-tiny living room. He'd been thinking, letting his mind drift, rather than doing what he'd been told. He'd probably pay for that now.

Thwack! A stinging pain, his ears ringing with the force of the slap. He braced himself for the next one, but he got off easy; there was only that one. Uncle Johnny musta been pretty distracted. He'd come back in a funny mood tonight, itchy, almost, like he was jumpy in his own pants. Mad and cursin', then acting like there was nothin' wrong at all.

Maybe it was because of the man in the shed.

Though he was all tied up and blindfolded, the man had throwed hisself so hard against the door, it had almost splintered open before Uncle Johnny had even knowed it. Jack was glad that had happened this evenin', after Uncle Johnny got home from wherever it

was he went most days. If the man had got away while
Jack was here alone, he had the feeling he'd be the one
who'da got beat with the strap instead of the poor, cryin'
man in the shed. The fact that Jack couldn't have done
anything, since Uncle Johnny locked him in the trailer
when he was gone, probably wouldn'ta even made a
difference.

Funny, that Tucker boy had never thought men could
cry, only girls and babies.

As for Jack? Well, he knew better. Oh, my, yes. He'd
heard men not only cry but sob, scream and beg. Sometimes he had to put his hands over his ears late at night
just to make the sound of it stop, even long after whoever had made those sounds was dead and buried in an
unmarked grave in the woods.

"Well, you gone deaf, boy?" snapped the big man at
the table. "Where's my supper?"

"It's ready," he whispered, quickly spooning the food
into a cracked bowl. Scuttling over, he put it down in
front of the man, offered him a spoon and a shaky smile,
too. "Not too hot, just the way ya like it. And I buttered
ya some bread."

Uncle Johnny scooped up a few pieces of the soggy
pasta and shoveled them into his mouth. He chewed,
swallowed, then muttered, "Not bad."

Jack waited, wondering if Uncle Johnny meant it and
would follow up the praise by pattin' him on the head or
tellin' him he could have some food for himself. Or if he
was just playin' possum, waiting for Jack to get closer so
he could whack on him again. Jack never knew.

Sometimes Uncle Johnny seemed to be like two people sharin' the same face and skin. He could be nice,
friendly-like with a big smile, sayin' things like "Call me
Daddy, son!" Then something would snap, and he'd be
mean as a snake. He even seemed like he had two brains
in his head. Each one talked with a different voice, and,

when it got real bad, they sounded like they was arguin'
with each other.

A while back, when he started to notice how bad Uncle Johnny could be when the mood came over him, he'd
started to think of the mean Uncle Johnny as someone
else. *Uncle Bob.* Not out loud, a'course, just secretly, in
his mind. He didn't know why; it just helped keep him on
his toes to remember which one he was dealing with.

He suspected Uncle Bob had walked in the door and
smacked 'im. But he wasn't sure who was sittin' at the
table right now.

Finally, when the bowl was almost empty and the
room had been real quiet but for the sound of his eating,
Uncle Johnny—and he thought it was Uncle Johnny now
'cause his eyes weren't all squinty and hard—looked at
him. "Well? Aren't you hungry?"

"Yessir!" he said, so relieved at that normal voice he
wasn't sure whether to laugh or cry.

"What are you waiting for, then? Have something to
eat," he said with a smile, as nice as could be, like he
hadn't just walloped him. "Growing boy needs to keep
his energy up."

As good as it was to see that smile, Jack knew it could
be wiped away in an instant. He could never count on it
stayin' for long. If he'd dared to have some food without
first bein' told he could, and Uncle Johnny had been in
an Uncle Bob kind of mood, he coulda ended up with his
arm in a sling. Better to wait to be invited, no matter
what.

Now that he had been, he hurried back to the stove.
His stomach rumbled loud enough for Uncle Johnny to
hear it, and from the table, he let out a laugh. "Hurry up
there, Jackie-boy. The grizzly in your belly is getting
hungry."

"Yessir," he mumbled, quickly spooning the few remaining pieces of food into the other bowl. He stood by

the stove, eating his scraps quickly, using his fingers. He didn't want to risk getting too close, for fear that Uncle Johnny would decide he did want the rest, after all, and take it.

Or, worse, that Uncle Bob would.

Before he'd finished, he heard a ringing sound coming from Uncle Johnny's pocket. It was the phone that he kept with him all the time, except when he locked it up in a trunk he kept in the bedroom, along with some clothes and other stuff Jack had never gotten a good look at.

Jack sometimes used to think he might make a call on that phone, if his uncle ever happened to drop it or somethin'. But he didn't know who he'd call. Tucker's mama and daddy and sister was dead and gone. He had nobody else, just the man sittin' at the table, the one Jack watched now with both loathing and a kind of shaky, terrified love.

Uncle Johnny pulled the phone out, looked at the numbers on it, and answered in a sociable voice, "Hello, there. What can I do for you?"

Jack smiled as he washed the dishes, glad the phone call wasn't a bad one. Maybe if Uncle Johnny stayed in this mood, he might let Jack listen to the radio after dinner. Maybe he'd even go out and get some ice cream that the two of them could eat outside while they watched the sun go down. He'd done that on occasion, a long time ago, but it hadn't happened since they'd come to this new place a while back.

Then he thought about the man in the shed, the way he'd screamed and cried. And Jack decided he'd rather stay in and listen to the radio, especially if he could turn it up real loud. Even if it meant no ice cream.

"You did?" Uncle Johnny said into the phone. "This morning? Are you sure? Goodness, that musta slipped my mind. Sorry about that!"

He was quiet again, and the next time Jack looked over, he saw those eyes get smaller. Squinty-like. *Uh-oh.* His legs wobbled, and he leaned against the counter, hopin' he was wrong but not thinkin' he was.

"What?" Uncle Johnny asked, his voice gettin' low, husky.

No. Oh, please, no.

"Who the fuck you think you're talkin' to?" The man sneered, his whole body curling up tight, all hard and mad. "Don't be thinkin' you kin order me around . . . You think I'm s'posed ta be skeered 'cause a some old bones in a wall?"

Closing his eyes, Jack reached for the scrub brush, knowing he had to get the dishes extra clean. He didn't want to do anything wrong, give the man any reason to get mad.

There would be no radio tonight. No ice cream. No sunset.

He only hoped there wouldn't be any beating, either.

Because Uncle Bob was back.

Chapter 6

When Olivia had agreed to attend a family brunch this morning to celebrate her sister's engagement, she'd thought the only hard part about it would be pretending she didn't dislike her future brother-in-law. Though her sister obviously saw something in him worth caring for, Drew Buckman did seem to go out of his way to make himself unlikable. Their father called him a tool. And their mother, always a little more blunt, referred to him as the nutless wonder.

Buckman was a corporate lawyer—strike one. He was also a pompous know-it-all—strike two. Finally, being seventeen years older than his fiancée, he was also a bossy, controlling jerk. He had Brooke looking to him for permission before she ordered something off a menu. *Strike three, you're out.* Not just the game but the whole ballpark. Except he wasn't, unfortunately. In six months, he would become a member of the family.

Her sister could do so much better. Brooke had always been shy, a late bloomer, and had started dating Drew—who'd been their senator cousin's best friend for decades—right out of college. She'd wanted a settled, steady, older man. Nobody dangerous, nobody too exciting. Like the tortoise who was content to go slow and steady, confident the trophy at the end of the race was worth skipping any exciting sprints, Brooke had never even considered taking a risk.

Olivia sometimes wondered if it was because of what had happened to *her* as a teenager. Brooke had, after all, been sleeping in the next room, just twelve years old, when Liv had been taken. She'd been the one to realize Olivia was gone the next morning. Maybe it wasn't so surprising she'd wanted a safe life and a safe man. Safe and, in Olivia's opinion, sad.

Funny, though, as it turned out, hiding her dislike of the future groom wasn't going to be the hardest part of the morning. Neither was trying to pretend it wasn't the weirdest thing in the world to have a big family gathering with her not-divorced parents and their significant others shooting under-the-breath gibes at each other. Nor having to listen to her senator cousin talk politics while his snooty wife talked about her designer clothes or simply name-dropped.

No. The hard part was trying to not let all of them know how utterly terrified she was.

Terrified, excited, hopeful, reluctant—all feelings that overwhelmed her when she thought about where she was going right after brunch: to examine the remains of a boy who had been haunting her waking and sleeping moments for more than a decade.

Gabe Cooper had agreed to her request. She didn't know whether he believed she could do what she said, but the skeptic had at least become open to the possibility. She appreciated it and liked that about him—his ability to move outside his comfort zone. One of the many things she found herself liking about the good-looking, thoughtful man.

Still, when she thought about this afternoon, she couldn't help shaking. The funny thing was, she needn't have worried about anybody noticing her mood. They were all too busy being shocked by the fact that she'd brought someone with her.

"You sure you're doing okay?" she asked in a low

voice, watching Gabe cast a dubious eye on a small dish of caviar on a nearby table. He seemed much more a beer-and-wings type.

And she liked that about him, too.

"Sorry. I don't have much experience with family gatherings," he said.

"Yours doesn't get together often?"

"I don't have one," he replied, his jaw stiffening. "At least, none I'm willing to claim."

She mentally kicked herself for asking. Though her family was a bit out of the ordinary, and she sometimes wanted to lock her parents together in a room and make them admit they still loved one another or finally just agree to get a divorce, she could not even imagine life without them. "Well, thanks again for coming. I appreciate it. We can leave in a half hour or so."

"I think I'll survive that long," he said with a slight smile.

She still couldn't quite believe he was here. She'd been half-joking when she'd suggested it last night. Yes, she needed someone to give her a ride home from the coroner's office, because she wouldn't be able to drive afterward. If today were like every other time, she'd be in a bad way, needing to curl up in a dark room, cry for a while, then sleep off the horror. She'd intended to take a cab, but he had insisted on driving her.

Problem was, she had this brunch, and the timing was tight. They had to be at the coroner's at noon, yet she couldn't bow out of this gathering, not just because it was for Brooke but because Richard would feel slighted. Her cousin was rarely in Georgia, spending most of his time in D.C., so the August recess was usually filled with Richard-centric events. *Yippee.*

When Gabe had found out she had an engagement she couldn't avoid that would make it impossible for her to get home in time for him to pick her up there, he'd agreed to come with her to her father's estate just out-side of Savannah. Having him come as her guest was a lot easier than trying to explain why she'd needed a cop to drive her when she left here.

The thing was, she hadn't had a date in a long time. And she hadn't brought a man around her family for at least two years. So what had sounded like a good idea last night after a glass of wine seemed crazy today, not least of which because, for a few minutes last night, she'd found it all too easy to think about being involved in some kind of personal relationship with the man. Espe-cially when he looked at her with that slight smile, laughed that sexy, husky laugh, drawled her name in that honey-smooth Southern voice or brushed up against her with that wickedly powerful body.

God, what was happening to her? She was rapidly growing addicted to a man she'd met less than a week ago. The simple truth was, she wanted him. Wanted to be in his arms.

Last night he'd held her for comfort, and that had been nice. But he'd continued to hold her in response to sudden, thick sexual tension and, for a little while at least, that had been nicer.

He'd let her go out of necessity. That hadn't been nice at all. In fact, it had left her wondering later that night when she was alone in her bed what might have hap-pened if she hadn't climbed off his lap.

Olivia didn't usually fall hard and fast, having been burned by enough men to be wary of ever letting her guard down around one too soon. Yet this rough-edged detective already had her wishing this were a real date. Preferably their fourth or fifth date, so it could end with them in her bedroom.

Admit it, you already want to go to bed with this man, whether you ever go on a real date with him or not.

It was true. And no matter how much of a proper

Southern lady her grandmother had hoped she'd be, she couldn't muster up much embarrassment about that fact. Olivia was a woman, she liked sex, and she was incredibly attracted to the man standing next to her. What else was there to say?

"Everybody's okay with us having to cut out early?" he asked.

"So they say." Olivia had told them she and Gabe had to leave early for another event.

"Good." He gazed around the living room, where everyone had gathered to socialize after the sumptuous buffet in the dining room. "Nice place your dad has."

"I guess." Her father's live-in girlfriend had recently redecorated the entire downstairs. The minute her mother had walked into the house, she'd sneered, disdainful of the beachy theme, with the pale blue walls and lightweight sand-colored wicker furniture.

Personally, Olivia agreed with her. The place looked like it wanted to be a Hollister store. Then again, the girlfriend was nicknamed Sunni, so maybe it was appropriate.

The nickname irritated her mother to no end. The fact that her mother had been the one to hire Sunni as a live-in housekeeper and au pair many years ago made the situation even worse. Mom had never quite come to terms with the fact that the young woman she'd liked and welcomed into her home had ended up replacing her after she'd left. "I don't know why he holds on to it," she admitted. The tiny pessimist inside her suspected it was because he knew it drove her mother crazy that another woman was playing hostess in her old house. But the much bigger optimist said it was because he still held out some hope, deep within, that this whole awful situation could be fixed, and he could reclaim the life he'd once had here with his family.

She sometimes wondered how Sunni felt about it. The

woman was either truly the sunniest-dispositioned person in the world, or she was one heck of an actress. Because despite an occasional edge to her tone and hardness in her eyes, for the most part, she always maintained that smile, acting like she really didn't care that her longtime boyfriend refused to divorce his wife and marry her. But Sunni had to know Elliott Wainwright well enough to know that if she pushed him to do it, he never—ever—would. Her father was a stubborn one. So she seemed patient enough to wait, content with the house, the cars, the jewelry and the lifestyle.

"Did you grow up here?"

"Uh-huh."

He sipped his drink—a virgin mary—then asked, "And, uh, your parents?"

"No, they're not divorced, and, yes, they're always like this."

"That's a little . . ."

"Dysfunctional?"

"I was gonna say 'unusual.' But that works, too."

"Neither wants to be accused of being the one responsible for ending the marriage."

He gave a pointed look at Sunni, who clung to Olivia's father's arm, and then at Carl, a tall, balding man hovering over her petite mother like a kindergartner guarding his juice box.

"Yeah. I know." Sipping her club soda and cranberry, she added, "It's ended in every way except on paper. Everything just sort of fell apart after what happened to me."

"It's a shame, but that happens in a lot of kidnapping or child murder cases. It's a marriage killer." He edged closer, just the tiniest bit, but enough for her to feel his body's warmth against her arm, bared by her sleeveless top. Her heart fluttered a little, startling her. She suddenly remembered her dream from last night, surprised she hadn't recalled it when she first woke up. Probably she'd just been glad there were no night terrors.

Definitely nothing terrifying. Something rather lovely instead. She'd dreamed about going to sleep in Gabe Cooper's arms, in the chair in the den, as if he'd never let her go after he'd pulled her onto his lap. It had been a nice dream, not at all sexual but incredibly intimate. Just like that actual moment had been.

"So, do you think it was really your kidnapping that caused them to break up, or was that the excuse?"

She blinked, trying to refocus. "It was a catalyst. Things were already tense because she didn't like the way they lived. She was uncomfortable with the Wainwright family's never-ending quest for more money, and she loathed the politics. She was a front desk clerk at one of my father's hotels when they met."

Her father's family had made their fortune off the high-end travel industry. It seemed the überrich still traveled a lot, even in a down economy, and business was booming. As far as she knew, there was enough money to keep several generations of Wainwrights comfortable.

Except her. She really didn't want anything to do with it, having enough of her mother's independent spirit to demand to go her own way. She'd gotten the house, and that was enough.

"My grandfather had died that March, and the governor wanted to appoint my father to his seat to finish his term. My mom hated the idea. Then I was kidnapped, and she *really* hated it."

"Why?"

"She thought it would make us more of a target." Glancing out the windows, she gestured toward a black limo parked by the detached garage on the other side of the lawn. Two large, black-clad men stood there, one leaning on the car, the other against the building. "Despite how my cousin lives, Mom had no interest in drivers and bodyguards. She wanted a normal life."

"Hate to break it to ya, but this place ain't exactly middle class."

"No kidding. That's why she took Brooke and me to Tucson and told my Dad if he wanted to stay married to her, he'd turn the governor down and come join us."

"And?"

"Well, he did turn the governor down," she said. "It wasn't a huge sacrifice. Dad had never wanted to go into politics; he liked running the business. His older brother was the political genius, but he died fifteen years ago. So when the time came, Dad deferred to Richard, my late uncle's son, who was an attorney, already a state representative, and who wanted the job."

Gabe glanced at her cousin. "Musta been pretty young."

"Only thirty. He just squeaked by on the age requirement. Crisis averted: God forbid there not be a Wainwright in Congress."

"Lemme guess. Your dad didn't go to Tucson, right?"

She shook her head. "Nope. Too proud, I think. And Sunni, our housekeeper and former babysitter, stayed here to take care of him."

"Guess she did the job a little too well."

"You could say that."

"Yet you still get along with her?"

Olivia shrugged. "I've known her since I was a kid. At first I felt a little betrayed. But Mom *was* the one who left. She practically issued an invitation to Sunni to take her place."

"Your Dad was probably pretty lonely and vulnerable without you all."

"Exactly, and Sunni was here to keep him company. Time passed; neither of my parents would make the first move either to get back together or to end it for good.

He stayed here, she stayed there, until Brooke and I moved back after college. Then she came back, too, with Carl in tow."

Gabe nodded, looking thoughtful, glancing again toward her parents, who stood with their significant others in a far corner of the room, examining some piece of brightly colored art Sunni had bought. Olivia felt sure her mother hated it on principle.

"That's pretty sad, actually," he mused.

Yes, it was sad. How funny that he'd said that rather than cracking a joke or pointing out how bizarre the whole thing was. *So much to like in this man.*

As if knowing the subject pained her, he quickly moved on. He shot her that grin, which took ten years off his face, made his green eyes sparkle and made her heart thud. "Are your mother and Sunni going to wrestle over who gets the mother-of-the-bride spot in the church?"

"Are you kidding? Mom would lock Sunni in a closet first."

"Nice that they're all so *friendly*. That'll be an interesting wedding." His sarcasm was obvious. The mood in here was not friendly; it was hard, edgy and sharp as glass.

"I told Brooke she should elope." Then she laughed. "I should have told her to run."

"You're against marriage?"

"Just the being married part." *Especially to a man like Drew.*

"I guess I can see why."

Maybe. But he didn't know all of it. It wasn't just because of her parents' situation or her dislike of the groom. She'd seen women murdered by their husbands—literally. Feeling what an abused woman had felt while her husband stabbed her, screaming with every plunge of the knife that she'd promised to love and obey him, she couldn't say much for the whole institution.

Suddenly, a voice intruded. "So, Gabe, I hear you're with the police department? Good for you, young man. We appreciate your public service."

Good lord, could her cousin Richard be any more of a dick? Not only was he incredibly patronizing, being only a dozen or so years older than Gabe, but he was just such a damned politician. He was always on, always glad-handing for votes, even at a family gathering.

"Thank you, Senator," Gabe said smoothly, not thrown by the condescending greeting any more than he'd been thrown by her father's questions about where he lived, her mother's about his past relationships, or her sister's about his plans for Valentine's Day. Her wedding day.

"How did you two meet?" asked Richard's wife, Tess, with that small, pasted-on smile she always wore. With the perfect hair and perfect face, she was the perfect politician's wife. "Did you pull her over for speeding? Our Olivia has an awful lead foot."

Our Olivia. Cheers to the second-most patronizing person in the room.

As if he could feel her rising tension, Gabe reached over and pressed a slightly possessive hand to the small of her back. It was a simple, casual gesture, but it rocked her hard. She almost found herself quivering, sensation rolling through her at the brush of this man's fingertips on her. Even through her blouse, she could feel the warmth of his hand and wondered what that hand might feel like traveling over other parts of her body.

You're making too much of it, she told herself. It was so easy to pretend they were here on a date, she'd let herself think it was a real one. Let herself imagine he had the right to touch her, and she had the right to seek his touch.

"Well, Gabe, how did you two meet?" Tess asked, sounding a wee bit impatient.

Olivia and Gabe exchanged a quick look. They'd gone

over this in the car on the way over, agreeing to say as little as possible. "We met through our jobs," Olivia said.

Her cousin-in-law tilted her chin up even farther, her nose flaring, like she smelled something bad. Tess hated that Olivia worked with eXtreme Investigations, without even knowing exactly what Olivia did for them. She had made comments that made it sound like Olivia was a prostitute for all the damage her "career" did to her cousin's reputation.

That was ridiculous. Few people outside the family even knew she worked for Julia. Because Olivia's ability was so unpleasant, she was asked to use it only in the direst circumstances, so it wasn't like they advertised her services as a death reenactor.

The groom-to-be, who never strayed too far from his good buddy Richard, even if his fiancée was in the room, joined them. Snapping his fingers, as if he'd just realized something, Drew said, "Say, didn't I just see you on the news yesterday? Something about a fire?"

Olivia held her breath. Gabe, though, replied easily, "Yep, I'm afraid I'm not much of a TV guy." He laughed softly. "The press office usually handles that kind of thing."

*Tsk*ing, her cousin's wife said, "I hope no one was hurt?" Knowing Tess, she was saying what was expected and wasn't interested. She confirmed it by immediately moving on. "It's a shame that you two can't stay longer; we wanted to show you pictures of our Paris trip."

Olivia checked her watch. Eleven thirty. "Oh, thanks for the reminder. I'm sorry, but we really have to go," she said, murmuring a firm goodbye to her cousin, his wife, and Drew. Then she looked around for her sister, who sat alone by the window, gazing outside. Her lovely profile was emphasized by the soft sunshine coming in through the pale yellow sheers, and again Olivia couldn't help thinking Drew wasn't nearly good enough for her.

Walking over, she said, "Sorry to leave you alone in the lion's den. But it can't be helped."

Brooke rose, taking one of her hands. "Oh, Livvie, I'm just glad you came." She cast a quick glance toward Gabe. "I can't believe you kept him a secret. He's so handsome."

"Not exactly handsome, but he is supersexy," Olivia said before she could think better of it.

Brooke chuckled, but even as she did, her face pinkened. Not for the first time Olivia had to wonder about her sister's relationship with her fiancé, because there were moments when her twenty-four-year-old sibling acted like she'd never been touched by a man. Certainly Drew wasn't demonstrative toward her; she'd never even seen him hold Brooke's hand.

But there was no time to talk about it now. There might not ever be a good time. What was she supposed to do, ask her sister if she was a virgin, then beg her to go out and get laid, at least once, before she stuck herself with Drew? Not very maid-of-honor-ish advice.

Gabe was saying his goodbyes to her parents, and Olivia joined them. "Thank you again, Sunni," she said, extending her hand to the other woman. One of those strange protocol moments—thanking the girlfriend while the wife was standing right there, flinty-eyed.

God, with a family like this, was it any wonder Olivia had never had a relationship lasting longer than six months, and Brooke was marrying a man old enough to be her father?

Sunni extended her arms and gave her one of those fake air-hugs and a kiss that landed about an eighth of an inch away from Olivia's cheek. "Thank you so much for comin', sweet pea. I'm sorry y'all can't stay. You be sure to bring your friend back any ol' time."

Nails on chalkboard—that voice. She noticed Sunni's accent had gotten decidedly more Southern over the years, and she suspected the woman affected it in order to fit in here. Though they'd never talked about her background, she doubted her father's girlfriend had been raised in rich surroundings.

Neither had her mother, of course. Yet the two women couldn't be more different. Mom was pretty, small, feisty and tough. Sunni was a walking bottle of syrup with a blond cap.

"Your daddy sure misses you. Don't be a stranger," Sunni added.

"I won't," she said, smiling politely. She kept that smile on her face for several minutes as they finished their goodbyes, went to the car, and started down the driveway. It felt stiff by the time they reached the two men standing by Richard's limo, both of whom quickly straightened and stomped out their cigarettes when they came into view. Since the big vehicle was blocking the drive—probably to stop any big bad terrorists or Democrats who wanted to get at Richard—the driver leapt behind the wheel to move it.

"Sorry 'bout that," the man said.

"It's okay," replied Gabe.

Glancing past him out the window, Olivia saw the bodyguard tug at his tight collar. Leaning over Gabe, she asked, "Has somebody brought you two down some cold water?"

"We're okay, ma'am. Got a cooler in the car," the man said with a broad smile. "It'd be crazy not to in this heat. I think the mercury in the thermometer's turnin' to lava today."

It sure seemed that way. The idea of another few weeks of August misery was enough to make her miss Tucson. At least Arizona didn't have the humidity.

But if you'd stayed in Tucson, you wouldn't have even heard of Julia, wouldn't have started working with eXtreme Investigations, wouldn't be getting answers about Jack.

And you wouldn't have met Gabe Cooper.

No, she couldn't regret being right here where she was.

That thought made a smile—a real, genuine one this time—curve her lips. But as they pulled out of the long driveway onto the main road, it faded completely away, not only because there was no need to keep it up once they were out of sight but also because, considering where they were going and what she was about to do, she had absolutely nothing to smile about.

Last night, when Gabe had told Olivia she could examine the remains, he hadn't been entirely honest with her. He'd never actually lied, but he also hadn't come right out and told her there was a string attached to his offer. A big string. Then again, it was a pretty big offer.

She could examine the bones, touch them, do whatever she had to. But she was not going to be alone when she did it. He would be in that examination room with her the whole time.

It wasn't only because of legal issues: If her kidnapping was connected to this murder that made her a witness. He couldn't let her do anything that might taint the evidence. But just as important, there was also the issue of how she was going to deal with whatever happened. Even somebody who made no claims to having any unique abilities could get a little freaked out over handling human remains. Seeing a pile of charred bones that you thought belonged to a murdered kid who'd once saved your life just set up the experience to be that much worse.

He'd seen her last night, mentally reliving that awful night, like something out of a horror movie she'd never been able to escape. Even a distance of twelve years hadn't been enough to keep her whole body from shaking, to prevent her voice from cracking, to stop tears from filling her eyes. Today could be a lot worse. So, no, she wasn't going in there alone. Period.

Did he really think she was gonna psychically connect with this dead boy? Well, as much as he had found himself liking her the longer he was with her, no, he wasn't ready to concede she had some kind of otherworldly powers. But he was open-minded enough to give her a shot. After all, if Sue-Ann Bowles's theory had any basis in truth, there could be another victim out there. And a little boy at risk was worth opening up his mind as far as it would go.

He hadn't told her about that—the possibility that her attacker's accomplice was still out there, doing what he did best. No point until they knew more.

So, he was staying. Those were the terms; she could take them or leave them. Which was exactly what he'd told her when they arrived at the coroner's office. They hadn't even gotten out of the car, and he was waiting for her to make up her mind about whether she'd obey his rules.

She stared at him, her big green eyes narrowing. "You're serious?"

"Yes, ma'am."

Her throat quivered as she swallowed. "You can't."

He crossed his arms. "Yes, I can. And I will. Otherwise, I'll drive you home right now."

"Detective—Gabe—listen to me. What I do, it's very . . . unpleasant."

No kidding.

"And it's a little scary."

"I'm a big boy. I think I can take it."

"I didn't mean you'd be frightened *of* me; more likely you'll be afraid *for* me."

He could only answer bluntly. "I'm already afraid for you, Livvie."

Her lips widened a tiny bit, just for a second, into a sort-of smile, as if she liked hearing him call her by the nickname he'd heard her family use. He liked it, too. It was less formal, less cool and well-bred than Olivia. Yes, she was elegant, beautiful, but she had such strength in her. He'd seen it. He appreciated it. To him, that strength belonged to Livvie.

Then the smile faded. "Nobody ever stays with me. I've always done this alone."

Which told him those coworkers of hers were cowards. "The clock's ticking."

She still didn't move for a good minute. He didn't sense they were involved in any kind of battle of wills here; she wasn't pulling some kid stunt, trying to wear him down until he changed his mind. This was more like somebody trying to find the strength to do something she didn't want to do. The fact that she had to try this hard to convince herself told him how serious she was about him not coming. Which only made him more determined to be there. If it was so awful nobody else could see it, it was awful enough that she shouldn't have to do it all by herself.

Do it. Do what? You don't even know that she's going to do anything!

Funny how he kept forgetting he didn't quite believe her. Only not funny. Not at all.

"All right," she finally said, her voice not much more than a whisper. "I agree."

He reached for the doorknob.

"But I have one condition, too. Whatever you see, whatever I say or do, you cannot interfere. Don't try to talk to me, don't touch me, don't do anything to stop what's happening."

He hesitated, not liking that any more than she'd liked his terms. "What if you . . ."

"Absolutely no interference, Detective. Whatever happens, it will be over in two minutes and ten seconds, and I can take it. Agreed?"

He thought about it, cursed under his breath, then hedged, not exactly promising. "Okay."

Getting out of the car, they headed into the building in silence. Gabe got her through security, then led her to the back, where they kept unclaimed remains. Nobody would be claiming this boy's until somebody could identify him.

Then, all too soon for his peace of mind, they were in a small examination room. A technician had wheeled in a steel table and placed it directly beneath a strong, overhead light. A sterile white sheet was draped across the top, not settling into a body shape like it usually would. Not when there was no body, just those sad bones.

He donned a pair of sterile gloves, then handed her a pair. She eyed them, looked at him, but didn't protest. Remaining silent, she tugged them on and then approached the table. He saw the way she trembled, though her spine was stiff and her chin upraised, determination visibly wafting off her. "Remember your promise," she said, not even glancing over.

"I'll remember." The answer was a technicality. He hadn't actually said, "I promise," and couldn't guarantee he wouldn't step in if he thought she was in danger. Only a fool promised something without all the facts. It was like a man "promising" not to get mad before his wife told him her secret—that she was messin' around. Gabe didn't make those kinds of promises.

Livvie reached for the corner of the sheet and lifted it slowly. Each inch revealed more of the charred skeleton below, starting at the feet. A few of the toe bones, phalanges, if he remembered his science classes, had broken off and lay positioned below the metatarsals.

His stomach clenched. He'd seen bodies before, God yes. *But here were such tiny little things. Some parent once counted those ten toes, tickled those plump feet.* At least, he hoped so. God, he hoped this kid had had some happiness in his life somewhere along the way.

He closed his eyes briefly, reminded himself to focus, then opened them again.

Olivia didn't make a sound. She just kept moving the sheet, careful not to touch anything below it. The bones had been cleaned since he'd last seen them, obviously for the coroner's examination—it couldn't be called an autopsy. It was damn lucky the means of death had been made obvious by the broken hyoid, at least obvious to the experts, not to a layman like him.

Judging by some awkward lines, bends where things should only have been straight, the boy had suffered other breaks. The skinnier bone below the right knee, he couldn't recall the name, was awkwardly bent, as if it had been snapped and had healed crookedly. So was one of the ones in the arm. And the right collarbone looked like it had been crunched at some point. God, did he hope it had been after death, not before.

"So small," Olivia whispered, her hand shaking as she finished removing the sheet.

"He was a young kid." Gabe shook his head in disgust, as he had the first time he'd seen this awful sight Monday at the scene of the fire.

Olivia whispered something else. From here, a few feet away, he thought it might have been *Is it you?* But he didn't ask her to speak up. Frankly he wasn't entirely sure what to do. Olivia had not said anything about what she intended or what would happen. She just calmly—if sadly—studied the remains, making no effort to handle them.

Maybe it wasn't going to work. Which, to be honest, sounded better and better to him the longer they stood here. He'd find another way to work this case, someone else to ID this kid.

Olivia lifted her hand to her mouth, like she feared

she would be sick. He reached for her, but she jerked away, muttering, "Stay back!"

Rather than being sick, she touched her lips with one finger, her pose pensive. Then, before he could say a word, she bit at her own fingertip.

"What the hell are you . . ."

Ignoring him, she yanked her head back, tearing at the latex with her teeth. She hadn't been biting her finger; she'd been biting the glove.

She spat the tiny piece out. Gabe realized what she was going to do about one second before she extended her index finger, a tiny bit of pink skin visible on the tip. "Don't!"

She did. With no hesitation, she pressed her bare skin to one of the tiny finger bones dangling from what had once been the boy's hand. It was the slightest touch, the barest of connections between flesh and bone, dead and alive.

But he knew right away it was enough.

God help her—and him—it was enough.

"Please . . . stop . . . hurts."

The plea wasn't screamed but barked from a hoarse, tight throat—the boy's painfully constricted one, through which he managed to take only the tiniest sips of air.

The throat Olivia now shared with him.

Hands wrapped tight, strong fingers, the thumbs touching in the hollow, pressing, twisting, cutting off the airway. Oh, God.

The pain was bad. But the scary sensation of suffocating—breathlessness—was worse. Too familiar and, oh, so much worse.

This wasn't just starting, the boy was already in utter agony, his organs pleading for something they weren't going to get.

Two minutes and ten seconds of this?

Stop. It's not really happening to you. It happened years ago, and there's nothing you can do for him now except try to solve his murder. So keep breathing.

That voice—her own—whispered in the reasonable, rational section of her brain, and Olivia wanted to obey it, visualizing herself drawing in deep, steady breaths. But it seemed impossible while her throat was closed, crushed. And how could she allow herself to breathe when the boy's breaths were denied to him?

In. Out. Slowly. Come on, do *it.*

Finally, she did. She inhaled a choppy mouthful of stale, chemical-tasting air. It tasted of the examination room—reality—where she stood before a table of bones in harsh, unforgiving light. She couldn't see any of that, though. Couldn't hear the tick of the big clock on the wall, couldn't feel the warm concern of the detective she knew was watching from a few feet away.

Don't interfere. Please.

Knowing she was being watched, she struggled to keep a part of herself separate, to remain aware of both lives she was living at this moment. Usually, she didn't bother to try to keep herself apart from the victims, almost as if she had to give herself over to their last moments, if only to honor them for the tragedy of their deaths. But now she did, sensing Gabe Cooper would try to stop her if he thought she wasn't all right.

You're not all right.

But she would be. Soon.

Unlike this poor boy, who struggled, fruitlessly swinging his small fists.

Olivia held the breath for a few seconds before pushing it out. She then repeated the steps, having to mentally go through each one. It was such a strange sensation, feeling the breath fill her lungs at the same time she felt them ready to burst from lack of oxygen. The air flowed through her windpipe even while it was also tightly crushed between a monster's massive, punishing hands.

Suddenly, all breath, all thought ceased as a voice filled his/her ears. "You betrayed us, boy. Now you gonna pay for it."

Even as she felt the boy's heartbeat slow, Olivia felt her own heart leap in her chest. The boy's stomach was empty; her breakfast churned within hers. His skin was clammy, cold; hers erupted with sensation. Every inch of her went on alert, every hair on her body standing upright, reacting to the hoarse, hateful voice. Even through the thick whisper, she heard the insanity, the barely suppressed rage. Just as she'd heard it that night.

She knew that voice. She'd heard it in her nightmares for twelve years now.

"You coulda ruined us, after all we done for you. So this is what you git."

It's him. It's both of them. Her would-be killer . . . and her savior.

There could no longer be any question. The child being strangled to death was Jack. Her kidnapper had come back too soon, perhaps right after Olivia had gotten away. He had realized the boy was not burying her as he'd been ordered to. And Jack had paid the ultimate price, his poor little bones all that remained to prove he had ever existed.

It was all true.

Olivia's body began to shudder uncontrollably. Her fingers curled into defensive fists, her legs wanting to run, her mouth opening to beg for this to stop. Only there was no air. No air.

Yes, there is. Breathe it in. Let it out.

She did, sucking in oxygen between nearly closed lips, sure if she parted them farther, they'd let out the scream building inside her.

As if time itself had opened a portal between them,

she suddenly realized the boy's airway had opened a tiny bit, too. The tight grip on his throat—their throat—relaxed for a second. Enough for a gulp of air, another plea. "No, Uncle Johnny . . ."

Uncle Johnny? Who's Uncle Johnny?

"You call him daddy, boy!" the man screamed, sounding utterly enraged.

Is someone else there? Why can't I see?

She'd been focused on breathing, then on the voice, and hadn't even availed herself of the most important ability—her sight. The last images he'd seen in his life. Seeing the photographs of Dwight Collier after he'd died wasn't enough. She had to look into his face, see the insanity in his eyes so she could finally overcome her fear of him.

She focused, pulling her attention off all the other senses, trying to make out the images. And she realized she was seeing—not well, not very clearly. A fine red mist appeared to be covering her vision. *Their* vision.

Broken blood vessels in his eyes.

But he/she wasn't totally blind. She blinked several times in a row, finally focusing in, enough to see the shape of him. The man was close, his big T-shirt–covered chest filling his/her vision, his hot, rank breath brushing the boy's/her face.

She saw thick, greasy, dark hair, but it hung over the angry face. He was almost too close, so she couldn't make out any of his features, just the hair and an inch of stubbled cheek. *Damn it.*

His broad body was pressed against theirs, his thick leg pressing the much smaller form against something hard. The barn wall? *No, too smooth. Cool. The camper?*

He shifted slightly, and the vision cleared, brightening. His body had been blocking out the . . . wait. No. That was impossible, it couldn't be right.

"You shouldn'ta done it, Jackie-boy."

"I ... din't ..."

"Don't lie. That little cunt's escape's all over the news!"

Hot tears burst from his/her eyes, streaming down the cheeks and drenching the lips with salty moisture. But there was a morsel of air, and they grabbed for it greedily.

It hurt. He couldn't quite take it in; his throat was damaged, crushed. Hers wasn't, and she knew she was filling her lungs, though it felt as though she weren't.

She tried desperately to make her brain work, to keep thinking, keep some part of herself lucid. She needed to make sense of this . . . what she was seeing, the impossible thing he had just said. But the coherent part of her was slipping further away as Jack's agony continued.

"This is too good for you," the man hissed. "Why don't you go like your girlfriend did?"

The word *no!* screamed in her brain.

She and the boy were spun around. She saw a large, old-fashioned washtub, filled with water. Not the high barrel he'd put her in but still very capable of fulfilling its purpose: drowning someone small and helpless.

Oh, God, no, not this. Anything but this.

The boy resisted weakly, and she struggled with him as she had before. But his small, already nearly dead form was no match for the powerful arms gripping him, pushing him down onto his bony knees beside the tub. Olivia's stung, too, as sharp rocks sliced into skin.

Then the monster looped an arm around the boy's waist—her waist—and bent them over, forcing his/her head down toward the tub. Olivia was sobbing now, flailing, desperate to not have to go into that water again, wanting to give Jack all her strength so they could escape this hideous nightmare.

To no avail. The water loomed ever closer.

It wasn't greenish-black and dirty, as she remembered. It was murky, yes, but not old, as if the tub had been freshly filled with untreated well water.

The details weren't right. Something was wrong here, very wrong. Her conscious mind realized that, even as the rest of her remained locked in the struggle for Jack's life.

An inch closer, and she suddenly realized the water was glimmering with beams of bright sunlight. And, in the brightness of that day, she saw another reflection. *His* reflection. *Jack's.*

Olivia moaned, grasping what was so wrong about all of this. Seeing that face so clearly was almost enough to break her mind.

I shouldn't be seeing you. I didn't see myself, how can I be seeing you? This makes no sense!

Closer still, the body nearly immobile yet still trying to jerk, making the tub shudder and the water splash.

Then, one more half-angry, half-recriminatory cry from the killer: "You broke my heart."

Lips almost touching the water now, its sulfurous reek filling his/her nose. A silent scream rose—hers, not his— its urgency growing until she thought her head would explode with the need to let it out.

"G'bye, Jackie-boy," the man said.

Then, right before the boy/she was pushed under, she heard a faint whisper. The final words of a boy making one last brave effort to reclaim the only part of himself he could in the last seconds of his life.

"My name is Zachary."

Chapter 7

Ty was getting a little worried. He hadn't heard a word from his partner for hours, and their last conversation had been pretty surprising. Gabe had called early this morning, saying he had arranged for his witness to examine the bones found at Fast Eddie's. When Ty had asked him about his change of heart, Gabe had admitted that he'd gone to see Olivia Wainwright and that she'd told him her whole sorry tale. That, combined with the conjecture of Sue-Ann Bowles, who'd stormed into the police station yesterday, had his stoic partner ready to consider using even the most unusual methods to solve this case.

Ty would have liked to go to the coroner's office, too, wondering exactly what this woman did and how she did it. But Gabe hadn't extended an invitation. So, instead, he'd come here to the precinct. He'd spent the day tracking down every case involving a missing six- to twelve-year-old Caucasian boy in the Southeast, going back twenty years.

There were more than he would ever have imagined, which depressed him to no end. Some had been solved, the child either returned or, in more cases, found dead. A lot of others involved suspected noncustodial parental kidnappings. But a whole bunch still remained.

He had a plan on how to sort them out, though. Doing some calculations based on what Mrs. Bowles had said, he figured that if her son and Brian Durkee had both been taken at around eight and killed at age twelve, the mysterious "Jack" might have been kidnapped somewhere around 1995. That narrowed the field considerably. Problem was, of those who were left, none of them sounded like the right kid.

"Hey, Wallace! Somebody's out here wantin' to see your partner. What is it with that lucky bastard, gettin' all these hot women chasing him?"

As always, Kinney's voice was like nails on a chalkboard in Ty's ears. "I'll be right out."

"Better hurry up. You don't put dibs on her, I'm takin' my shot."

Repulsed, Ty rose, determined to spare the unknown woman from Kinney's unique—vile—brand of charm. He left his desk and went out to the front of the building. The vestibule wasn't too crowded: a few uniformeds, the on-duty sergeant, and a leering Kinney.

And her. *Wow.* Her.

That old song from his favorite kid's show started repeating in his head: *"One of these things just doesn't belong here."*

Because she didn't belong in this dingy office surrounded by gruff cops talking b.s. and street crime. She was out of their league, something pretty and bright and innocent that didn't belong in this dark, mundane place.

The woman was of average height, not skinny but not voluptuous by any means. Her light gold hair fell to her shoulders, thick and lustrous, catching the sunlight streaming in from the windows. Her profile was equally as attractive—up-tipped nose, soft cheeks, nice lips. She wore a flowery sundress that looked like summer itself, and her high-heeled sandals emphasized her long legs. An absolute Southern beauty if he'd ever seen one, and Savannah had its share.

But judging by the frown on her face and the way she

kept her hands twisted in front of her, not a very happy one right now.

Straightening his tie, he walked over to her, offering her a friendly smile meant to put her at ease. "I'm Detective Tyler Wallace, Detective Cooper's partner."

"Brooke Wainwright," she said. "I need to see your partner right away. It's about my sister, Olivia."

Ahh. A sister, and just as pretty as the redhead whose picture he'd seen on that Web site yesterday. Again he noted the frown on her face, the tension in her body, and wondered what had gotten her so upset that she'd come down here to the central precinct on a Saturday afternoon.

As if seeing his confusion, she quickly explained. "Olivia and Gabe came to my father's house this morning." Her eyes narrowing, she added, "She told us he was her date."

His brain went blank. Ms. Wainwright might have made a statement, but she was, without a doubt, asking a question. The last place he wanted to be was in the middle of a lie between two sisters, so he hedged. "Is that right?"

"Yes. But this afternoon, I answered a call at the house from an FBI agent. I'm just glad I answered it, not my dad, because he'd lose his mind if he knew all this was starting up again."

"All what?" he asked, though he suspected he knew.

"My sister's kidnapping case. Special Agent Ames told me he heard from a Detective Cooper in Savannah who's working with Olivia on a case. Meaning her old case?"

Uh-oh.

"He couldn't reach Cooper, so he called, looking for Olivia. I've called her cell and her house, and she's not answering," the woman added, her voice rising, shaking a little, though she wasn't afraid. Merely very worried. "Are they here?"

"No, they're not. But I believe they are still together, and I'm sure your sister's fine."

"Where are they? And why? What exactly is going on? Is my sister in danger?"

"I'm sure she's fine," he repeated, meaning it. "Detective Cooper wouldn't let anything happen to her."

"Oh, right, he's a saint," she said with a sneer. "He came to our family's home under false pretenses today, lying to all of us."

He didn't point out that her sister had been behind the lie, sensing she wouldn't appreciate the comment. "Look, why don't we go to one of the back rooms where we can talk."

If she were going to go ballistic about Gabe allowing her sister to do her psychic act on a bunch of burnt-up bones, he'd prefer she did it out of sight of the public.

The minute they walked into an interview room, Brooke Wainwright crossed her arms over her chest, piercing him with a steady stare. "Tell me one thing. Does this have anything to do with the body of that boy that was found in that fire earlier this week?"

He didn't have much of a poker face. Because without a word from him, she muttered a soft curse, tightening her arms even more around herself. "Why won't this ever end?" she whispered.

He couldn't help reaching out, awkwardly patting her shoulder, trying to offer some comfort. "It will. If your sister can do what she says she can, this could all be over very soon."

The woman paled, and her mouth fell open. "She's not . . . tell me she's *not* going to do that. You can't possibly let her!"

"It'll be all right. She wanted to help."

"No, it will not be all right," she snapped, looking like she wanted to hit him. "Don't you get it? Every time she does it, a little piece of her dies, too! She carries the weight of them. All of them. And she never fully puts it down."

He remained very still, the reason for her concern sinking in. Gabe hadn't told him exactly what Olivia Wainwright intended to do, and he'd been picturing a misty crystal ball kind of moment in the coroner's office. Something odd but not dangerous. God, no. And he doubted Gabe had ever realized it could be, either.

Her sister wasn't finished expressing her opinion. Not by a long shot. She lifted a shaking hand, pointing an index finger at Ty in unmistakable warning. "If it's *him*, if it's the boy she's been looking for all these years, Jack, this could be the one that breaks her for good. And I swear to God, if anything happens to her, I'm going to hold you and your partner responsible."

As Olivia began to stir, shifting restlessly beneath the lightweight sheet on the bed, Gabe tensed, wondering how she was going to feel about waking up in her bed with him sprawled out right beside her. He and her silent green-eyed cat had both been watching her sleep for over an hour now, the cat from up on top of a bureau and Gabe from right here, in the bed. Even after she'd fallen asleep, he'd stayed put, not wanting to leave in case she woke up and started screaming again.

He didn't think he'd ever get the sound of her screams out of his mind.

She'd asked him to give her two minutes and ten seconds. He'd made it to the count of ninety-eight before jumping in and grabbing her. Yanking her hard against him to control the deep, violent shudders that racked her ice-cold body, he'd twined his fingers in her hair and whispered in her ear, "You're okay. It's over—it's done."

He couldn't have taken any more, couldn't have watched the tears continue to gush out of her eyes, couldn't have listened to the tiny gasps as she seemed to struggle for air. Couldn't have watched her fist flail in the air, swinging at nothing. Couldn't have stood by while her legs weakened and her body leaned against the table full of bones, which rattled and danced against the metal.

And Gabe could not under any circumstances listen to her scream again. One horrific, heartfelt cry had been wrenched out of her mouth, a sound so grief-stricken, so utterly hopeless, he wasn't sure he even wanted to know what on earth or in hell she'd seen.

So he had put a stop to it. Dragged her away, ended the connection of flesh to bone. He'd held her tight, not letting her go, allowing her to hammer her fists on his chest, to kick his legs, knowing he wasn't the one she was fighting in her mind.

Then, suddenly, within a couple of seconds she'd stopped. She understood that it was over and knew who was holding her. Knew she was safe.

He'd expected her to be angry. She hadn't been. Instead, looking utterly bereft, so pale it seemed as if all the blood had fallen out of her body, she'd merely pleaded, "Take me home."

That's exactly what he'd done. Fortunately, the coroner's office hadn't been busy, so not many people had been around to see him carrying a teary-eyed, trembling woman through the building and out to his car. He'd gently put her in the seat, buckled her in and driven her back to her place. She hadn't said a word the entire time, not even protesting when they arrived, and he came around to carry her again.

He liked and respected that about her. She didn't put up phony walls or pretend she was fine and dandy. She needed help, needed *him*.

He asked her where her bedroom was, and, following the shaky hand pointing toward the stairs, he carried her up. She kicked off her shoes on the way. But when they reached her room and he bent to lay her on the bed, she kept her arms around his neck and pulled him down with her. There was nothing sexual about the moment—he knew that. She just wanted to stay connected, touched by a warm, living human being. Death's cold hands had been way too close today, and she wanted—needed—life.

"It's okay. Go to sleep, sweetheart," he told her, smoothing her hair back off her face.

Nodding, she curled up on her side against him, her head on his shoulder, her hands curled together beneath her chin like a child saying a prayer. "Please don't leave."

"I'm not goin' anywhere."

Then, even as her eyes drifted shut, she whispered something else. Something that stunned and horrified him beyond measure.

"It *was* Jack. And he wasn't only strangled . . . he was drowned."

He was drowned.

He couldn't stop the words from playing over and over in his mind as he watched her sleep. If she really could do what she said she could, and, judging by what he'd seen today, he had no doubt she'd experienced something, then drowning would have to be the absolute worst thing for her to experience. To know the boy who'd helped her had died the same brutal death at the hands of the same vicious killer made it so much worse.

She shifted on the bed, moving even closer. He lay on his back, she on her side, facing him. Her lips were gently parted as she breathed, and he couldn't help but note how beautiful she was. Nor could he help noting the feel of her soft breasts against his side and the intimate way one of her thighs had ridden over his.

Don't, he reminded himself, closing his eyes, forcing his mind on other things.

But he was human and male, and he knew the longer

he stayed here with her wrapped around him, the more likely he was to remember that he was incredibly attracted to her.

Only a real low-life bastard would take advantage of this situation. And he'd worked his whole life to *not* be the low-life bastard that everyone had expected him to be, considering he'd been raised by his grandfather after his mama and grandmother had died.

"Gabe?" she whispered.

He glanced down and saw her looking up at him, sleepy-eyed but no longer tearful and not nearly as pale. "How're you doin'?"

"I'm okay. How long did I sleep?"

"Little over an hour."

"You stayed."

"I promised I would."

"Thank you." She moved her arm, extending it across his waist, and curled more tightly against him. And that bent leg moved higher on his, until all he could think about was the sensual feel of her as she moved around him.

Well, that and the horrific scene that had led to this moment, where they were twined together on her bed. The one she still hadn't explained.

"Olivia, what . . ."

"Shh," she whispered, knowing what he was about to ask. "I can't think about it yet. Can't talk about it. Let's just be still for a little while."

Be still? When all his blood was rushing through his veins, landing in certain parts of his anatomy with fierce determination? Yeah, right. Might as well ask a toddler to be still and not reach for his own damn birthday cake.

She's not your birthday cake. She wasn't his at all. He had no right to be reaching for her.

But she still needed him, needed to draw strength and security from him. No way was he going to fail her. So he did as she asked and stayed still, when what he really wanted to do was get up and put ten feet between them. Or else roll her onto her back, move over her and kiss the breath out of her mouth. Then move down her body kissing her everywhere else.

He didn't quite understand it and was sure nothing like this had ever happened to him before, but the truth was, he had a major case for the woman in his arms. He'd thought of nothing but her from the moment they'd met, admiring her more every time they spoke, desiring her more practically every time she moved.

He'd had affairs before, even thought he was in love once. But it had been a long time since he'd felt this mix of confusion and want, frustration and irritation, hunger and tenderness all at the same time, all directed toward the same woman.

Olivia had gotten under his skin fast.

She seemed to read his mind. Either that, or she'd been feeling the same spark and wanted something to happen between them, too. Because, without warning, without another word, even, she moved up and brushed her lips against his jaw.

He groaned, stiffening as a flood of heat washed over him. She smelled good—her skin, her hair, her breath. He wanted to lose himself in all those sweet, delicious scents.

She came closer, tasting her way to the corner of his mouth.

"Liv . . ."

"Just kiss me, please," she whispered, her longing evident. "One kiss."

One kiss? One kiss to drive out the bad memories and her fear and make them forget the tears that had filled her eyes and the screams that had filled his ears?

Not such a bad bargain—for either of them.

He bent to her, and their lips brushed lightly, once.

They parted, shared a breath, then met again, soft and quiet, new and fresh. Like every first kiss should be.

But, oh, she tasted so good and felt so right, and when she parted her lips and that delicate tongue swept against his, he was helpless to resist taking more of what she was offering. Their tongues met in a slow exploration that reminded him of what he so liked about kissing. The closeness of it, how personal and intimate it was—almost more intimate than sex. Not to mention how good it felt.

One thing he knew, this wasn't going to end with just one kiss.

It stayed languorous and lazy for a minute or so, then got more intense. He couldn't seem to taste her deeply enough. He sunk his fingers in her hair, twining them in the silky strands, and turned her head a little so their mouths could join more intimately.

Olivia shifted, moving up onto him. She didn't weigh much, and when that bent leg moved farther, so she could straddle him, he groaned, deep in his throat. Her breasts pressed against his chest, her nipples puckering against her shirt, tempting him beyond belief.

He hardly noticed when she tugged his dress shirt up out of his pants and slid her hand over his stomach. His skin sizzled upon contact, and every part of him that wasn't already hard got that way pronto.

He wanted to do the same, to touch her, stroke her skin. Fortunately, her soft, filmy skirt draped over his pants, not only leaving her warm sex pressed against his groin—*Lord have mercy*—but also baring her legs. He reached down to cup one bare thigh, marveling at how soft she was. How feminine. How perfect.

How goddamned strong.

And a witness. A goddamned witness

Not to mention an incredibly vulnerable woman who'd been through hell.

That did it. As much as it pained him, physically hurt

him, he let go of her leg and slowed the kiss, finally ending it. Olivia stayed close, still on top of him, her face an inch or two away from his. They both breathed deeply, raggedly. But before she could lean down to kiss him again, which he suspected she wanted to do, he carefully shifted out from under her.

Her whole body went stiff. "Gabe?"

"I'd say that was a little more than being still, darlin'," he said with a tender smile, wanting her to understand that he didn't regret kissing her even though he wasn't ready to do it again. "Now, I think maybe we should go downstairs, if you're feeling up to it."

She swallowed, her throat working with the effort, and her bottom lip, so luscious, so well kissed, trembled.

"It's not that I don't want to," he said, hearing the thickness in his voice. Oh, he most definitely wanted to. At this moment, he wanted to make love to her more than he wanted to hit his thirtieth birthday, and, frankly, he'd always kinda wanted to get that far, since everybody in his hometown had predicted he'd have a short, rough, wild life.

She nodded once. "It's not exactly the ideal situation, is it? Not to mention the fact that we met less than a week ago."

It seemed crazy that they'd only known each other for five days, considering how she now filled his thoughts. They'd shared some incredibly intense moments and some nice ones, too, the last few being right up there at the top. He hoped there'd be a chance for more of them.

Are you crazy? She's totally out of your league.

The inner voice sobered and disturbed him, mainly because it wasn't wrong. Olivia's grandfather had been a senator; Gabe was the abused grandson of a dirt-poor farmer. She lived in the Victorian District in a house that probably cost about twenty times his annual salary, and he'd been proud of himself for being able to scrape up the money to buy a tiny little two-bedroom condo a year ago. She was all soft Southern gentility, and he was one step above po' white.

There was no way this could go anywhere, and he'd been crazy to even think about kissing her, much less doing it. He needed to remember that, and, if necessary, point it out to her as well. But not now. Not when he was here, in her bed, because she'd put herself through a horrific, painful ordeal and had fallen asleep in his arms.

An ordeal they had yet to even discuss. "I think we should . . ."

His words trailed off when he heard a door slam, then a voice calling from downstairs. Olivia's eyes widened in surprise, and for the barest second he wondered if she'd forgotten to tell him she had a husband or live-in boyfriend lying around somewhere. Then he realized the voice calling Olivia's name was female.

"Livvie? Where are you?"

"That's my sister. She has a key," she whispered, quickly rolling off him, then sitting up on the edge of the bed. "I'll be right down, Brooke!"

Gabe sat up, too, trying to stuff his shirt back into his pants and wondering where his shoes had landed. He'd kicked them off when he'd realized he would be spending part of the afternoon in Olivia's bed with her. He sure hadn't anticipated what would happen when she woke up from her much-needed sleep.

They probably would have been fine, could have gotten themselves put back together, if her sister had stayed downstairs.

She didn't.

"Oh, thank God you're all right," she said as the bedroom door flew open. "I've been trying to reach you for . . . oh!"

Feeling like a kid caught making out by his girlfriend's parents, Gabe stood, uncomfortably aware of his lack of shoes and the untucked part of his shirt. Judging by the sister's expression, she had come to some obvious conclusions, and she definitely did not like them.

"You jerk!" the woman snapped. "How could you take advantage of her like this?"

"Brooke?" Olivia gasped, sounding shocked.

"She's vulnerable and came to you for help!" The woman stalked closer, almost shaking with anger. Funny, Gabe had considered her kind of a mousy thing this morning. Now she was more like a lion. And this lion had obviously been talking to somebody who'd filled her in on the true nature of his relationship with Olivia.

Olivia obviously realized that, too. "Brooke, you've misunderstood. Gabe carried me up here because I needed to lie down. I asked him to stay, and I just woke up," she explained, her voice calm and reasonable. "He was a total gentleman."

Yeah, right. Given his desire to rip her clothes off, *gentlemanly* was the last word he'd use to describe himself.

The apple don't fall far from the tree, boy, and don't you forget it!

Angry with himself for remembering what his grandfather's voice sounded like, much less one of his favorite expressions, he shook his head hard.

"I'm fine, really, Brooke," Olivia said.

It was probably the reasonable tone that got through to the other woman. She finally stopped glaring at him long enough to focus on her sister, whose upper arms she immediately grabbed. "Are you sure?"

"I promise. But, Brooke, what are you doing here?"

"We couldn't reach you! We tried everything, your house phones, cell phones. Then somebody you work with said you were here."

Somebody she worked with? *How the hell . . .*

"He saw Gabe carrying you into the house."

"Your coworkers stake out your house when you're not aware of it?" he snapped, disliking these people a lot, even though he'd only ever met one of them. But frankly, if they let Olivia do what she'd done today and, in fact, capitalized on it for "business," he felt nothing but disgust for the lot of them. If he had his way, Olivia would never get within ten feet of a dead body again for as long as she lived.

Olivia shook her head and lifted a hand to her brow. "Morgan."

"That's right!"

Shocked at the intrusion of another voice, Gabe looked over and saw yet another woman, this one a very attractive brunette, standing there. He recognized her immediately from the pictures on her Web site. This was Julia Harrington, owner of eXtreme Investigations.

"FYI, your partner's downstairs, too," Julia said with a smile that was almost a smirk. She might have come here out of worry for Olivia, but she looked amused at seeing a Savannah detective caught in a compromising position, since he was her natural enemy these days.

The enmity was pretty mutual as far as Gabe was concerned. He didn't know that he was ever going to forgive Olivia's colleagues for what they regularly put her through.

Then her words sank in, and he realized what she'd said. "Wait. *Wallace* is here?"

"Jesus, you brought an entire army and walked into my house?" Olivia snapped.

Brooke nibbled her lip, for the first time looking a little sheepish at her brash entrance. "I'm sorry. I was worried. I'm your sister, that's my job."

Huh. And to think he'd always wondered what it might be like to have a sibling. Right now, the whole concept didn't seem very appealing.

"Why don't we all go downstairs and let Olivia splash

some cold water on her face. She just woke up." He shot Julia Harrington a glance, daring her to say a word. She remained silent.

Olivia nodded her thanks. "I'll be down in a few minutes."

Pausing to grab his shoes, he found himself not giving a damn that Olivia's sister and boss were eyeing him like he was some low specimen who belonged on the bottom of hers. All that mattered was that he'd been here for Olivia when she'd needed him. It was the least he could do. Especially because, sooner or later, she was going to have to tell him exactly what had happened back in that coroner's examination room.

So much for seduction.

When Olivia had awakened in Gabe's arms, breathing in the warm, masculine scent of his body, feeling his muscled form pressed against her, the idea of sex hadn't exactly galloped into her mind, but it sure had come at a fast trot. Her senses had gone into overdrive, but this time they combined to entice her, not to terrify her. He looked so good, smelled so good, felt so damn good. And she'd wanted him.

She wanted to think it was only because she was attracted to him, had been affected by him from the moment they'd met, but she knew it was more than that. She needed physical connection. Needed to be touched, stroked, filled. She needed to feel the utmost physical pleasure, the most perfect delight life had to offer, in order to undermine the dark foundation that was trying to build up inside her soul.

Not just because of today, as horrific as it had been. The darkness had been coming on for a long time. *Every time you do it.*

But today . . . Oh, God, today had been beyond anything.

A little over three years ago, when she had told Julia Harrington she would work for her at eXtreme Investigations, there had been one condition, one absolute, completely inflexible rule. Olivia would help solve murders and cold cases if they really thought she could be of use. She would not, however, agree to be involved in any drowning or suspected drowning cases. Period.

Julia, who knew enough of her story to understand why, had agreed without reservation. So, the only time she'd ever experienced that horrifying sensation of her lungs filling with water had been when she was fifteen years old and it was really happening.

Until today.

Thank God Gabe stopped it. She'd started to go into that water, and then he'd pulled her away, breaking the faint touch between her and Jack's remains and breaking the psychic connection as well.

She had never been so glad to have somebody break a promise.

If she'd known the boy had actually been drowned after he was strangled, she would have had to think twice about touching him. Now that it was over, though, she couldn't bring herself to regret it. Not when the experience had uncovered such shocking truths. Which was why she needed to put all these thoughts and wishes and desires for Gabe Cooper aside for now. Because she needed to talk to him, needed to tell him everything.

She'd had a chance to think about it all the way home as she'd drifted off to sleep. She'd put it all together—all the clues, the visions, everything that didn't quite fit—and had come up with a whole new picture.

It changed everything. Nothing was as it had always seemed.

While the realization she'd made didn't shock her quite as much as she'd have expected it to, since she'd been thinking along these lines since yesterday, it did make her feel sick. Even now, hours later, and after that wonderful interlude with Gabe, she felt the horror trying to claw its way back into her.

"Don't," she told herself as the fear tried to take hold. "Don't let it."

Looking at her reflection in the mirror, she swallowed, then licked her lips. She'd done as Gabe had suggested and splashed some water on her face, though she still looked pale and drawn. Reaching for a facecloth, she wet it, then pressed it to her closed eyes, hoping to bring down the swelling her tears and fatigue had caused. As the coolness penetrated her forehead, she suddenly became aware of an unusual intermittent warmth on the back of her neck. Not like a breath, certainly, but more like warm air falling from a ceiling vent. But there were no vents in the bathrooms of this old house, only radiators that she hadn't turned on for months.

Strange. But on the strange scale, definitely nothing compared to the rest of her day.

Finally, after counting to sixty, she lowered the cloth.

And gasped.

The shower curtain had moved. It hung from a round loop on the ceiling, draping down over the clawfoot tub, and it had just visibly fluttered, as if someone had brushed past it. Someone who'd been standing behind her, between her and the doorway to her bedroom.

"Who's there?" she asked. Her mind worked frantically. "Gabe?"

Nothing.

He wouldn't play games with her, wouldn't stay silent if he were really in her room and knew she might have seen him. Nobody else in her house would, either. They all knew how unraveled she'd been earlier, or at least she assumed they did by now.

So who had been there?

"Nobody," she told herself in a firm voice.

It had been a blur, a trick of the eyes after she'd dropped the cloth and let the light back in. Nothing else at all. She was jumping at shadows now, and that was one thing she couldn't let continue. The horror in her life was compartmentalized; all the ugly, scary, dark stuff was only supposed to happen when she was working. Here, in her home, it simply wasn't allowed.

"Got it? Not allowed," she told her reflection.

Taking a quick glance at her face, she remembered she hadn't worn any mascara this morning, knowing it might be a crying kind of day. So no emergency makeup repairs were required. That was a good thing, because she'd kept Gabe and the others waiting long enough.

Stepping into the bedroom, she glanced around quickly, confirmed the emptiness, then headed out the door. Descending the stairs, she followed the sound of their voices, all coming from the den: two masculine ones, Julia's brusque, throaty drawl and her sister's light, lyrical tone. *God, how did Brooke get sucked into this?*

Entering the room, she found Gabe, Brooke, and Julia, of course, plus an extremely attractive man who looked a little like that actor from *Criminal Minds*— Shemar Moore. Wow, they grew them nice at the Savannah PD. At least she assumed this was Gabe's partner, Detective Tyler Wallace.

Gabe had been leaning against the fireplace, his hands in his pockets, when she came in. The pose was casual, but she saw the tension in his broad shoulders and the frown on his face. "You okay?" he asked, ignoring everyone else.

She nodded. "I'm fine."

Julia had been sitting on the edge of the desk, her long legs swinging as she talked to Brooke about heaven knew what. Now she hopped off and walked over. "I'm sorry. I wasn't trying to be nosy. It's just, when Brooke called, looking for you, and was so upset . . ."

"You asked Morgan to check on me?"

She nodded. "He told me a strange man had carried you into your house. I panicked, called her back, and we all raced over." She glanced at her watch. "Hell, we should probably listen for the doorbell; I bet you anything Mick will be showing up soon."

Oh, wonderful. "You called him?"

She merely shrugged, unrepentant. "Hey, we're a team, remember? But don't worry. I couldn't reach anybody but Mick."

Out of the corner of her eye, she saw Gabe grimace. It didn't take a genius to see that he didn't think much of Julia, though they'd only just met, as far as she knew. That surprised her; most men liked sexy, ballsy Julia a lot. Not that she had eyes for any of them. Olivia suspected her heart still belonged to a man who was thoroughly beyond her reach.

Gabe's partner walked over and extended his hand, which she shook. "We didn't get a chance to meet yesterday. I'm Detective Wallace—Ty."

"Nice to meet you." Though it would have been so much nicer to meet him and to see Julia and Brooke anywhere other than in her house minutes after they'd interrupted those wonderful moments in Gabe's arms.

Lie. It was over before they walked in.

Perhaps. But she liked to think she might have convinced him to change his mind.

"Now," Julia said, "Detective Wallace filled us in on what he knew, and he," she waved at Gabe, "told us the rest. Everything except the Final Jeopardy answers."

"Questions," she murmured absently.

"Whatever."

"Stop browbeating her," Gabe snapped. "Can you at least let her sit down?"

That sounded remarkably protective. Well, she supposed his protective instincts had gotten all worked up today. Frankly, that had been good, at the time. Now, though, she didn't need that. She just needed him—all of them—to listen. And to understand.

So, without hesitating, she told them what she'd learned about the final moments of the boy who'd once saved her life. They didn't interrupt, not once, though she saw Gabe's brow furrow in confusion when she mentioned one thing: that she'd seen the boy's face and recognized his reflection as the sunlight gleamed on the water in the washtub.

She should have known he'd be the one to realize something was wrong with that statement, even if he couldn't puzzle it out right away. He was quick, always thinking, alert and attentive. She admired that about him.

He'd also frowned when he'd heard the boy had called his attacker "Uncle Johnny," which in no way sounded like Dwight. But he'd probably assumed the kidnapper had used a false name.

Though it was difficult thinking about the most pitiful, heartbreaking part of it, she also shared one more detail, the one that had been so very hard to hear. "He said something at the end." She swallowed, trying to find some moisture in her very dry mouth. "His last words were 'My name is Zachary.'"

Brooke, who'd been sniffling since almost the start of the conversation, started to cry in earnest. Detective Wallace pulled a handkerchief out of his pocket—what a nice, old-fashioned thing for a young, modern man to carry around—and gave it to her.

"Zachary," Gabe said, looking relieved to have the boy's real name to go on. It was an excellent clue, and she knew it. That, in itself, was worth the ordeal she had gone through to learn it.

But it wasn't the most important thing. Oh, no.

"What happened after that?" Julia asked.

Olivia looked at her, blinking, her mouth opening,

then closing. She lifted her hand to her throat, trying to focus, wanting to help, but unable to think, unable to even consider thinking about the moment his face—her face—had gone into that water.

"What the hell do you think happened? He died," Gabe snapped, sounding angry. He strode over, stood beside the chair—the one where he'd held her on his lap just last night—and put a hand on her shoulder. "You don't have to say anything else, Liv. You can put this all behind you, forget about it."

A nice thought, but it wasn't true. She looked up at him, saw the concern and appreciated it more than she could say. "I need to tell you one more thing the man said."

"Yes?"

"When Zachary tried to deny letting me go, the man got angry, saying that word of my escape was all over the news."

He drew in a low, audible breath, understanding washing over his features. It all clicked in his mind, the way it had in hers. "The sunlight on the water," he mumbled.

She nodded.

"Christ."

"What is going on?" Brooke asked. "What are we missing?"

"You don't remember the details as well as I do, you were so young," Olivia said, tearing her gaze off Gabe to glance at her sister.

Gabe jumped in to explain. "Dwight Collier, the man everyone assumed had kidnapped Olivia and killed young Zachary, was himself killed in a shootout with police the *night* Olivia escaped."

Detective Wallace muttered a curse, and Julia gasped as it hit her, too. But Brooke, sweet Brooke, whose mind didn't work in warped, evil ways, still didn't quite see.

Olivia leaned forward, reaching for her sister's hand. "I heard the killer's voice, and I know he was the same man who had taken me, and . . . who did what he did to me."

Brooke squeezed her fingers tighter.

"Jack—*Zachary*—helped me escape, and I spent the night in the cemetery. But he was killed in the daytime. I saw the blue sky, I saw the gleam of sunlight on the water, and word of my escape didn't hit the news until the next morning, when they found me in the cemetery."

Hours after Dwight Collier was dead.

Suddenly, her sister saw the same thing they all did and looked every bit as dismayed. "Oh, my God."

Olivia knew it was true, didn't doubt what she'd experienced with her own eyes and ears, but it was still hard to take in. Yesterday, she'd voiced concern about an accomplice, wondering if someone else had walled up the boy's remains. In truth, Dwight Collier had been the accomplice all along, sent to pick up the ransom money and paying for that errand with his life.

Which meant the man who'd kidnapped Olivia, drowned her, then murdered Zachary, had escaped altogether. And he might very well still be out there.

Chapter 8

After he'd finished burying the rich businessman from Jacksonville, Johnny Traynor went into the motor home and headed for the kitchen to wash up for supper. He'd told Jack to have his food ready, and when he entered, his stare immediately went to the table to make sure he'd been obeyed. He saw a bowl filled with some canned stew, a plate stacked with bread, a box of crackers and a big glass of water.

Well, wasn't that fine.

"Good job, son," he said, smiling broadly at the boy, who stood in the corner, his eyes big and round in the near darkness. His smile quickly faded, however. "Why din'tcha turn the lights on? It's dark as a witch's snatch in here!"

The boy darted toward the lamp and flicked it on. "I din't think you'd wanna waste the gas from the generator. It ain't been dark but for a couple'a minutes, and I could see okay."

Johnny gave him a thumbs-up. "Smart thinkin' there, Jackie-boy."

Seeing the sticky, dried blood and dirt on his fingers, he paused for a second, confused. The dirt, sure—he'd buried a man, hadn't he? But the blood . . . he couldn't quite recall where that had come from. The body'd been all wrapped up in plastic, hadn't it? It'd been lyin' there on the ground, waiting to be buried when John had gotten back from . . . wherever he'd been.

Dang, he must be getting old; he couldn't remember shit these days. He'd come back from using the man's own keys to break in and rob his house, taken a nap, then . . . then buried the man rolled up in the tarp.

Wherever the blood had come from, he didn't want it on his hands while he ate the fine meal his son had prepared for him. Needing to wash, he headed to the sink, giving the kid a little hair ruffle as he passed. He'd been pleased with how well Jack had been behaving lately.

The boy ducked his head, probably feeling embarrassed about the praise. He was a shy one, quiet, maybe a little soft. But hopefully he would toughen now that he was getting older.

How old? How old is Jackie-boy?

Johnny paused and turned his head, thinking he'd heard something—a voice—but there was nothing, no sound at all but for the screaming bugs outside the trailer.

Screaming . . . the businessman from Jacksonville had screamed, hadn't he? Somewhere off in the distance.

"Don't matter," he mumbled under his breath. The businessman from Jacksonville was gone now. And there was lots more money waiting to be hidden away, along with the tens—maybe hundreds—of thousands of dollars he'd collected over the past two decades. Much of it—any ransom money, for instance—couldn't be used anytime soon. He knew better than to think those rich assholes would keep their word and deliver only unmarked bills. But someday, in a few years or so, when he was ready to retire, he'd dig it all up. Then he and his boy would move somewhere far away, live high on the hog.

But he won't be a boy anymore, will he? He'll be a man. A lying, untrustworthy man.

"You say something?" he asked Jack, who again stood in the corner, watching.

"Nossir, Uncle Johnny."

His hand flew out, the back of it meeting the boy's cheek in absent irritation. "I told you to stop calling me that. I'm your daddy, and it ain't right for you to call me anything else."

Tears filled up those eyes, and for a second, Johnny felt enraged by them. He wanted to put his hands around that throat and throttle the kid for being such a whiny, crying little pussy.

"I'm sorry . . . D-Daddy."

He sighed, his anger dissipating and his shoulders sagging as he finished rinsing his hands with a big jug of water. He oughtn'ta lost his temper like that. Hell, it was no wonder Jack occasionally forgot who he was talking to. Johnny had used dozens of aliases. Folks here in Savannah, which he considered his home, knew him by a name he'd used nigh on twenty years. While if he went up to Augusta for a spell, he might answer to Jimmy, or in Atlanta to Ralph.

Then there was the name folks who weren't quite as law-abiding called him. The people who wanted to hire him for a specialty job—like the fella who'd decided to act out that movie *Fargo* and have his own wife kidnapped so's he could get rid of her and keep all their money—knew him as Mr. Wolf. When anybody started nosing around, looking for the Wolf, he knew they had a special, sneaky job in mind.

Though they confused his poor, muddled son, simple names helped him blend in, be easily forgotten, which was part of the job. He didn't want to be remembered once folks turned up missing. It was a blue-wonder he remembered his *own* name sometimes.

"You're forgiven—just don't let it happen again." He cuffed the boy gently on the cheek. "Now, what say we have some supper? Buryin's awful hard work. No way to spend my afternoon off, I tell you that."

"No, sir, it sure ain't," Jack said, looking relieved. Like

a dog that had got strapped a bunch and was glad to get only a single kick this time.

That made Johnny feel bad but also a little bit angry. Who was the kid to act like he had it so tough? Didn't Johnny treat him right, put food in his belly and keep a roof over his head? And everything he did—robbing houses, snatching people and getting money for them—wasn't it so him and Jack could have a better life someday?

Of course it was. That's all it had ever been about. Him and his boy.

"Go on, now, get yourself some food," he said, gesturing toward the camp stove.

"Thank you, sir," Jack said, dashing over to get a bowl.

Johnny watched him, smiling at the boy's rapid movements, how fast he was despite being a little scrawny. And smart, too.

Smart enough to figure out how to get out of here. Have you looked at a calendar lately?

"Damn it." He waved a hand by his face, irritated by whatever bug was flying around inside, buzzing in his ear. "You leave the doors open again, boy?"

"Nossir," Jack said. "They was locked the whole time you was gone, remember?"

"You sassing me?" he snapped.

"No! I promise, Daddy. I wasn't sassin'. I just didn't want you to think I'd let any flies in. I know how much you hate 'em."

"Filthy little buggers." Then he stared at Jack, who stood over by the stove, shoveling food into his mouth the way a growing boy would. A growing boy—he surely was that. His pants were about three inches too short, showing a pair of dirty ankles and skinny bare feet.

Growing up.

He shoveled a spoonful of stew into his mouth. "You know I lock the door to keep you safe when I have to go to work, don'tcha, Jackie? And didn't I buy that fan and all that gas for the generator so you'd be nice and comfortable in here all day?"

"Yessir," he said, then quickly added, "Thank you."

Johnny waved a hand. He was glad the boy had remembered his manners and knew enough to be grateful. If there was one thing he couldn't abide, it was lack of gratitude in a person. "I'll always take care of you. I don't want anything to happen to you, not ever. You're my boy, and I hate having to leave you out here all alone."

"Maybe . . ."

"What?"

Jack's voice dropped to a whisper. "Maybe we could live in town."

Scowling, Johnny said, "Town's no place for you; there's nosy people there, cops and evil women. Plus there's druggies and perverts who hurt little boys like you. It ain't safe."

Johnny didn't mention that he had a place in town, not that he stayed there too often. He needed an address. No sense having people wonder where he lived. But Jack didn't need to know that. No point in the boy pining for somethin' he wasn't gonna get.

It was safe out here in the woods. Safe, secure and private. This time, he wasn't squattin' somewhere, having to worry somebody'd stumble across the two of them. He owned the twenty acres around them. He'd gone to a lot of trouble to buy it, having to get a fancy lawyer to set up what he called "an investment trust." The main thing was to do whatever he could to keep his name offa the deed so's it would be harder for anybody to trace him. They'd have to look real hard.

Licking his lips, still looking nervous, Jack went on. "But if we was in town, maybe I could come to work with you an' help you, and you could make sure nobody got me."

Johnny slapped his hand on his knee, tickled by the suggestion. A boy wanting to go help his father do his job—now that's what he called a perfect father-son relationship. But it wasn't exactly practical considering how little Johnny liked for people to know his private business.

He's only askin' so he can try to run away. That's what boys his age do, they run away.

His amusement fell right out of him, the smile disappearing to be replaced by a deep frown. His temple started to throb, and a low ache started building in the back of his head.

It came on fast. Just a little pain, then it flared into an agonizing throb. Something pounded at him, like somebody was hammering on his skull from the inside, trying to get out. He saw black spots and lifted a hand to cover his eyes. A whole bunch of blurry pictures went through his mind, and a voice whispered deep inside his head. An angry, familiar voice.

Some bones. A fire. The cops. Don't you remember the phone call? It's all falling down!

"I don't know what you're talking about."

"Sorry, Daddy," Jack said, probably thinking he was the one Johnny had been talking to.

It's that girl's fault. Oh, that girl. We shoulda killed that whore, that lying little bitch who caused all the trouble. We coulda done it a hundred times. Coulda reached out and snapped her filthy neck before she ever even realized she was in danger.

We gotta do it. Gotta finish it. Finish 'em both.

Johnny leapt up from the table, his fingers pulling his own hair, his eyes closed, face upraised. "Leave me alone!"

Look at the date. You know it's comin'. You know it.

"I'm sorry, Daddy. I'm sorry. I'm sorry," Jack cried, scurrying out of the kitchen.

Finish her. Finish him. Then we'll start over. Think of it: a nice, new, sweet-faced little boy, just eight years old, gap-toothed, all smiles and freckles, skinned knees and soft cheeks. He'll never sass you, never think of runnin' away. Never betray you. Our perfect little son.

Just like Jackie was once upon a time.

"No!" Johnny yelled, feeling like his brains were being dug out a spoonful at a time. The pain, the voices … God, why wouldn't it stop? Why couldn't he have any peace?

It's got to be done.

"I won't put my boy in the ground," he whispered. "Won't put Jack in the cold ground."

You won't have to. It'll be like he's playin' a game of hide-'n'-seek. Only he won't never be found.

A bunch of pictures entered his mind—dark corners, hidden crevices. Jack.

"No! Leave me be!"

I can't, and we both know why. You know I'm right. The time's coming when one of us is gonna have to finish this—and we both know it's gonna be me.

Then we'll start over.

If there had been any way Gabe could have swept Olivia out of her own house, away from her sister, his partner, and those annoying coworkers of hers—one more had shown up an hour ago—he would have, happily. But there had been no way. Because, somehow, in the telling of her tale, everyone in the room had decided they were part of this now and wanted to be involved in the investigation. Every damn one of them.

Including the "mousy" sister, who'd actually hung up on her fiancé the fourth time he'd called to ask her where she was and order her home. Having met said fiancé, the calls hadn't surprised him. Brooke's response, however, had. Every once in a while, Gabe had seen Olivia sneaking glances at her sibling, as if to make sure it was really her and not some body snatcher.

That whole thing he'd been thinking earlier about siblings came back to him. Brooke was here, fierce and protective, because she loved her sister more than she worried about displeasing her fiancé. Which was a nice thing to see, rare and sort of alien to him but nice.

"So whaddya say, Cooper?" asked Mick Tanner, one of the eXtreme Investigations guys, who seemed pretty normal, except for the thin leather gloves he wore on his hands. Gabe hadn't asked about the gloves, having an idea what they were for, given what he'd seen Olivia do.

That didn't mean Gabe liked him. He was prepared to dislike anybody Olivia worked with. *If you're such a great friend and care about her so much why do you let her do it?*

"Cooper?" the other man prodded.

"What do I say about what?"

"About letting us help?"

He frowned, noting that across the room Ty was doing the same thing.

"This is an official police investigation."

"A cold case," Tanner said, waving a gloved hand. "Come on, admit it. You know nobody at Central gives a damn about an old closed murder case, and you could use some help."

"They'll care if they know this boy's killer has killed two other boys."

"How are you planning to explain that?" Tanner asked. "How will your lieutenant react if you say an employee of eXtreme Investigations touched some remains, had a vision and told you the kid's killer was not who the police say he was."

Damn. Good point. He had been thinking of the results, not of the psychic means of getting them; anybody who hadn't been in that room when Olivia had touched that finger bone would question the truth of her story.

As for Gabe, well, he no longer questioned it. He didn't know why, or how, or what it meant, but he believed every word she said. Her reaction had been too extreme and her mood afterward far too crumbled, crushed under the weight of what she'd experienced, for it to have been an act. Plus, everything she'd said made sense. The biggest problem he'd had with her story was the time line. Now it no longer mattered. Of course the bastard hadn't carried out every evil act in that one, awful night; he'd been able to take his time. Hell, for all they knew, poor Jack had been killed a couple of days after Olivia's rescue.

In Gabe's mind, he pictured the man sending Collier to get the money. When all hell broke loose, he'd have gone back to the woods in a panic, not knowing if Collier would live to talk. He'd have packed up the boy and the camper and taken off to lie low somewhere.

When he'd heard on the news that Olivia had gotten away and that Collier, the "evil kidnapper," was dead, he'd probably decided Jack was both a traitor and a loose end. He'd had all the time in the world to kill the boy, then wall-up his body some night, because nobody was even looking for him. They'd all thought he was dead. Afterward, he'd ditched the cleaned-out truck at the bus station, wiped his hands and walked away clean.

It was vile, twisted . . . and sickeningly smart.

Mick Tanner apparently hadn't noticed Gabe's thoughts had wandered. "And what about the fact that the main suspect is the guy who tried to kill her, and now, despite the police reports from the time that say he's dead and gone, she's claiming he's still alive? You think they're going to be fine with that, admitting somebody screwed the pooch twelve years ago and let this psycho get away?" He rolled his eyes. "Sorry, friend. We all know that's not gonna happen."

He was seriously not liking this guy. That did not, however, mean Mick was wrong. In fact, his theories about the reaction Gabe would get to this were probably dead-on. Olivia was a former victim, and anybody might think she was looking for payback or resolution to her own crime. And, yeah, ass covering was alive and well at city hall and in the PD.

Hell. Nobody else at the station was going to touch this one with a ten-foot pole. Frankly, he was a little surprised Ty was still here. Then, again, considering how solicitously his partner was hovering over Brooke Wainwright, he somehow suspected an ulterior motive.

Brooke was an engaged woman, but engaged wasn't married. And her fiancé seemed like a real dickhead. So Gabe certainly wasn't going to be the one to warn Ty off.

"We can help. Let us," Mick urged.

"What is it you think you can do?" he asked carefully.

Mick lifted his hand, displaying the gloves, like ones a race-car driver would wear.

"I saw them," Gabe replied, his tone dry.

"They're hard to miss," the other man said with a grin.

"I assume it's to keep you from touching something you don't want to touch?"

"Uh-huh."

"So why don't you use something a little less obvious, like a doctor's glove?"

"What, and get mistaken for a proctologist all the time? No, thank you," Mick said with an obvious eyebrow wag, trying to keep the mood light.

Julia chuckled, as did Olivia. Gabe didn't. This guy wasn't answering any of his questions. "So, back to the point. What exactly do you do?"

"I know things."

"Yeah, yeah, you're all psychic."

"I'm not," Julia said from across the room. "I don't have a psychic bone in my body."

Well, at least she admitted it.

"I'm not really psychic, either," Mick said. "I can't tell the future."

"So what *is* your trick?" Ty asked, sounding half-amused, half-interested.

Mick glanced at Olivia. "Do you mind?"

"Your call," she said with a shrug.

Mick nodded, looked around the room and didn't seem to see what he wanted. Saying "I'll be right back," he walked out of the den, heading to the formal dining room, which looked like it was all set for the queen and her family to sit down for tea. Gabe had glanced in there yesterday and hadn't liked the heavy, antique furniture, room-darkening drapes and prissy, rose-patterned china displayed in a glass-front hutch. It didn't suit Olivia, who, though feminine and graceful, was in no way prissy. Not with the steel she had running through her spine.

When Mick came back, he was carrying a cup. One single rose-patterned teacup.

"Don't you dare drop it," Olivia warned him. "That thing's valuable."

"Hey, no hinting," Mick said. Putting the cup down, he took off one of his gloves.

Gabe took a step back, having a sudden, vivid memory of what had happened that afternoon when Liv had torn one fingertip off hers. From beside him, he felt the brush of her hand. He looked down at her, sitting on the edge of the couch, and she mouthed, "It's okay."

Yeah, he hoped so. Because he sure as hell wasn't carrying this guy upstairs and climbing into bed with him.

Across the room, he saw Ty leaning forward on his chair. Brooke was doing the same thing. Julia, obviously used to this dog-and-pony show, wasn't even watching, instead staring at something out in the hallway. Frankly, he didn't want to know what it was.

Once his right hand was ungloved, Mick reached down with the left one, picked up the teacup, and deposited it in his bare palm. Fortunately, he didn't start to shudder, shake, or scream. He only scrunched his eyes shut, then nodded.

"Well?" Olivia asked.

"Your grandmother, she liked her tea with lemon but no milk."

"This is the South, darlin'; that's how all the best people take their tea," Julia drawled. "Come on, you can do better than that. Impress us, hotshot."

Mick chuckled, not offended. "Okay. Wait."

A long silence, then he spoke again. This time, his voice was a static monotone, like he was describing a series of boring pictures in his mind. "You've never sipped anything out of this cup, Olivia. Your mouth hasn't been on it, though your hand has. You've washed it, cleaned it less than a month ago, but it hasn't held anything except dust for at least ten years."

Olivia nodded once, though Mick's eyes were closed and he couldn't see her do it.

Gabe crossed his arms over his chest, still waiting to be wowed.

"The last time it was really used was at a bridge luncheon in January of 1999."

"My grandmother loved bridge, but she stopped playing when my grandfather died."

What rich, old Southern woman didn't play bridge?

"A woman named Agnes Bedford drank out of it," Mick added. "She wasn't very happy. She and her partner, Bitty Bates, just couldn't get it together."

"Agnes and Bitty were my grandmother's best friends. Debutante class of 1933."

Okay, a little more interesting. But he still wasn't convinced Mick didn't know Olivia well enough to know the names of . . . her dead grandmother's friends? *Hmm*.

"Your grandmother used the set for her bridge club meetings because she knew 'the girls' were all so impressed by it. Something about where it came from. . . . Other than that, it was used once a year at Easter, and children under fifteen weren't allowed to touch it."

Brooke laughed softly. "I used to stick my finger on the plates when she wasn't looking."

Gabe couldn't deny growing more interested, but the skeptic in him could still come up with a rational explanation for all of this. The late senator and his wife were very well known; her best friends might have been mentioned in society articles that Mick could have seen. What old lady didn't like to lord it over her friends a little with her best china, and who wouldn't insist that the kids not touch it?

"Tell us something you couldn't possibly know," Olivia charged, correctly reading Gabe's skepticism.

Mick nodded. "It is a family heirloom, a wedding present to your great-great-grandmother. The wedding was . . . *umm* . . . spring of 1863, I think?"

Interesting? Or utter bullshit?

Olivia rose to stand beside him, frowning at his lack of faith.

"That's right, Mick." Then she took Gabe's arm and pulled him with her as she walked over to a bookshelf on the far wall. Still silent, she reached up, pulled down a leather-bound book marked "The Wainwright Family: A Genealogy" and put it into Gabe's hands.

He guessed that rich, old Southern families did things like print up entire books about their family history. If anybody were to do that for his family, it'd have about two pages, the only names in it being his, his mother's, his grandmother's and his grandfather's. His mother had died when he was nine, his grandmother six months after that. As for his grandfather, well, he was too mean to be courteous enough to die and leave the earth to better folks. Gabe had never met his father—his mother wasn't even allowed to mention his name once her daddy had let her "come crawling back home with her no-good little bastard" when she had no place else to go. Gabe had been about two at the time.

So, yeah. Fuck genealogy.

"Tell me the ancestor's name, and then tell me who gave her the gift," Olivia ordered Mick, from across the room, though her attention remained on Gabe.

While Mick concentrated, Olivia flipped the pages, stopping on one with an old, tintype-style wedding photo of a very dour-looking man and his equally constipated-looking, frumpy bride. Gabe couldn't help whispering, "The happy couple?"

With a smile tickling her lips, Olivia nudged him in the ribs with her elbow. *"Shh."*

"Uh, seriously, Liv?" Mick said. "Your great-great-grandmother's name was Bathilda?"

Olivia tapped the tip of her finger on the caption beneath the photo.

Bathilda Chester Wainwright.

"Her father was German," Olivia said. "Yes. Now, who gave it to her?"

Mick thought a second more, then said, "Cool!"

"Who was it?" asked Ty, obviously intrigued.

"President and Mrs. Jefferson Davis," Mick said. "Old Jeff himself picked up this very cup to examine it when shopping for the gift in Richmond."

Again, Olivia tapped something on the page. It turned out to be a list of the guests who had attended the wedding. The honored president of the Confederacy and his wife were right on top.

Son of a bitch.

"Oh," Mick muttered. His eyes flying open, he put the

cup down suddenly, as if needing to get it away from himself.

"What?" Gabe asked.

Mick's jovial demeanor had faded, his smile no longer conveying a good mood. In fact, his suddenly clenched jaw said it was anything but. "The whole box was wrapped in lace and tied with blue silk ribbons," he said, his tone dripping distaste, "by Mrs. Davis's house slave, who dropped one of the matching cups. She didn't have a very good day."

Everyone fell silent for a moment. Then Ty asked, "Is he for real? Seriously, for real?"

Gabe was wondering the same thing. But he couldn't deny the evidence was strong; he was holding the book right in his hands. There was no way Mick could see it. There certainly had been no time to set this whole thing up as some elaborate scheme, nor did he think Olivia ever would. He'd already accepted the fact that he'd seen evidence of a true, inexplicable phenomenon yesterday in that examination room. How could he deny it existed in this form?

Yeah, this might be for real. Crazy, impossible. But real.

Mick tugged on his glove, not saying anything more, then sat on the couch, remaining silent. Suddenly it hit Gabe how tough it would be to have an ability like that. How difficult it must be to go out in the world, unable to touch anything without fearing some random object's dark history would overwhelm you at any given time. He'd once read that paper currency was one of the dirtiest things you could touch because it had been handled by so many people. God, how would this guy even manage to pay for a cup of coffee without a glove on his hand?

The very idea of it saddened him, and he found his instinctive mistrust toward the man fading. No, he wasn't ready to toast marshmallows and sing "Kumbaya" with anybody Olivia worked with, not if, as he suspected, they exploited her abilities to her detriment. Still, he couldn't deny he felt sympathy for Mick Tanner. Olivia could avoid touching human remains for the rest of her life if she chose to. Mick didn't have the luxury of never touching anything.

Mick looked over at him, the twinkle gone from his eyes. They held a long stare, during which the man silently admitted that it was just like Gabe was imagining. Bad. Painful. Ugly.

But also, Gabe suspected, very useful when it came to solving crimes. Especially when it came to solving *cold* crimes. Like this one.

It could never be as bad as what Olivia already went through to help solve this case.

He thought about the case, thought about the evidence, thought about the murdered boy. He also thought about the information he'd read in Olivia's file early this morning, before he'd come here to pick her up to take her to the family brunch. The file had mentioned evidence gathered at the scene after Olivia's rescue. A cigarette butt. An old spoon. The broken tip of a knife. All normal items but items that could very well tell a story if only the right man was there to listen to it. And the right man was practically begging for the chance to listen to it.

"So what do you think, Detective?" asked Julia, as if sensing he was waffling.

What did he think? *Hmm.* He *thought* he was actually giving this some serious consideration. He *thought* he was about to take an off-the-wall chance he would never have considered two days ago. He also *thought* he might live to regret it.

Before he went any further and actually decided, though, he needed to make a few things clear. He stared at the owner of eXtreme Investigations. "This would be totally off the record."

She lifted both hands, holding them palms out. "Not a problem."

"I mean before *and* after. I don't want to see some newspaper article next week about how the Savannah PD is now working hand in glove . . ." he glanced at Mick, "no pun intended, with your company. And any kind of payment is out of the question."

Julia rose, lifting one dark brow over a dark eye. "Olivia is one of us. We're here for her, not for you, not for any money and not for the company. Understand?"

"Got it," he said, glad they had laid it all out. He had suspected as much, but it was better to be up front about what was expected of everyone in this situation.

"Let's start by giving it a day, okay? Tomorrow, totally outside regular office hours, just some like-minded people putting their minds together to work on a problem." That sounded perfectly reasonable . . . and like something that might not cost him his job.

You're dreaming. If this thing goes south you can kiss your job goodbye.

He ignored his inner pessimist. "Ty, you really up for this? You know we're walking on thin ice here, right?"

"I know, but you bet I'm in. This dog will hunt."

Gabe shook his head and *tsk-tsk*ed. "Not so good that time."

Ty grinned. "Well, how about, 'Why, yes, partner, that's a fine idea. I'd be happy to.'"

"That's better," Gabe said, ignoring everyone's confusion. If they were going to spend time with Ty, they'd figure it out soon enough. Or, as Ty would probably put it, right quick.

"So, that's it?" Julia asked. "We're agreed?"

Gabe turned the whole situation over in his mind one more time, considering what his lieutenant would have to say, what the press would make of this. But in the end, he came back to the same thing: If it helped get justice for that murdered boy and peace for Olivia, and helped prevent more people from being hurt, how could he possibly refuse to even try? "Okay, I think we've got a deal."

He only hoped it was one he didn't live to regret.

After a few more minutes' conversation, they all agreed to get a fresh start in the morning at the eXtreme Investigations offices. Julia left first, with Mick following her out. Ty was next. Then it was just him and Brooke, standing on either side of Olivia by the front door. Liv's sister eyed him like he was some despoiler of innocents.

"Thank you, Brooke," Olivia said, giving her sister a soft kiss on the cheek, setting their departure order without actually putting it into words.

The blonde frowned, looked at Gabe, then back at her sister. "Are you sure you're okay?"

"I'm fine," Olivia insisted.

Brooke licked her lips nervously, as if unsure she should say anything, then did, anyway. "Have you, you know . . . done it yet?"

Gabe stiffened, shocked that the sister would ask that with him standing right there.

"No, but I promise, I will," Olivia replied.

He suspected he'd gotten the wrong impression about what Brooke had been asking. The woman confirmed that by turning her attention toward him. "You make sure she does what she needs to do to let this go. Understand?"

Again, the mouse had become a lion. Funny what family loyalty could do to a person. Then Brooke left, and it was just him and Olivia, standing in the front hall. There probably should have been some awkwardness, considering that several hours ago they'd been kissing passionately in her bed. But there was none. Gabe was too focused on Brooke's comments to even stress about what had happened earlier. "What did she mean by 'let it go'?"

Olivia cleared her throat. "I have to let go of what happened today."

He got it at once. "You mean, when you touched the remains?"

"Yes."

"That means you *can* let it go? Get it out of your head entirely?" he asked, incredibly relieved. One of the things he'd been dwelling on while she'd slept earlier was the thought that all these things, these dark, awful deaths, never fully left her consciousness. Which would be enough to break anyone, sooner or later.

"No," she replied, "it's not like that."

Hell. "So what is it like?"

She tilted her head, visibly considering how to describe it. "It's . . . I guess it's like going to therapy. I don't suppose you've ever been."

"It's been recommended by a woman or two over the years," he said, his voice dry.

The rejoinder got a tiny smile out of her, as he'd intended it to.

"But no," he added, "I've never been on the couch."

"I have. And what I do now, to get out from under this, is something like what I used to do then. First I accept it, embrace the fear and horror of it. Then I wash it away, clean it from my mind, and allow myself to feel triumph over having risen above it."

He only stared. He'd been hoping for some psychic magic trick, something that would erase this from her memories, and she was talking about channeling that dumb book *The Secret*? Positive thinking and all that crap?

"I know it sounds . . ."

"Wait. You accept and *embrace* it?" he asked, focusing on that part of her explanation.

Olivia turned away from him, walking slowly back toward the den, not asking if he wanted to stay. As if she just couldn't stand up and have the conversation any longer.

He followed, of course. This time, when she sat down on the sofa, he was the one who went to the wet bar. He poured her a glass of cranberry juice, splashed some club soda in it, as he'd seen her do, then brought it over and handed it to her. "Drink. Breathe. Then we'll talk."

"Bossy," she mumbled, not sounding like she minded. He wondered how often Olivia actually let anybody take care of her. While she was so busy throwing herself in front of every ugly, murderous bus her friends and co-workers asked her to, how often had one of them just put a foot down and made sure she took care of herself? Did anyone? Ever?

The whole thing infuriated him more every time he thought about it. He had no claim on Olivia, but if he did, he'd do everything in his power to make sure she stopped hurting herself like this. There were other ways to solve crimes; he'd believed that every day of his life, right up to and including this one, when he'd seen proof of things he'd never known existed.

The world would go on spinning if Olivia Wainwright never touched another dead human being. And that's the world he wanted this beautiful woman to live in.

After taking a few sips, Olivia put the glass on the table. "Thanks."

"You're welcome," he said, taking a seat beside her. He leaned back on the couch and stretched an arm out behind her. Olivia curved into him, fitting into the crook of his arm like she was meant to be there, and they'd done this every night for a decade. He might not know what color toothbrush she used or whether she drank her coffee with cream—or, hell, if she even drank coffee—but he suspected he knew her more intimately than almost anybody else in the world. He'd been there to catch her after she'd walked through the fire and had seen her in the kind of open, exposed moment that changed people. Changed relationships.

It had definitely changed theirs. He didn't think he was ever going to get over this need he had to just be there for her. Be a real hand to grab in the dark, a warm body to touch.

Finally, she told him the rest. "Embracing it, facing it, that's the hard part. I didn't want to say anything to Brooke, but sometimes it takes a while before I'm up to it. Because in order to move past it, I have to let it back in, all the memories, all the feelings . . ."

"Fuck that," Gabe said, the reaction instinctive, as was the tightening of every muscle in his body. Then he mumbled, "Sorry."

"It's not a great process, I know."

"It's a rotten one," he replied, dropping his arm off the back of the couch to drape it over her shoulders. He ran his fingers up and down her arm, reminding her that she wasn't alone. He had the feeling he could be content doing that—reminding her she wasn't alone—for a very long time. If she'd let him.

"It's all I've got," she said. "It's not perfect, but it helps keep the nightmares at bay."

His hand stilled for a moment; then he resumed stroking. He'd been wondering if she would have trouble sleeping tonight, given the way she'd begged him to stay earlier.

Nightmares born of your own dark imaginings were bad enough. But inviting them from the minds of dozens of murder victims? Unfathomable.

"You've gotta stop, Liv," he murmured, not even thinking about whether he had the right to say it, just knowing he had to.

She stiffened.

But he wasn't backing down. "You can't keep doing this to yourself. You cannot face an entire lifetime of this, You know that, right?"

"It's not usually as bad as it was today."

"Oh, right, sometimes you just get shot, huh?"

"There are worse ways to go."

"There are a whole lot of better ones, too!"

"I know that," she admitted. "Have I told you about how I found out about this ability?"

Come to think of it, that had never come up. It wasn't exactly casual, cup-of-coffee conversation. "No."

"It was a year after the kidnapping. My grandmother, the one who left me this house, had died. Mom brought Brooke and me back from Tucson for the funeral services." Sounding half-weary, half-resigned, she admitted, "It was an open casket."

"Oh, no," he muttered, envisioning it.

"Oh, yes."

"You, *uh* . . ."

"I loved her hair. It was long and white, just beautiful, and she was very vain about it. So when I went up to say goodbye to her, I reached in to smooth it near her cheek . . . and suddenly I was lying in a bed, my head turned to the side, looking at a bunch of pictures on a bedside table."

He gulped, trying not to think about the fact that she'd been sixteen, just sixteen years old and a year off a nightmare that would have crushed a lot of people.

"I saw my grandfather's face, a family portrait of me and Brooke with our parents. My late uncle, Richard and Tess . . . a whole little Wainwright family gallery."

"Did you recognize the place?"

"Of course, it was her bedroom at the assisted living center where she'd moved after her stroke. We'd been back to visit Dad a couple of weeks before, and I had visited her every day."

She was probably very glad of that, now. "What did you do?"

"I didn't really do anything. I was just shocked, watching. I saw her try to lift her right hand, but it fell to the bed; she'd lost much of the use of that side. So she reached with her left one, stretching so far. Her fingers were trembling, and I could hear her harsh breaths."

He closed his eyes, silent, knowing she needed to tell him this, for her own reasons.

"Then she was able to get grandfather's picture. She brought it close. The vision got blurry, like I was looking through tears, and I saw her trace her finger across his cheek."

Saying goodbye?

"That was when I became aware of a tightness in my chest. I felt weak, couldn't breathe well. Grandmother's left hand was sagging by this point, she had to rest the picture on her chest."

"She was having a heart attack?"

"Mmm hmm."

"Nobody came to help?"

"Honestly, Gabe, I don't think she pushed the button to let anybody know. Because I heard her say something, her voice was soft, but clear in my head. She looked at my grandfather and said, 'I think I'll be seeing you soon, my love. Thank God.'"

He pictured it, remembering what she'd told him— that the grandfather had died the year before. It sounded as though his widow had just wanted to join him. He'd seen that kind of love, a lifetime of it, in movies, of course. God knew he'd never had any firsthand experience with it. The whole idea of it, decades of happiness together, so much love you didn't want to live apart, seemed so impossible. And yet so incredibly beautiful.

"Was there anything else?" he asked, clearing his tight throat.

She laughed softly. "Yes. I heard her say one more thing before her breath stopped. Her voice was louder, almost quarrelsome, like the flamboyant, eccentric old woman I'd known. She said, 'And I expect you to be waiting there with my two-olive martini!'"

He smiled at the image, understanding so much about the woman from those very last words. "I'd like to have met this grandmother of yours."

"I wish you could have," she replied, sounding not sad but merely winsome. "She was one of a kind. Fascinating, difficult. Wonderful."

So far, every member of her family seemed fascinating, except, of course, her cousin Richard, who was pretty much a blowhard, which seemed about right for his line of work.

"What happened . . . afterward?" he asked.

"The pain ended. Everything went dark for a few seconds. Then I opened my eyes, and I found myself on the floor of the funeral home, flat on my back, having supposedly screamed and fainted." She gave an exaggerated shudder. "Grandmother would have been appalled at such a spectacle." Turning a little, she pulled back so she could look up at him, as if wanting to make sure he understood her point. "So, you see, it isn't always horrible. This ability of mine gave me one of the most perfect memories of my grandmother I could ever have asked for."

Her green eyes were wide, clear and dry. She spoke from the heart, and, honestly, Gabe could see her point.

In that one instance. That one, single instance.

"I'm glad you have that," he told her gently, "but, Liv, does that one good memory wipe out all the vicious, horrible ones that have to be building up inside your head? Do you think your grandmother would want that for you?"

Her breath caught, and he heard the tiny gasp in her

throat. But she didn't pull away, didn't glare, didn't get angry. Instead, she remained silent, thinking about his words. Then, finally, she admitted, "No, I guess it doesn't, and I suppose she wouldn't."

She was seeing sense.

"But knowing I've helped solve the murders of so many people, given them justice and peace, and stopped others from being hurt? That goes a long way toward balancing the scales."

Chapter 9

Olivia arrived downtown a half hour before this morning's scheduled nine a.m. meeting. She knew Julia well enough to know her boss would be there early and wanted a chance to talk to her before the others showed up. The others being her coworkers and the two Savannah detectives who had suddenly found themselves working with their former enemies.

She wasn't sure how Gabe and his partner felt about it. They hadn't even discussed that part of this whole working-together idea, even though she'd spent a couple of hours curled up against him on the couch last night. Talking. *Only* talking.

At first, they'd talked about ugly things, sad memories. But then, as the night had grown deeper and he'd continued to stay, their conversation had rambled. As if they'd both suddenly realized they'd been all wrapped up in darkness from the minute they'd met, and maybe it was time to stop, take a mental health break and just talk about absolutely nothing that mattered.

They'd talked movies and TV shows, cars and sports teams. She'd told him he was a cretin for preferring country music to jazz, and he called her a snob for insisting it was just wrong to eat a big, sloppy burrito with your hands.

Then they'd laughed. They'd laughed a lot.

By the time he'd left, at around one—without any-

thing more than a soft brush of his lips on her temple—
she'd been so relaxed, in such a good mood, she'd gone
to bed and hadn't had a single bad dream. She'd still
woken up early, tense for some reason, but there had
been no nightmares. Giving it some thought this morning, she realized that was probably exactly what he'd
intended.

She'd told him she wasn't ready to chase away the
darkness her usual way, so he'd found another one. She
could love him for that, she really could. *What a man.*

Still, with all their talking, they'd never touched on
how he felt about her coworkers and the joint endeavor
they were about to undertake. He wasn't the only one
who might be having cold feet; she wasn't sure how
Aidan would react, either, considering he was the one
who'd practically had his face printed on Wanted posters
by the local police. But it was worth a try. The two detectives had agreed to give it a shot, to pool their resources,
off the books, at least for a day or two, just to see what
happened.

Just to see what happened . . . Hmm, hadn't that been
what she'd been thinking about when she'd kissed Gabe
Cooper yesterday? The problem was, she had not been
satisfied with what had happened. It had been incredibly
nice, but she'd wanted more. A lot more. Yet last night,
when she'd been in his arms, she hadn't pushed it, knowing she liked him, liked being with him, as much as she
wanted him.

She definitely wanted him.

Olivia hadn't had a no-strings affair in, well, ever.
Honestly, she wasn't sure she wanted one now. Something about Gabe pulled her strings but good. She had
the feeling that if she did become more intimately involved with him, those strings would only grow tighter.

It didn't help to remind herself that she hadn't known
him long. The point was, she knew him in the ways that

really counted. Not his history or his background—she already knew his family was a touchy subject.

The important stuff, however, she got. She knew his character. Oh, that she knew exceedingly well. There was also his tenderness, his smarts, his sense of humor, his loyalty, his determination. All the things he possessed in spades, many of them things she hadn't learned about the other men she'd been involved with, even after a period of months.

When this was over, when she had the answers she'd been seeking, she'd slow down and look at this picture through more rational lenses. Right now, though, she was taking things as they came. If that meant another kiss coming her way, she'd be all right with that. If it meant him coming back to her bed, that'd be even better. Anything beyond that, she couldn't think about right now, even if she really did like thinking about the bed one.

Pulling into the parking garage attached to her building, Olivia drove down the first ramp, then all the way around to the back of the structure, aiming for her standard reserved spot on the bottom level. When she got there and pulled in, though, she realized she'd been pretty silly, driving past row after row of empty spaces. She'd been on autopilot, oblivious to the fact that the place was practically empty. The eXtreme Investigations offices were located in a slick office building that also housed more traditional companies run by lawyers, accountants and hedge fund–manager types, most of whom didn't operate on Sundays.

She sometimes wondered what visitors to the high-rise thought when they looked at the building directory and saw that business with the funny name, the funny punctuation, and the really funny reputation. She'd certainly been taken aback by it when she'd first heard about the place. Then she'd met Julia, realized the former cop was about as far from a new age quack as anybody could get and knew she had stumbled into something very serious and very special.

Speaking of Julia . . . "Ha!" she mumbled, spying the woman's car parked in her regular spot two spaces down. So Olivia hadn't been the only one who'd been on auto-pilot this morning.

Despite not having had any bad dreams, she'd still awakened very early this morning, before dawn, and had been unable to get back to sleep. Eventually she'd realized the tension she'd been feeling was due to the strange, discomforting sensation that somebody was watching her. She'd thought about that shadow, that movement in the mirror earlier, and had grown a little worried. She'd even gone downstairs to double-check all the locks, though she knew she was probably being para-noid. But considering she'd realized last night that the man who'd tried to kill her was not rotting in his grave and could still be out there, she probably had reason to be jumpy.

When she'd gone back to bed, she'd forced herself to think about other things, more pleasant ones. Past and present were banished, and she focused on Gabe, on the wonderful hours they'd shared the night before, maybe even on the future.

"Don't go there," she reminded herself. She didn't need to let herself get any more distracted by Gabe Coo-per. They had a case to work on, a case that mattered to her, a lot. For the first time that she could remember, members of the SCCPD and agents from eXtreme In-vestigations were working together, collaborating. She wanted this to go well, for any number of reasons.

Speaking of other members of the team, she noticed that Mick's car wasn't in his spot. Not surprising. He was almost always late. Aidan's wasn't in his, either. She hadn't expected it to be, honestly, because he and his girlfriend had gone away for the weekend. She'd specifically asked Julia to not interrupt them by calling Aidan back and hoped her boss had listened.

As for Derek, the other agent at eXtreme Investigations, he rode a big, badass motorcycle, which suited Derek's big, badass personality pretty well. He was definitely the rebel of the group, and it wasn't merely because Mick had the playboy role sewn up, while Aidan was the brainiac. *Hmm.* And Julia was the boss. So what did that make her?

The freak.

She thrust that thought out of her head, angry at herself for even allowing it to surface. Then, reaching for the door handle, she got out and locked the car. Her eyes on the elevator sign, she headed across the dark, shadowy lot so she could ride up to their tenth-floor offices.

Dark and shadowy, indeed. It was broad daylight outside, but that light didn't penetrate far under the cover of five stories of concrete parking deck. She wasn't exactly underground—Savannah's elevation didn't allow for that—but the bottom floor was slightly below street level.

The distance between her spot and the elevator suddenly looked a lot longer than usual. Maybe it was the shadows cast by the pillars and half walls of the deck, or the click of her heels on the cement, or just the fact that it was so utterly empty, but the place that always seemed so normal and commonplace now felt a little creepy.

A low, furtive scrape interrupted her thoughts, like the sound of a shoe dragged on the pavement. She cocked her head, curious more than startled, wondering if she'd missed seeing Derek's motorcycle in the designated bike area. It was one level up, directly overhead, and he might be walking around right now, too.

If he got here before you, he's probably already upstairs.

Another sound, a soft rustling, came from behind her.

She spun around, not sure what she expected to see . . . but saw nothing. Just her car and Julia's and a vast expanse of shadowy, empty parking lot, striped with lines, stained with occasional splotches of engine oil and skid marks. Perfectly normal.

You're hearing things.

But she still didn't move, listening intently. Olivia hadn't lived a normal life; she was attuned to certain sights, sounds and sensations, especially those related to danger. This, well, she wasn't entirely sure what this was. Her pulse had quickened, yes. But whose wouldn't? Beyond that, she didn't feel any panic clawing at her, sensed no evil or imminent peril. Only mystery.

She cocked her head, sure that she would hear a car driving on one of the upper levels or the mechanical noise of the elevator in motion. Or even the buzz of an insect.

But all was silent. Not a car horn, not a voice, not a whisper, not even, she suddenly realized, the sound of her own heartbeat. It was as if she were in a sense-deprivation chamber, all sound blacked out.

Like being underwater.

"Stop it," she told herself, speaking loudly, her voice jarring in the silence. She had needed it to be; she'd wanted to disturb that silence and break its power.

Swallowing, she swung around again and took several firm, deliberate steps, her low-heeled sandals creating a staccato *tap-tap* that matched her heartbeat. She breathed steadily, the gasoline-tinged air sharp in her nose. Not panicked, not even truly afraid.

Until there came another sound. A low, soft, splashing sound.

Her rational mind thought *water main break.*

Her more primal one . . . went in another direction.

This time, she called out, "Who's there?" and looked over her shoulder.

O-liiiiii-via.

Shock rolled over her. Her leg muscles stiffened, her knees locking up so quickly that she almost tumbled to the ground. She began to feel light-headed as that whisper floated around her, wrapping her in its eerie embrace, echoing in her ears.

Had she really heard that? Had someone truly said her name, or was she still messed up in the head after yesterday's horror fest? She waited, craning her ears, trying to understand, but didn't hear a thing, except, perhaps, her own nerves, which were making her so damned jumpy.

"This is ridiculous," she muttered. "There's nobody here." It was shadowy, yes, but not utterly dark, and she didn't think a person could actually be hiding close enough for her to hear him whisper her name without her seeing him.

A dark thought occurred to her. *Unless he's hiding behind Julia's car.*

Even more ridiculous. But not impossible.

No way was she going to go over there and find out. This wasn't some TV movie with a stupid woman who'd go off and investigate a scary noise in the big abandoned parking lot. She might be feeling more nervous than afraid, but still, she'd seen that creepy movie *P2*, about the woman stalked in a parking garage, and was not up for a reenactment.

Now about twenty feet from the elevator, she started toward it again, not quite running—still not entirely sure she'd heard anything at all—but not dawdling, either.

Olivia!

"Who the hell are you?" she snapped, skidding to a stop once more as that odd, disembodied voice called to her again, now sounding like it had come from above her. One thing had struck her this time—it didn't sound like a real person speaking, and yet she had heard her name clearly.

Then a strange thought entered her mind. No, she'd never seen Julia's ghostly friend—or friendly ghost—but she didn't doubt Julia had, so she believed he was around. Just yesterday, in fact, he had been watching her, had reported back to Julia that Gabe had carried her into her house. Which was kind of annoying, to be honest, thinking a ghost was spying on her.

Could he be watching her now? And was she somehow becoming aware of him? Having experienced death so many times, perhaps her own sensory perception had been altered. What if she, too, might now be able to interact with the ghostly remnants left behind by those who had died? What if he somehow sensed it and was trying to make contact with her?

"Morgan?" she whispered.

A long moment and then that strange whisper that seemed to come from all around her but also inside her own head.

Maybe you should drown her.

"No!" she cried, panic washing over her. Her stomach heaved and she dropped her purse as she ran toward the elevator. She lost a shoe but didn't even slow down, driven by a ravaging fight-or-flight impulse that was telling her to fly.

She skidded to a stop as she reached the control panel. "Please hurry," she begged as she punched the Up button. But the door didn't open. The elevator was on some floor high above her head and would take its own sweet time getting down here. She didn't have much time.

"Oh, God," she whispered when the realization hit her.

It was already too late.

Her skin began to prickle, her hair standing on end, her whole body going on red alert. Because she felt the presence, the weight of something pushing against her like a thick cloud of warm air. She wasn't crazy, she wasn't imagining things; someone else was here now.

Right behind her.

"Who are you?" she asked, somehow finding a reserve of calm deep within her. She was able to shove away the instinctive revulsion those whispered words had caused in her and realize what was going on here.

No man was stalking her. Something else was.

She didn't bother to turn around. She didn't need to look, because there was nothing to see. All her eyes would show her was empty parking lot. The presence behind her didn't have shape or form here, she understood that now.

It only had voice.

O-liiiii-via . . . I'm sorry I told him to do that to you.

The truth leapt into her brain, and a name came to her lips. The wrong name. She didn't say it, instead uttering what she knew to be the right one. "Zachary?"

Sorry.

"I'm the one who's sorry." Tears formed in her eyes, spilling down her cheeks. Olivia clenched her hands together, lifting them to her face, tipping her forehead onto her fist. "I shouldn't have left without you." She'd regretted that decision ever since that night, never more so than yesterday when she'd seen, heard and felt exactly what that monster had put him through because he'd helped her escape.

The presence moved closer. She could feel it pushing harder against her back. The feeling was unlike anything she'd ever experienced, and she couldn't quite define it. Not solid but not purely a vapor, either. There was a tingling sensation and a hint of pressure. It felt as though the air itself had gained the barest whisper of mass, like tiny wildflower petals picked up and tossed about by a gust of wind.

Nor did she feel cold, as she'd always seen in the movies. This was warm, comforting, heartbreakingly tender. She suddenly had a vision: his ethereal form pressed up behind her, his skinny arms slipping around her waist and his cheek resting against her spine. A hug from beyond the grave, because he thought he needed to be forgiven.

"I forgive you, Zachary," she whispered. "I forgave you a long time ago. And I thank you. You saved me."

The warmth increased, the soft blanket of butterfly-light pressure spread even wider, as if he wanted to envelop her entire body. She had pleased him.

You need to save Jack.

Shame made her drop her head, her chin hitting her chest as her hair fell over her face. "I didn't save you. I'm so sorry for that."

I hafta go now. I think I can go now that they found me.

Found him? Found his bones?

My mama's waiting at the station. She's been waiting on me a long time.

"What station? Your mother's . . ."

She died a long time ago and she's been awful sad, but I'm pretty sure she'll be happy now that I can go, too. Bye, Olivia.

"Wait, Zachary!"

Don't forget, you have to save Jack. He'll be twelve soon. His time's almost up.

Her thoughts had been in a crazy whirl; she hadn't really been focusing on individual words, more on the experience as a whole. Part of her had listened, part of her had grieved, while yet another part had wondered if she'd completely lost her mind. But now certain things he'd said started to sink in.

She sucked in a shocked gasp. "Are you telling me there's another boy?"

The pressure lightened a little, as if he were pulling

away, diminishing, the substance and form he'd put together out of air melting apart. Then one final whisper in her brain.

There's always another boy.

Her stomach clenched. She thought she'd be sick. Especially as he continued to pull away, and she found herself missing the comforting warmth, the delicate weight of him against her body. "Wait, Zachary. Please, you have to tell me more!"

There was no answer, nothing but silence. The air grew more buoyant, that pressing sensation having disappeared completely. Noises started to return: the whirring of the elevator equipment, the ding as it reached her floor, the throaty hum of traffic on the street above her. All of which told her one thing: Zachary had finally moved on.

Gabe knew as soon as he saw Olivia's face that something was wrong.

He'd arrived a couple of minutes ago, had been standing with Julia Harrington at the reception desk in their darkened office suite, when he heard the elevator doors open in the hallway. He'd glanced toward them, taken one look at Olivia, who was wide-eyed and pale, and his heart had leapt into his throat.

"What happened?" he asked, rushing toward her.

"I need to talk to Julia," she insisted.

"I'm here, honey," the woman said, taking Olivia's arm and helping him lead her into the office. The three of them went to a leather sofa in the waiting area, the women sitting down, Gabe squatting down in front of Olivia.

She looked strange. Upset, yes, but not afraid. Or even worried. In fact, judging by the frown tugging at her brow and the twist on her mouth, he'd have to call her mood determined.

"What is it?" Julia asked.

Olivia responded with a question of her own, which surprised them both. "When Morgan first came around, could you see him? Or did you just hear him?"

Julia didn't even hesitate at the strange question. She merely answered it: "I saw him, but later I realized I'd been hearing him for quite a while. He'd been talking to me in my head; I thought his whispers were my memories of him talking."

"Who is this Morgan?" Gabe asked. He'd been curious since yesterday, when he'd heard this Morgan guy had seen Gabe carry Liv into her house.

Olivia's boss cast him a quick sideways look, replying, "Morgan Raines. He was my partner on the Charleston PD."

Oh, right. She'd been on the job. Gabe had known that, but he'd forgotten. He suddenly began to feel a little bad about being so hard on her.

"Morgan's been dead for almost eight years," the woman added.

Which pretty much made the "feeling bad" thing dissipate. He had a sudden urge to stick his fingers in his ears and sing "La la la" in order to drown out the conversation. God help him, he was getting in so far over his head that he couldn't even see the surface of the water anymore.

Olivia licked her lips and nodded. "Have you ever, uh, *felt* him? Morgan, I mean?"

The brunette blinked, then shifted in her seat, looking uncomfortable for the first time since he'd met her. Which led Gabe to believe he really didn't want to hear her answer, because he suspected he'd thereafter be hearing "Unchained Melody" and picturing Patrick Swayze and Demi Moore having ghost sex. The very idea made him rise to his feet and walk over to the reception desk, lean against it and cross his arms over his chest.

"I'm sorry," Olivia said. "It doesn't matter. The point is, I did. I felt him."

Julia's jaw dropped open. "Morgan?"

"No!" Looking at Gabe with eyes that pleaded with him to believe her, she explained, "The boy. Zachary. I . . . he . . . I couldn't see him, but I heard him. And I could, I don't know, feel him there with me, like I was draped in a warm blanket made of air."

"Yes," Julia said, sounding shocked. "That's how it is. Where? When did this happen?"

"A few minutes ago, down in the garage. Though, I suspect he tried to connect with me yesterday at my house. Something happened right before I came down to meet with you all."

Julia suddenly stiffened, her eyes widening. "Oh, my God! Morgan told me about this."

"About what?" Olivia asked.

"He told me the other day that somebody like *him* was trying to get to you."

Olivia was shaking her head, still visibly shocked by whatever had happened down in the garage. "Why? How could this happen? I've never had any kind of encounter with a ghost."

"According to Morgan, there are plenty around. They stay; others depart right away."

"Via some sort of station?"

"Yes!" Julia clapped her hands together, smiling. "Oh, God, it's so wonderful to finally have somebody to talk to about this."

Olivia didn't look like she considered it wonderful. More confusing and nerve-racking. "Has Morgan ever explained it to you? How it works, why you can see him?"

"Well, I know he stayed because he was worried about me and because he wanted—still wants—to help catch the people who had him killed."

Gabe couldn't deny being interested by that statement. If he were to die in the line of duty, and if there really were an afterlife, he'd probably want the same thing. Justice, even if it was from beyond the grave.

"I think I heard him and eventually could see him, because I was with him when he died. I shared his final moments."

Olivia shook her head slowly. "I wasn't there when Zachary died."

Julia reached over and covered Olivia's hand tenderly, offering her warmth but also, Gabe thought, lending her strength for what she was about to say. "Liv, honey, don't you see? You might not have been there, but you actually lived his death. You experienced it with him."

Olivia let out a long, slow breath, thinking about that. Gabe could only imagine what was going through her mind—probably the first thing that had popped into his.

She'd lived a lot of people's deaths. A whole lot.

"If it's any help, I don't think anybody else has ever, um, tried to reach you before," Julia said. "Morgan told me right away about this one, and I'm pretty sure he'd know. I bet the rest just moved on. This boy, though, felt he had a reason to stay."

"I don't think he could leave," Olivia whispered, sounding terribly weary and sad. "Not until his remains were found." Then she looked up at Gabe, pushing her sadness aside, getting back to business. Important business. "Zachary told me some things you need to know."

Part of him—the traditional, rational part that didn't believe in woo-woo stuff—wanted to walk out of there so he didn't have to admit the woman he was majorly attracted to had just said she'd had a chat with a ghost. Another part, the Gabe who had watched her put herself through such hell yesterday, then asked him to stay with her and watch her sleep afterward, couldn't do it. He couldn't let her down like that, couldn't say, even without words, that he thought she was imagining things.

Which was, of course, the first thing he'd thought. Old habits died hard, and it wasn't going to be easy for him to let go of his instinctive skepticism overnight. First sharing someone else's death memories, now ghosts? Lord, wouldn't his grandfather be cackling right now at the thought of how off the reservation Gabe had gone with his thinking in just a few days' time. At this rate, he'd be out of a job by the end of the week. Taking up with psychics, letting one of them handle evidence? What the hell was he doing? If he had any sense at all, he'd put an end to this right now, walk out the door and go back to a normal life and a normal murder investigation.

Unfortunately, he didn't seem to have much sense when it came to the green-eyed redhead watching him with trepidation, waiting for him to either tell her he believed her or else break her heart.

You know you believed her yesterday. Why is it so hard to accept this?

Besides which, he'd been raised in the church. If he believed in the spirit—the soul—why was it so crazy to think that occasionally spirits outstayed their welcomes?

"Why don't you tell us what happened?" he asked, not exactly giving her what she wanted but not refusing to, either.

She did as he asked, but there wasn't much to tell. An apology, a moment of penance with a boy she felt she owed . . . whose brush with the afterlife wouldn't include that?

But then she said something that floored him.

"The worst thing is, Gabe, I think this monster has another little boy, right now. And that his time might be running out."

Gabe straightened, dropping his arms to his sides. He had not told Olivia anything about Sue-Ann Bowles's visit, or the possible conclusion both he and Ty had reached because of it. "Why do you say that?" he asked, keeping his voice low.

"Zachary told me, twice, that I needed to save Jack. The second time he mentioned that he was almost twelve and his time was running out."

Gabe thought he managed to keep the shock off his face. But maybe not.

How could she possibly know that? Thanks to Mrs. Bowles, he and Ty had already realized the age of twelve seemed to be some personal trigger point for the man they were dealing with. But no way could Olivia know.

"At first, I thought he was talking about himself, but then I realized he wasn't. He would never call himself Jack, not considering the last words he said on this earth."

Julia blew out an audible breath. "We have to assume the monster who kidnapped him is the one who changed his name."

"Exactly," Olivia replied. "So maybe he did it again, kidnapped another boy to use as a slave and is calling this one Jack, too, for some twisted reason."

They were going on the assumption that there were only two victims, while Gabe knew there could very well be at least four. It was time for him to bring them up to speed on that, and he would, as soon as Ty and the others arrived. Ty was bringing all the information he'd already dug up on missing boys; he'd spent much of yesterday morning working on it.

Gabe suspected it was a good thing he had. Whether a ghost had told her or not—and, honestly, he couldn't come up with any other explanation right now—he already believed Olivia's theory that the man who'd tried to murder her had not been killed by police. And, frankly, a man who'd kidnap a boy and a teenage girl and then drown them both wasn't the type of leopard who'd change his spots.

Of course he would do it again. Having gotten away with it the first time, the whole world thinking the perp was dead, what on earth was there to stop him?

We're going to stop him. Too late to help Sue-Ann Bowles's son or the Durkee boy. But hopefully not too late to save this latest "Jack" he was holding captive now.

Before he could say that, he heard his cell phone ring and pulled it out of his pocket. Seeing the Atlanta area code, he caught Olivia's eye. "I think this might be your FBI agent friend."

She nodded. "Please tell him I said hello."

Julia pointed toward an open door, which looked like it led into a shadowy conference room. "You can go in there and talk."

"Thanks." He headed for the door, not because he didn't trust the two women to hear the conversation but because he wanted to be able to listen closely to what the man said without being interrupted by every new arrival.

"This is Detective Cooper," he said, answering on the third ring. He pushed the door shut behind him and flipped on a light, then sat in one of the chairs circling the large conference table.

"Special Agent Steven Ames here, Detective," the man said. He had a deep voice, gruff, and sounded older. Olivia had once mentioned he'd been fatherly toward her at the time of her kidnapping, which had been more than a decade ago, so he figured this guy was probably at least in his fifties by now.

Gabe apologized for having missed the man's calls yesterday, not telling him it was because he'd been busy watching Olivia go through her psychic nightmare.

"No problem. It gave me a chance to check out the

crime wires from Savannah. I suspect you're calling about the remains found in that bar fire. Was it him? Was it Jack?"

Impressive that the man remembered so much about the case. "Yeah, looks like it."

"How's Livvie taking it?"

"About like you'd expect." He had already decided to lay it on the line with Ames, since the man had worked this case long before Gabe had ever heard of it—or, at least, aspects of this case. "The thing is, Agent Ames, the evidence we've come up with so far doesn't really fit in with the story everyone has settled on from that night."

A beat. Then Ames murmured, "It wasn't Collier."

"No, sir, I don't believe it was. I think it's likely he was sent on an errand to pick up the money, but the real kidnapper got away."

"I never thought that son of a bitch was smart enough to pull this off, at least not without some inside help."

"How smart did he have to be to grab a helpless girl and lock her in a barn?" he asked, hearing his own barely subdued anger. The ease with which that monster had intruded on Olivia's life, completely upsetting it, changing her future, her family, everything, simply infuriated him.

"You might be surprised. See, at the time, I was having a hard time figuring out a couple of things. Why he'd wait so many hours to try for the ransom money. Guess he was busy."

Walling up a child's body perhaps.

"How the bastard disabled the security system was another big question," the agent added.

"There was an alarm?" he asked, not having noticed that in the file.

"Uh-huh. He broke in through a small window in the laundry room, one of the few that wasn't wired—guess they thought it was too small."

"Did you think, later, after Olivia told you about Jack . . ."

"That maybe he had the boy climb in, then open the closest door for him? Makes sense."

Yes. It did. Tragic sense.

"However it went down, he got in and found the main control panel inside the pantry of this huge old house on a dark, moonless night, probably without turning any lights on. And he disabled the alarm so none of the motion detectors would go off as he went upstairs to the girls' side of the house."

Picturing the scene, Gabe felt sick. Liv and Brooke had been so young, so vulnerable. If he ever had kids, which wasn't something he pictured easily, not given his own childhood, he definitely wouldn't have them sleeping farther than screaming distance from his own room. And his shotgun. He didn't doubt Olivia's parents loved their children, but the rich sometimes had strange ideas about how to spend their money. Living in humongous houses that separated you from your loved ones wasn't his idea of smart.

"Did Livvie tell you how he got her not to scream?" Ames asked.

"I read it in the file." Standard operating procedure for maniacs. "He threatened to kill her sister."

"Yep. So she didn't make a sound, he knocked her out, then carried her right down the stairs and outside. All without anybody hearing a thing."

Gabe mulled it over, realizing right away why Ames had been disturbed by the whole scenario. It sure didn't sound like the work of some punk whose previous crimes hadn't included anything worse than petty theft, a few drug violations, and drunk and disorderly. Something like this would have taken planning and steel nerves, neither of which was usually associated with drunks or drug abusers.

"Then there was the fact that he took her at all. The Wainwrights are rich, no doubt about it, but they're not the richest people in Savannah by a long shot. The house is out in the boonies, and any criminal slimeball would know they had gates and alarms, plus servants. So why go to all that trouble when you could just as easily stalk and snatch some superrich debutante trying to piss off Daddy by hanging out at a sleazy club on Abercorn?"

A very good question. What had drawn the monster's eye to the Wainwrights? To Olivia? Kidnapping for profit wasn't really that common a crime, not in this area, at any rate. So what had put the big bull's-eye on her?

"Did you ever suspect anybody else?"

"Well, I sure was thinking inside job, if that's what you're asking."

Gabe whistled. It hadn't been. But now that Ames mentioned it . . . "And?"

"Between the night she was taken and the night Collier was killed picking up the ransom, we practically shone flashlights up the assholes of every handyman, maid, repairman, deliveryman, florist, gardener, caterer or friend who was in that house during the previous six months. We'd barely made a dent when the word came in that she'd been found."

Suspecting he already knew the answer, Gabe asked, "You wouldn't happen to still have the names of those folks, would you?"

The other man laughed. "Does a wicked old man sin on Saturday nights and pray on Sundays? Hell, yes, I do."

Liking the agent more and more, Gabe gave him his e-mail address and asked him to send the list as soon as possible.

"Will do. And, Detective, if you're right, I sure hope you get this bastard. It never sat right with me, us not finding that boy." He cleared his throat. "I'm damn sorry to hear he was killed."

"You and me both, Agent Ames. Thanks for the help."

Though Johnny Traynor wasn't fool enough to ever spend the ransom money and didn't make a whole lot at his day job, he did have a fair amount of cash at his disposal. That was because of his special jobs, the contract work he did on behalf of other people who didn't have the brains, the balls, or the entrepreneurial spirit to do them themselves.

He really shouldn't do that type of work anymore—he knew that. Interacting with other people in any of his illegal activities could be dangerous. Accomplices meant witnesses.

It could also, however, be lucky. Just look at what had happened when he'd paid a loser fifty bucks to go pick up the ransom money for that Wainwright bitch all those years ago. If Johnny hadn't hired him, he, himself, might have been the one killed by the cops.

"Sneaky little whore," he mumbled under his breath, feeling sick thinking of her. What a mess she'd made of things, running away like that, forcing him to pull up stakes and move before he was ready, just a couple of steps ahead of the law. Lucky for him, most cops were so stupid they couldn't find their own heads if they weren't wearing a hat. After they shot down that Collier fella, it'd taken 'em hours to get out to the old barn. He'd been long gone.

Still, they weren't the ones he truly hated. She was.

Because she'd tried to take Jack away from him.

She hadn't succeeded, o'course. His boy was just fine, out here enjoying the sunshine with his daddy, the way every boy should on a beautiful Sunday mornin'.

That didn't mean him and the little whore were

square. He always knew that bill would come due some-day, and she'd have to pay it. That was why he'd kept tabs on her over the years.

He'd thought about going back and taking care of her and had desperately wanted to. But he was a man of his word. He'd promised his accomplice he'd stay away from the girl, agreeing that killing her might bring too much unwanted attention. The police thought her kidnapper was dead; why get anybody sniffing around, wondering if her murder today had anything to do with what happened back then? He'd been biding his time, waiting till nobody would even remember she'd ever been snatched. Then he could strike. Promise or no promise.

He could reach out and get to her anytime he wanted to. Hell, this very week she'd been practically under his nose.

He'd been cutting her next-door neighbor's lawn for the past couple of years, hadn't he?

She'd seen him hundreds of times—had come within two feet of him a few weeks ago when that damn cat of hers got out—yet she'd never recognized him. Never spared him much of a glance at all. Most rich sluts like her didn't, looking down their nose at quiet, hard-working old Lenny, who'd been cutting lawns in Savannah for more than a decade. He was invisible to them yet had a respectable, normal life that allowed him to blend in, even if he did have to live it under an assumed name. Everybody knew him as Lenny; very few people had any idea he'd been born Johnny Traynor or that him and his cousin was raised in the same foster home after their mamas got killed in a car wreck.

His foster parents had been the first two people Johnny had killed.

With good reason.

In one way, Johnny hated the Wainwright bitch for

not recognizing him. In another, he was glad, not to mention proud of what a fine job he'd done holding that girl if she'd never gotten one decent look at him.

That might not matter. If she gets in our business, we're gonna have to kill her right away. And she's tryin' that. Why else would she be talkin' to the po-lice?

Vicious, lying whore. She hadn't fallen far off the tree, that was for sure. Her parents were equally as rotten. Buncha untrustworthy, double-dealing scumbags as far as he was concerned. He shoulda known that hers wouldn't be an easy ransom job, that the family would get the police and the FBI involved. He'd been told that they wouldn't, *promised* that they wouldn't, but they had. You couldn't trust nobody nowadays.

"Except people who are just as guilty as you are," he mumbled, chuckling.

The only reason he trusted the people who hired him for his special projects was because they, too, were up to their necks in whatever crimes they paid him to carry out. He'd kept more than one of them in line over the years by reminding them of that fact, though most times they'd parted ways amicably, pleased with the results of their dealings. Which was why he was still in the murder-for-hire or occasionally kidnap-for-hire business.

Business was good.

So good, he had about fifty thousand dollars cash tucked away in a safety deposit box, left there in case of emergency or if he needed a quick getaway. Now, for the first time in a while, he was thinking about raiding that cash for something else: a birthday present for Jack.

Nothin' too fancy—a good boy didn't need much more than a fishing pole to entertain himself, not that there was any water near the camper. But someday he might take Jackie out to hook a catfish or two. So a rod and reel would be good. And maybe a baseball bat, a nice, heavy wooden one, the kind that still cracked when it connected with the sweet spot, not those pussy aluminum ones that didn't do much more than *tink*.

He'd like that, a fishing pole and a baseball bat. What boy wouldn't want those things for his tenth birthday?

Twelfth. He's gonna be twelve.

No, that wasn't right. A man oughta know how old his own son was, oughtn't he?

Confused, he put down his knife, which he'd been using to scrape the dirt and damp grass out of the soles of his work boots, and called, "Jackie-boy? You excited about your birthday this week?"

The boy, who'd been washing some clothes with jugs of water in a big washtub outside the camper, lifted his head and pushed his floppy hair off his face with a sudsy hand. "It is?"

"Course it is!" he snapped. "You stupid or somethin'?"

The boy swallowed, hard. "Uh, I don't know what month it is; we ain't got no calendar."

Johnny got mad at himself. The boy hadn't been saying he forgot his own birthday; he just didn't know the date. Hell, in Georgia, all summer months were so damn hot, who could be expected to know June from August? "Today's August fourteenth. And your birthday's the sixteenth. That's only two days away."

The boy remained silent, watching, wide-eyed.

"How old you gonna be again?" Johnny asked, reaching up to scratch behind his ear with the handle of the knife.

"Well, I guess if my birthday's this week, I'm gonna be twelve, sir. Last year, on my birthday, you gave me eleven whole dollars 'cause I was eleven."

That was right. How had he forgotten that? Or, had he not forgotten? Maybe Jack was trickin' him.

It's true. I told you. Twelve. The bad year. The dirty, lying, cheating year.

Johnny stared hard at his son. "You sure?"

Jack nodded quickly, then ducked back to finish the wash, which, for some reason, irritated him badly. Why did the boy have to be so squirrelly? So timid? Johnny rarely hit him; it wasn't like he had it so tough.

His anger grew. Here he'd been thinking about doin' something nice for the boy for his birthday, and this was how he was repaid?

"Little whiny bastard," he muttered under his breath.

"Huh?"

"Shut up. I wasn't talkin' to you," he snapped. Then, for good measure, he flung the knife from his hand. It spun through the air—Johnny had always been good at knife throwing—and plunged into the dirt a few feet from the boy, blade down.

Jack shrieked with fear, and he jerked so hard, he fell back into the wash water with a loud *ker-splash*. It was quite a comical sight. The boy looked like a drowned pup, dirty, gray soap bubbles dripping down his chin and his clothes all sopping wet.

Johnny couldn't help it. He slapped his hand on his knee and proceeded to laugh until he was fit to bust. Jack, who'd been terrified a minute ago and who now looked on the verge of tears, finally smiled weakly. Then a little more, until at last he laughed, too.

A man and his boy laughin' together in the sunshine, was there anything better? In Johnny Traynor's opinion, it was moments like these that made bein' a father just about the most beautiful thing in the world.

"Now, son," he said, once the hilarity was done, "what should we do for your birthday?"

Chapter 10

So far, the joint task force of two Savannah detectives, plus the owner and three agents from eXtreme Investigations, seemed to be going pretty well. Sitting around the large conference room table, Olivia had to take a moment to be thankful for the presence of every other person in the room. They were here for her. She knew that.

Oh, sure, Gabe and his partner were doing their job. But they were here, in this office, working with her and Julia, and Mick and Derek, because they had faith in her and believed what she'd had to say. Or at least believed it enough to do some further investigating.

She wasn't stupid. She knew it had been a big stretch for Gabe to accept what she'd told him about what had happened down in the parking garage. It had been an even bigger shock for his partner. Yet both of them had set aside their own skepticism and attacked the case as if the information she'd provided had come from a live witness rather than a dead one.

Probably the most shocking thing about this meeting, for Olivia, anyway, was when Gabe had finally shared *everything* he knew with her and with everyone else.

For a second, when he'd told them about the visit from that grieving mother, Sue-Ann Bowles, Olivia had felt a flare of anger rise within her. Gabe had kept this from her, not saying one damn thing about the possibility of there being another boy at risk right now.

But her anger hadn't lasted for long. It didn't take a brain surgeon to understand that trust didn't come easy for him. He was opening up, little by little, but he was a long way from the kind of man who would put forth conjecture and theory in place of cold, hard facts.

She respected him for that.

That didn't mean she wasn't still reeling from his revelation. Olivia still couldn't quite believe it. That psychopath hadn't killed only Jack; he might have gone on to kill two other boys? *With another one out there, perhaps with only weeks or days to live?*

The idea revolted her, and she was sure of only one thing: No matter what happened, no matter what this ragtag group managed to uncover together, Olivia would not give up until that monster was caught and every little boy was safe from his brutal hands.

"So, that's it, then? We've gone over all the details and everyone has the game plan?" asked Julia, leaning back in her chair. She was sitting on the opposite side of the table, having offered the head position to Gabe, subtly reminding everyone in the room who was in charge. Julia might be a bulldozer, but she did have some tact.

"I think so," said Gabe. He glanced at his partner. "Ty's going to take Mick over to the evidence graveyard and try to dig out whatever's left from Olivia's kidnapping case."

"After that," Ty said, "I'm going back to the station to weed out these missing kids cases a little more. Looking for a boy with the first name Zachary."

"Plus a deceased mother," Olivia said.

Ty, who she was really starting to like, if only for the great smile and the cute way he kept trying to slip Southern expressions into his decidedly non-Southern vocabulary, nodded. "I tell you, I think we might be able to get somewhere now."

She would bet he'd rather go back to the precinct and

get to work on that list immediately rather than escort Mick to the evidence lockup. Then again, considering how fascinated he'd looked by Mick's teacup performance, maybe not.

Gabe turned his attention toward Derek, who was, as usual, sitting a little apart from the group, over by the window. Though a good guy, Derek was a bit of a lone wolf. He definitely looked the part, right down to the faded jeans, the tight black T-shirt, the engineer boots and the chain looping from his belt to his back pocket. With the clothes, the motorcycle, his longish hair and unshaven face, he looked more like the kind of guy the police would be investigating rather than one who'd be helping with an investigation. His attitude usually didn't help matters, either.

Surprisingly, though, he'd been pretty receptive to this whole working-together idea. Normally, Derek didn't play well with others. Olivia had never had any problems with him, except for the fact that he was a little irritable on occasion, but he and Julia had gone toe-to-toe a few times. And she knew Mick's sense of humor sometimes grated on his nerves. Despite that, they all still respected one another, which was why he stayed.

That was a good thing; Derek was incredibly gifted.

"Julia and Derek are going out to the site of the old barn where Liv was held to see if there's anything left to find," Gabe said, "and to do whatever else it is they're going to do."

Olivia knew what they were going to do. Derek—dark, dangerous-looking Derek—had a good eye. A really good one. In fact, it was so good, he was able to see the imprint a violent death left on the world. Not cognizant ghosts, like the one Julia saw. *Or the one I spoke with?* These were more like photocopies: It wasn't real; it was Memorex.

If anybody else had been killed around that barn,

Derek would see an imprint of it. Not who did it— he only saw the victims. Still, the knowledge of exactly where and how somebody had died could be very important. He'd give the information to Julia, and she would give it to Morgan, who would leave for a while, then come back with some useful tidbits. Like whether the person who'd died was still "lurking around" somewhere, or if he or she was beyond his reach.

For the first time, she wondered where Morgan got those tidbits and where those spirits lurked. Did he go to the station Zachary had mentioned? And what was it, some kind of railroad depot between this world and the hereafter?

Sometimes she wished she had been left with some memories of what had happened during the two minutes and ten seconds she'd been dead. Had she gone to that station? Been unable to afford the fare? Missed her train? What?

"And Olivia and I," Gabe said, looking her in the eye as if he realized she'd been drifting, "will go over the names Agent Ames e-mailed me, find out what those people are up to now and see if we can come up with another possible suspect."

"I'll do my best," she told him, though she knew her parents should probably be the ones to help him with that list. She might remember some of the names, but she wouldn't recall them all. But she still didn't want her parents to know any of this was happening, not until it was absolutely necessary. Bad enough that Brooke had gotten sucked into this.

Olivia had promised to call her sister this morning to let Brooke know what was happening. As much as she hated to admit it, Olivia figured Brooke might be able to help. "Brooke was pretty young, but she was at the house during the days I was missing. She might recognize some of the names I don't."

"Want me to go pick her up?" asked Ty, with a quick, suggestive lift of his eyebrows.

Interesting. It appeared the handsome detective had a mild crush on her baby sister. She only wondered whether Brooke had noticed and what she thought of it. Considering Brooke was engaged, she probably wasn't interested. But considering she was engaged to a jackass . . . Olivia couldn't help hoping maybe she was.

"You need to go with Mick," Gabe told his partner, rising to his feet.

Everyone else followed suit, exchanging phone numbers and other information, then leaving two by two. Meanwhile, Olivia made a quick call to her sister, who promised to come in immediately, sounding excited at being involved. Olivia only hoped that excitement didn't get Brooke into any kind of trouble—with her fiancé or anyone else.

Soon, Olivia and Gabe were alone in the silent conference room, alone for the first time since last night. He stood at the head of the table, a few feet away, busy reading over some paperwork, and she took a long moment to stare at him: the masculine profile, the perfect mouth, the strong, slightly stubbled jaw.

Memories of how it had felt to taste him, to touch him, washed over her. Her fingers tingled as she remembered touching that flat stomach, rippling with muscle. Oh, had she wanted to keep touching him. All over.

A sensation that was part awkwardness and part anticipation slipped through her. She'd been wondering since last night if he'd kissed her back strictly because he felt sorry for her and because she'd practically leapt on top of him. God, she hoped not. She didn't know what she would do if she found out this intense attraction was strictly one-sided.

There was one way to find out, she supposed. "So, about what happened yesterday . . ."

"At the coroner's office?" he asked, immediately frowning.

"No, uh, afterward. In my room."

Unfortunately, his frown didn't ease up by much. "Yeah," he said, not meeting her eye, "I'm sorry about that."

"I'm not," she said with a simple shrug.

He turned slightly away from her, busying himself with the files, opening them and spreading some lists out on the table.

"Hello? Did you just drop out of this conversation?"

"I didn't know we were having one."

She walked around the table and pushed a chair out of the way so she could stand toe-to-toe with him. "Well, we are. I'd like to know what you're thinking."

He thrust his hand through his hair as if frustrated, then asked, "You want the truth?"

"I would prefer it, yes."

"Okay, truth. I think we should forget it ever happened. Last night was great. I loved hanging out with you, getting to know you. But what happened in your room . . ."

"So you'll be my friend, you just don't want to kiss me."

He blew out a hard breath. "Kissing you—that was a mistake."

Olivia paused, letting herself process that, not reacting immediately. Ghosts in parking garages notwithstanding, she was a pretty calm, deliberate person. She didn't like to make snap judgments and preferred to analyze the reasons for things that happened.

He'd said, "It was a mistake." Not "I wish I hadn't kissed you," or "I didn't enjoy it."

Which didn't necessarily mean he *did* wish he hadn't kissed her, and she would lay money he *had* enjoyed it. The way he wouldn't meet her eye told her that much.

So if he had liked it but didn't want to repeat it, there had to be a reason. "Is it because of who I am?"

He didn't answer right away and still wouldn't look at her, preferring to shuffle papers from one corner of the table to another. Which was answer enough.

She stepped back, hurt—devastated, actually—but determined not to show it. Her grandmother would have been proud as the unemotional, aloof, proper Southerner in her responded, "Well, thank you for being so candid." Then, to her annoyance, the emotional, non-aloof, nonproper woman seized her vocal cords. "I mean, it's not like it's the first time my freak quotient has driven a man away."

His jaw dropped, and his green eyes flashed. Gabe grabbed her upper arms, forcing her to remain still. He pressed closer, so close one thick jean-clad leg slid between her legs, bare under her summery skirt. The contact made her a little weak in the knees.

"Don't ever say such a thing again. It's got nothing to do with that."

"You just said . . ."

"I said it was because of *who* you are, not *what* you do."

He wasn't making sense. "And who am I, other than the weird psychic investigator who gets her jollies by repeatedly getting murdered?"

"Damn it, Olivia," he said, his fingers tightening on her arms. Not painfully, just providing evidence of his frustration. "I meant your name. You're a Wainwright, a senator's cousin, for Christ's sake."

"Not by choice, believe me," she muttered.

He ignored her. "You live in a house that's about ten times bigger than my condo."

Relief suddenly washed over her. It was about the money, the difference in their backgrounds. She found such things ridiculous in this day and age but knew others did not, especially in the South. Gabe didn't seem like the type who would be bothered by such things. But if he was, she needed to make him understand that just because she'd been raised a certain way didn't mean she had the same lifestyle now. "I live in that house not because I could afford to buy it but because my grandmother left it to me."

He rolled his eyes and dropped his hands, freeing her arms. His eyes flashed, and she suddenly realized that had been the wrong thing to say.

"Want to know what I stand to inherit from my grandfather, my only living relative? Nothing but the strap he used to beat me with."

She froze, hearing in that one sentence so much more than he had probably meant to say. Her heart ached, and a sudden hot anger flashed through her to think of him being treated that way by anyone, especially somebody who was supposed to love him. What the hell was the matter with this world, anyway? "He's still alive then?"

"He's too mean to die," he muttered.

"And your parents?"

Sounding weary, as if he wished he hadn't opened this can of worms, he rubbed his hand over his jaw and admitted, "I never knew my father. My mama died when I was a kid. It was just me and the old man, living in a farm shack for a whole lotta years."

She didn't even want to picture it, wondering how on earth this thoughtful, kindhearted man could have turned out to be so good after being raised in those circumstances. Talk about rising above your past. He was living proof that determination and a good soul could triumph over adversity. Of course, she'd witnessed that once before. Poor little Jack—Zachary—had been raised by a monster yet had saved her life.

Unable to resist, needing to connect with Gabe, she lifted a hand and brushed it against his face in a simple gesture of tenderness and empathy. His cheek felt a bit rough—he hadn't shaved today—and the result was a sexy, sandpapery feeling. An image flashed through her mind, and she wondered what that hint of roughness would feel like against her skin—her neck, her breasts. Elsewhere.

He allowed it for a moment. Then he turned away from her, his jaw as stiff as granite. "Look, Olivia, I'm not playing the poor-little-poor-kid card here, okay? I'm fine. I have a good life, and I'm happy with it. But the point remains, you and me, with our histories, our backgrounds? We're worlds apart."

"Yes, of course, because my life's been so utterly charmed," she murmured.

He lifted a hand and rubbed his eyes. "Hell, I'm sorry. That was a stupid thing to say."

She held up a hand to stop him. "Don't be. I wasn't saying it to play the poor-little-rich-girl card. I merely wanted to remind you that we have a lot more in common than you think." She stepped close again. This time, his back was to the table, and he couldn't evade her. "Okay, other than that, is there any particular reason you don't want me to kiss you again right now?"

"There is the fact that you're a witness."

"Come on, we're way past that point. Anything else?"

He eyed her warily. Opened his mouth. Then snapped it closed.

"I thought not."

She didn't ask, wasn't tentative about it, she simply looped her arms around his neck and pressed her body firmly against his. Leaning up on her toes, she brushed her mouth against his. Their lips met softly, tasting, caressing, and then widening so they could deepen the kiss.

Liv tilted her head, loving the way he started slowly sliding his tongue in and out of her mouth, tasting her, sharing each breath and making secret promises about how much pleasure he could give to her. Not that she had any doubt of that, not considering she felt weak and boneless yet still electrified and excited at the feel of his mouth on hers.

He slid his hands to her hips, cupping them, tugging her more firmly against his hard body. They lined up perfectly, her sensitive breasts scraping that brawny chest, the hollow in her thighs cupping his rising erection.

Olivia moaned, and he pulled his mouth away, sucking in a deep breath. She feared he was going to stop—*oh, God, please don't stop*—but instead he kissed his way down her jaw to her neck. He tasted her skin, sampling her in little nibbles all the way to the hollow of her throat, holding her in his strong hands as she leaned back to urge him on.

Tangling her fingers in his thick hair, she turned, drawing him with her, until her back was to the conference table. Gabe lifted her by the hips until she sat on the table's edge. He covered her mouth again, this time kissing her hard and deep, his tongue possessive and demanding. Olivia's legs shifted apart instinctively, and he stepped between them, and that was instinctive, too. Like he belonged there.

Oh, she wanted him to belong there, wanted him to stay there. Wanted him to pull off her clothes and make love to her right there, on top of the table. She wanted the pleasure of it, the eroticism of it, the wickedness of it. And the mindlessness, she wanted that, too. Wanted to forget everything else except how good and right it felt to be here, with him, like this.

As a knocking sound blasted through the cloud of hazy pleasure in her brain, however, she realized she wasn't going to get what she wanted.

He pulled away from her, lurching back, staring at her, breathing heavily. Olivia did the same, feeling breathless and dizzy.

Not so dizzy, though, that she didn't hear the voice calling from the hall outside the office suite. "Livvie? It's me, Brooke. Come let me in!"

Gabe straightened, shook his head, adjusted his jeans, then muttered, "That sister of yours. She's got some timing."

Indeed she did. But at least this time she'd knocked.

Though the old barn that had once served as a prison for a young girl had been torn down at some point over the years, Julia and Derek didn't expect to have any trouble finding the spot on which it had once stood.

Using GPS and police reports from the case, they made their way through the thick woods and scrub. Typical of Georgia, the woods ranged from dry and piney, to boggy and wet, to tangled and thick, with old, creaking oaks and wild plum trees. And moss, everywhere the moss, which some thought was pretty but which most locals knew was a virus, a blight on the landscape. Julia loathed the stuff; it looked like big clumps of witch's hair strewn over everything.

There had been no real road, just the hint of a path. Maybe even the same one the kidnapper had used to haul his camper back here, with a dozen years' added growth. It would have been hard to spot now, maybe even more so then, if someone had taken pains to conceal it.

"Almost there," she said, tapping him on the back. Julia rode behind Derek on his motorcycle, clinging to his broad back, her legs locked around his lean hips.

Not an unfamiliar position, actually.

Ducking a low-hanging branch, she found herself glad for the helmet, which had probably spared her from a nasty scratch. She'd thought that at least they might have a respite from the brutal heat here in the shade. But the trees overhead merely locked in the hot air and humidity until it felt like they were in the bowels of an enormous greenhouse. Oppressive didn't begin to describe it.

She spotted their intended destination first, pointing to a few remaining boards and the hint of a foundation on the ground. "There it is," she said, leaning close and raising her voice to be heard over the whistling wind and the motor.

Nodding once, Derek stopped the bike about ten yards away, skidding a little in the dirt. Julia took it in stride, not worrying that they'd fall over. Derek knew how to handle his machine; he just liked to live dangerously, to walk on the edge.

Cutting the engine, he pulled off his helmet. Julia did the same, then stepped off the bike. Her legs shook a little, the vibration of the powerful machine seeming to have seeped into her limbs. "Do you see it?" she asked.

When he didn't reply, she glanced at him and realized he wasn't looking toward the remnants of the old barn at all. He wasn't even pretending to listen to her, his avid attention focused to the left, where there was another small clearing. Perhaps where the camper had stood?

"Jesus," he whispered, the word sounding like it had come from a tight, dry throat.

That was when she knew their trip out here had been worthwhile.

He cleared his throat, took a deep breath that made his broad chest move, then turned his head about thirty degrees to the left. He stared intently at nothing that she could see, still and silent as the grave. Then came another quarter turn of the head. Now she could see his face clearly, noting the blaze of anger in his dark brown eyes and the disgusted twist of his lips.

Oh, yeah. They'd hit pay dirt.

"How many?" she asked, not sure she wanted to know.

"Three so far."

Three people murdered in this small, innocent-looking patch of woods. And those were just the ones Derek could see from here on the bike.

What a strange world he must live in and how cautiously he had to tread in it. Derek never knew when he rounded a corner if he was going to be presented with the violent images of a phantom body flying through a car windshield or someone being flung back after being shot in the chest. Deaths happened everywhere. The quiet ones eluded his sight, but the violent ones, oh, they left their mark.

"Are you all right?" she asked.

"Yeah, fine." Shaking his head as if to clear it, Derek finally turned to look at the ruins of the old barn, which she'd pointed out to him.

That didn't help. His whole body stiffened, his head jerked and a small groan emerged from his throat before he muttered, "Well fuck me."

"What is it?"

"It's Liv," he said, his deep voice not much more than a whisper. "Young. Just a kid. But it's her, no doubt about it."

Shocked, Julia followed his stare, even though she knew she'd see nothing.

But Derek definitely did. He was focused on what had once been the side of the barn. Where, she knew from hearing Olivia's story, there had once stood a large barrel full of water. His eyes were narrowed, his teeth clenched, judging by the stiffness of his jaw, but he wouldn't look away.

"I don't understand. She's not dead," Julia said, confused, as she often was by the abilities of these people she worked with day in and day out.

"No, but she was," he replied evenly, not a hint of doubt in his voice. "Remember, these aren't ghosts, they're visible memories of violent deaths. She might have been brought back, but I'm telling you, I am watching her being murdered . . ." He lifted a hand and pointed. " . . . right over there."

The horror of it hit her: Olivia was someone he knew, someone he worked with and liked. "Will you be able to focus in spite of that?" she asked. "I mean, is it going to stop?"

He finally dropped his hand, then turned his head to look at her. "No, it won't stop. It's like the world's most gruesome instant replay, a loop, happening over and over again."

His friend. Their friend. Being murdered. And he was the eternal witness.

Awful. Oh, God, it was so awful, she didn't know how he stood it. How did any of them stand it? Mick was exposed to every ugly thought that had crossed the minds of every person who'd touched anything he touched. Derek had to watch people die. Olivia kept getting murdered, for God's sake. And Aidan, though his psychic gift was slightly less brutal, was forced to feel helpless, getting impressions from people in trouble, knowing he couldn't always find them in time. Couldn't save them.

She wouldn't want to be them. Not for anything. She had her ghost, and that was enough.

Something suddenly occurred to her, and her heart skipped a beat. "Wait. If you can see Olivia and she's still alive, maybe those other people are, too!"

Derek simply stared at her, long and hard, silently asking her to think about what she'd just said. It did sound impossible. Olivia had survived because of the boy. But there was no way one boy could have saved them all.

Seeing her shoulders sag as she acknowledged that, Derek muttered, "I need to walk."

She knew he was experienced at this, that he'd dealt

with it all his life, but before he left, she still had to ask, "Are you sure you're okay?"

He nodded once. "Yeah. I'll be back in a little while."

He didn't wait for a response but simply walked away. Alone. Like always.

Except, of course, when he was in her bed.

Funny how well they'd gotten along there, though it hadn't happened very often and hadn't for quite a while. But their affair had been nice, the sex fantastic, the lack of expectations of anything more, on either side, great as well.

They'd eventually acknowledged how tricky it was to sleep with someone you worked with, especially since Julia was the boss. So it had ended. That had been a little poignant but not heartbreaking. Especially because they weren't in love with each other and knew they never would be. But every once in a while she found herself wishing Derek would find someone he *could* love and would come out of the self-imposed exile he seemed to have chosen.

"They're not, you know."

She jerked her attention from Derek's retreating back to the man she saw standing beside her. He'd waited until Derek was out of earshot, knowing that if he showed up sooner, she wouldn't talk to him.

When this whole thing had started eight years ago, she'd gotten her fill of looks from people who'd thought she was crazy, talking to herself or to thin air. So she'd laid down some ground rules, one being that she wouldn't even acknowledge Morgan if anybody else was around. He'd had a grand old time doing crazy stuff in the periphery of her vision, trying to distract her, but had found her a tough nut to crack. Finally, he'd relented.

"Who's not what?" she asked.

"They're not still alive."

Oh, hell. If anybody would know, it would be him. "Are you sure?"

He nodded. "Yeah. Because they're all still here."

She caught her bottom lip, looking around. "You mean ..."

"Uh-huh. Not what your *friend* is seeing. The real deal."

Morgan didn't particularly like Derek, he'd made that clear before, though she wasn't entirely sure why. Maybe he knew about the affair, maybe not. Julia had never mentioned it, not asking his permission or begging his forgiveness.

She had loved Morgan Raines when he was alive. She still loved him now.

But he couldn't keep her warm at night.

"You can see them?" she asked, still unsure how this worked even after all this time.

He nodded, gesturing toward the other cleared area where she'd thought the camper might have been. "The old man is lying over there, like he's taking an afternoon nap in the sunshine." Pointing toward the edge of the trees, he went on. "The younger one's leaning against that sapling." Then a final gesture, toward where the old barn had stood. "And the woman's walking in circles, wringing her hands."

Julia tried to fathom it, looking at each spot, one after the other, seeing nothing but dappled trees, scrub and grass—a typical spot on a typical day ... in a place claimed by the dead.

It broke her heart. Like so much about her relationship with Morgan broke her heart.

"Are they aware of us? Or of each other?" she whispered, feeling like she'd stepped into a holy, sanctified place.

"I don't think so," he said. "Or they just don't care. They're not going to leave until somebody finds them."

Almost nonchalant, as if this whole thing was utterly normal, Morgan bent down to pick up a long piece of grass. He drew it tightly between his thumbs and brought it to his lips, blowing hard as if to whistle on it. But not a sound came out.

Sometimes Morgan seemed to forget he was dead.

She never did. Not ever.

Remembering what Olivia had said that morning, about the reason Zachary had given for staying around, she asked, "Do you mean their bodies? Is that why they're still here?"

"Yeah. It's a *thing* over here, I guess. Not a rule, more like a guideline. You gotta look out for the shell, even if you're no longer in it."

She peered toward the tree line. "Do you know where their 'shells' are? If they were here, wouldn't the police have found them after Olivia was rescued?"

"Not necessarily." He stepped closer, following her stare, then looked to the left and then to the right. "I'm pretty sure they're deep in the woods. I think I could find them."

Finding them, bringing them into the light, that would set them free. Which, to Julia, sounded like one of the most important things she or anybody else could ever do.

"Will you, Morgan? Will you please?"

"For you, babe? Anything."

Anything. If only he could give her the one thing she desperately wanted, the one thing she'd dreamed of for eight years.

One more moment—one real, true moment—with *him.*

When it came time for Brooke to leave, Olivia insisted on going down with her to her car. Which meant Gabe was going, too. He didn't think he'd need to protect her from any ghosts—it appeared Liv's one and only phantom encounter was over—but he was taking no chances.

They'd spent the past few hours going over every name on Agent Ames's list. Gabe had been surprised at how many of them Olivia had remembered. Just as surprising, given how young she'd been, was that Brooke was able to fill in the blanks on almost a!! the rest. So, for right now, it didn't appear they'd need to involve the parents in this.

They'd ruled out some names right away, based on Olivia's memories, and Zachary's. The women. Any non-white men or any under twenty; her captor had been older than that.

Still, there had been quite a few names left. Those would require more research. Gabe intended to go to the precinct and run reports on them.

When they reached the bottom floor, they headed out to the street, where Brooke had parked. "You sure you don't want to go with your sister?" Gabe asked Liv. "Take a break?"

She shook her head. "I'd rather follow you to the station. If we only have one day to work together, I don't want to waste any of it."

Remembering what he'd said—about this group coming together for this single day—Gabe understood her meaning. "Listen, I'm not the type to mess with a good thing." Boy, did that have some double meaning, like how he felt about what was happening between them personally. No matter how much he'd told himself he couldn't get any further involved with her, not one single part of him regretted what had happened between them up in that conference room this morning. "As long as this keeps working, I'll stick with it."

She nodded, looking relieved. "Thank you."

"You're welcome."

He meant it. Over the past several hours, hell, the past couple of days, he felt like his worldview had been gradually altered. Like he'd been wearing dark glasses, and they'd been tugged off his face, little by little, until now he was seeing things in a whole different way.

Not just Olivia. All of it. Her friends. The supernatural. eXtreme Investigations.

He froze for a second as the realization hit him: He'd become a believer. Him, the hard-nosed, slightly hardheaded good ol' boy. He now truly believed that these people he hadn't even known a week ago had an open-door relationship with some spiritual other side. Through mind, touch, sight, or soul connection, they somehow knew things nobody should be able to know. There was no rational explanation. Which simply left the irrational one as truth.

One thing his realization made clear was that he owed Olivia an apology. He'd said he was sorry before for the way he'd acted the other day at the police station. But he hadn't apologized for dragging his feet, doubting her every step of the way, not allowing himself to be convinced because the things she told him didn't fit into his worldview.

Before he could even think how you apologized for something like that, a car pulled up into an empty spot behind Brooke's. Mick got out of the passenger seat, Ty the driver's. Neither of them looked particularly happy.

"Any luck?" Gabe asked. He feared he already knew the answer.

Ty shook his head. "That place is like the warehouse where they hid the Ark of the Covenant at the end of that Indiana Jones movie. It's huge, full of boxes and cartons, stuff going back decades. I swear, I think I saw a section marked Civil War Murder Convictions."

Mick added, "We couldn't find the paper trail, much less the evidence from Liv's case."

He'd been afraid of that. With a case this old and supposedly solved, it would have been a miracle if the evidence hadn't been destroyed. An even bigger one to actually find it.

Ty and Mick joined them on the sidewalk, both greeting Olivia's sister, who hadn't been there when they'd left. Ty, in particular, had an extremely warm smile for her. "You doing okay today?" he asked, sounding solicitous, tender.

"Yes. Thanks again for calming me down yesterday. I'm sorry if I came across as . . ."

"Persistent?"

"I was going to say pushy."

He *tsk-tsk*ed, shaking his head even as he flashed her that grin that Gabe had seen charm a lot of women. "What man wouldn't like to be pushed by a beautiful woman every now and again?"

Brooke glanced away toward her car but not before Gabe saw the tiny smile his words brought, not to mention the hint of color rising in her cheeks. She seemed younger than her years, maybe a little immature, without a hint of Olivia's broader, not to mention darker, worldview. Which made her nice, sweet, but not nearly as fascinating to him as her sister.

Ty, however, seemed to like her a lot.

For a second, he considered putting a word of caution in his young partner's ear; after all, Ty was very experienced, while Brooke, he imagined, was not. He didn't figure it was his business, though. Plus, he'd never heard Ty use that gentle tone with a woman before. He was usually brash and flirtatious, not that he hadn't been flirting with Brooke, but this seemed a little more tender, serious. Like he knew she wasn't one of his usual conquests. And the way Brooke kept stealing glances at the man made Gabe suspect Ty's interest was returned.

Watching them, he had to concede that they could be good together. But they could also be heading for a world of hurt. Not only the race thing—this being the Old South—but she was also rich and engaged to a powerful, controlling lawyer. Lots of checkmarks in the "Forget it" column.

Part of him, though—the part that liked Brooke and Ty, not the part that simply *dis*liked her fiancé, Drew Buckman—hoped they might be able to make something of this. One thing was sure: He doubted she'd ever find a man with a bigger heart than Ty.

Mick looked back and forth between Gabe and Olivia. "You two have any luck?"

He told the man what they'd found out and what the next step was. Then, curious about how Mick had handled his field trip, Gabe asked, "Things were okay for you there?"

Mick lifted his gloved hands, which was answer enough.

"Gotcha."

"I have to admit, I was tempted to take them off when I saw a box filled with underwear from some panty-obsessed cat burglar," Mick added.

Olivia and Brooke both groaned. But Gabe couldn't prevent a small grin, seeing the mischief in the other man's expression. Mick was growing on him.

From up the block, a horn blew, intruding on the quiet Sunday afternoon. A car approached, moving fast; then the driver pulled up beside Brooke's vehicle, double-parking.

"Uh-oh," Olivia whispered.

He realized why when he saw Brooke's fiancé exit the car, his expression stormy. He stalked toward her. "Where the hell have you been? Why haven't you returned my calls?"

"I'm sorry. I . . ."

"You left one message that you were going to see Olivia at work and then ignored me the rest of the day?"

Beside him, he felt Mick tense, as Gabe had. But Ty,

who was closer than either of them, stepped right into Drew Buckman's path. "Can I help you, sir?"

Buckman sneered, "Get out of my way."

He tried to go around him, but Ty, completely unintimidated, shifted sideways, blocking his way again. "I think you need to calm down," Ty said, his voice low, tight and controlled.

Protectiveness rolled off his partner and belligerence off Buckman; the tension was thick enough to feel from five feet away. It was a case of hate at first sight if he'd ever seen one.

"Drew, I'm sorry. I was about to call you," Brooke said, stepping toward the two men. She was twisting the straps of her purse in her hands, looking nervous, like a kid caught doing something she wasn't supposed to.

"Get in my car, Brooke," he snapped, not even looking at her.

"Mine's right . . ."

He wheeled on her, sticking out his index finger. "I said get in the damn car."

Gabe had grown up in a household where men who turned red in the face and yelled quickly segued into men who struck. No way in hell was Olivia's sister getting in that car with him.

"Brooke," he said, his voice low yet firm, "why don't you go with Olivia?"

Liv gave him a grateful look, visibly relieved he'd stepped in. She grabbed her sister's arm. "Let's go visit Dad."

Perfect. He'd caught the vibe off Mr. Wainwright yesterday and knew he didn't like his future son-in-law. Buckman wouldn't get past the man.

"Don't you walk away from me!" Buckman ordered.

But Brooke did. She and Olivia headed for the entrance to the parking garage. Which meant Gabe and the other three men would be staying right there, waiting for

Liv's car to pull out and move on down the street. Buck-man wasn't leaving until the women were well on their way.

To think he'd considered the man merely an asshole. It was pretty obvious Drew had a temper. While he didn't imagine Olivia's sister had low enough self-esteem to actually marry a man who'd hit her, he doubted it would take long after the wedding for that hand to fly, and hard.

"Now," Gabe said, walking over to block Buckman's retreat to his own vehicle, "let's stand here and calm down while the ladies get on their way."

"Damn it, Cooper, what the hell is going on here? I can't reach Brooke for almost two days, and now you're treating me like I'm some kind of criminal?" Buckman sounded blustery, offended. That didn't, however, hide the underlying rage that still seethed deep inside him. He might have calmed his tone down, trying to get himself under control. But Gabe knew bullshit when he heard it. This man was holding on to his violent anger by a thread.

"And who the hell does this boy think he is?" Drew added, jerking a thumb toward Ty.

Gabe leaned in, grim, that word, *boy*, grating on him like nails on a chalkboard. He couldn't even imagine how Ty felt about it. "That *man* is my partner, Detective Tyler Wallace, to whom you oughta show a little respect, if you can't manage courtesy."

Brooke's fiancé took a small step back. "I'm sorry. I'm really worried about Brooke. This is unlike her, not being in touch with me for days. I thought something had happened to her."

Days? Christ, was he exaggerating much? They'd all had breakfast together yesterday.

"She talked to you four times yesterday afternoon," Ty said, not buying that crap either.

Buckman's jaw fell open. "How would you know that?" He took a threatening step forward, his beefy hands clenching into fists.

The gleam in Ty's eye said he'd perhaps expected such a reaction.

Damn it, partner, you don't go wavin' a red cape if you're not a professional matador.

"Olivia's working on a rough case, and her sister got worried and wanted to spend time with her. That's it. So how about taking things down a notch?"

The man sniffed, drew himself upright. "Well, why didn't she tell me that?"

Gabe suspected she had tried. This man didn't seem like his ears were open much of the time. Just his mouth. Wanting to keep things on a friendly basis, however, he didn't say that. "I'm sure she intended to fill you in."

Buckman nodded. "Fine. Whatever. Now, am I free to go, *officers*?"

"Of course," Gabe said.

His wounded dignity pushing his head high, the man turned and walked to his car without another word.

As Buckman drove away, Ty lifted a hand and waved goodbye. "Gee, what a nice guy." Raising his voice, he called, "Nice to have met you. Have fun storming the castle!"

Gabe had to laugh, recognizing the movie reference. He'd been a little unsure about his new partner at first, thinking he was too young, maybe a bit too lighthearted. Now he found that was one of the things he liked best about the other man. A great sense of humor was a rare quality in a cop.

Mick, who'd remained silent during the confrontation, cleared his throat. "Okay, so now that Douchey Mc-Doucheface is gone, somebody want to tell me what the game plan is?"

Ty dug his keys out of his pocket. "I'm outta here. Going back to the station to dig back into those missing persons cases."

"I'll be right behind you," Gabe said, knowing his partner had been dying to do that since Olivia had come up with the missing boy's real name. "I need to see what I can find out about the rest of the people on this list I got from Agent Ames. Mick, why don't you wait here and serve as point of contact? I'll call and let you all know what I find. Then we can regroup."

Ty had already walked back to his car and gotten in, waving goodbye as he pulled away from the curb, and Mick turned toward the entrance of the building. Gabe was about to go to his own car when his cell phone rang. "Cooper," he answered.

"Detective Cooper? It's Julia Harrington. Where are you?"

"I'm about to get into my car to go to the station."

"Well," she said, "I think you're going to want to take a detour."

"Why?"

She told him. And Gabe realized she was right.

He was definitely going to be taking a detour.

Chapter 11

Working alone at his desk late Sunday afternoon, Ty wondered, not for the first time, what had drawn his partner out to the woods to meet up with Julia and Derek. Gabe had been sketchy on the phone, as if he, himself, wasn't exactly sure what he would find out there. Ty had offered to go, too, though he hadn't wanted to since he'd been itching to get back to the missing persons files. Gabe, probably realizing that, had told him to just keep doing what he was doing.

So far, Ty had scoured every possible resource—the FBI's NCIC database, NCMEC, all the state records—and he was still coming up empty. Oh, there were a few boys in the right age group and time period who'd disappeared and had never been found. But adding the name Zachary to the search parameters did nothing but eliminate those who were left. He'd tried mixing things up, wondering if Zachary was perhaps a middle name the boy had gone by, and still got nowhere.

So maybe his name wasn't really Zachary. You ever think of that? Yeah. Maybe Gabe's new best friend had had a close encounter of the I-should-be-institutionalized kind.

He couldn't deny that everything Olivia Wainwright had said seemed possible, despite the fact that the way she got the information sounded totally off the wall. Plus he'd seen the stuff Mick could do. And it wasn't like he didn't know anybody else who believed in ghosts. To this day, his grandmother kept up a running conversation with his grandfather, who'd died when Ty was a baby. She always said Grandpa was sticking around to make sure she didn't marry somebody who'd spend his hard-earned money. Now that he was considering Olivia Wainwright's story to be a plausible one, he suddenly felt a little bad for all the times he'd wondered if his dear old granny was succumbing to Old Timer's disease.

Still, to be basing an entire murder/potential missing-child investigation on the word of a woman who had gotten her information right from a ghost's mouth?

"What the hell are we thinking?" he mumbled, pretty sure he knew the answer. Gabe was thinking about Olivia, and Ty was thinking about Brooke. And both of them were probably thinking with their Southern brains—the ones below their belts—rather than their Northern ones.

Brooke sure was a pretty one—sweet and quiet, hair as bright as sunshine and a smile to match. Damn, did he wish he'd met her before she'd let that lawyer slide a ring onto her finger.

It isn't a wedding ring yet. Which was definitely something to keep in mind.

"What are you doing here? Aren't you off today?" a voice asked.

Looking up and seeing one of the other detectives, Bill Waczinski, he admitted, "I should be, but I was following up a lead. But it looks like I came in on a wild-goose chase." Knowing the older man had been on the job a long time, and figuring he might have some fresh ideas, he asked, "You got any experience with kidnapping cases?"

Waczinski lifted a brow. "You catch a kidnapping?"

"I'm working on that cold case, the kid whose bones were found at the Fast Eddie's fire."

"Trying to ID him, huh?"

"Yeah."

"You go through NCIS?"

"Of course. And every other damn database I can think of. Figuring out the age of the skeleton and the time it was there, I've narrowed it down to a kidnapping in the late nineties, but I haven't found squat. None of these stranger-kidnapping records seems to fit."

"Well, what about the nonstranger ones?"

Ty's brow furrowed. "What do you mean?"

"Hell, you are new to the job, ain't ya?" Waczinski said, though he did not sound condescending, merely sad, as if thinking of all the dark, ugly things Ty could look forward to learning in the next twenty years in law enforcement. "Think about it: Out of the hundreds of kids that get snatched every year, how many of them are taken by strangers?"

"Not many," Ty admitted.

"No shit. So don't you think it's time to start with the noncustodials?"

Ty slowly nodded, his mind working frantically. As soon as he'd begun this snipe hunt, he'd pretty much discounted cases of familial kidnapping, because the Bowles and Durkee boys had been taken by strangers— very likely the same stranger. Besides which, the idea was too disturbing, thinking Zachary might have been killed by someone who'd known or been related to his family. But Waczinski was right; noncustodial kidnappings, cases where one biological parent took the child from the other parent who had legal custody were by far the biggest piece of the pie chart when it came to child snatching.

"Worth a shot, isn't it?" the other detective said. Then he headed for the door. "I'm outta here. See ya tomorrow."

"Sure, thanks," Ty replied, his mind already churning

with this new possibility. Kicking himself for not broadening his thinking to begin with, he turned to his computer and began keying in new parameters. This time, he added back all the kidnapping cases that had been flagged as likely being familial, which increased the result pool a hundredfold. Then he zoned in on the sex of the child—a boy. His age in 1999—about twelve. His race—Caucasian. Description—brown-haired, small build. And, of course, his name—Zachary.

He pushed "enter" and stared hard at the screen while awaiting the results.

And in seconds, found what he'd been looking for all along.

"Gotcha," he whispered, a little stunned at how easy it had been once he'd looked in the right place. Because the picture that popped up on the screen, of a Georgia boy who'd been kidnapped many years ago, bore a strong resemblance to the forensic drawing that was, right now, sitting on Ty's desk. The child had been younger, but the similarities could not be denied.

His middle name had been Zachary, not his first. But lots of kids went by their middle names. If Zachary's what he'd been called throughout his life until he'd been forced to change it to Jack, that's what he'd whisper with his last breath, wouldn't he?

Ty pushed the image out of his head, not wanting to think about those sad, final moments Olivia had described. They'd been too real, too vivid. Too damn awful. Not for the first time since he'd heard the story did he think Olivia Wainwright must be the unluckiest person in the entire world for God to have given her an ability like *that*.

"So maybe He's making up for it by giving her Gabe," he mumbled under his breath. Because the two of them did seem to shine with life when they were together. Maybe they were just what each other needed.

Reaching for a pencil and paper, Ty began to make

notes about the case as he quickly scanned the record. Then he read something that made him want to howl with frustration. "No way!" he muttered, his theory totally blown to hell with that one entry. Because in the "suspected kidnapper" section of the report was a name and picture, not of a man, but of a woman ... who was identified as the boy's own mother.

"Damn, damn, damn," he muttered, snapping his pencil in half.

It definitely had not been a woman who'd kidnapped Olivia Wainwright all those years ago. Nor had it been a woman she'd seen in her vision of Zachary's death—if such a vision was to be believed. And hell, he was so deep in this now, he might as well believe it.

So disappointed he could hardly stand it, he sighed, then leaned close to the screen, figuring he'd read the report anyway. It was fairly straightforward, saying this mother had been involved in a bitter custody dispute with her ex-husband. When the court had sided with the father, citing the mother's inability to provide for the child, she'd allegedly grabbed him and taken off, assisted by one of those secretive groups who helped women hide from their exes.

He tabbed down, continuing to read, checking the updates that had been added over the years, mainly out of curiosity now. Near the bottom of the screen, in one of the final updates on the case, he saw a surprising notation. "Deceased?" he whispered. "She *died*?"

Zachary told Olivia his mother was dead.

Was this possible? Might he still be on the right track after all?

He couldn't figure it out, couldn't see how everything fit together, but each new question only made him more determined to find answers. Truly fascinated now, he dug some more, following links like a mouse after a trail of bread crumbs.

Turned out the mother's body had been found in a wooded area in Virginia in the summer of 1995. She'd been murdered and had apparently remained a Jane Doe for several months until she was finally ID'd with dental records. Of the boy, there was no further mention.

But they couldn't have found him, dead or alive, or the case would have been closed. Yet it remained open, active, twenty years after charges had first been leveled against the mother.

One other case remained open: the mother's murder. The ex-husband had been questioned, of course, but then released, as had a suspicious drifter. But nobody had ever been charged, and the case remained unsolved to this day.

Everything he read was making him think this might not be a dead end. With thoughts whirling in his head, Ty dug out another pencil from his desk drawer and started making notes. A time line seemed a good place to begin.

In 1991, at age three, Zachary had been kidnapped by this mother.

The mother had been murdered five years later.

Her body had remained unidentified for several months.

Being on the run, the woman would have kept a low profile, moving a lot. It was doubtful Zachary would have stayed in one school for long and probably didn't have friends. So nobody had been close enough to report either the mother or the child missing. Which was why it had been months before anybody even knew Zachary's mother was the Virginia Jane Doe.

"Jesus," he whispered as the whole scenario took shape.

Had their perp killed a woman in order to grab her son? And, if so, how fucking lucky could that bastard have gotten? He'd chosen his prey, probably not knowing that the mother, herself, had kidnapped him and had been living in hiding. Nobody to notice, nobody to report the crime, nobody to hunt for the boy.

Zachary had been the utterly perfect victim.

As if that weren't bad enough, even the authorities had screwed up, nobody bothering to go back in and change the designation on Zachary's case from a suspected noncustodial kidnapping to a stranger, child-in-peril one.

Getting thoroughly disgusted by the whole thing, he went back to his time line.

"Kidnapped again by an unknown subject at age eight," he said, tapping the tip of his pencil on the pad. "And likely killed four years later, in 1999, at age twelve."

Just like the Bowles and Durkee boys.

Ty waited for the tingle to start, the excitement of knowing he was on to something big here. He had the feeling he'd solved at least one big mystery—the identity of their Jimmy Doe.

He didn't tingle. Yeah, his heart was beating fast, but he wasn't feeling triumphant or proud at having put this much together. This whole story was too damned heartbreaking for that. Instead, he felt a grim determination wash over him.

Gabe had warned him this case would probably affect him like no other, and his partner had been right. Ty wanted to solve this mystery more than he'd ever wanted anything in his life. He was going to see this through, get justice for that kid—for all those kids—no matter what it took. He might have found a huge piece of the puzzle, but there was still a bunch missing.

Who had kidnapped Zachary? Who had killed his mother? Who was the mysterious new "Jack" the sicko had now? And, most important, how long did that boy have to live?

Going back to the screen, Ty made a few more notes and another list. This one was of names and contact information. He started with the detective who'd investigated the Virginia murder, then continued right on down to the last known whereabouts of the father and the only other living relative named in the file, the father's cousin.

Ty didn't know how he was going to handle those conversations. He sure wasn't ready to tell a grieving father or another family member that he might have discovered the remains of their loved one. But he needed to talk to them. Still, he figured it would be safer to start with the detective.

Reaching for the phone, he wondered if this detective would remember the case and hoped he wouldn't mind getting a call about it on a Sunday evening. One more thing that he hoped: that he'd have very good news to share with his partner whenever Gabe got back from doing whatever it was he was doing out in the woods.

Right before he dialed, he made a mental note. He really needed to call his granny and tell her to give his grandpa a big hello from Ty the next time she saw him. Because he now knew spirits could reach out from the land of the dead.

In reaching out to try to help solve his own murder, this lost little boy, Zachary, had made Ty a believer.

Though tired, Olivia didn't think about getting ready to go to bed Sunday night. Instead, she prowled the house, did a load of laundry, scared Poindexter half to death by deciding to vacuum the den and kept checking the phone to see if Gabe had called with any further updates.

Honestly, she wasn't sure what was happening. She only knew Derek and Julia had found something out in the woods where she'd been held, and Gabe had been out there with them well into the night. Olivia had offered to come out, too, though she'd felt queasy one second after she'd suggested it. Still, if she could have been of help, she would have done it, which was exactly what she'd told Gabe when she'd left her father's house several hours ago.

Her father. Ouch. He had been angry at Drew. But he'd also been angry at Olivia and Brooke for keeping him in the dark. While going there in order to get her sister away from her jerk of a fiancé had been a great idea, it had also exposed them to their father's curiosity, not to mention Sunni's nosiness. It hadn't been twenty minutes before Brooke had spilled the beans about exactly why she'd been out of touch with Drew for so long, and then the questions had come hot and heavy. Olivia had felt as if she were being interrogated on a witness stand.

She'd hated to tell her father that all this had come up again. As soon as she had, she'd seen tears in his eyes, tears he tried to pretend he wasn't shedding. When she'd told him they had found the mysterious Jack and relayed the poor boy's fate, her father had simply taken her into his arms and held her, like he had so many times after the kidnapping when she'd cried out her memories and her fears. Sunni—always perky and, well, sunny—had seemed a little embarrassed by the raw emotions flying around and had made herself scarce while Brooke and Olivia told him the whole story.

He'd wanted to call someone. Do something. Get the chief of police on the phone and the district attorney, and his lawyer, and Richard, and her mother.

Oh, God, her mother. She'd made him promise not to even think of telling her anything yet. One scared parent was bad enough; two was more than she could deal with right now. Especially if they started turning on each other, playing the blame game they'd taken such delight in playing twelve years ago.

If it weren't for your money and your name, nobody would have come after our baby.

Well, if you don't like the money and this life, why did you decide you wanted this house?

I didn't want the house. You wanted the damn house.

I bought it for you!

And on and on it had gone until the language of tenderness had been wiped out and bitterness and rancor had consumed their entire vocabulary. Yet they still loved each other, despite Sunni, despite Carl. Of that, she had absolutely no doubt. Which just made the whole thing so unbearably sad.

Hearing a car, she leapt up, went to the window and peeked through the blinds. Someone had just parked at the curb. She saw the dome light go on as the driver's-side door was opened. Smiling as that light shone on a familiar head of thick, brown hair, she dropped the blinds and went to let Gabe in.

"Hi," she said, greeting him before he'd even reached the bottom porch step.

He looked up at her, his face weary and smudged. "Hi, yourself."

"You look like you've been playing in the dirt."

Slowly coming up the steps, he replied, "Not playing. Not by a long shot."

Gesturing him in, she shut the door behind him. "Would you like a beer? Or coffee?"

"No, thanks. I'm gonna head home and take a shower. I just didn't want to leave you hanging. Figured you should know what's going on."

Whatever it was, she knew he was dreading telling her. "Okay then. What happened?"

He replied, calmly telling her what Morgan, Derek and Julia had discovered out in the woods this afternoon—ghosts. And graves. Three altogether.

Olivia's head spun, and she felt a little queasy. She didn't know those people, yet they were connected in a deep, primal way, as only those who'd shared a horrifying experience could be. Like battlefield brothers who could never forget the scars they'd earned together. She and these three people—and poor little Zachary—they'd all been murdered by the same man.

"Morgan was able to find the bodies?" she asked when he'd finished.

"He told Julia where they were buried." He shook his head. "It's such a damn mess, Liv. It wasn't like I could call in a search team and say a ghost pointed out their graves. Absolutely the only break we caught today was that the property had been seized for unpaid taxes years ago and nobody ever bought it, so it's owned by the county."

She assumed that meant the legal issues were a little easier.

"In the end, it was Julia who just used her cell phone, called nine-one-one and made an anonymous tip about finding some human remains while she'd been out walking in the woods."

Simple. Smart. But had it been plausible? Would the authorities, however, see anything to back up her claim? Treading carefully, not wanting to ask the man if he'd been playing the role of grave digger today, she asked, "Was her story believable?"

He nodded once, grimly. "Yeah."

Which was all she needed to know about that. "So then what happened?"

"A squad car was dispatched. The patrolman actually did his job and came deep enough into the woods to find the site. He called for backup, and I made sure I responded to the call." He leaned a shoulder against the wall, then rubbed his face, fatigue rolling off him. "They're going to go over the area tomorrow and will find the other two graves. I'll make sure of that."

Talking more to herself, she said, "If one of them saw *him*, got a better look ..."

"Forget it!" Gabe's voice cut through her musings. "You're not going near them."

Remembering what he'd said last night while he'd held her so tenderly in his arms, she knew where his vehemence was coming from. "But I can help."

"I don't want that kind of help, Liv. It comes at too high a cost."

"I'm willing to pay it."

"I'm not," he snapped. "Let's get one thing clear. I'm putting my foot down on this. You don't do any more of your tricks on my watch or on my case. I've gone out as far on this psychic limb as I intend to, and I'm not going an inch further, not when it comes to you."

Sure, he wanted her to think that was it. But she wasn't stupid. She knew he was worried about her. She also knew something else—that he cared about her.

"I understand," she said quietly, knowing she couldn't argue. This situation was difficult enough without her being childish and demanding or throwing a fit because she'd been shut out. He'd already done so much, she could honor this one request.

Realizing how difficult this whole thing was for him—walking a line between his job and his oath as a police officer on one side and his willingness to work with her and her colleagues on the other—she had to again count her blessings that he'd been the one to land this case. She put a hand on his arm, feeling the bunched muscles tense beneath the sweaty male skin. "I won't, okay?"

He hesitated, then shook his head, slowly, his gaze locked on her face. "I'm swimming upstream here, Liv. I have no idea what the hell I'm doing, but I couldn't make myself stop, even if I wanted to."

Now she understood why he'd needed to come here rather than call to tell her what had happened. It was as if he needed to see her to convince himself he was still doing the right thing, as if he trusted her, drew some kind of strength from her. Maybe it was because he'd been there, had borne witness when she'd connected with Zachary. It wasn't easy for anybody to let go of a lifelong certainty that some things couldn't possibly exist—it had been hard enough for her. For a blunt skeptic like him? Well, she had to admit, the man's courage in stepping out onto this huge limb with her stunned her a bit. Hell. Everything about him stunned her a bit. It had from the minute he'd saved her life last week.

"Thank you, Gabe," she whispered. "Knowing someone who has so much to lose is putting this much faith in me . . . well, I can never express how much I appreciate it." Unable to help it, she moved closer, her hand tightening on his arm, until they stood just a few inches apart.

"I'm not good at ignoring my head and going with my heart," he said, his voice low.

His tone and the way he looked at her made her wonder if they were still talking about just the case. There was something intimate in that stare, in the way his eyes dropped to her lips and his own parted on a slow breath. She sensed he was referring to something a lot more personal. Like the fact that he'd been telling himself she was out of his league, that they were wrong for each other . . . when his heart was saying *to hell with all that*.

She desperately wanted him to listen to his heart, to touch her, to finish what they'd started this afternoon in the conference room. But she'd initiated both their intimate encounters. If Gabe really needed to get his head involved in whatever crazy—yet also wonderful—thing was happening between them, he needed to make the next move.

"Are you sure you don't want to sit down, relax, and have a beer?" she asked, leaving it entirely in his hands.

He hesitated, as if tempted, then looked down at himself. "I'm a mess. But, maybe I could use your bathroom and at least wash my hands before I go?"

She pointed toward a half-open door down the hall. "It's right there." Then she added, "I'll be in the den—with your beer. If you're really stressed about being dirty, just jump in the shower while you're in there. Towels are under the sink."

She didn't add that she was having a hard time wondering how she'd feel sitting one room away while he stripped out of his clothes and washed every inch of that big, broad body in her downstairs bathroom. Some things were just better left unsaid. Or unthought.

Going into the other room, she almost held her breath, waiting to hear either the sink or the shower. One would indicate he intended to simply say goodbye, then leave; the other that he had reconsidered and might stick around awhile.

After a long moment, she heard the shower go on.

Olivia smiled. So far, she suspected his head was making the same decisions his heart would have. That made her happy, not just because she hadn't been able to stop thinking about the intimate moments they'd shared, but also because she'd just gotten used to being in his company over the past few days. It was amazing how quickly she'd gotten used to having him there.

She liked spending time with him and wanted more of that. Maybe, someday, they'd even get to spend *normal* time together—going out for dinner, taking a walk—but for right now, even tense, crazy, madness-is-all-around-us time would do.

Something was building between them, something insistent, something real. It wasn't just sexual—although, yes, they were going to have sex sooner or later, of that she had no doubt.

There was more, though. Having spent so much time with him over the past few days, she realized she liked him, very much. More than liked him, really. In fact, he seemed like exactly the kind of man she could love. That combination of blunt strength and sweet tenderness was nearly irresistible. When you threw in the intelligence, the determination, the flashes of wit, the inherent kindness, and an overwhelming sexiness, he added up to her perfect man.

She honestly hadn't been sure men like him were still around, much less living in Georgia, working as cops.

Her mind whirling with all those thoughts, she didn't even notice he was finished with his shower until he walked into the den. At which point she couldn't think a single damn thing.

Because he'd put his jeans back on . . . but nothing else.

The jeans looked great. The nothing? Absolutely amazing.

Olivia's heart leapt. The man was just stunning. No pale, lean, nine-to-five body here; he was built like a boxer: small waisted and lean hipped but so muscled and toned through the arms, chest and shoulders that he looked capable of lifting a car. His bare chest gleamed with moisture and steam from the shower, and his muscles rippled with every movement as he toweled his still-wet hair. Droplets fell from the damp strands, landing on his shoulders and sliding down. They left faint zigzag lines that disappeared into dark, wiry chest hair that swirled over the top of his chest.

"I'm gonna run out to my car and grab my gym bag. My workout clothes have to smell better than these," he said.

She tried to speak with too dry a mouth. Lifting her glass, she sipped her water, then managed to mumble, "It's fine. You don't have to."

"Hey, are you okay?"

She managed a tiny nod but kept her attention on her drink, not on him.

He apparently noticed that and misinterpreted. Moving closer, he put a hand on her shoulder. "Liv, what's wrong?"

She closed her eyes, breathing deeply as two strong scents filled her nose: clean and male. Gabe moved his hand to her hair, running his fingers through a few long strands, and she quivered a little. Did this smart man really have no clue what he was doing to her?

"What is it?"

No, he obviously did not. "Nothing. Just . . . go, do whatever you have to do."

Before I do something I don't want to do—like trying to encourage you to think with a part of your anatomy other than your brain.

It wasn't his heart she was referring to.

How could she not be thinking of that when he was standing right beside her, his jean-clad legs a few inches away? He was so close she felt the warmth as the moisture evaporated off his skin. The man was the most sexually exciting creature she had ever seen in her life, he was half naked, and, given where he was standing, his groin was probably no more than eight inches from her right cheek—not that she was looking. Hell, no.

Her voice obviously hadn't convinced him, because Gabe suddenly dropped to one knee beside her chair. "Talk to me. What is it? Are you upset about what I told you? Do you want me to go?"

Men could be so incredibly dense. Finally swinging her head to look at him, she snapped, "I'm trying to be honorable here, okay?"

His eyebrows almost shot up into his hairline. "Excuse me?"

"You said you weren't used to following your heart instead of your head, so I'm trying to back off, let you really think about what you want and not influence you either way."

"Influence me?" he said, sounding innocent, but she'd

swear a hint of mischief lurked on those incredibly soft lips.

"Gabe," she said, speaking through almost clenched teeth, "I'm not going to make the first move *again*, damn it, and then have you later say your head wasn't in the game. So if you want me, you'd better do something about it."

That was a risk, but she was tired of dancing around this. She wanted him badly but on open, aboveboard terms. No seductions, no stolen embraces driven by pity or anything else.

After a moment that lasted just a couple of seconds but felt longer, Gabe did something about it. Without another word, he cupped her face in his hands and leaned in close.

She had a moment, one single moment to think, *Thank God.* Then he was kissing her, tasting her, answering all her questions with warm, deep thrusts of his tongue. He was hungrier than the other times they'd kissed, as if desperate to memorize every inch of her mouth. It was as though he wanted to claim her, make sure he kissed her so well and so deeply that no man would ever come close to giving her this kind of pleasure again.

Somehow, she already knew none would. Certainly none ever had before.

Without pausing, he dropped those powerful hands to her hips and tugged her forward. Olivia parted her legs, all her feminine instincts taking over. There was no deliberation, no thought, just pure reaction to the feel of him, his smell, his hot, hard body pressed against hers.

"Mmm," she groaned when she let her hands begin traveling over that muscular form. She kneaded the powerful shoulders, then felt her way down his chest, twining her fingers in the crisp brown hair that ringed his nipples until he hissed against her mouth.

Gabe seemed to want to touch her just as much. He

reached for the front of her sleeveless blouse and tugged, hard, sending buttons flying in all directions. Not that she gave a damn.

"I'll replace it," he mumbled against her lips.

"No need; I stock up at the dollar store."

He laughed softly, and she wanted to swallow that laughter down, loving the light, happy way he made her feel. She wished she could bottle this euphoria to drink from later, a constant reminder that she *could* feel light of heart, could flirt and be silly and fun and have a sexy, playful relationship with a man. This man.

Of all the things she so found so perfect about Gabe, that was one of the biggest. Though they'd been surrounded by darkness almost since the moment they'd met, he could, at times, make her feel so carefree. Like she was just a typical twenty-seven-year-old with no baggage and with nothing but brightness and all kinds of possibility laid out in front of them. As if they could just be normal, be at the start of something wonderful.

We are.

She didn't question the whisper in her mind; she knew it was right. They were starting something wonderful; she only hoped the evil around them didn't bring it crashing down.

"Liv, you take my breath away," he said, staring down at her, his eyes narrowed, lips parted as his deep, audible breaths passed over them.

She smiled, more sure of herself as a woman than she'd ever been in her life. Because she saw how much he wanted her. Hunger, lust, desire—they dripped from the man.

"Take me to bed, Gabe," she ordered.

He nodded. "Yes, ma'am."

He stood and picked her up by the waist, looping an arm beneath her bottom. Olivia wrapped her legs around his hips, wanting to cry at how big, hot and hard he felt.

All that heat would soon be inside her, driving away any remnants of cold, making her forget what her body had ever felt like before he'd been a part of it.

He groaned, as if he could feel the heat of her through his jeans and her slacks, then bent to kiss her again. That kiss continued, deep and wet, as he walked all the way upstairs and straight to her bedroom. He didn't reach for the light; the moon was full and shiny, gleaming through the door that led out to the balcony. And a million stars seemed to have burst through the humid sky to brighten this one perfect night.

When they reached the bed, he sat on its edge, keeping her on his lap. She scratched his back lightly, loving the way his tongue moved in and out of her mouth like he was already making love to her. His kisses both filled her up and made her desperately hungry for more.

Moving his mouth across her cheek, he kissed her, nibbling lightly, right down to her neck. Olivia liked the direction he was heading and leaned back, trusting him to hold her, not to let her fall. Funny how much she trusted this man already. He hadn't let her fall emotionally throughout the roller-coaster ordeal of the past few days, and she knew, down to her soul, that he would move heaven and earth to make sure nothing ever hurt her physically.

"Please," she murmured, arching her back further, needing a more intimate caress.

He noted the invitation and responded to it, moving his mouth down her throat, sinking his lips into the hollow and pressing a hot openmouthed kiss there.

"Close but not quite," she said, both delighted and a little frustrated by his slowness.

He chuckled, the sound almost evil. "Patience isn't one of your strongest suits, is it?"

"I'm very patient. I waited for you to make up your mind about this, didn't I?"

This time he didn't chuckle but laughed deeply. "Yeah, that took all of ten seconds."

"See? I'm infinitely patient."

She proved it by resisting her urge to twine her fingers in his hair and pull him down to her breasts, where she so wanted his sweet, lovely attention. The feel of his chest hair against her bare skin had shot her awareness level into the stratosphere, and she held her breath, waiting for the thrilling scrape of his cheek or the brush of his lips against her puckered nipples.

"Oh, yes," she groaned when he finally kissed his way to the top curve of one breast. She stroked his back, arching toward his mouth, needing even more. "Please, Gabe."

He didn't make her wait any longer, deftly removing her bra and then bending down to kiss one taut peak. She moaned as he flicked his tongue out for a taste and cried out when he closed his mouth over it and sucked deeply. Pleasure roared through her. Olivia's breasts had always been incredibly sensitive, and the electric delight rocketed in every direction, landing especially hard between her thighs. She jerked against him, needing to be naked, needing him inside her.

There was a lot she wanted to do with this man. She wanted to taste every inch of him, to feel his mouth on the most intimate parts of her body. But mostly, she just wanted him to fill her up, to make her warm and whole, to remind her that she was every inch a woman.

"Please," she whispered, reaching for the waistband of his jeans. "I want you inside me."

He moved to her other breast and whispered, "We're just getting started. We've got a lot of rungs on the ladder before we get to the top and jump off."

She cupped his cheek, forcing him to look up at her. "We have all night. Fill me up. Then we'll climb back down and hit every single rung, I swear to God." Some more than once.

With his wide gleaming smile, he looked a little wolf-ish. But he didn't argue.

Sliding off his lap, Olivia stood in front of him, reached for her zipper and unfastened her black slacks. She let them fall to the floor. Wearing nothing but a pair of skimpy panties, she stared down at him, seeing his gaze roam over her. Anticipation and hunger gleamed in his eyes, and he looked almost unable to help himself as he leaned forward and pressed a warm, openmouthed kiss to the hollow below her right hip.

"Liv, please, just two rungs down the ladder," he begged, moving his mouth along the elastic edge of her panties. She felt his warm breath flow through the nylon into the curls covering her sex and shuddered, having to drop her hands onto his shoulders as her legs went weak. "Or one. Give me just one."

"Uh . . ."

He didn't wait for permission. Instead, with wicked intent, he merely tugged her panties off and continued to taste her into near incoherence. A cry built up in the back of her throat as warm, wonderful waves of pleasure began to roll through her. Olivia was shaking so hard, he had to support her, holding her by the hips. And when an orgasm washed over her, she tossed her head back and let out a low cry of delight.

That seemed to snap whatever restraints had been holding him back. Gabe rose to his feet, tore his jeans off and reached for her again. She held back for the briefest moment, wanting to see him—all of him—and the sight was enough to make every part of her that wasn't al-ready soft, warm and ready get that way on the spot. She was nearly desperate to feel that thick erection pressing into her, going so deep he'd imprint himself on her.

Knowing they hadn't discussed the issue, she said, "I'm on the pill. And I've, *uh* . . . Well, I haven't been with a lot of people."

He obviously understood what she was getting at. "It's been a long time for me, too, Liv. I don't do casual sex, and I never have . . . in case you were worried about that."

"I wasn't."

"Good," he whispered as he maneuvered her around, until her back was to the bed. Then he pushed her down onto it, following her, kneeling above her. "I'm glad that's taken care of, because I am dying to feel you wrapped around me, without any kind of barrier between us."

There was none of any kind, prophylactic or otherwise. Her own need to protect herself from a world that hadn't always been kind about the things she'd seen, his to keep up a tough-guy, uncaring façade to prove he'd risen above his childhood—all of that had fallen away. Now they were just two people who were falling for each other, giving in to the emotions and desires that had been nipping at them in tiny bites of awareness since the moment they'd met.

"I've wanted you so much," he told her as he moved between her parted thighs.

Liv bent one knee, curving up to welcome him. "I've wanted you, too." She wrapped her arms around his neck and drew him down for a kiss, even as he moved his hands down to see whether she was really as ready for him as she claimed to be.

She cried out against his mouth when he slid his fingers between her slick womanly folds and jerked when he slid one inside her.

"Top rung," she reminded him, certain he had to realize she had meant what she'd said. She was ready, her body wet, soft, waiting to be filled. She wanted him inside her, now.

"Then we go down?" he asked, his eyes gleaming with erotic wickedness.

She nodded. "Oh, yeah. We definitely go down."

"Deal," he said, then moved closer, replacing his warm, strong fingers with that equally warm erection.

Olivia closed her eyes, held her breath, feeling him begin to slide into her. He was so restrained, so determined that they'd both feel every sensation, every inch of connection.

She felt it. Oh, God, did she feel it. Olivia savored every moment as he moved deeper, possessing her both physically *and* emotionally, the way no man ever had before. Until, finally, he drove all the way into her, bringing a tiny gasp to her lips.

He froze. "Are you okay?"

She couldn't speak for a second, focused solely on the amazing fullness, the heat, the pleasure of it. Then, finally she whispered, "So okay, I might never be not okay again."

Her answer seemed to please him; he smiled and kissed her again, whispering sweet words against her lips. He told her how beautiful she was, how good she felt, how much he'd wanted her. All of those words echoed the thoughts that had been going on in her mind.

They began to move together. There was no awkwardness, no first-timers-getting-acquainted trepidation. Their two bodies seemed to become as one, each gentle thrust met, each powerful one welcomed with a groan or gasp of delight. As he filled her with deep, deliberate strokes, Olivia began to feel everything else—the dark thoughts, the worries—vanish. There was only this wonderful, passionate man, making her feel better than she'd ever thought she could.

He kissed her like he had never tasted anything more perfect than her mouth and made love to her like he never intended to stop. Every moment was better, more fantastic than the last, each caress so evocative and every touch wrapped in sensuality. Until finally, after Olivia had ridden yet another wave of pleasure to its shattering culmination, Gabe cried out his release against her hair, joining her at last.

Afterward, he rolled over onto his back, taking her with him so she lay across him. She felt his heart pounding against her cheek and the movement of his chest as he drew in deep breaths that finally began to slow.

They were still for a long while. She had no idea what time it was; she just knew the room had brightened as the moon moved in the sky. It shone through the uncurtained glass doors, bathing their bodies in soft, gentle light. Above them, the ceiling fan swirled lazily, sending streams of air to cool their heated skin.

"Gabe," she eventually whispered, her voice lazy, sated and thick with sex.

"Yeah, darlin'?"

"Thanks for pushing me out of the path of that car."

"Pushing doesn't sound heroic enough. I didn't push you; I swooped in and carried you."

She chuckled. "Okay, thanks for carrying me then. You really are my hero." *In so many ways.*

He ran his fingers down her back, caressing the sensitive spot at the base of her spine. "Yeah, well, thank you for not getting run down by it before I could reach you."

"It wasn't a very auspicious first meeting," she admitted.

She felt him stroke her cheek, pushing her hair back. Then, putting his index finger below her chin, he tipped her face up so she would meet his eyes. "However it happened, Olivia, whatever the circumstances, I have the feeling that every day for the rest of my *life* I'm gonna thank God for bringing you into it."

Watching Olivia's balcony doors from the shadowy backyard of the house next door, Johnny blew out an angry breath. He wasn't gonna be able to grab the whore tonight.

He muttered a curse, not worried that somebody might hear him. The family who lived in this house had gone on vacation—who'd know their schedule better than the good old lawn guy who was supposed to come by and water every other day?

"Damn, them people are stupid," he muttered. Stupid and trusting. He could go into that house and clean it out, top to bottom. They'd never checked no references, never even wondered if Lenny was his real name. They just knew he worked cheaper than most other guys and did a good job, so they kept him around.

The timing of their trip had been perfect, considering he was ready to take care of the little bitch he'd hated for more than a decade. He'd come here at around nine, after doing some research for some other business he would be taking care of later, and had started watching the house. He'd been waiting for the lights to go off, which would indicate Olivia Wainwright had gone to bed.

He had been so excited at the thought of waking her up again. A hand clamped on her face in the middle of the night. A familiar voice whispering that she'd better not scream, or else he'd kill her sister. A knife pressed to her throat. She'd be downright sick in the head.

Confusion would make her slow. Memories would make her crazy. Fear would be her undoing.

"But not tonight," he snapped, so frustrated he wanted to break something.

Because the damn woman had brought that cop up to her room. He'd seen a pair of shadows passing by an upstairs window.

She'd ruined his plans for tonight, when he'd been ready to grab her, take her, end this.

He had it all worked out in his mind, what he was gonna do to Olivia. Just smothering her or shooting her in her bed—like he intended to do to his other victim tonight—was too good for this one. He wanted her in his power, wanted her to be afraid, wanted to gobble up her terror, gorge on it.

He wanted her to see Jack and know that no matter what she'd done, nothin' could come between him and his boy.

But no. She wasn't alone. He'd have to wait until tomorrow. The cop might be there all night, but he couldn't stay 24/7. He glanced at his watch, realizing how late it was. But the night wasn't a total loss. He had another victim on his list. He'd planned to grab Olivia, knock her out, and leave her tied up in the back of his truck while he ran his other errand. He'd thought it'd be quick, secretive, not too messy. An in-and-out job to eliminate the threat that had arisen. Now, though, he guessed he'd just go take care of that errand without her.

That's just fine. Now maybe I can have some fun, take my time. You don't have to do this, no need to rush through it. I'll handle everything.

Johnny rubbed his forehead, feeling the tingling of a headache, then reached into his pocket and grabbed the small bottle of aspirin he always kept on him. He dumped a few in his hand, popped them into his mouth and chewed, the familiar tart, acidic taste comforting and soothing as a cool cloth on his brow.

For a second, he couldn't remember what he was doing. He'd had it planned: take the girl, run that other errand, eliminate the threat quickly. A silenced gunshot in the dark while his prey was sleeping. He didn't take pleasure in killing; he preferred to just do it and be done.

No, no. That'll be too easy. You just leave it to me. 'Cause I do take pleasure in it.

He'd heard the voice more clearly that time and didn't confuse it for a buzzing insect or a passerby on the street. His mind cleared, came into focus, and he acknowledged that he was hearing the whispers of his old friend, his secret, invisible friend, who always seemed to show up when things was really bad for Johnny. Like when he was bein' hurt, or beat, or when those evil people who'd taken him in as a kid did their nasty things to him and all the other foster kids they was getting paid to take care of . . . like his own little baby cousin. His one remaining connection to his old life.

Everything's gonna be just fine.

Yes, he thought it would. Because it appeared that tonight, like always, his secret friend would take care of everything.

Chapter 12

Armed with a search warrant, which had been easy to procure, given the human remains already found, as well as the ownership of the property, Gabe had gone back out to the woods early Monday to hook up with the search crews. He hadn't even gone in to the precinct, having met with someone from the DA's office who'd obtained the warrant, then with the team leader, who was bringing out the dogs and the ground-penetrating radar.

They wouldn't really need either one. He knew where the remaining two bodies were buried. But he had to keep up appearances, pretend he didn't have the information.

It was damned frustrating, a waste of time, and he intended to keep steering the search to make sure the bodies were found quickly. He wasn't going to spend another whole day in the woods, not when there was a child to find. He wanted the graves exhumed and the remains delivered to the coroner so they could try to find out who these victims had been.

Learning their identities was the first step in finding out who'd killed them. They just needed one break, one single, tiny break—a suspect the police had never charged, a name that popped up in more than one investigation.

Please, God, just give me one break here.

He wanted to finish this with real investigative police work. Nothing supernatural. Not that he didn't appreciate the help of the eXtreme Investigations group. In fact, they had proved invaluable. Thing was, he couldn't very well say, "Sure, y'all come on and give us a hand . . . uh, except you, Liv, you're not allowed."

Worrying about her, wanting to protect her, was a lover's prerogative. After last night, he had definitely earned the title of lover. Damn, had he ever earned it—in a night he wouldn't forget as long as he lived.

Still, he'd seen her face when he'd refused her help last night; he knew she'd agreed to mollify him. But if this case stayed cold and he didn't get something going fast, not only Olivia but also all the rest of her people would probably be bugging him to change his mind.

"Forget it," he mumbled as he watched the search crews running the GPR over the wooded ground about ten yards from where he knew they were gonna hit pay dirt.

Knowing things were about to get a lot busier, he grabbed his phone and dialed the precinct. He hadn't spoken to Ty since yesterday, when his partner had dropped Mick off outside the eXtreme Investigations office.

Gabe had been so busy throughout the evening, then so distracted by what happened with Olivia, that he hadn't even checked his messages. So he hadn't realized until this morning that his partner had called last night. Sounding excited, Ty said he thought he'd found a major lead to the identity of little Zachary and would be in touch with more information as soon as he had it.

Equally as excited, especially since the victim pool was widening and they should soon have other names to tie to Zachary's, he'd been trying to reach the man all morning. Ty hadn't been answering his cell or the phone on his desk. Being pretty busy himself, Gabe hadn't been too worried about it, but now it was going on nine thirty, and it just wasn't like his partner to stay out of touch. Especially when they were working a major case.

Finally deciding to try a little harder, Gabe dialed not Ty's direct line or the central operator but the phone number of Bill Waczinski, one of the other detectives on the squad.

"Hey, it's Cooper," Gabe said as soon as the other man answered. "Have you seen Wallace this morning?"

"What'sa matter, Coop, you lose your rookie partner?"

"I caught that case out in the woods, where the remains were found. Ty's been working on something else."

"Yeah, I know I saw him yesterday. He was trying to ID the kid from last week's fire."

"When did you see him?"

"About five, right before I left. He was still at his desk."

Hearing a few shouts, Gabe realized the guy holding the radar equipment had just spotted something. He covered his free ear, wanting to finish the conversation, already knowing things were about to get a lot busier on site. "What about this morning?"

"Not hide nor hair," Waczinski said. "Usually the kid's the first one here, putting the coffee on—you got him well trained. I had to make it myself when I got in. Hold on a second." He heard the big man's footsteps. Then the detective came back on the line. "Nope, I think you've got an AWOL partner: His desk is cleared, computer off, chair pushed in. I don't think he's been here since last night."

Gabe had been just a little concerned before he'd called in. Now his tension went up a notch. The muscles in the back of his neck tightened, his skin prickled. He thought frantically, wondering if Ty had said anything about an appointment or anything else. He could think of nothing. "Okay, thanks Waczinski. I'll try him at home. Maybe he's sick or something."

Or maybe he ended up going to find Brooke Wainwright last night, just to make sure she was okay after the altercation with Buckman. And maybe the two of them got carried away? Hell, stranger things had happened. Though he didn't like the idea of his friend getting mixed up between a woman and her fiancé, he couldn't help hoping it was something like that rather than anything . . . else.

Ending the call, he saw the searchers converging on the spot where body number two, the woman, if Morgan was to be believed—and so far, he hadn't been wrong— would be located. But rather than joining them, he made another call. He knew he wouldn't be able to concentrate until he found out where Ty was.

He tried his house and got the machine. Tried both calling and texting the cell. He considered calling Olivia. He wanted to say good morning to her, anyway, since he'd had to get up and leave her bed at a little after dawn so he could go home and get fresh clothes. But what was he gonna say: *Hey, do you think your sister cheated on her fiancé last night and might be shacked up in a hotel somewhere with my partner right now?*

Having another idea, another possible explanation, he dialed Julia Harrington. Maybe Ty had contacted her about the case and she'd given him some other lead this morning.

"Morning, Cooper," the woman said as soon as she answered. "How's it going out there?"

"Pretty well," he told her. "Looks like they've found the second victim. Listen, have you heard from my partner this morning?"

"Detective Wallace? No, not a word."

That tension started again, but he didn't give it too

much power over his imagination. Ty could have woken up this morning with a toothache and gone to the dentist. He could right now be numb with Novocain, with a drill boring at him. Or he could be with Brooke—and could be the one doing the drilling. Crass, perhaps, but those explanations were better than some of the alternatives that were flashing in his mind. He suddenly wondered if this was how parents felt when their teenager was late coming home or stayed out all night.

"Do you want me to ask Olivia or her sister if they've seen him?"

His heart skipped a beat. "Her sister?"

"Yes, she came in a little while ago. She's with Liv in her office."

"Shit." *The dentist then. Or car trouble. Or phone trouble. Or maybe he had been with Brooke and had gone home to get cleaned up.*

"What's wrong?" Julia asked.

"I haven't heard a word from Ty since yesterday," he admitted. "He's not answering any of his phones, didn't show up at work. It's not like him."

"*Hmm,* no, that doesn't sound like him," she said. She didn't really know him, but anybody who'd spent even a few hours with Ty would realize the young man was earnest and hardworking, not the type to blow off his responsibilities.

"Hey, Cooper, you'd better come over here," the leader of the search team yelled. "We've got something!"

Julia apparently heard. "Sounds like you're about to get pretty busy. Listen, let me see what I can find out, and I'll get back to you, okay?"

"Okay, thanks," he said. "But do it discreetly, would you?" He didn't want Olivia or her sister thinking he suspected Brooke of stepping out on her future husband.

"You bet, a covert operation all the way."

Gabe disconnected the call, then strode the twenty yards to the search team, who were staring at a radar screen, talking excitedly, like a bunch of treasure hunters who'd spotted a sunken galleon full of gold. Hell, he guessed in their line of work this was like hitting a jackpot. Finding a human body buried in the middle of nowhere was a good day for them. He had to concede, in this case, Julia and Morgan's way had been a little more effective timewise.

Giving the team his full attention, he watched as they slowly unearthed the plastic-wrapped skeleton that Julia had said had been under the ground for at least fourteen years. It took a while; forensics was on-site, photographing and taking notes every step of the way. The dirt had to be cleared off layer by layer, saved to be sifted through later. Though he'd always thought that side of police work would be pretty dull, he couldn't deny being interested by all the steps they took to preserve the evidence.

Any residual evidence might be well and good down the line, but he needed information now, today. Because if this psycho had a child, and his days were numbered, Gabe couldn't wait around to find out whether this woman had been shot or stabbed. He wanted the name. Just the name.

"Any ID on her?" he asked, once the entire skeleton had been brought aboveground.

"Nah, nothing," one of the technicians replied. Then, his brow furrowed, he asked, "How do you know it's a her? You been taking nighttime anatomy classes?"

Gabe felt his face redden. He was so not cut out for this clandestine crap. "No, just a fifty-fifty guess."

He was saved from having to answer any more questions by the ringing of his phone, which was hooked to his hip. Grabbing it, he saw Julia's name in the caller ID box and immediately walked away to answer it, his eyes down so he could watch the uneven ground for any obstacles. "Have you heard anything?" he asked. His tension had grown in the hour he'd been waiting for her call.

"Cooper. . . ." A woman's voice, Julia's, but low, broken. Her hitchy breaths were audible over the phone lines. "Oh, God, Cooper, I'm so sorry. It's bad."

He froze midstride, jerking his head straight up, like a puppet being yanked by the string. The hot, sunny day seemed to grow forty degrees colder as a chill washed over him, making him shudder. "Don't," he ordered, his mind not working, denial the only reaction he could muster up. "Don't you fucking say it, Julia."

Don't you dare. You're wrong. It's impossible.

"I found Ty's address and sent Morgan to check on him," she whispered, her voice so thick with tears and emotion, it was hard to make out her words.

"Don't, don't," he kept repeating, unable to say anything else. His throat was closing up. The ground started to spin beneath his feet. A shadow seemed to have crossed the entire sky, darkening the world, and a deep well of panic and horror began to build inside him. He grabbed the trunk of the nearest tree, his fingers digging into the bark so hard he thought they might snap.

"Someone must have broken in. Morgan says it looks like there was a fight. Ty's on the floor."

Jesus Christ. His partner down, attacked in his own home? Could this really be happening? Could he accept it, believe it, based on some damn psychic and her doubly-damned ghost?

No, he absolutely could not. He had to see for himself. If something had happened, then his partner needed him. Gabe threw off the shocked lethargy and started to run toward his car, the phone at his face. "I'm on my way," he snapped.

She said something else, something low, three words that didn't sink into his brain. Gabe snapped the phone shut, barking an excuse of an emergency to one of the other officers as he dashed by. He threw himself into the driver's seat and started the car, mentally calculating the fastest way to Ty's house.

"Hold on, partner. Hold on," he mumbled as he flew down the dirt path, taking each turn as fast as he could, skidding on dirt and taking out a few small trees as he went.

When he'd been a kid and the old man had been in one of his beating moods, Gabe used to sneak out of the house and run—far, fast—until his lungs hurt and his feet ached and he could run no more. He'd once told his mama that it felt like he was running to beat the devil.

Today, he was once again running to beat that devil, trying to stay ahead of some ugly, awful beast trying to grab him from behind. The dark monster wanted to swallow him, force him into a hideous place where kids were kidnapped and women were drowned.

And partners were murdered.

"No," he yelled, slamming his hand on steering wheel. "No, damn it. Hold on, Ty. Hold on, man. I'm coming."

He kept repeating it, saying it louder and louder, to drown out not only the scream of the monster coming at him from behind but also the echo of those three little words Julia had said . . . the ones he'd refused to hear, absolutely would not acknowledge.

It's too late.

Olivia stared in horror at Julia, not believing what she'd just heard the woman say into the phone. *Ty. Oh, God, no, please, not Ty.* Not that handsome, funny young man who had such an obvious crush on her sister.

She'd just walked Brooke out after spending a couple of hours talking to her sister about her plans to end her engagement and had come back to apologize to her boss for the personal intrusion on their workday. She'd been standing right outside the slightly open door when she overheard the conversation. It occurred to her as soon as Julia disconnected the call who she had been talking to. "Oh, God, was that Gabe? Did you just tell Gabe his partner was murdered?"

Julia's head jerked as she spied Olivia in the doorway. Her eyes teary, she nodded.

"How do you know?" Olivia asked, stalking into the office, angry, shocked and horrified, not wanting to believe it, even though the hot tears bursting from the corners of her eyes said she already did. "How could you know that?"

"Cooper called here this morning, asking if I'd heard from Ty, because he hasn't been able to reach him since last night," Julia explained, her voice quiet, calm, in contrast to Olivia's rising emotions.

Understanding washed over her. "You sent Morgan."

"Yes. He found Ty lying in a pool of blood in his house."

Wanting to throw up, Olivia swallowed down the reaction and spun in a circle, looking around the room. "Is he still here? Well, ghost, are you here, damn it?"

Julia walked around from behind the desk and grabbed her hand. Olivia pulled away, not wanting to be comforted, not wanting to share any grief-stricken moments over a young man neither of them had known well but both had recognized as someone pretty special. She just wanted information. "Is he sure?"

Julia nodded once.

"You know where Ty lives?"

Lived. Oh, God. Lived.

"Olivia, what are you . . ."

"Do you really think I'm just going to sit here and do nothing while the man I love is on his way to find his best friend's murdered body?"

Julia's mouth fell open on a gasp, though Olivia didn't

know whether the woman was more surprised by Olivia's determination or her use of the word *love*, which she hadn't even thought about—it just seemed to come so naturally from mouth.

"Well?" Olivia snapped.

After one more second, Julia broke her own cardinal rule and, glancing toward the love seat, said, "How far is it from here?" She paused, nodded once, then looked at Olivia. "Okay, we might be able to get there before Gabe." Then she turned away and grabbed her purse off her desk. "Let's go."

"You . . ."

"You don't really think I'm letting you go there alone, do you? I'll drive."

Olivia spun around and followed her, both of them brushing past Aidan McConnell, who'd returned to the office this morning after a romantic weekend getaway with his girlfriend. In his world, none of this had happened, none of it even existed.

"Is everything all right?" he asked, frowning, as if he knew the answer to that question. Maybe he did. He hadn't been around for a few days, had no idea what they were working on . . . yet Aidan always had a way of knowing things. He confirmed it by asking, "Who died?"

"No time to explain," Julia said. "Ask Mick or Derek to fill you in on what we've been doing when they get back."

Not even waiting to see if he agreed, they left the office, took the elevator down to the parking lot and got into Julia's car. She drove as quickly as she could, but even that didn't seem fast enough for Olivia, who leaned forward in her seat, as if she could mentally make the vehicle go even faster. She just kept picturing Gabe's face this morning, when he'd woken her up with a smile and kiss. He'd been happy, tender. Though he knew they still had a long road to travel, he'd almost made her believe it when he'd promised her that things would get better, that last night was the first step in a brighter future for both of them.

Now, just a few hours later . . . God, what a nightmare.

"Here's his street," Julia said, her voice tense, tight.

Liv saw Gabe's car in front of a small house in a neighborhood of new homes. The car was parked crookedly, the door not even closed, as if he'd leapt out before the vehicle had come to a stop. She did the same thing, unfastening her seat belt and yanking at the door handle even as Julia pulled in. Leaping out, she ran across the lawn to the small porch and saw the wide-open front door.

And there she stopped. Because Gabe was sitting right in the doorway, facing out, his elbows resting on knees, his face buried in his hands.

Those broad shoulders were slumped, his whole body was shuddering and he was trying to suck in deep, shaky breaths. But he couldn't quite manage it because each time he did, a strangled noise emerged from his throat.

Just as grief had its stages and its rituals, it also had its sights and it had its sounds. Olivia had experienced a lot of them. And she knew this sound, this helpless, enraged sob that came from someplace deep within Gabe. As if he were holding in the memories of his happy, smiling friend at the same time as he tried to swallow down the awful reality of what had happened to him. There just wasn't room inside him yet for both.

Olivia slowly ascended the outside steps, mourning with him, feeling his grief, stricken at the sight of him, crushed and heartbroken. She knew he'd come here in a panic, determined to save his friend.

She also knew, since he was sitting here, that it was too late. Far too late.

She shifted her gaze over his head and glanced

through the open doorway for a brief second. That was enough. She had to close her eyes and look away, though she knew what she'd seen would stay with her forever.

Ty Wallace had apparently fallen right behind the door, which blocked most of his body from sight. But his arm was extended, and his hand, Ty's limp hand, was clearly visible on the floor just a couple of feet behind his partner. Palm up, fingers loose and open, the pose so normal but for the red streaks that dripped down from his pinkie onto the white carpet.

Olivia squeezed her eyes tighter, not to shut out the sight but to keep her tears from falling freely down her face. Her heart was breaking, but she knew Gabe's had shattered.

He had so few people in his life. He'd opened up to her a little during the night, told her a bit more about his family—losing his mother and his grandmother. She knew he had few friends and that he counted his partner as his best one.

And now Ty had been taken from him, too.

It was cruel. Unfair. This man deserved so much better.

And God knows Ty had.

Finally, when she felt she could keep herself together, she opened her eyes and stepped closer, murmuring, "Gabe?" before dropping a hand on his head, tenderly stroking his hair.

He didn't look up, didn't move, didn't acknowledge her at all. He merely kept shaking, trying to control himself, keep his emotions in check, like men were taught they had to do.

She dropped to her knees between his legs, then reached up and gently touched the backs of his trembling hands. Still saying nothing, he took her fingers between his, squeezing tightly, holding on to her like he needed to hold on to something or else go completely out of his mind.

She knew that feeling, that cold, desperate feeling. Like you were being lifted by a big, random wind, tossing about in a storm, just needing something to ground you, keep you in place.

He could squeeze until her fingers broke; she'd take it and offer him anything else he needed.

As if he'd heard the thought, he suddenly let go of her hands, wrapped his arms around her shoulders and hauled her up against his body. Clinging tightly, he buried his face in her neck. She felt the hot moisture of his hidden tears against her skin and tunneled her fingers into his hair, holding him close, giving him the privacy he needed while also being his foundation, his rock in this sudden, violent storm. She kept her eyes closed, not wanting to look past him into that house, not wanting to see sweet, sexy Ty like that.

"I'm sorry," she whispered. "So very sorry, love."

"I was too late," he muttered, the words muffled, coughed out. "Hours too late."

Hours. There was nothing he could have done. Nothing she, Julia or Morgan could have done. Someday he'd be able to hear those words. But she doubted he'd ever fully believe them, any more than she'd fully believed them when he'd told her the same thing about Jack.

"Can you tell . . . Do you think it was a robbery or something?"

"No. This was *not* a robbery," he said.

Hearing a sound behind her, she turned her head and opened her eyes to see Julia, watching from a discreet distance. The other woman held up her phone, making a dialing gesture, silently saying she'd called 911. Olivia nodded once.

"Gabe, the police are probably on the way," she said. "Julia called nine-one-one."

He remained silent for a second, and she felt his muscles bunch, as if he were undertaking a mighty struggle to bring himself under control. Finally, though, he loosened his tight grip on her and lifted his head. Olivia turned her face to his and saw the paleness, the tracks of moisture on his cheeks, the red eyes.

"He was on to something," Gabe said, shaking his head slowly, as if trying to get his own thoughts straight. "He left me a message last night, said he was on to something big, thought he'd identified the boy."

She sucked in a shocked gasp. "Are you saying ..."

"Yeah. I think whatever he stumbled onto is what got him killed."

She caught her lip between her teeth, biting hard to keep the tears from falling, knowing she had to be strong. Olivia just hadn't envisioned this. Her mind had gone to other places—a robbery gone bad, some domestic dispute. It hadn't occurred to her that Ty's murder could be related to their case; after all, he hadn't been nearly as involved as she or Gabe, or even Julia.

But it appeared she was wrong. He *had* been.

"You're sure?"

He lifted his shoulders in a shrug and said simply, "You met the guy. He didn't have an enemy in the world. He was the nicest cop, the most ..." His voice broke a little, and he sniffed. Then he finished. "The most decent man I've ever known."

Hearing sirens in the distance, Olivia began to think, quickly trying to sort through all the little details, all the pieces of the puzzle. This changed things. She'd come here to comfort a lover, to help mourn a new friend. Now, though, if Gabe was right, if this murder was connected to the case, then she might have been the one who'd brought the eyes of a monster onto that sweet guy. She'd been the one who'd started digging all this muck up, pushing Gabe and his partner to believe her when she'd said she recognized the forensics sketch.

Good lord, if she hadn't ever turned on the TV set the other day, hadn't seen that sketch, Ty Wallace would probably still be alive.

"I'm so sorry," she said, knowing she sounded horrified now, not merely aggrieved.

He noticed, stiffening, lifting a hand to her cheek. "What are you saying?"

"If I hadn't . . ."

"Don't even go there," he ordered. "Ty was doing his job, a job he loved. This has absolutely nothing to do with you, do you understand me? Nothing."

So he didn't blame her. That was something at least. But she knew she'd blame herself for a while, always wondering.

There was only one way she could make sure something good came out of this, one thing that would perhaps enable her to forgive herself—and perhaps allow Gabe to let go of some of the guilt she knew he'd be carrying, too.

They had to find the boy, Jack. *Had to*.

"Gabe," she said, speaking carefully, "is there anything you think we should do, before the police get here?"

She didn't put it out there. Didn't make the offer, knowing how he'd acted last night to the very idea of her touching the victims found in the woods. But, God, this was his friend, his partner. This man deserved justice. *And Jack has to be found*.

He didn't catch her meaning, still looking a little dazed. He put his hands on his knees and slowly rose to his feet, careful not to touch the doorjamb or the open door. She had no doubt he'd gone inside to see if there was any way he could save his friend. Then his cop instincts had kicked in. He'd come out here to grieve, doing nothing to contaminate the scene further.

He extended a hand to help her up. "I guess we oughta get our stories straight," he muttered, sounding so tired, so sick of the games and machinations.

"The truth should suffice," Julia said from the lawn below. "Your partner didn't show up for work, you grew concerned when you couldn't reach him." Then she looked at Olivia. "Your girlfriend knew you were coming over here and was worried about you, and showed up a few minutes later."

That was the truth. A skimmed-down version but the truth nonetheless.

"I guess," he muttered before crossing the porch and slowly descending the steps. He looked at Julia for a moment, as if he wanted to say something. Olivia had the feeling he didn't know whether to thank her or tell her he hated her guts for being the one to bring him such evil, life-altering news. In the end, he said nothing, just nodding once and then walking past her toward the street to wait for the emergency vehicles.

Olivia watched his every move, noting the slump in his shoulders, the trudge in his step. He seemed a little shell-shocked, too filled with grief to think of anything else.

She understood; she felt almost as crushed.

But she was still able to think clearly.

Apparently, so was Julia. The other woman cleared her throat and gave her a pointed stare from a few steps below. She cocked her head, listening as the sirens drew closer, probably no more than a couple of minutes away.

"Well?" Julia asked, leaving the decision in Olivia's hands.

She was torn. On the one hand, she knew Gabe wouldn't want her to put herself through it—he'd made that clear last night. On the other, she knew he'd move heaven and hell to solve his partner's murder.

Olivia could solve it. Right now, right this minute. Not only solve it, she might also be able to save a child's life.

She could sit right on the step where he'd been sitting, extend one hand two feet into the house and place the tip of her finger against one of Ty's. She wouldn't have to go inside, wouldn't disturb any possible evidence, wouldn't touch anything else except a centimeter of his partner's body.

Gabe was leaning against a tree by his car, keeping his back toward them, his hand raised to his face. Grieving privately, trying to get it out before his coworkers showed up and the situation changed from the site of a friend's death to a crime scene.

The sirens. Louder now.

Ten blocks? Eight?

Julia continued to stare. Silent. Nonjudging. Saying she'd support her either way.

Unable to resist, Olivia turned and looked over her shoulder into the house. Her eyes immediately went to that helpless hand, and she was struck with a deep, nearly inconsolable sadness for all the things Ty would never have, never hold, never do.

That hand would never brush the cheek of a woman he loved, never wear a wedding ring, never tickle his child's feet, never again wave goodbye to a friend.

All that glorious potential was wiped out, his empty hand full of nothing but the remnants of possibility that could have been the rest of Ty Wallace's life. Like dark streams of smoke and ash, those hopes for the future eluded his grasp, dissipating into the ether of lost dreams and unmet expectations.

Tears streaming down her face, Olivia made her decision.

Ty had died because he'd wanted to save a child's life. His sacrifice deserved to be honored . . . and shared. Even if it would hurt her terribly to share it.

She slowly lowered herself to the metal doorstep on which Gabe had been sitting. Not touching the door or the jamb, or the carpet, mindful of every possible finger-print, hair or fiber, she reached inside, noting the cooler air against her skin. She hesitated for just a second while she mentally prepared herself, then extended her hand.

She thought she heard someone yelling in the distance. But it was too late.

By that time, Olivia had already brushed her fingertip against Ty's cold, dead skin.

Monday, 1:15 a.m., eleven hours ago

Ty usually had no trouble sleeping. Once his head hit the pillow, he was almost always out immediately, sleeping like the dead. His granny called that the sleep of a righteous man. He called it the sleep of a dog-tired one.

Tonight, though, he'd had trouble. He'd been tossing and turning, running everything over in his head. The case, of course, but also the big pit of psychic quicksand he and his partner had somehow walked into. He'd seen and heard stuff in the past two days that would stay with him the rest of his days. Just thinking about the story Olivia had told, about experiencing the final minutes of that boy's life, was enough to make him want to get down on his knees and give thanks that he'd never had a near-death experience.

One of these days he intended to ask Gabe how he really felt about it. There was no way his partner could disguise the fact that he was falling for the woman—and Ty wondered if the man had really given it a lot of thought, what being involved with someone like that would mean. Marrying her, having kids with her, with what was in her head? How could he ever do it?

"Okay, head, empty out—time to sleep," he muttered, staring up at the ceiling. He tried to picture sheep up there, jumping over a little fence, but that just made him hungry. He hadn't had his mom's roast lamb with mint jelly in a long time.

Knowing his partner was a night owl, he thought about calling him, but honestly, until he had solid news to share, he didn't really want to. Part of him hadn't been disappointed not to have reached Gabe earlier tonight, because Ty had almost as many questions as he did answers.

It wasn't that he'd had no luck with his investigation.

No, he hadn't spoken with the detective who'd handled the Virginia Jane Doe murder case. The man had retired a few years back, and nobody was around on a Sunday evening who could tell Ty how to contact him.

And no, he hadn't been able to reach the father of the missing child who he thought might have been their Zachary. The man's last known number had been disconnected, and a quick property search showed his house—his last known address—had been sold almost twenty years ago.

Ty had searched online, looking through driver's license records, arrests and criminal cases, and hadn't found anything on the man. He knew he'd be able to run a more extensive search on property and tax records in the morning when he could get some help, have live people to talk to. But he had exhausted what he could do on a Sunday night.

With one option left, he'd crossed his fingers and tried calling the only other relative named in the case file, the father's cousin.

To his surprise and delight he'd gotten through. The man's only relative had sounded nice enough at first. At least until Ty had mentioned the missing boy and his father. Then the voice on the phone had gone from friendly and confused to wary and cautious.

That's what was keeping him up.

Gabe had been telling him for a year that the best detectives learned to rely on their intuition. That while cold, hard facts were most important, knowing how to recognize that churning in your gut or the tightening in the back of your neck could also be critical. And his Spidey senses had been tingling up a storm during that telephone conversation, which he replayed in his mind

Johnny's gone. He left the country. His heart was just broken to pieces when he lost his baby boy—that was awful, what his wife did, stealing Zachary away.

When Ty had asked where Zachary's father was now, he'd been told this "Johnny" had joined the army and hadn't come back for a visit in more than ten years.

It was possible, he supposed. It would explain the lack of local records. Still, Ty hadn't been completely convinced.

Mainly because his stomach had churned. And the back of his neck had felt tight when he'd hung up at the end of the conversation.

That cousin knew something. He'd lay money on it. Hopefully, tomorrow, he and Gabe could figure out how to get that information.

Knowing he wasn't going to be able to get back to sleep, Ty got out of bed, having decided to go do some more surfing on the Internet. See if he could find out anything else about this family.

"Gonna be an early morning," he muttered, eyeing the clock. But being awake and working was better than being awake and tossing around in his bed. So he headed for the kitchen, poured himself a glass of water, then went into the tiny spare room he used as an office. He turned on his laptop and, while it fired up, flipped open the folder with the report on Zachary and his mother. He'd skimmed it earlier, but now he read a little more carefully, paying special attention to any mention of the rest of the family.

It was while reading a transcript of the father's statement to police, when he'd reported that his wife had kidnapped their son, that the tension he'd been feeling became a full-on frenzy.

He stared at the father's name. Then stared at the boy's name. Then stared at the nickname the father had used for him.

Then remembered every word Olivia had said about Zachary's last minutes.

"Oh, no, you didn't," he whispered. "You son of a bitch, no, you did *not*."

He read it again.

She took him. I love him—I still love her, too—it broke my heart when she left me, officer. But him, my son— God, why would she do such a thing? Why would she take my little Jackie-boy when he's all I got?

"You motherfucking piece of shit," he snapped, hearing his own anger in the darkness. As it all washed over him, the whole, ugly truth, he lurched out of his chair, needing to go get something stronger to drink than water. "Bastard, hanging's too good for you. What kind of father would do that?" he muttered as he walked out of the office into the dark living room.

He didn't even see the man until he charged forward, the gleam of moonlight reflecting against the long, sharp blade in his hand.

Ty was caught totally off guard, never in a million years expecting something like this, so he was a bit slower to respond than he might otherwise have been. But he did respond. He instinctively threw up his arm, to ward off the blow. He gasped, taking a deep slice to the forearm, glad only for the fact that the hunting knife had missed its intended target—his chest or throat.

The shadowy figure came at him again, from the right, and Ty spun around, knocking over a table and lamp. He kicked out with his right foot, making contact with a beefy leg. But his bare foot barely slowed the bastard down, and the knife arced through the air, cutting into the back of Ty's calf.

"Ah, God!" he cried, pain exploding through him. "Christ, who are you? What do you want?"

"You shoulda minded yer own bizness," the voice said. "Left me and Jackie alone."

He suddenly got it and knew he was fighting a madman, fighting for his life. Despite the pain, he found some well of strength and startled his attacker by launching forward, barreling right into his chest. They both fell, rolling across the floor until they slammed into the couch. Ty ended up on top of the man's back, and he swung his left fist, hard, hitting his assailant in the kidneys.

The man grunted in pain, squirming, but Ty hit again. He looked frantically around, seeing nothing close enough to use as a weapon. The knife had flown out of the man's hands, too far for either of them to use it, and Ty's service weapon was holstered in his bedroom.

He punched a third time as the man bucked, pushing himself up to his knees, taking Ty with him. The room had begun to spin. Glancing down, Ty saw blood gushing from his leg.

He tried to hold on, knowing if the man got up, it would all be over. Ty's right arm was hanging useless by his side, and he wasn't sure he could walk on his leg, which still throbbed with the kind of pain he hadn't known was possible.

It was a losing battle.

Though he tried desperately to wrap his good arm around the man's thick neck, he just couldn't hold on, growing weaker with every second that passed. His attacker finally threw him off and staggered to his feet. Ty rolled onto his knees and glared at the other man, hating him, wanting to lunge forward and rip him apart with one hand and his teeth if he had to. But he could barely see his attacker much less do anything to hurt him from here. He was several feet away, it was too dark, and Ty was too badly hurt.

He considered diving for the knife, or trying to roll—or hell, crawl—to his room, which had never looked so far away. But before he could do either one, he saw the killer pull something out of his pocket.

A gun.

Fuck.

His assailant raised the weapon, pointed it. Ty lifted a hand, palm out, as if to ward him off. But he didn't beg, didn't plead. This bastard had come here for this, to kill him. There was no mercy in his veins. What he'd done to poor little Zachary—John Zachary Traynor, who his father had called Jackie-boy—was eternal proof that he had no soul.

Ty was about to die. His life was ending at the age of twenty-six.

Knowing that, his mind churned frantically. He had seconds at most, and while he wanted to think about his parents and his granny and his brothers, and his partner, and oh, God, how he wanted to think about Brooke Wainwright's pretty smile and her soft hair, he knew he didn't have that luxury.

He had to leave a message.

"Liv," he muttered, "he killed his son. His own son. Zachary was Jackie-boy. Tell Gabe—look at the noncustodials. Tell him the name John . . ."

Pop.

He flew back, landing on the floor a few feet from his front door, wondering why he hadn't heard much of a shot or why it didn't really hurt. Had it been some kind of tranquilizer. . . ?

Jesus. He moaned, unable to make any more sound

than that. The fire had started, the burning in his chest; his mind just hadn't caught up to the pain till now. *Real gun. Real bullets. Just silenced.*

He looked up, gasping for air, knowing something vital inside him had been hit, wasn't working anymore. Because he couldn't catch his breath, couldn't even feel his heart beating.

But his mind worked. And the things he'd wanted to think about suddenly flooded it.

He pictured the faces of the people he loved, remembered the way his Dad had taught him how to fish, and his Mom had made the best pumpkin pie at Thanksgiving, and his granny had called him every Sunday night to ask if he'd gone to church. He'd missed her call tonight and figured he'd call her back later in the week.

She'd be waiting on that call forever, now. *Sorry. So sorry.*

He heard heavy footsteps, barely noticing—or caring—that his killer had gone to pick up his knife and was now coming back. Ty knew he should look at him, should try to fill his eyes with every detail, hoping Olivia would see, would recognize the man despite the darkness.

But he was almost gone . . . almost gone. . . . He didn't want his murderer's image to be the last thing he ever saw in this world. And he was tired, very tired; he could hardly keep his eyes open.

So he stopped trying. He closed them and let his mind drift. His thoughts landed on one last image, one last lovely thought.

How he would have liked to have gotten to know her.

"Such pretty blond hair," he whispered.

And then he died.

Chapter 13

Gabe felt like he was moving underwater or in slow motion. He'd been standing by the street, trying to dry his goddamn face before the first responders showed up. Then something had made him glance over his shoulder to see what Olivia was doing. From across the small yard, he saw her lean into the house, her hand extended, as if she was reaching to grab something.

What is she doing?

But the thought had immediately been replaced by a sick certainty that he already knew.

She wouldn't. She'd promised. She wouldn't do that, not without saying anything. Not without asking, not without giving him the chance to say absofuckinglutely not.

Only, she was.

"No, Livvie, stop!" he yelled, his own voice sounding distant to his own ears.

She didn't stop; she couldn't—it was already too late.

He hesitated, hearing the sirens no more than a minute away. Two at most.

Two minutes ten seconds.

"No!"

He wouldn't allow it. This was his partner, his friend. Ty had just died. He was still lying in a pool of his own blood, in his own house, and Gabe hadn't even processed that yet. Olivia couldn't just . . . just . . . reach out and take his death like she had some right to it.

He felt sick. Afraid for her, furious at her. And all these feelings combined to finally get his brain working and his feet moving. He raced toward the house, yelling at her to stop, almost barreling right over Julia, who stepped directly into his path.

"Wait!"

He grabbed her upper arms and moved her out of his way.

"Damn it, Gabe, just wait a minute," she said, pushing in front of him again. "It's already started. Let her do what she has to do."

Gabe thrust a finger in the woman's face. "She doesn't have to do it—don't you get that? All you people who call yourselves her friends make her feel like she does. You encourage her to do something that not only tortures her but eats at her soul, one tiny bite at a time."

Julia's face paled, and her eyes widened in her face, as if nobody had ever said such a thing to her. How could these people claim to know her and never have realized, never have seen the truth? This so-called gift was actually a curse, and she used it at her own peril.

"How can you not have noticed that Olivia doesn't just experience these deaths, that she, herself, dies a little every fucking time she does it? Now get out of my way."

She lifted a shaking hand to her mouth and stepped aside. Gabe launched up the steps onto the porch, even as he heard the sirens right up the block. He grabbed Olivia, trying to pull her away.

She resisted.

Glancing inside, he saw that this time she hadn't just made a finger-to-finger connection. She'd actually clasped Ty's hand and was holding on tightly. As if she knew Gabe would try to stop her.

Damn right.

He was about to reach in and pry her hand away when he heard her mumble something. Olivia's eyes were closed, her whole body shaking, tears flowing down her cheeks. Then she whispered something else. "Tell Gabe, 'Look at the noncustodials.'"

He froze, shocked into complete immobility.

Tell Gabe.

Ty had left him a message? Was that even possible?

His young partner had heard about what Olivia could do and had believed it—or at least believed it was possible. Knowing that and figuring she might try to use her abilities to find out what had happened to him, he'd used his last coherent moments to try to help solve his own murder . . . and find that boy.

Right to his dying seconds he'd been thinking not of himself, of the life that was slipping away with every tick of the clock, but of saving somebody else.

Olivia suddenly jerked hard, one of her hands flying to her chest. She cried out. Gasped for air. Gabe didn't know what the hell to do, torn between his desire to pick her up and carry her out of here and his loyalty to his partner. He owed it to Ty to listen to his last words, didn't he?

It had been a while—nearly two minutes, he felt sure. It was almost over. So, in the end, he simply knelt behind Olivia, pulling her back against his chest but not trying to loosen that tight grip she had on Ty. He wrapped an arm around her shoulders, supporting her, burying his face in her hair and whispering, "You're okay. It's all right. I'm here, Liv. You're not alone."

Please come back.

She relaxed a little, her breathing slowed to a crawl, her muscles eased and her whimpers stopped. The first ambulance pulled up out front, the siren screaming. But above the din, he heard her say one more thing, something he couldn't understand. Something about pretty blond hair.

Then she released Ty's hand and sagged back against Gabe.

He sent up mental thanks for a second before rising and picking her up in his arms. As he began to carry her down the steps, Julia hurried over, and one of the members of the ambulance crew ran up as well. "Let us help her, sir," he said.

"She's fine, she just fainted." He gave the man his name and badge number, adding, "My partner's lying in the house, but you can't help him."

"Are you sure? Maybe . . ."

"I'm sure," Gabe said, feeling the emotion well in his throat again. "He's gone."

As Gabe carried Olivia to Julia's car, setting her on the passenger seat, a police car pulled up. "Turn on the air conditioner," he told the brunette before turning away to go speak to the first officer on the scene.

He knew he'd be telling this story again and again today, so he made it quick, sharp and succinct. Yes, he'd been worried about his partner—they could check his phone records, confirm that with Waczinski. His girlfriend, Olivia Wainwright—yes, that Wainwright, the senator's cousin—had been worried, too, being a friend of Ty's as well. They'd arrived within a couple of minutes of each other, him first. He'd confirmed his partner was dead, then stepped outside and found Olivia and her friend there. Olivia had fainted when she'd spied Ty's hand. Her friend was about to take her home.

Smooth. Easy. Even almost true.

After that first conversation, it got easier. He immediately got on the phone and called his lieutenant, knowing every damn member of the squad would be here in a half hour. The SCCPD went a little crazy when one of their own died. And Ty was especially well liked.

He deserved the attention he was going to get.

Gabe was about to go talk to the forensics guy who'd just shown up when he saw Julia waving at him, trying to get his attention. Olivia was awake, watching him from inside the car, her wide eyes dominating her pale face. She looked heartbroken and remorseful, and maybe even a little frightened, as if worrying about his reaction.

She should be. With every minute his fear for her had receded, his anger had grown. He felt like one of those parents who'd yanked his kid out from in front of a speeding car, then promptly slapped him—furious at her for putting herself in danger and for scaring him so badly.

Angry that she'd gone behind his back—literally—and done something she'd promised him she wouldn't. He counted to ten, knowing he had to stay calm. She was grieving, just as he was. She was also in pain, affected by the experience.

And she had something to tell him.

Walking over, he slowed down enough to hear Julia mutter, "Don't you be mean to her."

He ignored the woman, then squatted down beside the open car door and looked at Olivia's tear-racked face. "Are you okay?

"I'm sorry."

His jaw tightening, he tabled that apology for discussion at another time. "I'm gonna be tied up here for a while."

"You can't," she said, her mouth trembling. "You have to go to your station, look through Ty's phone logs, his computer history."

With his heart thudding, since he already knew the answer, he asked, "He left me a message?"

She nodded. "I heard him as clear as bell. He said my name; he knew I'd hear him."

That much he'd already figured out.

"He told me to tell you to look in the noncustodials. Do you know what that means?"

He did. "We've been trying to ID Zachary in files of kids kidnapped by strangers. There's another whole classification: kids taken by their noncustodial parents. We just assumed he wouldn't be there, that all these kids were snatched by the same sick stranger."

Olivia rubbed a hand over her eyes, and her voice was filled with disgust as she told him the rest of it. "It will be there. Because Ty said something else. Zachary wasn't killed by a stranger."

The possible explanation hit him a second before she said it.

"He was killed by his own father. His real father."

Stunned, he could only stare, thinking of everything she'd told him about the boy's death. His awful, brutal death. At the hands of his own father?

He wondered why he was shocked; he'd seen lots of horrible, abusive parents. And he'd seen firsthand what a grandfather could do. Still, this seemed especially brutal. "You're sure?"

"Positive. He also mentioned the name John, right before . . ." She reached up and rubbed her chest, as if feeling the impact.

Gabe knew what bullet wounds looked like. He knew how his friend had died. He clenched his back teeth, not letting his thoughts be derailed. He'd mourn Ty forever, but right now a low, boiling anger had begun to build within him.

He wanted the man who'd done this. Wanted him badly.

"If you can find the right case, you can retrace Ty's steps."

Agreeing, he added, "And once I find out who he talked to, I'll know how the bastard found out Ty was on to him."

Then he'd get him. Oh, hell, yes, would he get him.

Having to ask, since they'd already come this far, he took one final step into her dark nightmare. "Did you see anything?"

She shook her head, her fine red hair falling down to curtain her face. "Nothing useful. It was dark, shadowy." He saw the way her throat worked as she swallowed. "If it matters, he fought his heart out. And it was over pretty quickly."

His eyes burning, he nodded his thanks.

It mattered.

Silent, he rose to his feet. Olivia looked up at him searchingly, as if wanting to discuss this more. Not just what she'd learned, but how she'd learned it. "Gabe, I . . ."

He put a hand up, stopping her. "Don't say it. I'm not ready to hear it."

"You can at least let me say I'm sorry. I did what I thought I had to do. And it worked."

Glaring, he said, "Oh, the ends justified the means, right? But how long until those means send you right around the bend, Liv?"

"I'm fine," she insisted.

"Yeah, sure you are. Tell me, how do you expect to ever have any kind of normal life—maybe settle down, get married, have kids—when you've got a nightmare playing out in your brain twenty-four/seven?"

She winced when he said those words, as if that possibility—a life with him—had been on her mind. Hell, it had been on his, too, as crazy as it seemed since they'd only known each other a week. But it had been far too easy to imagine.

He was falling for this woman, hard, and fast, heart, mind and body. And one thing he knew for sure: They wouldn't have any kind of life together until she got this monkey off her back. She was like a heroin addict who was never gonna be made whole and well and strong until she kicked the habit.

"It's not always . . ."

"Like hell it's not. You live in a horror movie all the

time. It's wrong, it's unhealthy and eventually it's going to make you want to put a bullet in your head."

He heard her gasp, saw her jerk a little and realized he'd done exactly what Julia had asked him not to do. He'd been too hard on her, not that Olivia didn't need to hear these things, but now wasn't the time, and this sure as hell wasn't the place.

Feeling like an utter shit, he muttered, "I'm sorry. I shouldn't have said that."

"You've obviously given it some thought."

"Well, I'm not thinking too straight right now." That was certainly true. "Listen, I've got to get to work. My lieutenant's going to order me off the scene as soon as he gets here. He'll probably tell me to go home for a few days. I'll make an excuse to go by the precinct first and track down everything Ty's been up to."

She nodded once. "That's a good idea. Will you please call my office and let somebody know if you need help?" She sounded as though she didn't think he'd trust her enough to call her directly. "Promise me you won't do anything without backup."

No backup. Yeah, right. He didn't have a partner anymore; Ty was gone. That reality was going to sink in any minute now. Or any decade, maybe.

"I won't," he told her. "Now, let Julia take you home. Try to get some sleep. I know you need it." He wanted to reassure her, tell her he hadn't meant the things he'd said. But how could he do that? He had meant them. He regretted having said them now and in that way, but he'd meant every one of them. He loved her, deep down, he truly suspected he did. But damned if he would ever stay by her side and watch her kill herself a little at a time.

In the end, though, he simply said, "Take care of yourself. I'll come soon, and we'll talk."

Before he could leave, she reached for his hand, saying, "Gabe? I'm so sorry about Ty."

He squeezed her fingers, thanking her for the senti-
ment and silently offering her the reassurances he
couldn't verbalize just yet. "Yeah, so am I, Liv. So am I."

Johnny had figured Olivia would be alone at her house
at some point today. Sooner or later her boyfriend was
gonna find out his partner was dead, and she'd come
back here to be all sad by herself while he played super-
hero crime solver.

That partner—the thought of him still made him ball
his fists in impotent rage. "Dirty fighter," he snapped, still
sore from where the man had punched him in the back.
Bastard had been strong; he had bruises as big as dinner
plates on him. "Shooting was too damn easy for ya."

At least he was gone, that particular threat elimi-
nated.

He wasn't stupid enough to think he was in the clear.
The cop could have told his partner what he'd found out,
so Johnny was probably gonna have to kill him, too. But
the woman just had to go first. He wanted to take her,
terrify her, then cut her throat.

Johnny sat in his van, the one he used to haul around
his landscaping equipment. The one everybody in Olivia's neighborhood had seen a hundred times parked in
dozens of driveways. Right now, it was parked in the one
beside her house, and from here, he had a perfect view
of her balcony. Olivia was home, upstairs in her room.
Alone.

She'd looked like shit when her friend had helped her
into the house, half-dragging, half-carrying her. The
flashy brunette had helped her up the stairs to her room,
and when she'd left, she'd closed the front door softly,
like she hadn't wanted to wake anybody up.

An afternoon nap. Perfect.

It wasn't an ideal situation. It was daylight, for one
thing. And the woman might not be totally out. Yet he

couldn't wait. He was running out of time, needed to finish this, enjoy her while he could, then put her in the ground. A quick packing job, then he and Jackie would be on their way to who knew where to lie low for a while.

He'd promised he would go away for a while, and he tried to keep his promises, though he wasn't always successful. Aside from the promise, he couldn't take one more frantic phone call, one more interrogation from somebody who should have learned years ago to stay out of Johnny's business. Then again, his cousin's phone call about that cop had come at a pretty good time yesterday. If not for that call, Johnny might not'a knowed Wallace was on to him.

His cousin was the one who'd asked him to leave town for a while . . . the one he'd made the promise to. She was all worried about him, thinking his mind had split apart when he'd lost Jackie.

Ha. If only she knew Jack was safe and sound, tucked in the camper.

Knowing he had to act now, before people started getting home for dinner, he headed into the neighbor's backyard and then leapt over the fence. A dash across a few feet of open grass, and he was on her back patio. He'd already tested her locks and knew exactly which door to jimmy.

"No alarms," he mumbled, "not like when you was a kid."

Not that the alarm had been a problem—hell, he'd had the code, hadn't he?

He was inside ninety seconds after he'd left the van. Reaching the stairs, he suddenly hesitated, sure he'd heard something. A creak, or rustle. He peered into the room he'd just come through, then into the one closer to the door, seeing a curtain moving.

An air vent. Had to be. It was cold as a pig's ass in

here. Hell, right now he felt a chill washing over him like somebody'd dumped a bucket of cold water down his shirt.

Johnny turned to the stairs, lifted his foot, and suddenly stumbled forward, like he'd tripped over something, though nothing was there. He almost fell, but managed to right himself.

"Get on with it," he whispered, climbing the steps with slow, cautious determination. He ignored the strange feelings this place brought out in him—the feeling he was being watched—and went straight into her room.

She was, as he'd expected, on her bed, sound asleep, curled up on her side with her hands clasped under her chin. He stared at her, Johnny's nostrils flaring and the black rage building inside him as he thought of what she'd done, what she'd cost him. *Jack. Oh, God, Jackieboy . . .*

He crept closer. The woman on the bed hadn't made a move or a sound. Nor did she, not until he slapped his hand over her mouth.

Then she came awake right quick.

She launched up, grabbing at his hand, her eyes about popping out of her head. But unlike the last time, when terror froze her, she fought hard, scratching and kicking. So he couldn't enjoy her moment of panic.

He simply had to lift the gun he was holding and slam it down hard on her head.

Though still angry at him for saying whatever he'd said to hurt Olivia this afternoon, Julia couldn't help feeling very sorry for Gabe Cooper. He'd spoken in a moment of horrible stress, in the midst of tragedy, and she had no doubt he regretted it.

Because the man loved her. She could see it on his face, hear it in his voice. She'd known it the minute he'd nearly ripped her head off for letting Olivia touch Ty's remains.

Concern like that didn't come out of liking someone. He'd fallen for her friend in a big way, just as Julia believed Olivia had fallen for him.

There was something else: For the first time since the day Olivia had walked into her office and offered her services, Julia had stopped to think about exactly how much those services were costing. Not in terms of dollars but in terms of Olivia's well-being. Everyone was always very solicitous of her, asking her to do her thing only when there was no other choice, knowing it had to be awful. But nobody realized just *how* awful—that it could be killing her little by little. Nobody but Gabe Cooper, whom she hadn't even known a week ago.

She eyed the man, watching him dump a bunch of printed-out pages onto the conference table. He'd just arrived, loaded with files, looking grim and determined.

The first question he'd asked had been about Olivia. Julia let him know she was home, sleeping. The second was whether they'd help him, since he'd been ordered to go home and stay away from the investigation into his partner's murder. Standard operating procedure, she knew.

And not damned likely to happen. No more than she'd stayed out of Morgan's.

Quickly introducing Gabe to Aidan, whom he'd not yet met, she asked, "So what have you got?"

"I think I've found our boy," he said, tapping a printout on the table. "I did just what Ty must have done: dug into the noncustodials. I used the dates we had, rough information about the victim and the names Zachary and John."

He had made copies of a basic info sheet, and he dealt them to everyone sitting around the table. "John Zachary Traynor. Only child. Kidnapped by his mother at age three."

He told them what he'd learned so far, which hadn't been much beyond that, adding, "I had more to go on than Ty did—he didn't even have the name John at first." Dropping his eyes, he muttered, "Ty made sure we got the message. He also made it clear that the boy was killed by his biological father—who I've identified as John M. Traynor."

Aidan looked away, one case haunting him, like always.

"I printed out his initial kidnapping case file, then had to leave before my lieutenant decided to have me escorted out."

"Did he put you on official leave?" Julia asked, wondering if Gabe still had his shield and weapon. It wasn't unheard of for partners to be sent home for an unarmed cooling-off period.

"No," Gabe said, eyeing her from the other end of the table. Which meant he was armed.

"Now we need to go from here, figure out whatever else Ty might have, make the same moves he would have so we can find out who took him down."

Julia nodded, reaching for the printout. "I'll read every page of the initial report," she said, knowing that, as a former cop, she had the best eye for it. "Interviews, background on the divorce, see if there were any psychologist reports on the boy. If the divorce was a bad one, there should have been something in there about it." Given what had happened, it wasn't hard to read between the lines and assume the mother had taken the child away from an abusive situation. She'd had reason to fear for her son.

"I'm good with computers," Mick said. "How about letting me have a crack at finding out some more information about John M. Traynor."

Gabe eyed him sharply, as if to ask whether this crack would be legal or not. Mick merely held his gaze, not saying a word, neither admitting nor denying.

"Be careful," Gabe said with a nod.

"Why don't I go use my laptop to run through all the crime databases, unemployment and driving records, see if I can get a bead on where the mother was while she was in hiding," said Aidan. "The father had to have tracked her down somehow. It might help to know how."

Derek opened his mouth, though what he was about to say, she didn't know. Because suddenly a familiar voice called her name. She sat up straight in her chair, glancing over her shoulder out to the reception area. The new receptionist had just left for the day, mumbling about the strange, frantic goings-on here, and Julia wasn't sure she'd be back tomorrow.

"Julia!"

"Excuse me," she mumbled, rising to her feet, about to go find Morgan in her office. But before she had to, he materialized here, in the conference room.

"What is it?" she asked, seeing his nearly panicked expression. The other men in the room all turned to look at her, but she ignored them. "Morgan, what?"

"He took her. I tried to stop him, but there wasn't a damn thing I could do. Then I tried to follow but lost him. But I know who he is. I saw the name of his company on the van."

"Wait. Who, what are you saying?"

"Olivia. He took Olivia."

Julia staggered back against her chair, sending it spinning. Mick, who'd been closest, reached out and grabbed her arm so she wouldn't fall to the floor. "What is it?"

Terror filling her, she caught Gabe's eye from across the table. She told him.

And watched the man go from determined cop to utterly enraged lover.

Chapter 14

She hurt.

Olivia's head throbbed. Every time her heart beat it felt as though someone had stuck a spike through her temple. She tried not to move, thinking before she opened her eyes, trying to understand what was wrong, what felt so different.

She realized immediately that she wasn't in her bed. The ground was hard beneath her, rough, shaley dirt scratching at her bare skin. And it was hot, so very hot, like being inside the trunk of a car.

"No, oh, no," she whispered, suddenly remembering waking up, feeling that hand on her face, seeing him above her.

History repeating.

Almost. It hadn't been dark this time, and he hadn't bothered to cover her eyes. So she'd recognized him immediately. The man who'd terrorized her and haunted her for years had worked right outside her back door, right under her nose, all this time. He'd been cutting the lawns of all her neighbors, circling her house, again and again, like a great white on the prowl.

She breathed deeply, not allowing fear to rise inside her. She wasn't the same girl she'd been, wasn't helpless and weak. In pain, yes, but not helpless.

Finally opening her eyes, she remained still, studying her surroundings. The small building in which she was im-

prisoned looked like a shed of some kind. Wood walls, dirt
floors, corrugated metal roof. Only a hint of light shone
through the seams, and she figured it had to be close to
dusk, several hours since she'd fallen, exhausted, into her
bed, needing to sleep away the horror of Ty's death.

Gabe will be looking for me.

She'd given him the clues, Ty's clues. He'd use them.
He'd track this man down, and he'd find her.

In the meantime, though, she needed to prepare herself for her kidnapper's return. She didn't think of him
as Lenny, the name he'd used in recent years. If her suspicions were correct, his name was John. Ty hadn't been
able to finish telling her whether the name John had belonged to father or to son, but she suspected she knew
the answer: both.

Jack was a common nickname for John. A father
named John might want to call his boy Jack rather than
Junior.

Jackie-boy.

What a monster. She didn't think she could feel any
worse about what had happened to the boy who'd saved
her life, but the thought that he'd died at the hands of his
own father—because he'd helped her escape—was
enough to drive her mad with regret.

*Not now. You don't have time for this. Besides, maybe
he's finally happy. He's with his mother, away from the
man who'd abused him.*

Maybe. It was cold comfort, but maybe.

Suddenly hearing a noise outside, she slid closer to
the wall, trying to see out the sliver of a crack at the base.
She couldn't make out a thing, but she could hear something that was getting louder.

A vehicle. But whose—John's or someone else's, her
attacker's or her rescuer's?

There were no sirens. Nor did she imagine any rescuer
was just going to come driving up.

It was probably him.

Glad he hadn't tied her up, Olivia reached down into the pocket of her pants, hoping he hadn't searched her while she was out. "Yes!" she whispered when she felt her key ring. She'd pocketed it this morning when she and Julia had left the office to head to Ty's house.

Digging it out, she felt everything on it, fingering a round tube—a mini flashlight. And then a thin, flat metal object—a tiny folding knife.

Her father had bought her the key ring years ago, after the kidnapping, telling her she should always have something to use in case of an emergency. She didn't imagine he'd ever thought she might try to defend her life with a two-inch knife, dulled to near uselessness. But it was better than nothing. If the killer got close enough to her—maybe thinking she was still unconscious—she might be able to stab him in the eye. Not kill him, probably, but hurt him enough to run.

You're not running.

No. She wasn't running this time. Not if there was a chance there was a boy here who needed her.

So she probably ought to try really hard to kill the bastard.

The car drew closer, until it passed right by, making the tiny shed rattle. A little farther, then it stopped. Olivia stayed very still. She wanted him to think she was still out cold—defenseless. Or else scared out of her wits.

Suddenly, to her shock, she heard a woman's voice call, "Johnny? Where are you? Damn it, get out here!"

Olivia gasped. Did he have an accomplice? Was some demented woman helping him with his crimes?

A door creaked open nearby. "Well, fancy you coming all the way out here for a visit," a man's voice said, sounding like he was no more than twenty feet away. Heavy footsteps landed on what sounded like metal, then on crunching gravel.

He'd walked down a few steps onto the road.

She knew this scenario, had been through it before. He was living in a trailer or motor home, probably out in the woods somewhere. But was he living alone, or was there a boy inside, staying quiet as a mouse, ordered to by the man who'd gone outside to see who'd come to call?

"Did you kill that man?" The woman's voice rose with every word, and she was almost screaming as she repeated, "Did you kill that man?!"

Ty. Was she talking about Ty?

"Answer me, damn you!"

Olivia's stomach clenched, her heart tripping a little in her chest. There was something about that voice ... something ...

"Now what the hell didja expect me ta do?"

"You said you'd leave," the woman said, sounding on the verge of tears. "You swore you'd just go and never come back."

"You'd like that, wouldn'tcha, little cousin?"

A cousin? The monster had a female cousin? Did she know what he was, what he'd done?

"I never would have told you he'd called if I knew you were going to do that. Damn it, Johnny, why couldn't you just leave?"

He laughed, a low, evil chuckle. "Aww, I'd miss ya too much. I like our talks."

"You like tormenting me," the woman cried. "There's something wrong with you."

"And you like that when it suits your purpose, don't you? Fuckin' whore, usin' me to get what you want, then throwin' me aside once ya got it."

"I never wanted you to kill anyone. Not ever."

"Well, aren't your hands lily white, then? Go on, get back in your fancy car and get outta here."

No. Please. Don't leave. Olivia didn't know what to do.

If she screamed for help, would she just be putting the woman's life in danger, too? The man had killed his son; what on earth would prevent him from killing another relative?

"Fine," the woman snapped, walking away, "but I'm through lying for you. The next time my phone rings and a police officer asks me if I know where you are, I'm giving him directions."

"Well, then, won't we have fun sharin' a jail cell?"

Her footsteps stopped. "You wouldn't."

"O'course I would."

"All this time, all the help I've given you, the money . . ."

"You paid me to do your filthy work. Don't go actin' like it was charity."

"You're a bastard."

His heavier footsteps pounded across the gravel, and the woman shrieked.

"Don't touch me! I left a note sayin' where I was going. If I'm not home in an hour, somebody will come out here lookin' for me."

Olivia listened for the sound of fists or a slap, but didn't hear it. The woman's threat had worked. That meant he might be forced to let his cousin go, even if she saw or heard something she wasn't supposed to.

Olivia weighed her options, knowing they were few. She could lie here and wait, hoping to surprise him with her tiny knife, or she could try to grab at the one lifeline that had been thrown to her.

Praying she was doing the right thing, she slowly rose to her feet, moving to the wall of the shed. Then she drew in a deep breath and screamed as loud as she could.

As soon as she stopped she heard the woman's horrified voice. "No, tell me you didn't. Tell me it's not . . ."

"Well, sure it is, darlin'." His tone vicious, he added, "Why don't we say hello."

Olivia hadn't been sure what to expect. That the other

woman would get in the car and drive away in a hurry, going for help? That she'd question her cousin? But not this. Not that he'd bring her here and open the door. God, what would she do if he threw the woman in here with her? *Stab him before he can slam the door*.

She tightened her grip around the knife. Standing by the door, she waited, every fiber in her body on alert, knowing she had one chance at this.

She heard the clink of chains, then the sound of rattling keys.

"Don't. Please, don't. No, stop," the woman was saying, sounding on the verge of hysterics. "You can't, you mustn't let her see . . ."

The words stabbed at her, their meaning both cloudy and terrifyingly clear. Olivia focused, listening to the voice, not to the words, realizing it was familiar somehow.

The door began to swing open. Olivia forced all other thoughts out of her mind, knowing she had to leap and stab first, then deal with whoever this mystery woman was.

But she didn't get the chance. Because the woman was suddenly pushed into the open doorway, blocking Olivia's path out, preventing her from getting at the man.

It took a second for her eyes to adjust; the lights from the motor home shone brightly in her face, blinding her. She blinked, trying to make out the figure in front of her, seeing a slim body and an arm, which was clenched in a beefy male hand.

She lifted her eyes until she was finally able to see the face.

Recognition exploded through her like a cannon shot.

"Sunni?" she whispered, not understanding. "What are you doing here? What . . . how . . ."

"She came to visit her family," the man said.

It was impossible. Olivia's father's live-in girlfriend

was related to the man who'd kidnapped and tried to kill her? There was no way it could be a coincidence. No way at all.

"Ya got it, don'tcha, sweetie? She took that job baby-sitting you precious little angels so's she could get close and help me plan the kidnapping. We was supposed to get rich."

Olivia gripped a beam on the wall, shocked, betrayed. Utterly enraged. This woman, this awful woman, had worked her way into Olivia's childhood home, destroyed her entire life and her family, for ransom money? And then, to add insult to injury, Sunni had stolen her way into her mother's place in her dad's life?

"I didn't want him to hurt you. He wasn't supposed to hurt you," Sunni said.

Olivia reacted from the gut. "You traitorous bitch," she snapped, then, unable to stop herself, spat right in the woman's face.

"Liv, I . . ."

Whatever Sunni had been about to say was cut off when the man yanked her away.

"I'll be back for you later," Johnny said.

Then he slammed the door shut before she even had a chance to raise the tiny knife, much less use it.

Gabe was like a man possessed.

When Julia told him what Morgan had seen, his first impulse had been to go straight to Olivia's house to find out for himself.

But he didn't. Because, as he'd already acknowledged, Gabe was a believer. He had no doubt Julia had inter-acted with a ghost, nor did he doubt that the ghost had seen Olivia get spirited away by some guy driving a lawn care van.

What a perfect way to stay close, to keep an eye on her. Just another anonymous worker in the neighborhood. Her gaze had probably skimmed over him hundreds of times, never seeing the danger he presented.

One thing was sure: His name wasn't Lenny. It was John Traynor.

"Damn it, Mick, have you got anything yet?" he asked, urging the other man to go further into a secure county property database. "There has to be something."

All of them were working as hard and fast as they could, trying everything they could think of to find Traynor. They'd searched records under his real name as well as his false one and had found out just about everything there was to know about the man. And every one of them sure down to his or her bones that he'd killed his ex-wife and kidnapped his son back when Zachary had been eight.

They'd found his last known address—he was long gone. Had tried reaching his only known living relative, a female cousin—all but one of the contact numbers had been disconnected, and there had been no answer at that one.

Aidan, feeling useless, had insisted on going over to Olivia's house to see if he could get any kind of psychic vibe about where she might be. And it was Aidan, whom Gabe didn't even know, who put them on the track that might actually help them find her.

He'd called from the driveway. He'd knelt there, touching the dirty tracks left by the most recent vehicle, and had had some kind of psychic vision.

A big stand of tangled woods. A trailer. A shed. A chain looped across a gravel driveway with a Private! No Trespassing sign hanging from it.

The most critical detail: The chain and sign had looked new.

Which led Gabe to the only possible conclusion: Traynor couldn't be squatting on some random public land like he had before. If he'd blocked the road, put up signs, he had to feel confident that they'd be obeyed, meaning he had the right to post them.

He'd bought land somewhere.

"He's got to be there," he said, watching as Mick keyed through page after page of records, looking for any transfers of wooded, undeveloped property of ten acres or more, going back a decade.

There were a lot. Too many. This would never work.

"Wait," Mick suddenly said, snapping his fingers. "I've been looking for individual buyers; this is the fourth or fifth property I've seen that was bought by some kind of holding or development company."

Which wouldn't be hard to set up, not if you had a little bit of money to hire a lawyer. And if he'd had money to buy the property, obviously he could afford it.

"Can you cross-reference the names of these companies with his name or alias?"

Mick clicked the keys, his gloved hands flying over them without a single misspelling. He'd obviously become very adept to life with gloves.

"Oh, my God, here he is!" he said, raising his voice so loud that all the others, who'd been working in the conference room, came racing into Mick's office. Every one of them looked hopeful, all of them having spent the past several hours worrying about their friend.

Gabe had been prepared to not like these friends of Olivia's—and he still didn't like that they hadn't even thought about how her gift was affecting her. But right now, he couldn't think of four other people he'd rather have on his side when he went to find her.

Mick smashed his index finger on the print button. "He bought it three years ago, a big section of woodland west of I-95, between here and Brunswick."

Gabe had already grabbed the page off the printer and was punching the address into his GPS.

"I guess we're not exactly doin' this by the book?" Derek asked.

Gabe knew what he meant and realized he'd completely put aside his job as a police officer. He wasn't waiting for a damn warrant or for anybody's permission or approval. He was going out there, finding Olivia and bringing her home.

She'd left.

Olivia hadn't even quite managed to accept Sunni's vile betrayal as truth before she'd heard the woman scream at her cousin, then get in her car and drive away. Leaving Olivia here to die. This woman who'd babysat her as a child, who'd pushed her and Brooke on the swings, who'd been to family dinners and shared holidays and who slept in her father's bed had abandoned her to the ruthless hands of a psychotic monster. Not once, but twice.

The woman had pretended to love Dad, but people like Sunni didn't understand the concept of love. If she were capable of any kind of real emotion, she wouldn't have been able to just drive away from here, knowing her cousin would never leave Olivia alive to testify against either of them.

Olivia had been waiting for Johnny to come back, but so far, he hadn't. After the car had driven away, he'd yelled, "Seeya later, O-livvv-eee-a. Time for my supper." He'd stomped up the stairs and gone inside, the door slamming shut behind him.

Alone in the dark, she remained alert, preparing. Sunni's presence had caught her off guard, but she still had the knife, which she'd now begun to scrape on a tiny rock, sharpening the blade. "It's not over yet," she whispered.

Suddenly, she heard a noise, a low, scraping sound from outside. She tensed, trying to determine where it had come from, sure only that it had not been from the direction of the camper. That squeaky door had remained firmly shut, and not a single footstep had crushed against the gravel.

"Olivia?"

She tensed. *Sunni.*

The woman had come back, obviously on foot, and crept up to the back of the shed.

"I'm going to get you out."

Olivia hated the woman, wanted more than anything to tell her to go screw herself, but no way was she going to turn away a chance of rescue.

"How?" she asked.

"I have spare keys to everything out here."

Johnny had given her a spare key to his torture chamber. There was familial love for you.

"I have to work fast once I go around to the front; if he looks out the window, he'll see me. Just be ready to run as soon as I get the door open."

Olivia moved to the door, stretching a little, flexing her calves, testing how quickly she could bring up the knife.

No, she didn't intend to use it on Sunni—not that the thought wasn't tempting.

She was going after Jack.

Finally, after what seemed like forever, she heard the clink of the chain and the rattle of the lock. Sunni muttered a curse—obviously the wrong key—then tried again. And again.

"Hurry," Olivia ordered, wondering how long it would be before Johnny looked outside.

"There!" The chain moved, separated, and the door slowly opened.

Sunni stood there, staring at her with guilty, tear-filled eyes ringed by dark circles where her makeup had smeared. She stepped out of the way, letting Liv out, then carefully pulled the door closed again, looping the lock over the chain.

Liv darted around behind the shed, crouching down, waiting for Sunni to finish. Once she had, she joined her, sniffling. She reached out, trying to take Olivia's hand.

Liv yanked back. "Don't touch me."

"Livvie, I'm so sorry."

"Shut up. I don't want to hear it."

"I know you hate me, and you have reason to. But please, at least believe that I never meant for you to get hurt. Johnny was supposed to get the money and let you go."

Sure. Trust the psychotic to do the right thing. "Yeah, right."

"You don't understand how it was for Johnny and me. We grew up together in foster care. We never had anything and just wanted a little money to make a new start."

"Cry me a fucking river."

As if realizing there was no way Olivia was going to listen to her, Sunni let out a self-pitying sigh, then said, "Come on. My car's about a half mile away, through the trees."

"I'm not going anywhere," Olivia said. "Not without Jack."

She'd run the last time, sure she'd be back in time to save a helpless boy. He'd paid for it with his life. She wasn't making that mistake again.

Her cousin's child; Zachary had been this woman's relative, too.

"You're delirious," Sunni whispered. "He hit you in the head. John Zachary is dead. He's been dead for twelve years."

"Murdered by your loving cousin."

"You're wrong. He died in an accident," Sunni replied, shaking her head. She had obviously been telling herself a fairy tale so she could sleep at night. "Johnny loved his son. He would never have hurt him."

"Yeah, but he *did* hurt him," Olivia snarled. "He lost his temper, got furious because he thought Jack had betrayed him by letting me go, and he murdered him."

And he'd been doing it again, every four years, ever since.

"No, no!" Sunni insisted.

Disgusted by the bitch's self-delusions, Liv sneered. "You really don't know anything about that cousin of yours, do you? Ever since he murdered his own son, he's been kidnapping other people's boys, holding them for years, then killing them when they get too old for him to pretend they're Jack. And one of those helpless boys is inside that trailer right now."

Sunni's mouth fell open, and she let out a tiny cry. She might be the world's greatest actress, having pulled off the part of loving girlfriend with that drippy Southern accent that was nowhere to be heard now. But it was at least possible that she hadn't realized just how evil her cousin was.

Cold comfort, though.

"There's something wrong with him; there always has been. He heard voices, claimed that someone else was telling him what to do or that the mysterious someone else had just done some of the things Johnny got blamed for. He had a hard life. We both did."

"Boo hoo," she snapped. "Say one more word defending him, and I swear to God I'll slap your face." Then, trying to hold on to her fraying temper, she added, "Go ahead, get out of here. Just call nine-one-one. I'll stay here and wait for them, unless I see him making a move on the boy."

Sunni shook her head quickly, looking over her shoulder at the trailer, where all remained still and ominously silent. "I'm not leaving you . . ."

"For God's sake, we don't have time to mess around. At least call the police."

"My phone's in my car."

Stupid, *stupid* woman.

"Then I guess you're leaving me." Liv put a hand on her back and pushed her toward the woods. "Go."

From behind them came a squeaking sound.

The door.

Oh, God, go!

Sunni went, darting into the woods. Liv could hear the snapping of limbs and the rustling of leaves, and prayed Johnny did not.

He yelled something, and her heart stopped. Then she realized he hadn't been yelling at Sunni . . . but at the boy, who had just emerged from the camper.

"Jack," she whispered, knowing that wasn't his name.

He was small, undernourished, scrawny. Pale. His brown hair was long and shaggy, his skinny shoulders slumped under an ill-fitting old T-shirt. He stumbled a little as he trudged down the stairs, and he kept his head down, trying to make himself small, unnoticed.

He looked broken.

"Do you know it's only a few hours till your birthday, Jack?" the man said. "And I got you a present. Gonna give you somethin' that'll make you know what it means to be a man."

He cast a sly look toward the shed. Olivia, realizing what he meant, wanted to puke, wondering if there was any evil, any degradation beneath him.

"And after you get your cherry popped, we're gonna have us another kind of fun together. You know all those times you asked me what I was doin' out in the shed and what those funny noises were? Well, tonight, you are gonna find out."

So, he wasn't going to kill Jack right away. He was going to make him a rapist and a murderer first.

Olivia gripped the pen knife, knowing that the moment Johnny came close enough to see the lock had been opened, she'd have to act. She only hoped the boy wasn't so brainwashed that he'd try to help his captor.

They walked closer, the man clapping the boy on the back. Then suddenly, from the woods behind her, Liv heard a snap, and a small cry.

Johnny heard it, too. "What the hell?" He reached into his pants and pulled out a gun Liv hadn't even seen. Good lord, she'd thought she could go up against this man with a knife, given what he'd done to Ty?

"You worthless bitch!" he howled.

For a second, Olivia was sure he'd seen her face, peeking out from behind the shed, but he soon proved otherwise.

"You shoulda never come back! I woulda let you go, you dumb whore!"

Then he was running, darting into the woods. He ran right past the shed—right past her—and kept going. Olivia could just make out a blond figure running away from him, zigzagging through the trees, crying, "Johnny, no!"

Sunni had come back, and she'd drawn him away.

Olivia and Jack had a chance, just one chance.

And she was taking it.

Not giving it another thought, she ran out from behind the shed, charged to the boy, swooped him into her arms, and ran as hard and fast as she could in the other direction.

Gabe drove like a madman, not really giving a damn that, beside him, Mick was hanging on to the dashboard and, in the backseat, Julia was clutching the door handle. The siren was on the roof, blaring at everyone in his way to make room. Somewhere behind him, Aidan and Derek were following, but they'd fallen back, not having the power of a tricked-out, eight-cylinder police car made for pursuits.

"There!" Mick said, pointing to the exit.

Gabe flew down the ramp, taking the curve so fast he thought the two inner tires would lift off the ground. "Which way?"

Mick looked at the GPS. "Right, then one mile. It should be on your left. Hopefully you'll see a new chain and a No Trespassing sign."

And if he did, Gabe was driving right the hell through them.

"Your ghost show up back there yet?" he asked Julia, eyeing her in the rearview mirror.

"No. I'm sure he's still looking."

He saw the small gravel driveway, right where Mick had said he would . . . and it did, indeed, have a metal chain with a shiny new sign. Knowing he was probably ending his police career for bursting onto a potential crime scene without a warrant or any provable probable cause, Gabe gunned the engine and drove right through the chain, tearing down the two posts that had been holding it up.

"Guess we're not going for the element of surprise," Mick said.

"No time."

There were no streetlamps, of course, and the woods overhead blocked out much of the sky. It wasn't full dark out on the road, but here in the woods, he couldn't see any farther than the distance of his headlights. He tapped the high beams, gaining a few extra feet, and kept following the narrow road, twisting and turning around hairpin curves and over downed limbs and brush.

Ahead, he suddenly spotted something—a glow in the woods. Some kind of light. His foot nearly hit the floor, taking the gas pedal with it, and he heard Julia fly around in the backseat. But he couldn't slow down.

Olivia, please, God, please be okay.

Suddenly, ahead of him, he saw a shocking sight and hit the brakes. A blond woman, her hair tangled over her face, obscuring it, came staggering out of the woods, clutching her stomach. Her hands were covered with blood, which dripped down freely, drenching her body.

"Who the hell is that?" he asked.

Julia was already getting out of the car, reaching for the gun at her hip. Mick joined her, and together they raced to the woman.

But Gabe didn't get out. They'd do what they could for her, but right now, he was focused on getting to Olivia, finding the shed Aidan had seen in his vision, since that's where the psychic had been sure she was being held. Those lights ahead, probably coming from the camper, were only yards away, he couldn't just sit here and stare at them.

He hit the gas again once Julia and Mick reached the woman's side. They waved him on, silently telling him to do what he had to.

Rounding one more curve, he suddenly emerged into a clearing and spied the mobile home. And the shed. He lurched to a stop, jumping out and running toward it, calling Olivia's name. But the word died on his lips when he saw that the door was wide open and nobody was inside.

"Gabe!" a voice cried.

Olivia.

He spun around, charging toward the sound, past the camper, into the dark woods. He knew a predator was out here, knew he was deadly. But Gabe was like a predator now, too. He was filled with rage and deadly purpose, wanting to save the woman he'd begun to love and avenge the partner he'd lost.

His weapon in his hand, down by his side, he paused midstep, hearing noises from two directions. A woman speaking somewhere to the right, a child's answering cry.

And to the left . . .

"Jack! You get back here, boy!"

"There you are," Gabe whispered, melting back against a large live oak, disappearing into its shadow. He waited, hearing the branches breaking as the murderous bastard lumbered through the woods, bellowing the boy's name again and again.

"You're not getting anywhere near him again," he mumbled, meaning it.

The man suddenly stopped yelling and stopped running, too. Gabe held his breath, not making a sound, knowing that, like any other deadly animal, John Traynor smelled danger.

Gabe was no murderer; he wasn't lying in wait to shoot the man down in cold blood. He'd just wanted Traynor to come closer, close enough so that there would be nowhere to run once Gabe leveled his gun on him and ordered him to freeze.

But he was still too far away. He could break left or right, disappear into the woods, where Gabe didn't dare randomly shoot for fear he'd hit Olivia or the boy.

"You're never going to hurt him again," a voice said, loud and deliberate. Olivia's.

She was close. Not more than a few yards away, though he couldn't see her. But she hadn't been talking to him; she'd been talking to Traynor. Baiting him like a bear.

Just like a wounded bear, Traynor bellowed, then lurched out of hiding, enraged by her voice, losing all caution. Which was obviously what she'd intended.

Gabe counted to five, watching the man step closer, sure Olivia had already taken cover again and was well hidden. Traynor drew even with him and then moved on past. Exactly two steps past.

"Freeze, you son of a bitch," Gabe snarled as he leapt out from his hiding place, putting the barrel of the gun against the man's lower back. "Drop that gun."

He'd expected him to do it, to know he had nowhere to go, no possible chance to get away from Gabe before he would be shot. But he was still operating on animal instincts. Those vicious, cornered-animal instincts must have told him to fight. He began to swing around, the muzzle coming up as he prepared to fire.

Somewhere out in the trees, Olivia cried out. The boy sobbed.

"Don't," Gabe ordered.

But it was clear the man wasn't going to stop. He intended to kill or be killed.

Knowing which of those two options he preferred, Gabe didn't even hesitate. He just pulled the trigger.

Traynor dropped. Gabe stared down at him, already knowing this man who'd killed so many, including the best friend he'd ever had, was never going to get up again.

Which was just fine with him.

"Gabe?" Olivia cried, running toward him through the trees. She held a boy in her arms, a gangly boy, not too big, but then neither was Olivia.

He jogged toward her, reaching out and taking the child from her arms. The boy, who looked like he was in shock, came without protest, staring down at the ground where the man who'd made his life miserable lay in a pool of blood.

"Are you okay?" Gabe asked, reaching out to touch Olivia, stroking her cheek, brushing his thumb across her bottom lip.

She curled her face into his palm, kissing his hand. "I'm fine. I think I really am fine at last."

Chapter 15

After she arrived home from Ty's funeral, Olivia kicked off her black shoes and sat down on her front porch swing. She hadn't used it in months—nobody used porch swings in the height of a Southern summer.

It was *still* the height of summer—still August, still hot, still miserable. But for the first time in at least two months, there was a hint of coolness on the breeze. Like Georgia had decided to take pity on her residents and send a tiny breath of fall a couple of months early, just as a tease.

It wouldn't last. But she'd take it while she could.

Pushing her bare feet against the plank floor of the verandah, she set the swing in motion, watching kids ride their bikes down the street, waving to one of her neighbors who was emptying groceries out of her car. They were living their lives. Normal lives. Normal families.

Normal days.

Would they ever be that way for her? Was normalcy something she could even understand at this point in her life much less strive for?

Most important, was she living her life the way she should be, or had her choices driven all chance of normalcy away for good?

That question had plagued her for a long time but never more so since Monday, when Gabe had looked at her with both anger and emotion in his eyes and told her what he thought of the job she'd been doing so far—the job of living the life she'd been given not once but twice.

She thought of Ty, whose murderer was now where he belonged, six feet under the ground. As was the murderer's cousin, who'd destroyed lives out of greed yet tried to do the right thing in the end.

She thought of John Zachary, who was finally at peace.

She thought of poor little Tucker Smith, whose parents had come to town as soon as they'd gotten word their boy was alive. He'd probably need years of therapy, but maybe, just maybe someday he'd be all right. He certainly seemed to have the love of good people—a family that sick monster had told him was dead.

She thought of Brooke, who'd broken her engagement this morning, and cried at the funeral this afternoon, mourning something she'd caught just a glimpse of that was now forever beyond her reach.

She thought of her parents, who'd listened to every word she'd said, realized how badly they'd been manipulated, and had then clasped hands, saying nothing but still somehow communicating more than they had in at least a decade. She knew they both blamed themselves—her mom for bringing Sunni into their lives, her dad for keeping her there. They might never be together again, but for now, they were united in sheer regret.

Then she did something she rarely did: Olivia thought of herself.

She considered her future, what she wanted, what she longed for, how she intended to fill her thoughts and her days.

And none of those things included death, hers or anybody else's.

She wanted life. She wanted it desperately. Wanted to be filled with laughter every minute of the day rather than sorrow. Wanted to go to sleep and dream happy dreams about the people she loved, not strangers living their agonizing final moments. She wanted to feel alive, rather than like she had one foot in the grave at any given moment. Wanted that light, giddy feeling of being young and free and in love . . . the one she felt when she was with Gabe.

Gabe. He was the one she wanted all those things with. The man who was, at this very minute, walking up the sidewalk, having stayed behind in the car to finish a phone call while she came to the porch and dropped onto the swing.

Gabe said nothing. He simply sat down beside her and draped an arm across her shoulders, letting his fingertips brush her arm. She pushed her toes against the floor again, setting them swinging, and they swayed together, the silence broken by the creak of the old hooks anchored into the ceiling.

"Are you all right?" she asked him, knowing today had been beyond awful. Burying a fellow officer was hard for any cop. Burying a friend and a partner was something few ever had to experience. She wished to God he hadn't been one of them.

"I'm okay. Ty's parents called to say they were getting ready to head to the airport."

"I'm glad I got the chance to meet them."

He continued to caress her arm, sighing deeply, so much more on his mind.

She knew one thing that wasn't worrying him—his job. She guessed that having a U.S. senator call your boss, the mayor, the chief, the media and everyone else to thank a young police officer for saving his cousin's life and bringing a cop killer to justice was enough to keep anybody employed. Gabe would probably end up getting a commendation.

Ty already had. Posthumously.

"What are you thinking?" she finally asked.

"I'm thinking about you. About us," he admitted.

She shifted so she could look up at him. "Funny, I was just thinking the same thing."

"Liv . . ."

She lifted a hand, putting her fingers over his lips. "Please, let me say something."

He nodded.

Swallowing hard, she admitted, "I gave Julia my letter of resignation."

His eyes widened in shock. "You did?"

"Not because you wanted me to," she was quick to point out, "even though I know you did."

"I didn't necessarily want you to quit your job. Hell, I'm no caveman."

"I know. You just wanted me to stop doing the most important part of it."

He didn't deny it.

"And that's what I decided to do." She shrugged helplessly, having to admit the truth, even to herself. "You were right. It was breaking me. I kept telling myself I was helping, doing what needed to be done. That the ends did justify the means. But they don't. Not if what I'm doing ends up destroying me, which it would."

She could never have a normal life unless she stopped. Her sanity would slip away, along with her security and her peace of mind. It might not happen right away, but it would happen. In the meantime, being so sure of that bleak inevitability, she would never *allow* herself to have a normal life. She'd never trust herself to give her heart completely or to accept his.

And she would never—ever—inflict her inner darkness on a child.

Olivia wanted children—she always had. She just hadn't allowed herself to think about the choices she faced, the decisions she would have to make, before she could even dream of having them.

"I'm finally ready to put down all this baggage I've been carrying around," she told him, knowing no other way to put it. "It's too much to haul. From now on, I'm only going to lift what I've bought and paid for myself."

He understood and smiled at her, bending to kiss her temple. "You're sure?"

"I'm absolutely certain," she said, meaning it. "Whether you and I have a future together or not—and please don't be terrified by me saying this, but I hope we do—I've realized I want one for myself. Even if I spend my days alone, I need to spend them in my own head, with my own problems, my own fears, my own dreams. Good and bad."

He moved his mouth down to her cheek, kissing her again. Then farther, to her mouth. Right before he brushed his lips against hers, he murmured, "We have a future, Liv."

A bright one, she hoped.

A bright, beautiful shiny one filled with love.

And life. So much life.

Epilogue

Three months later

Arriving home after the first day at her new job, Olivia walked into the kitchen to start dinner, already anticipating making a nice roast, perfect for a fall evening. Okay, so it was Georgia, and it was still seventy-five degrees outside, but she'd take what she could get when it came to autumn, her favorite season.

She was tired, and her feet hurt—who knew showing people works of art in a gallery would involve standing every single minute of the day?—but that was okay. Maybe it wasn't as challenging or exciting as the job she'd given up, maybe she wasn't making a huge difference in the lives of other people, and maybe she kind of hated modern art, but a job was a job.

The difference in her private life made it completely worthwhile.

She couldn't remember a time when she'd been happier. Gabe had moved in with her a month ago, finally acknowledging that living in a house that she owned didn't mean he was sponging off her. Considering she'd been unemployed and he'd been footing the bills, the opposite had been true.

It had been wonderful. She slept beside him every night, drank coffee with him in the morning, made crazy-wild love so often she was never entirely sure when the next orgasm was going to strike.

She was madly in love with him, and he felt the same way toward her. And life, oh, life was so very good.

There had been dark days, certainly, and sometimes when she looked at him, she knew he was thinking of his lost friend. His new partner seemed like a good guy, but she knew Gabe wouldn't let his guard down, wouldn't let him get too close. It had hurt too damn much the last time.

She sighed. "He misses you, Ty."

"Hey, you can't miss what won't leave."

Olivia dropped the roast she'd just pulled out of the refrigerator. It landed on the floor with a wet splat, but she didn't even notice as she spun around, her heart beating crazily as she realized someone was in her house.

Then she saw who it was. "Would you stop doing that?" she said, letting out a shaky laugh. "Damn it, Ty. I thought we agreed you wouldn't just pop up like Casper and say stuff to scare me."

Tyler Wallace, who'd appeared to her for the first time two weeks ago, when he had simply showed up in her car as she'd been driving to a job interview, gave her a sheepish look. "Sorry, I haven't got the hang of this myself yet." He looked at the floor. "You gonna pick that up before the cat eats himself into a case of food poisoning?"

Dex, as if hearing himself being talked about, hissed toward the empty corner where Ty stood. She sometimes wondered if Dex could see Ty, too. If so, they were the only two creatures on the face of the earth who could. Bending down, she scratched the cat's head, then picked up the unfortunate hunk of lumpy raw meat.

Glancing at the clock, she said, "Gabe's going to be home soon."

Ty smiled, looking a little winsome, sad that he could see his friend, reach out and touch him, but that Gabe never knew he was there.

Well, he knew, he just couldn't see or hear him.

Not keeping secrets had been one of the first promises they'd made to each other. So she'd told Gabe that very first night after Ty had come back into her life.

At first a little freaked out about it, he'd come to accept it, knowing that Ty's decision to stay here hadn't had anything to do with revenge or anger about his murder and that he wasn't trying to draw Olivia back into a world of pain, vengeance and brutal, ugly death.

Ty had just been lonely. He'd told her that the only member of his family who'd died before him was his grandfather, who had been a cranky, boring miser when he was alive and was equally as cranky, boring and miserly now that he was dead. "Granny was right," he'd said. "That man makes Scrooge McDuck look like the patron saint of charity."

He wasn't here all the time, but Ty came often enough to keep her on her toes.

Huh. To think three months ago she'd lived here alone, spent her days and nights by herself, with only her cat to talk to. Now she had two men around: one, her love and future husband and, hopefully, someday the father of her children; the other, his dead best friend.

It was weird, but somehow they were making it work.

"So how was your first day on the job?"

Olivia rolled her eyes.

"You know, Liv," Ty said, moving past her to sniff the wine she'd just poured, "you do have another option."

"I don't do that anymore. Remember?" And she couldn't be happier about it.

"I mean, if one ghost was enough to get Julia Harrington started in the psychic detective business, wouldn't two make it even better?"

She gaped. "Two? Meaning you? You want to go work for Julia?"

He shook his head. "Nah, she can't see me. You're the

only one who can." He wagged his eyebrows up and down, looking so cute and flirtatious, like he always had when he was alive.

"Come on, you know you want to."

Go back to work for eXtreme Investigations? Yes, some days she did want to. She missed her friends, missed working with them to solve a cold case that had baffled people for years.

She didn't miss what had once been the hardest part of her job, but she definitely missed the rest.

Could it work? Could she really go to Julia and say, "Me and my ghost want to come hang out with you guys?"

"It's crazy."

"Aww, don't even start arguing with me about this," he told her. "I've been told I'm so stubborn, I could argue with a wall . . . and win."

She had to hand it to him. Ty had gotten better at the Southern speak since he'd died. She wondered if there were a lot of dead Georgians hanging around on whom he'd been practicing.

"Let's do it, whaddya say? It'll be fun."

Her pulse picked up a little, excitement making her thoughts churn.

Maybe it really was possible to have the best of both worlds: some semblance of her old job and her new life free from the personal darkness she'd had to endure to do that job.

"What would Gabe think?" she said.

"What would Gabe think about what?"

This time she dropped the head of lettuce she'd been about to wash for salad, not even having realized that Gabe had come home much less that he'd walked into the kitchen. "Damn it, I'm going to make the two of you start wearing bells on your collars."

"Every time a bell rings, an angel gets its wings," Ty said, solemnly. Then he snorted. "Just kiddin'. What the heck would I know about angels?"

She rolled her eyes. "Your friend is a dork," she told Gabe.

Smiling faintly, Gabe murmured, "Hi, partner."

Ty lifted a hand, reached out and placed it on Gabe's shoulder, whispering, "It's good to see you."

Gabe stayed very still, his head cocked, as if he'd caught a faint whisper on the air, though she knew he would say he'd imagined it.

But who knew? Who could possibly say what strange things could happen at any time. Maybe Ty would appear to Gabe someday, or maybe he'd decide to head to that station she'd heard about, hop on a train and see what came next.

No one really knew, did they?

"So, what would I think about what?" Gabe asked as he came around the island to kiss her lightly on the lips.

She turned into his arms, cupping his face in her hands, looking up at him with every ounce of emotion she felt for this sexy, warm, tender, amazing man. The well of it ran deep, overflowing, filling her completely. And it was the same for him, she knew beyond any doubt.

One more thing she knew: Gabe was going to hate the idea of her going back to work for Julia Harrington. At least at first.

But he'd come around.

She was never going back to that awful, dark place where she'd lived for twelve years. Would never use her deadly ability again. Would never break her promise to him that she was finished with that part of her life.

Once she reminded him of that, she'd make him realize that he and their life together meant more to her than anything, and she wouldn't risk it if he truly didn't want her to.

Then she'd remind him that both his girlfriend and his late partner were ganging up against him.

Oh, yeah. He'd definitely come around.

Did you miss the first book in the thrilling
Extrasensory Agents series?
Read on for an excerpt from

COLD SIGHT

by Leslie Parrish

Available now from Signet Eclipse.

Until last night, nobody had ever read Vonnie Jackson a bedtime story.

Though she'd lived for seventeen years, she couldn't remember a single fairy tale, one whispered nightie-night or a soft kiss on the cheek before being tucked in. Her mother had always been well into her first bottle, her second joint, or her third john of the evening long before Vonnie fell asleep. Bedtime usually meant hiding under the bed or burrowing beneath a pile of dirty clothes in the closet, praying Mama didn't pass out, leaving one of her customers to go prowling around in their tiny apartment.

They definitely hadn't wanted to read to her. Nobody had.

So to finally hear innocent childhood tales from a psychotic monster who intended to kill her was almost as unfair as her ending up in this nightmare to begin with.

"Are you listening to me?" His pitch rose, her captor's voice growing almost mischievous as he added, "Did you fall asleep, little Yvonne?" But that mischief was laced with so much evil that it almost seemed to be a living, breathing thing, as real as the stained, scratchy mattress on which she lay or the metal chains holding her down upon it.

Most times, such as now, the man who'd kidnapped

her spoke in a thick, falsetto whisper, his tone happily wicked, like a jolly elf who'd taken up slaughter for the sheer pleasure of it. Every once in a while, though, he got angry and dropped the act. Once or twice, when he'd said a word or two in his normal thick, deep voice, she'd felt a hint of familiarity flit across her mind, as if she'd heard him before, recently. She could never focus on it, though; never place the memory.

Maybe she was crazy. Maybe she just recognized the twisted, full-of-rage quality that made men such as him tick. She'd seen that kind all her life. She'd just never landed in the hands of a homicidal one. Until now.

"Sweet little girl. So weary, aren't you? I suppose you fell asleep, hmm?"

She shook her head. Even that slight movement sent knives of pain stabbing through her skull and into her brain. Whether that was from the drugs he'd been shoving down her throat or from the punches to the face, she couldn't say. Probably both. The pills he'd given her hadn't made the pain go away. Instead they'd intensified it, brought her senses higher until every word was a thundering cry, every hint of light in her eyes as blinding as the sun. And every cruel touch agonizing.

The first beating had hurt. The subsequent ones had nearly sent her out of her mind. Only the solid, steel core of determination deep inside her—which had kept her going despite so many obstacles throughout her life— had kept her from giving in to the urge to beg him to just kill her and put her out of her misery.

"You must want to go to sleep, though."

"No," she whispered. "Go on. Don't stop. I like it."

Oh, no, she didn't want to fall asleep, as welcome as it might have been. Because it was while she slept, helpless against sheer exhaustion, lulled by his singsong bedtime stories or unable to fight the effects of the drugs, that he came in and *did* things to her. She'd awakened once to find him taking pictures of her, naked and posed on the cot. Though his face had been masked—one of those creepy, maniacally smiling "king" masks from the fast-food commercials—he'd rechained her and scurried out as soon as he realized she was fully conscious. As if he didn't have the balls to risk letting her get a good look at him.

Maybe he's afraid you'll escape and be able to identify him.

Yeah. And maybe a pack of wolves would rip him to pieces in his own backyard tomorrow. But she doubted it.

One of these times, she suspected she would wake up and find herself in the middle of a rape. So, no, she did not want to fall asleep.

"I don't know—we've read quite a lot. I'm worried you might have nightmares. Did you, last night, after hearing about the little piggies who got turned into bacon and sausage patties?"

She suspected the story didn't end like that. If it did, parents who called it a bedtime story had a lot to answer for. As for her nightmares . . . Well, she was living one, wasn't she?

Vonnie swallowed, her thick, dry tongue almost choking her. "I'll be fine. Please read to me some more."

The words echoed in the damp, musty basement room in which she'd been imprisoned for three days now. Or four? She had been unable to keep track, even though she had noted the sunshine coming and going again through the tiny window in her cell. She had been too out of it, couldn't make herself focus.

How long had it been since the night he'd grabbed her? And when had that been? *Think!*

Monday. He'd attacked her while she walked the long way home from a nighttime event at her new high school, to which she'd just transferred because they offered more AP classes than her old one. Mistake number one. Her old school had been a block from her crappy home.

"Well, if you're sure, I suppose we can read a little more about those naughty children."

Knowing he expected it, she managed to murmur, "Thank you."

"You're welcome, dear. I'm glad you like this story. It's no wonder their parents didn't want Hansel and Gretel—awful, spoiled brats, weren't they? Most parents hate their children anyway, but these two were especially bad."

If it wouldn't have caused her so much pain, she might have laughed at that. Because he was saying something he thought would hurt her, when, in truth, he'd just reinforced what she already knew. Her mama had made that clear every day of her life.

Most parents would be proud of their kid for doing well in school, but not hers. All she'd said was that Vonnie had been stupid to transfer. Stupid to go to the evening event. Stupid and uppity, thinking getting into the National Honor Society mattered a damn when she lived on the corner of Whoreville and Main.

Normally she'd have been at work serving chicken wings and fending off gropey drunk guys by that time of night on a Monday. But no, she'd had to go to the meeting, had to act as if she was no different from the smart, rich white kids with their trust funds and their sports cars. She'd been cocky, insisting it was no big deal to walk home alone after dark through an area of the Boro where no smart girl ever walked alone after dark. Not these days, not with the Ghoul on the loose and more girls missing from her neighborhood every month.

The Ghoul—the paper had at first said he was real; then that he wasn't. Vonnie knew the truth. He was real, all right. She just wasn't going to live long enough to tell anybody.

"Hansel and Gretel didn't know that the starving

birdies of the forest were eating up their bread-crumb trail, waiting for the children to die so they could poke out their eyes," he read, not noticing her inattention. "It was dark and their time to find their way home was running out."

Time. It had ceased to have any meaning at all. Minutes and hours had switched places: minutes lengthened by pain, hours shortened by the terror of what would happen every time he came back from wherever it was he went when he left her alone in the damp, cold dark.

And Vonnie knew, deep down, that her time was running out, too.

"Did you hear me?" he snapped.

She swallowed. "Yeah."

"Good. Don't you fall asleep. I'm reading this for you, not for myself, you know."

She suspected he wasn't reading at all, merely Wes Craven-ing up a real bedtime story.

"Now, wasn't it lucky that they were able to find shelter?" he added. "Mm, a house made of gingerbread and gumdrops and licorice. Imagine that. Do you like sweets, pretty girl? Want me to bring you some candy? Sticky, gooey candy?"

She swallowed, the very thought of it making her sick. Not that she wasn't hungry, starving even. But the foul-smelling air surrounding her, filling her lungs and her nose, made the thought of food nauseating. She didn't like to think about the other smells down here—the reek of rotten meat, the stench of human waste. And something metallic and earthy, a scent that seemed to coat her tongue when she breathed through her mouth.

Blood. At least, that was what she suspected had created the rust-colored stains on the cement floor.

Those stains had been the first things she'd noticed when she regained consciousness after she'd been kidnapped. And ever since, they'd reiterated what she already knew: This guy had killed before, and he intended to kill her. It wasn't a matter of if; only when.

There was no escape—she was chained, drugged, and had been terrified into utter submission. She had no idea where she was, or when it was, or if the door led to a way out or just another chamber of horrors.

Vonnie didn't even try to comfort herself with thoughts of escape. It did no good to pump herself up with the memories of all the other times she'd gotten herself out of difficult situations—put there through either her own gullibility or by her mama's greed.

Don't go there, girl. Just as much darkness down that path.

No, she didn't want to think those thoughts. Not if they were going to be among the last ones of her life. Because so far, at least, this nightmare hadn't included sexual assault.

"Well, maybe the candy shouldn't be too sticky," he said, tutting a little, like a loving, concerned parent, not that she had firsthand experience with one. "I know your jaw must hurt from when you made me hit you the other day. Maybe I could chew it up, make it nice and soft for you, then spit it into your mouth just like a mama bird with her little chick."

Though she hadn't figured there was anything left in her stomach, she still heaved a mouthful of vomit. But she forced herself to swallow it down. She wouldn't give him the satisfaction of seeing that his mere words had made her sick. Nor could she let him know just how disgusting she found the thought. Giving the monster ideas to try on her when she finally did pass out was a stupid thing to do, and Vonnie Jackson might be beaten and chained, she might be poor and the daughter of a drug-addicted prostitute, but nobody had ever called her stupid.

"Why was she doing it, do you suppose? Why did she want them to eat all those sweets?" When she didn't reply, his singsong voice rose to a screech. "Answer me!"

"Fattening them up," she said, the words riding a puff of air across her swollen lips.

"Yes! You're so clever; that's what they say about you. Such a smart, clever girl who was going to escape her pathetic childhood." He *tsk*ed, sounding almost sad. "And you nearly made it—didn't you, Yvonne? Oh, you came so close! High school graduation next May, then off you'd go to college on one of your scholarships, never to see your slut mother or the hovel you call home again. All that work, all that effort. Wasted."

She didn't answer, didn't even flinch, not wanting him to see that his words stabbed at her, hurting almost as much as his fists. Because getting out was all Vonnie had worked for, all she had dreamed of for as long as she could remember. And the fact that this filthy monster had taken that chance from her made her want to scream at the injustice.

"Ah, well, back to our story. Yes, indeed, the witch was fattening them up," her captor said. "But do you know why?" He hummed a strange tune, repeating himself in discordant song. "Why, why, why? Do you know why?"

Her eyes remained open as she listened to that crooning voice deliberately trying to lull her into much-needed sleep. Her body wanted to give in to it, to let go. If she thought there was a chance she might never wake up, she would have gladly embraced the chance.

But she wasn't that lucky. And she knew she would regret it when she awoke and found out what he wanted to do to her. So Vonnie forced herself to shake her throbbing head, knowing the sharper the pain the less she'd be inclined to give in. "Why?"

He laughed softly, not answering. Just as well. She probably didn't want to know the answer to that question, given the way he was turning these nightly stories into tales from his twisted crypt of a mind.

"You'll just have to wait and see. Patience, sweet . . ."

His sibilant words were interrupted by the sound of banging coming from somewhere above. Before Vonnie could even process it, she heard a clang of metal. The small sliding panel in the door, through which he watched her, talked to her, and tormented her, was slammed shut. The narrow column of illumination that had shone through it, one single beam of blazing light in the darkness, had been chopped away like the head off a snake.

Another bang from above. She tried to focus on it, tried not to let the relief of his leaving make her give in to exhaustion. That noise, the way he'd reacted to it, was important, though it took a second for her to process why.

Then she got it. He had been startled. The creature had been surprised out of his lair by something unexpected. Or someone?

Oh God, please.

Hope bloomed, relentless and hot. What if someone else was out there? For the first time in days, she realized he hadn't taken her to the bowels of hell but to somewhere real, a place that other people could come upon. A mailman, a neighbor? Anyone who could help her?

An internal voice tried to dampen her hopes. That might not have been someone banging on the door at all, but merely a loose shutter or a tree branch. Besides, it was dark out, maybe even the middle of the night—no mailman worked these hours.

The police. Maybe they're looking for me.

It was a long shot. But long shots were all she had right now. "Help me. Somebody, help me," she whispered. "Please, I'm here!"

She didn't think about what he'd do when he came back. Didn't stop for one second to worry whether he'd find some new way to punish her.

No. Vonnie Jackson simply began to scream as if her life depended on it.